DEATHRIGHT

A Mythic Fantasy

BOOKS BY E. ROSE SABIN

THE ARUCADI BOOKS:

ARUCADI: THE BEGINNING

MISTRESS OF THE WIND
BRINGERS OF MAGIC
A MIX OF MAGICS

ARUCADI: SCHOOL SERIES

A PERILOUS POWER
A SCHOOL FOR SORCERY
WHEN THE BEAST RAVENS

TRAVELS THROUGH ARUCADI:

BRYTE'S ASCENT

THE TERRANO TRILOGY:

SHADOW OF A DEMON
THE GIFT OF THE TRINDE TREE
TOUCH OF DEATH

SEDUCTION OF THE SCEPTER

WERE HOUSE

DEATHRIGHT

HOUSE OF DREAMS

GRANDY'S GRAND INVENTIONS (A Children's Chapter Book)
TO THE FAR SIDE OF THE FOREST (For Teens)

DEATHRIGHT

A Mythic Fantasy

E. Rose Sabin

Arucadi Enterprises, LLC
St. Petersburg, Florida
2016

ISBN: **0692634622**

ISBN-13: **978-0692634622** (Arucadi Enterprises, LLC)

And as the same thing there exists in us living and dead and the waking and the sleeping and young and old: for these things having changed round are those, and those having changed round are these.

Presocratic philosopher Heraclitus of Ephesus, c. 560 BCE

Fragment 205, from G.S. Kirk and J.E. Raven,

The Presocratic Philosophers, a critical history with a selection of texts

PROLOGUE

A TALE OF CREATION AND DESTRUCTION

"Tale Weaver, spin us a tale."

"What sort of tale would you hear, my people?"

"A tale of birth and life and death."

"A tale of love and hate and vengeance and reconciliation."

"A tale of wrongdoing and forgiveness."

"A mystery."

"A romance."

"A fantasy."

"A riddle."

"A revelation."

"Ah, *that* tale. Always that tale. Very well, then …

"In the place where chaos is transformed into order, where time is born from timelessness, where being springs from nonbeing, all things are in flux. That state of flux gives rise to stars, to worlds, to gods and men, to sprites and fiends and other entities beyond our understanding. So was born our world and many others, and so sprang forth the gods who rule those worlds and the fiends who aspire to plunge them into the flux from which they arose.

"Now it chanced that the twin gods Makor and Molor agreed that they would together rule a single world. Makor would shape the world and all its beings, striving for beauty, for perfection. Molor would examine Makor's work for any fault, any imperfection, and when he found a flaw in any portion, he would destroy as much as needed to remove the flaw. So Makor built and Molor tore down, and Makor rebuilt, aiming for perfection. But always Molor found some way in which the world fell short, and so the cycle of destruction and re-creation continued and the world endured, neither achieving perfection nor shattering and returning to chaos.

"Makor was strong and fair and glowed with an inner light. He was called Makor the Golden. Molor, swarthy, with large silver wings, was known as Molor the Winged.

"This world of theirs was Belbrevis, our world. Its beauty and grace drew the attention of other creatures of the Flux: those who admired Belbrevis and wished to make a home there, and those who hated it and wished to return it to chaos. Of the former are sprites called *falas*, beings spun of light and sound who sing songs of such beauty that they cause pain to any mortals who hear them. Of the latter are the Flux fiends, who stretch and twist and collapse time, trying to drag it back into timelessness. Because Makor and Molor together kept the world in perfect balance, the fiends could not prevail and the world endured."

"So our world will not end?"

"All worlds end, my young friend. But do not fear. All the ages of humankind are but the blink of a god's eye. I have not finished the story. Shall I continue?"

"Yes, let us hear the rest."

"Let us know how the story ends."

"I'll tell you more, my beloved people, but how the story ends I cannot say. The end is not yet written.

"The great goddess Uta, first to arise from chaos, spins the strands of life and time and weaves into an ever-changing tapestry all worlds, all lands, all lives. Uta has a daughter, Zera, fairest of all gods. Some say Uta bore her after mating with a Flux fiend, and that is why Zera is sometimes erratic and unpredictable and has the power to move back and forth in time. Whether that account is true I cannot say. I only know that Zera upset the careful balance between Makor's building and Molor's tearing down. And this is how it came about ...

"Makor saw and loved Zera, and although Molor counseled against it, Makor wed the lovely daughter of Uta and built for her a palace on the peak of the highest mountain on Belbrevis, where he could dwell with her, and they two could look down on their world.

"Now Zera took note of the falas and the beauty of their song. She loved their fair melodies, but she saw that the songs of the falas were so sweet and so haunting that men who heard them were driven mad, some with envy and lust, others with the sheer joy of the song.

"Seeing this, Zera begged Makor to gather up the falas, transform them into birds, and confine them in cages where she and he alone could hear their lovely songs. At first Makor refused, but Zera used all her wiles to persuade him until he yielded and did as she bade.

"Makor's capitulation enraged Molor, who favored the falas. He summoned his twin to say, 'You have upset the balance which has so long been maintained between us; for this caging of the falas, Brother, is an act of destruction, not of creation. You have usurped my role and stepped outside the bounds of our agreement.'

"And so began a feud between them that ended when Makor agreed to meet his twin at a crossroads below the mountain on which he and Zera dwelt. He came to the place expecting a parley, but Molor swooped down on him, his great silver wings spread wide. Saying, 'You have become imperfect, my twin, and I must carry out my duty and destroy you,' he raised a mighty sword and slew his brother, who did not defend himself.

"And so Makor died, and Zera grieved and swore vengeance on Molor. She claimed her consort's body and hid it in a secret place until she could find a way to bring him back, for gods should be immortal, and his death, she said, was the greatest fault of all.

Molor, his anger still hot, had anticipated Zera's hope and divided Makor's essence into seven parts. These he scattered about the world and also spread through time.

But as Molor's anger cooled, he grieved, for he loved his fallen brother. Instead of warring with Zera, he sued for peace. For lost Makor's sake he ceded most of the world to Zera, keeping for himself a lush valley and the forested hills around it. His portion was the fairest, most perfect part of our world, and he settled it with the best and bravest of the people. He carved out the River Rethe to mark the boundary between his land and Zera's.

"It is said that men cannot comprehend the ways of gods. Zera plotted against Molor, and Molor devised countermeasures that are beyond our understanding yet affect our lives in countless ways, bringing strange twists and turns, causing confusion that borders on chaos before snatching us back from the brink of annihilation.

"Still Uta spins, and Zera and Molor are threads in her great tapestry, and we too are threads, lesser yet essential parts of the design. So Zera and Molor plot, and the world stumbles on."

"But surely, Tale Weaver, that isn't all of the story."

"No, my dear friends. There is much more. But that must wait for another day."

1

LORD'S-KILL

I looked up when a man I'd never seen before came into the field. He wore the silver and black uniform of a Manor House servant. He spoke to our overseer, and the overseer pointed my way. The man walked to me.

"You are Korth? You are ordered to come to the Manor House. Now!"

I couldn't move. Why would a field slave be called to the Manor House? They must be going to punish me. But what could I have done wrong? I obeyed every order I was given.

The man got the look that my overseer gets before he uses his whip. I cringed when he leaned closer. But he only looked around and then whispered, "It's time."

Time? Time for what?

His brows pulled together. "Time for Lord's-Kill," he whispered when I didn't move. "You have to hurry."

Lord's-Kill! I'd been brought from cutting stone in the quarry and put to work in the Manor House fields just so I could be trained. One day a week I was called away from the other field and garden slaves to a place where nobody could watch, and from midafternoon to time for slaves to return to the longhouse a man taught me the way of Lord's-Kill. I don't know why they chose me. They didn't explain, and I didn't dare ask. My trainer said I'd get something special if I did the job well.

I followed the house servant. We stopped by a pump, where he ordered me to wash my hands and face. I pumped water and splashed it on my face and hands, and we went on to the Manor House. I was turned over to a big woman with a mean face. She grabbed my arm and took me to a washroom and scrubbed my hands and face all over again. I guess I hadn't gotten them clean enough at the pump.

"You still aren't fit to enter the dama's presence," she said. "Or Lord Brid's. But you'll have to do. I'm told his time is short."

After making me wrap cloth around my boots so as not to track mud through the house, she took me through a large kitchen. Servants were fixing food, and the smells made my mouth water. But the woman didn't stop. She took me into a room where the man waited—the one who'd trained me.

He was tall and very strong. I never knew his name. I never asked it or why he taught me how to do something he could have done himself.

"Korth," he said when I reached him, "this is the hour for which I've prepared you. Lord Brid lies near death. He is waiting for you. You must be quick and merciful. I have taught you how. Don't fail. I'll take you to Dama Koralie now."

I nodded.

He frowned and gave me a stern look. "This is a great honor,

Korth. You should be proud, not frightened."

"Yes." I was too scared to say anything more.

He led me into a sitting room finer than anything I'd ever seen. Fancy chairs and tables and more furniture I didn't know names for. I stood in the center of the room.

Dama Koralie came in. Immediately I bowed my head. I didn't dare look at her face. I was afraid of Dama Koralie. Everybody said she knew witchcraft and had truck with Flux fiends and they taught her how to move back and forth in time. I didn't understand any of that. I did know the dama was more powerful than anyone but the manor lord. And the old lord had been sick for a long time, so the dama was now in charge of everything. She spoke for Molor. No wonder I was scared of her. Everybody was.

She didn't speak to me. She asked my trainer, "Is he ready? He knows what he must do?"

"He is well trained, Dama," my trainer answered. "But he *is* a slave, and unlearned in all else. I—"

"So long as he does as he's been taught, nothing more is required. Time ebbs. Decio, take him to Lord Brid's bedchamber."

An old manservant took me by my arm. "This way," he said and led me from the room and up a wide stairway to a great chamber. And left me there.

In a bed far wider than the one our slave overseer slept in I saw one very old man. I'd never slept in a bed or even seen one besides Overseer Vicca's, and though this one had been described to me, until now I couldn't imagine it. The overseer slept in the slave quarters on a bed by the fireplace, while we slaves slept in hammocks hung from the rafters. I didn't know beds came as big as the one the old lord was in.

With such a wide bed, how could I get close enough to do what I was supposed to do? I'd been told I could kneel on the bed, but that didn't seem right.

The old man's eyes opened as I drew near. They were blue like a sky covered with thin white clouds. Could he see?

His mouth opened, his lips moved, but no sound came out. One hand lifted from the cover and waved toward a table that held a glass of water. I got it and leaned over the wide bed and held it to his lips. He took a few sips, but most of it dribbled down his chin.

I guess it helped a little. "Korth," he said. How did he know my name?

"Do … it … quickly." His voice sounded like the noise made by stalks of grain when they scrape together in the wind.

I put the glass of water back on the table and leaned over him. His eyes closed and his lips curved upward in a small smile. "Time," he murmured.

I had to put one knee on the bed and lean way over until my upper body was touching the covers and my face was right above his. I did exactly as I'd been taught. I wrapped my hands carefully around his throat. Breathing through my mouth, I put my hands around his neck … just … *so*. I felt the ridges of his windpipe under my fingers. That told me where to press. Quick and hard.

He gave a single shudder and let out one last breath.

I breathed in deeply as that final breath escaped him. And I got an odd feeling, as if his dying breath came into my open mouth and part of him came with it.

I wiped my hands on my shirt to get rid of the old man's sick-sweet smell. That didn't help. I blew my nose on my sleeve and shook my head hard. Keeping my eyes fixed on the carpet, I returned to where the dama waited. I stopped in front of her long black skirt. The skirt rustled. Sharp points of silver shoes showed under it.

"Finished so soon, Korth?" Her voice crackled like flames.

I nodded without lifting my head. "I did it just the way I was taught, Dama."

"Make certain he's dead."

To be sure she wasn't talking to me I looked up just enough to see the same old manservant hobble off. I waited, staring at the design on the carpet. Green vines and brown ones with withered leaves, twisted together—life and death. Not a thing I would have noticed before. New thoughts prickled through my head. I looked away from the design, looked at my feet instead, and followed the wrinkles in the cloth wrappings they'd made me put over my boots.

The man came back and said, "He's right, Dama Koralie. Brid Lord Terral, Twelfth Lord of the Manor Lands, is dead. The deathright has passed. Hail—"

"That's enough." Her voice was sharp, angry. It frightened me. But then the dama said more softly, "You may go, Korth. You've fulfilled your duty."

When I lifted my head to find my way out, I saw the staff the dama leaned on. It was plain wood except for the head carved at its top where her palms rested. Between her wrinkled fingers a dark, ugly face peered out with yellow eyes that glittered. I clenched my fists to keep from making the sign to ward off evil. They'd beat me if I did that in front of the dama. Eyes lowered, I backed from the room.

A woman waited outside the door. She gathered her robe close like she was afraid it might touch me. She led me down narrow stairs and out the garden door into a cold rain. We reached the high wrought-iron gate, and I looked around, hoping to see either my trainer or the messenger who'd brought me to the Manor House. The woman held the gate open.

"You're done here, and I'm getting wet," she said. "Go back to the longhouse."

I stepped through, and she slammed the gate shut. I hurried down the path through the rain. I felt confused and betrayed. I'd done everything just the way I'd been taught. Where was the special reward my trainer had promised?

But a slave couldn't complain. I'd been assigned a duty, and I'd obeyed. I had no right to expect a reward.

Cold and hungry, I broke into a run. Cook would have hot soup ready by the time I got back. The rain came down harder. I pounded along the last section of path, dashed into the longhouse, and shook myself.

"Hey! Stop! You're getting us wet," shouted one of the men gathered by the fire. The others glared. Even the fire hissed its anger.

Soup bubbled in the iron kettle hung over the fire pit. Its smell drew me. The others were already eating. Pushing past them, I grabbed my bowl from its peg, hurried to the steaming kettle, dipped the bowl into it, and scooped up some soup.

The back of my neck twitched like a spider was crawling on it. I turned around. Overseer Vicca had come in. He was staring at me. The scar that zigzagged from his right eye to his ear and back to the corner of his tight-lipped mouth gleamed white. He must be angry because I'd left my work in the garden. I waited for his curses.

He knew I'd been sent for. Maybe he knew I'd killed the old lord and meant to punish me for it. I tensed, waiting for the bite of his lash. The hush across the longhouse told me the others waited, too. Nothing happened. I sneaked a glance at our overseer. Master Vicca hadn't moved. The moment of danger passed.

The men started talking again. I backed to the side of the room and squatted on the dusty plank floor to bury my face in my bowl and lap the thick broth, too hungry to care that it burned my tongue. When I looked up from the empty bowl, Master Vicca was gone. He probably wouldn't come back until we slaves had all gone to our hammocks.

I would've joined the men around the fire, but the hard looks even from those who were usually friendly warned me away. Master Vicca's cold gaze had marked me as out of favor, and so to be avoided.

I didn't care. I was tired and I'd heard the jokes and stories many times. I did love the tales of the twin gods Makor and Molor. Now, though, the part about Molor killing his brother bothered me. How could a god die? How could that part of the tale be true?

These and other thoughts tunneled through my mind like hungry worms. I never had thoughts like them before I sucked in the old lord's dying breath. Confused, I helped myself to a dipper of dark ale from the barrel in the corner, drank, and headed for my hammock.

Yago stepped in front of me. "Change places with me," he said. "My hammock's too far from the fire."

He had no right to ask that. Our places were assigned. But his fists and hard look made me nod and back away. With Master Vicca already mad at me I didn't dare get in a fight. Yago knew that.

Yago's hammock was in the far corner of the longhouse. It stank of sour sweat. I lay down, wrapped in my poncho.

I awoke shivering and sweating at the same time. In the dark the glittering eyes of the thing I'd seen on Dama Koralie's staff floated before my face. I'd dreamed about it. I could still hear its high-pitched, mocking laugh. I'd been in a pit like some of those in the quarry where I used to work. Blasts of steam were coming out of cracks in the pit floor. I dodged pillars of slag, heaps of smoldering coals, and pools of molten lava. My leaps and twists were useless. The fiend unfurled leathery wings and flew like a hot wind. Everywhere I turned, the beaked face grinned into mine.

I listened for a hint of its movements, heard nothing but snores and the deep breathing of sleeping men.

I'd never had a dream that scared me so.

A floorboard creaked. My muscles tensed. I tossed my poncho aside and rolled from the hammock to stand staring wide-eyed into the darkness. The red glow of the cookfire's dying embers reminded me of the fire pits of my dream. The dream thing's mocking face flashed before me.

A shadow blotted out the glow. A dim form stopped next to my hammock—the one where Yago slept. The fiend!

As I eased closer, I made out an upraised arm holding something that caught a red reflection from the dying fire. A knife! He was going to kill Yago.

I hurled myself forward. My arms clamped around broad shoulders. I wrestled the figure to the floor and threw myself on top of it. A blade grazed my cheek.

I groped for the throat to use the form of defense I knew best. I squeezed just as I'd squeezed the old man's throat. It wasn't easy this time. He struggled while I squeezed tighter. I crushed the ridges under my thumbs. The body went limp.

My cheek stung. With the back of my hand I wiped blood off it. I pulled the dead man closer to the cookfire so I could see him in the faint glow of the coals.

The overseer! I'd slain Master Vicca!

The punishment for a slave who killed his overseer was to be shoved onto a sharp stake. I'd seen slaves die screaming and crying, the ground turning red, the awful stick tearing through their guts.

I listened, expecting someone to yell an alarm. Snores and heavy breathing told me the men all still slept. Even Yago. He'd never know I saved his life.

I felt my way back to where I'd slept and snatched up my poncho. I pulled on my boots. The man in the next hammock groaned and turned. I froze and held my breath. He muttered something and then lay quiet. I waited until I heard him snore.

I picked my way among the hammocks and pried at the door's iron bolt. It gave with a thud. I shoved the door open and ran into the damp, dark night.

2

PATHFINDER

The fear of being pushed down onto a stake drove me into the woods beyond the longhouse, where I could hide. Running wildly in the darkness, I crashed into trees, fell over shrubs and rocks, picked myself up, and fell again.

Branches snagged my poncho and clawed my skin. My forehead slammed into a large limb. I staggered, fell over an uplifted root, and lay stunned. A throbbing ache in my head replaced the imagined pain in my gut. Despite that ache, clear thoughts came to me. Could they be a gift from the old lord?

My crime must not yet have been discovered. If it had been, the manor guards could easily have caught me. I'd most likely been thrashing around in circles. A little stream flowed through the heart of the wood, and I hadn't crossed it. If I could find and follow that stream, it would lead me to the River Rethe. If I could get across the river, I'd be out of the Manor Lands. Safe! And free!

I sat up and strained to hear over the croaking of frogs and the tinny insect chorus. Instead of the gurgle of flowing water, the mournful call of a night bird reached my ears. Drawn by the haunting cry, I stood, weaving a bit, and staggered off to find the source of the sound.

The call came again, more distant. I moved after it, drawn through the darkness as by a cord. Branches caught my clothing, dangling moss tickled my face, and sticky strands of spiderweb veiled it, but I crashed into no more trees. The unseen bird seemed to lead me around them.

The cry ceased. Trees no longer pressed in on me. The darkness seemed less thick. I'd reached a clearing. I stepped forward and cracked my shin against something hard. My groping fingers found stone. Worked stone. I clutched it, explored its shape. A low, round pillar carved with some design.

I knew that shape. I'd set up such stones when I'd worked for a while in the Manor burial garden. It was a grave marker. But who could be buried here in the wood?

The lords and ladies of the Manor were laid to rest in a walled garden on the far side of the Manor House. The lord I'd killed would sleep there. Servants and bondsmen were interred in long, narrow trenches between the fields of barley and rye. No stone marked their burial places. The corpses of slaves were burned. I'd never seen the burial lots used by freedmen, but I didn't think they used grave pillars, and I couldn't imagine why one would be set in such an isolated spot.

Why am I so curious about this place? Why am I wasting time here puzzling over a grave marker when they're going to kill me? I've never been curious about such things. The thoughts I'd been having were all new. Words came into my mind that I didn't know I knew. The blow to my head must have stirred things up in my brain.

Again my hands traced the shape of the stone marker down to the damp earth. Thorns stabbed into my hand. I trailed my bleeding fingers along the ground until I found and broke off a spiky, ground-hugging limb. A grave planted with thorns? Holding the branch, I inched away from the pillar. I stripped a few thorns from the branch so I could grasp it and wave it back and forth.

Trees pressed close and shared whispered secrets with the wind. The branch helped me find my way through the blackness, snagging in leaves and tangling with tree limbs before I blundered into them. A curious feeling built within me that this branch, smeared with my blood, was helping me find the right paths. I named it Pathfinder.

The burbling of the brook came to my ears. My branch had found the way! It led me to the bank of the stream. I removed my boots, held them in one hand, wielded Pathfinder with the other, and waded into the shallow water.

I tried to cross straight to the other side. Pathfinder had other ideas. It found a solid wall of bushes on the far side. I couldn't climb up onto the bank. I had to walk in the stream, skidding over slippery rocks. The icy water tugged at my ankles and numbed my feet. I waved my arms to balance myself, slid this way and that, but never quite fell. Pathfinder protected me until it found an opening where I could scramble up onto a grassy bank.

I sat and dried my feet on the frayed border of my poncho, rubbing hard until feeling returned in a volley of needles. I drew on my worn and ragged boots but didn't rise. With Pathfinder held in front of me, my head drooped forward onto my left knee. My eyelids slid shut. I stretched out my right leg. It would be so good to sleep awhile.

Pathfinder tugged. My eyes popped open. I lurched to my feet and discovered that Pathfinder had caught in a tear on my right boot. I worked it loose and trudged onward.

The darkness dissolved into tree-shaped shadows. The sky lightened. A red glow crowned the tallest trees. Soon the sun spread the treetops with golden fire. I'd never noticed things like that before. I wouldn't have known how to describe them.

I came out of the woods onto a grassy sward, a broad blue ribbon beyond it. Sun glinted on the swift-flowing water. Pathfinder had led me to the Rethe, the boundary of the Manor Lands. I had only to find a bridge and cross to safety. And freedom. I knew little of the world beyond the Manor Lands, but this I did know: In the Manor Lands I was a slave; outside them I'd belong to no one.

With a glad cry I flung my arms wide and turned west along the river. Pathfinder caught the edge of my swirling poncho and forced me to turn to free it. I worked it loose from the tattered threads and lifted it. It pointed east. I shrugged. The Rethe ran from east to west, so in either direction I'd be following the course of the river. Since I had no idea in which direction I'd find a bridge, one way seemed as good as another.

A brisk breeze carried barks, bleats, cackles, and squeals intermingled with cries of vendors, shouts of herders, tinkling bells, and the songs and shrieks of excited children. I shaded my eyes against the morning light and its reflection in the river. Squinting, I saw booths spread on the greensward between wood and river. A market! The freedmen on the fringes of the lord's estate often held markets, but I'd never been allowed to visit one. Now I had to hurry through before they learned I was a fugitive fleeing punishment for a terrible crime. With Pathfinder beating the air before me, I trotted into the lane between two rows of booths.

I pressed forward, delighted by the brightly colored awnings shading the booths and drawn by the mouth-watering smells of cooking fish and frying sweetcakes mingled with the odors of animal dung and straw.

The stares and startled cries of the freedmen puzzled me. Women shrank back; children darted between the booths and peered fearfully around the wooden supports. A few men grabbed sharp stakes; others scowled and planted themselves in front of their wares as though to protect them. One man hoisted a heavy iron chain and edged into the lane. Legs apart and shoulders hunched forward, he blocked my path.

I halted and stared. They must have learned of the murder of Master Vicca. I turned, hunting a way of escape.

"Tatterman! Tatterman!" a child taunted from behind a wagon. Others crept from hiding and took up the shrill refrain.

Tatterman. I'd heard the old tales, used to frighten children. Tatterman attacked little ones with a whip of thorns. With an unaccustomed flash of insight I pictured how I must look, coming out of nowhere, poncho in shreds, trousers ripped, boots scraped and slit, hair a leaf-and-twig-filled tangle. And Pathfinder in my hand.

A yellow cur streaked toward me, barking wildly. Fangs bared, it lunged for my leg. I smacked Pathfinder down on the dog's snout. It leaped back, shook its head, and scurried away yipping, tail tucked between its legs.

"I only want to pass through," I shouted above the din. "I mean no harm."

The man with the chain flexed it between his hands. The children screamed louder. "Tatterman! Tatterman!"

They were not attacking a runaway slave who murdered his overseer. They were not drawing away from a lordslayer. They were defending themselves from Tatterman.

I dropped my hands to my side and backed slowly away from the man with the chain. "I'm not Tatterman," I said.

The man swung the chain. Its links struck my knee, sending fiery pain up and down my leg. I stumbled backward. Someone behind me shoved me back toward the flailing chain. I reached for it, caught its end. The impact jarred my arm, but I hung on, threading my sweaty fingers through the links.

My muscular opponent grasped his end of the chain with two hands. I held mine with only one and wielded Pathfinder with the other.

A powerful jerk wrenched the chain from my hand. A smelly barrage of overripe tomatoes and rotten eggplants pelted me. I threw up both hands to ward off the bombardment. But the sight of Pathfinder in my upraised hand stirred the crowd to an even greater frenzy. The chain crashed against my unprotected chest. I doubled over, gasping for breath. Someone jerked Pathfinder from my hand. A yell told me its thorns had taken revenge.

The chain smashed down on my back. I pitched forward. The world vanished in an explosion of fire.

Slowly my battered senses returned. I lay sprawled face down in the dusty path, my chest a mass of pain. Every breath brought stabs of agony. I opened my eyes, tried to lift my head. My attackers circled round me. In the dirt beside my outstretched hand Pathfinder lay in ruined bits.

3

THE FASCINATOR

"Tatterman's awake," someone shouted.

"Ho, Tatterman. Where's your whip of thorns?" another taunted.

Jeers and catcalls arose from the encircling crowd. "Tatterman's beat, Tatterman's beat. Can't hurt us. Tatterman's beat."

The man with the chain stood near me. He grinned and swung the chain over my head. I lay still, hoping they would tire of their sport. But they grew bolder. A young boy dodged through the circle of legs and aimed a savage kick at my hip. I twisted away. The sudden movement caused a sharp pain that tore a scream from my throat.

The outcry brought more laughter and insults from the crowd. Other boys, some barely more than toddlers, followed the example of the first. Most of their kicks were timid and poorly aimed and caused no hurt, but some landed on my bruised back and side. Teeth clamped together to stifle my screams, I tried to defend myself. But the kicks kept me gasping for breath and the chain fanned the air above my head.

One awkward boy loped toward my head, apparently meaning to stomp my face. In his excitement he put himself right in the path of the swinging chain. I grabbed his ankle and yanked him down before those heavy links could bash his head. He toppled onto me, bringing such a wave of pain that I blacked out for a few moments.

When I came to, the boy had been hauled off me, but his chums were redoubling their attacks, shouting and screaming at me. They thought I'd meant to hurt their friend instead of save him. Some grabbed up sticks so they could cudgel me from a safe distance. In helpless agony I waited for death.

A yell penetrated my fading consciousness. "The goats! They're loose! They're heading for the forest."

The circle of feet burst apart in a flurry of dust. Bleats and the bawling of kids rent the air, followed by squeals and crashes.

"The pigs! Catch the pigs!"

The man with the chain shouted a curse and pounded after his fellows. Women darted in to grab the children. One boy, yanked away in the act of aiming a kick at my nose, stomped his bare foot in a fit of temper. His heel slammed onto one of Pathfinder's dismembered thorns. The foot jerked up again. The boy clawed at it, hopped up and down on his other foot, and yowled until a woman caught him up into her arms and carried him out of my sight.

"Serves the little bastard right." The deep-voiced comment came from outside my range of vision. I tried to turn my head and winced with pain.

"Lie still and let's see what they've done to you," the voice ordered. "You're safe for a while. My daughter set the pigs and goats loose and chased them toward the woods. They'll be hunting them for hours."

The speaker bent over me—a tall, bearded man with a wide nose and deep-set eyes of startlingly bright blue. He lifted my poncho and gently probed my back and sides.

"Fools," he muttered. "They'd have let the children kill you, and what would they have threatened them with when Tatterman was dead?" Fingers prodded and poked, producing stabs of pain.

"I'm not Tatterman." I got the words out between grunts and groans.

"Of course not. But you'll never convince these ignorant villagers of that."

His words brought fresh fear. This was no freedman. The village men wore baggy cotton trousers and short plain tunics. I twisted my neck for a sidelong glance at my rescuer. His knee-length green kirtle hung over black silk trousers. Both garments were plain and unbordered; I searched in vain for the insignia of the Manor House.

He turned his head toward my face. I averted my eyes. He laughed.

"A Tatterman with the reactions of a slave? Come, man, look me in the eye. I won't have you whipped."

Slowly I turned my eyes and looked directly at his face. The brilliant blue orbs probed me; I could not break away, though I trembled from trying. When my gaze turned back to the ground, it was because he released me.

"Ahhh. I was not wrong about you."

I lacked the courage to ask what he meant.

Light footfalls sounded behind me. I tensed. Was one of the children returning?

A girl's voice, light and musical, said, "Hurry, Father, before one of those stupid goats heads this way."

He straightened. "Help me get him to his feet. I've found cracked ribs and bad bruises, but he'll be able to walk." To me he said, "There will be pain, but it'll be bearable if you follow our instructions and move exactly as we tell you."

I nodded.

The daughter's firm hands gripped my shoulders. The delicate scent of lilies swirled around me.

"Lie still." The man's sharp order ended my attempt to turn my head. "We're going to turn you onto your back and sit you up. Hold your body stiff and let us do the work. Don't twist."

I tensed and gritted my teeth. My fingers swept across the dirt and closed around small bits of Pathfinder.

They lifted, turned me, and eased me down. The man released my feet and came to stand by my shoulders. His daughter stood on the other side of me.

I saw first a full red skirt. Red! No one wore the color sacred to the goddess Zera on this side of the Rethe. Dama Koralie would have this girl flogged if she saw her.

Maybe the girl didn't know. I guessed her to be little more than sixteen. I thought of warning her, but when her gaze met mine I became too flustered to speak.

Her eyes were the same brilliant blue as her father's. Her hair, in surprising contrast, was a rich, glossy black. It flowed over her shoulders like night. She had a small nose and lips that smiled easily.

"Young man, I asked if you were ready to sit up." My cheeks flamed at the man's rebuke. I couldn't speak. How quickly I'd revealed myself an ignorant and ill-mannered slave. I shut my eyes because, lying on my back, I could look nowhere but up.

"Come, you can't lie here all day. Take his shoulders, Lisha."

I flinched at the touch of her hand, but she dug her fingers into my shoulder, her father caught hold of my other shoulder and braced the back of my neck, and they raised me to a sitting position. I squinched my eyes shut and clamped my teeth together and somehow managed not to scream.

"Open your eyes, man. You've given no offense."

I opened them but kept them downcast to avoid a chance glimpse of the girl. I followed my rescuer's instructions in all else, and with his and Lisha's help I gained my feet.

Lisha and her father led me through the market. My chest ached and I limped from the blow on my leg, but now that I was on my feet I felt my strength returning. I lifted my head enough to look past my guides at my surroundings. Though shouts and animal sounds told me the hunt continued, many women and a few men had returned to their booths. No children were around, and no one tried to stop us, though some made warding signs as we passed.

We walked the length of the row and exited the market on the east. On the greensward, men and boys chased squealing, grunting pigs. A few goats were tethered to trees. I was nervous about going among the men.

Lisha took my arm and pointed to a cheerful yellow tent set up at the end of the last row of booths along the river. At her touch a surge of warmth coursed through me.

A wooden wagon rested beside the tent; I saw no horse or other draft animal to draw the wagon. We reached the tent, and Lisha drew the flap aside. I bent to pass through. Pain stabbed my chest. At my gasp Lisha dropped the flap and caught my arm. I pulled away and tottered past her into the tent.

Sunlight filtered through the yellow silk and filled the tent with golden light. The tent was larger than it looked from outside. Sheepskins carpeted the floor. A low table held a bowl of fresh fruit, a bottle of amber liquid, six crystal goblets, and a chunk of banded rock. A paneled screen concealed what must be the sleeping area. Painted on the screen was a scene of snow-covered mountains. High on one peak a gold-domed temple gleamed. Awed by the splendor, I felt awkward and stupid, painfully aware of my threadbare clothes, the dirt that caked my body, the crime that stained my soul.

"I am Savnar," my host announced. "Welcome to our home."

I stared at the carpet. Why did this man insist on treating me as an equal when he could see I was a slave?

Lisha whirled in front of me, red skirt flaring, eyes sparkling as the river had sparkled in the morning sun. The sight of her made my heart sing.

"You must tell us your name since we have told you ours," she said.

I looked away. "I am called Korth," I mumbled, forgetting in my confusion the likelihood that Manor Guards would come asking about a slave named Korth.

"You're safe here," Savnar said. "The freedmen will not enter this tent. They fear me, yet they won't send me away because they value my services."

"They have hired Father as a fascinator," Lisha explained. "They need protection from crop failure, from barren wives, from winter-blight, from getting lost in the woods." She giggled. "I hope those who have not yet been fitted with fascina remember not to run into the woods after their pigs."

My confusion deepened. If the freedmen had hired Savnar, wasn't he their servant? But the appointments of his tent, his and Lisha's clothing, and their behavior indicated high station. And why had Savnar said the freedmen feared him?

What rank did a fascinator hold? That of merchant? Or craftsman? I strained to recall whether I'd ever been instructed on the degree of homage due a fascinator. No slave was permitted to own amulets of even the simplest type, so those of my station had no reason to have dealings with a maker of fascina, amulets that protect their wearer from evil.

The fascina I'd seen around the necks or wrists of freedmen had been crude trinkets crafted by an apprentice or journeyman. Though I'd seen no samples of his work, I was sure Savnar was no apprentice.

He smiled. As though he read my mind, he said, "I answered their call because it served my purpose. No man commands me. Now, come. Let's get that shirt and poncho off you and tend to your broken ribs."

"Lord Savnar, I can't let you …"

"I am only Savnar, not lord. And you must accept our help. Lisha!"

His call brought her to my side. Together they lifted my poncho off my shoulders and over my head. To my intense embarrassment, Lisha unbuttoned my shirt and eased it open. Her movements were gentle and deft. Savnar helped me lift my arms so she could peel the shirt off them.

"What are you holding so tightly?" he asked, looking curiously at my clenched fist.

I'd forgotten the fragments of Pathfinder I'd swept up and clutched all this time. "Nothing," I stammered. "Pieces of a stick with thorns. I brought it from the woods. I used it to defend myself. The men took it from me and broke it."

"Let me see. Open your hand."

I uncurled my cramped fingers. On my straightened palm, gritty with sand, lay three small chunks of wood, one with a thorn attached. Savnar grasped my hand and stared at them, then walked to the table, picked up the striped stone, and returned to my side. He held the stone above my palm and passed it slowly over the fragments. A warmth radiated across my hand.

"Where did you find the stick?"

"I broke it off a bush growing by a pillar in a clearing."

"A pillar? What kind of pillar?"

I was afraid to speak aloud my conviction that it was a grave marker. "I—I'm not sure," I said. "It was night. I couldn't see. I found the pillar by stumbling over it and the bush when its thorns stabbed my finger."

Savnar nodded and replaced the stone. He carefully plucked the three bits of wood from my palm and placed them on the table beside the stone. "I'll craft a fascinum for you with these, but first we'll finish repairing you."

Savnar turned back to me and probed the bruised area on my chest and side. The pressure made me cough and the coughing brought pain so intense I reeled and would have fallen had not Savnar supported me.

"Lisha. Get Korth a soporific."

Lisha left the tent but was back in seconds. She pressed a goblet to my lips. "This will ease the pain."

She tilted the goblet. Eyes closed, I sipped the liquid. It was cool and tart and tingled as it went down. My coughing eased. I wanted only to sleep.

"Lower him gently." Savnar's voice floated toward me from far away. I felt the cloud-soft carpet beneath my back. The last thing i recalled was the fragrance of lilies and Lisha's soft touch on my hand.

4

LISHA

I struggle up a wall of rock. My nails dig into its surface; the toes of my bare feet scrabble to find tiny cracks. Spiderlike, I scale the nearly vertical walls. At last, gasping for breath in the thin air, I pull myself up onto what I think is the top.

It's only a narrow shelf. I face another sheer rock wall striped with bands of different colored stone. At its top, high above, sunlight gleams on a golden dome.

A temple. I have to reach it. Lisha waits there. But I can't scale the wall.

I have to try. I cling to the wall and ascend bit by painful bit, the divisions between the bands providing meager holds. I climb until I can no longer see the ledge I left. I gain a flat surface and haul myself onto it.

Another ledge. Another rock wall. On its height, distant as before, stands the temple where Lisha waits. I beat my fists against the cruel stone and sob.

Hands caught my wrists, held them still. A sweet voice said, "Hush, Korth. Wake from your dream."

I opened my eyes. Limned in golden light and the scent of lilies, Lisha knelt beside me. Directly behind her was the temple of my dream. I blinked and gaped. My senses, befuddled by sleep, were slow to grasp that the temple was painted on the screen behind Lisha. The scene on the front had depicted the temple high in the mountains, as in my dream. This side of the screen showed the temple close and surrounded by jungle. Trailing vines and large trumpet-shaped flowers crept toward it. Tropical birds in iridescent plumage glided around the golden dome.

Streaming through the tent's yellow fabric, sunlight gilded Lisha's skin, linked her to the temple, and transfigured her.

Goddess. Zera.

An urge to prostrate myself overrode the pain in my chest. I rolled onto my side and rested the weight of my upper body on my hands.

Her voice immobilized me in the act of lowering my face to the carpet. "Tell me your dream, Korth."

A touch of her hand released me from my awkward position, let me sit with my legs stretched out in front of me. As though still dreaming, I looked into her face.

She smiled. "Tell me your dream," she said again.

Like blue magnets her eyes drew mine and would not let them go. For the first time since being taken from my mother while still a very young child, I looked directly at a woman as I spoke.

Slowly, searching for the right words, I described the rock wall, the ledges, and the ever-distant temple. I omitted only one detail—that I'd been driven by the certainty that Lisha waited there. I concluded, "I woke and saw you sitting in front of the temple. You looked so like a goddess I wanted to bow to you."

Her laughter rippled like wind chimes. "You have interesting dreams, Korth. Do you dream often?"

"I almost never dream. Yet this is the second one I've had in two days."

"And what was the first? You must tell me that one, also."

I couldn't refuse her, but the telling didn't come easily. I searched for words to describe the fiend, could not find any, and said simply, "It was the thing carved on the knob of Dama Koralie's walking stick. Some power gave it life." I told her how it chased me into the pit and how I dodged it around pillars of slag and streams of lava.

"And what happened when you woke from that dream?"

She'd trapped me. The force of her eyes compelled me to confess how I had killed Master Vicca to save a fellow slave. I expected her to quail in horror and dash off to fetch the authorities.

She didn't flinch. Instead she leaned forward. "Listen to me, Korth. You killed a man who would have killed you." Her face was solemn, the laughter gone from her voice. Outside a cloud must have drifted over the sun; her golden aura dimmed. "What you saw in your dream was a Flux Fiend, a disruptor of order and time. The dream was a warning. Be wary."

I only half understood her words. She did not despise me for killing my overseer. That much was clear, and that was all I cared about.

Lisha rose in a fluid motion. "I've kept you talking too long. I'll bring you breakfast."

Her words made me aware of a gnawing hunger. "I'd planned to beg something in the market. I'd be grateful for a bit of food. But breakfast? I must have slept for hours."

She grinned. "For a whole day. The attack happened yesterday. So, breakfast it is."

She slipped around the screen. I scratched my head, adjusting to the peculiar idea of having lost a day. I rubbed my hand over my face. Freed from the befuddlement I felt in Lisha's presence, I became aware that I'd been bathed and my face shaved. I wore no shirt, but strips of white cotton cloth were wound tightly around my chest. My trousers had been washed and mended so neatly I could scarcely find where they'd been torn. My feet were bare. Where were my boots? They were tattered and scarred, but I had no others.

I looked around. My gaze fell again on the painting on the screen. I could now see it in its entirety. Cracks and holes marred the temple façade where roots and vines insinuated themselves into the walls, crumbling the rock. The damage was confined to that portion of the temple that had been concealed by Lisha's body, so when she had sat in front of it, I'd seen it as whole and beautiful.

I walked around to the other side of the screen to look again at the other painting. But what I noted immediately was that the tent was empty.

Cold tendrils of fear clutched at my stomach. Suppose Lisha had run to the Manor Guards to report my presence. Suppose her offer of breakfast had been a pretext to allow her to leave without arousing my suspicions. They could have hidden my boots to keep me from leaving before the guards could be brought. I'd flee barefoot. Better to have my feet hurt than to be impaled.

I sped toward the tent flap and nearly collided with Lisha. The tray she carried tilted at her abrupt halt. Milk splashed from a large mug and spread a stain on her white bodice.

Stammering an apology, I took the tray from her hands.

She snatched up a napkin and dabbed at the stain. "Where were you going in such a hurry?"

"I was hunting my boots." It was a weak excuse, but how could I tell her I was running away?

Her amused smile made me think she guessed the truth. "Your boots were ruined, but you need not worry. My father will find you a new pair in the market."

I gawked at her, stupefied by the kindness Lisha and her father were showing a worthless slave.

She laughed and said, "Set your tray on the table and eat before the food gets cold. Help yourself to fruit from the bowl on the table to finish off your breakfast."

Besides the mug of milk, the tray held a loaf of bread still warm from the oven, a plate of fried fish cakes, steaming hot, a bowl of leeks and cucumbers. I inhaled the rich aroma. Never had I had fare as rich as this. I set the tray on the table between the bowl of fruit and the banded rock, tossed a pillow into place in front of the table, dropped onto it, and grabbed for the bread.

My stomach knotted. I drew back my hand and looked helplessly at Lisha. "Lady, I may not eat in your presence."

"Of course you may, Korth. Why do you insist on playing the part of a slave?"

"I *am* a slave."

She shook her head, sending her glorious hair scudding about like a thundercloud. "You are not a slave, Korth. You broke your bonds when you killed your overseer."

"That couldn't free me. It put me under penalty of death."

She tossed her head again. "You acted to save another. Others may condemn you, Korth, but do not condemn yourself. I tell you, you are not a slave."

"If I'm not a slave, what am I? I've no rank. I'm nothing."

Her hands rested on her hips; blue flame sparked in her eyes. "Very well. Be nothing. That's better than being a slave. It's a starting point. It frees you to *become* something."

I gaped. My mind reeled.

Her hands dropped to her side, her brow smoothed. "Be at ease. I won't spoil your breakfast."

She darted from the tent before I could think what to say.

Not a slave, she'd said. Being nothing was better than being a slave. I guessed she was right, but a slave was all I'd ever been.

I was born into slavery. I never knew my father, and I remember my mother only vaguely. Her face is a blur, but I recall that she was very thin, and on the few occasions that I tried to hug her, usually wanting consolation because of some hurt, she let me huddle against her but gave no other comfort. Her bones felt like sticks poking me. I was still small, probably little more than four years, when she handed me over to the quarry boss. I think she was relieved to be rid of me. She was his housemaid, and my fellow slaves all said he must be my father, but I never believed it, for I look nothing like him. My skin is fair and my hair light, but he was a brutish man, big and hairy. He walked with his shoulders and head thrust forward, like a bull. His wide face, dark skin, and black hair added to the resemblance. He was a cruel man, and I hated him. He wasted no time in putting me to work in the quarry. Too small to wield a pick, I was made to carry water to the men, one bucket at a time. I struggled with the heavy bucket, at first falling often beneath the burden and spilling most of the water, being cursed for my carelessness and stung by the overseer's lash. I developed muscles that eventually let me carry a bucket on either end of a yoke across my shoulders. In a few years I'd grown strong enough to turn the buckets over to a younger child and take up the pick. I chopped stone from the quarry until I was brought away and put to work in the fields and trained in the rite of Lord's-Kill. My life changed then, but I was no less a slave. Now my life had changed again, but I could scarcely conceive that the change made me something other than a slave.

The wonderful smell of the fresh bread and tangy odor of the fish cakes drove out these thoughts Lisha had stirred. I attacked the feast, stuffing food into my mouth faster than I could swallow, washing it down with gulps of the cold, sweet milk. I consumed everything on the tray and turned to the bowl of fruit, snatched up a pear in one hand and an apricot in the other. Alternating a bite of one with a bite of the other, I reduced them to core and pit and stretched my tongue to lick the juice that dribbled from my mouth. My gorged stomach pressed uncomfortably against my aching ribs. I stood, belched, and paced around the tent to settle the food.

Remembering my earlier intention, I paused in front of the screen and studied the painting of the temple. I circled the screen several times, comparing the temples on each side. They were alike, and I wondered why they had been placed in two such different settings.

I returned to the table and looked at the stone. The fragments of Pathfinder were no longer beside it, but the stone itself interested me. Memory of the heat it had radiated when Savnar had passed it over my hand made me afraid to pick it up. I peered at the colored bands so like those of the rock wall of my dream. Gathering courage, I reached out and stroked the rock with a fingertip, expecting a burning heat. Instead I felt the cool texture of ordinary rock.

Lisha burst into the tent and raced to my side. She clutched my arm and pulled me toward the screen.

"Guards," she panted. "Hurry!"

She shoved me behind the screen, pushed me onto the cushions, and dropped beside me. "They're almost here."

Her whisper was smothered by loud voices and the stomp of booted feet. My heart pounded. The flimsy screen would provide little protection from Manor Guards. With no place else to hide, I huddled against Lisha. Her nearness excited me. The heat of her body, the heady scent of lilies made me forget my danger.

Savnar's voice floated around the screen. "True, I gave assistance to a man the villagers had badly beaten. I didn't know he was an escaped slave. I assumed he was a freedman like them."

"His status should have been obvious from his clothing." Without seeing him, I could visualize the harsh-voiced speaker: shiny black boots, black trousers, a razor-sharp axe thrust into a wide belt of black leather. Tan tunic, a circular patch on its sleeve bearing the Manor insignia, the double-edged sword of Molor, silver on a background of glossy black. A mace held in chain-mail gauntlet to display the wicked spikes. His face … my imagination failed. I had never dared look at the face of a Manor Guard.

If he were alone I might have a chance against him, despite his weapons.

"To you the clothing would reveal his status. I am a stranger to this land, unfamiliar with its forms of dress and other customs." Savnar spoke courteously, but his voice held no tinge of subservience.

"His manner would prove him a slave." A second voice, with a clear ring of authority.

"He didn't linger long enough to permit me to study his manner," Savnar said. "I've told you he ran into the forest after the freedmen disappeared."

"That better be true, Fascinator," said a third speaker.

I was hopelessly outnumbered.

"Waste no more words," the second voice ordered. "Search the tent. What's behind that screen?"

I got ready to rise and defend myself. Better to die of a crushed skull than suffer the slow torture of impalement.

Lisha slid behind me and wrapped her arms around me. "Don't move," she breathed in my ear.

I leaned against her soft breast, and my heart slowed its frantic pounding. The scent of lilies swirled around me. I grew dizzy and my eyelids slid shut.

5

GIFTS

A fragrance of lilies wafts through the jungle. Sunlight, pure and golden, beams off the temple's dome and spreads out over the creeping vines and flowering shrubs. I edge through the dense undergrowth. Vines catch at my feet, snaring me. I fight free and struggle on. A bird with brilliant plumage swoops toward me. I wave it away, but others dive at me, their sharp beaks aimed at my head. I dash for the temple door.

I tug at it. How can it be locked?

I slam my fists against the carved wood. Hollow echoes mock me. Talons extended, the birds plunge. Claws grip my hands.

"Korth, relax. You're safe." At Lisha's whisper the jungle dissolved and the familiar tent rematerialized around me. My head lolled against Lisha's soft breast.

I pulled away from her. What delusion had I experienced? Where were the Manor Guards?

As if in answer, a voice floated back to me from somewhere outside the tent.

"You're free, Fascinator. You may stay and ply your trade. But befriend no more runaway slaves."

I stood and stared at the painted jungle on the screen. "I was there." I pointed to the temple. "I got to the door but couldn't get in."

I swung around. Lisha had also risen. Our eyes met. I did not lower my gaze. "What happened, Lisha? Why didn't the guards see me?"

"Didn't you tell me just now that you were in the jungle, in front of the temple?" Her smile teased. "You weren't here."

"But that wasn't real. It couldn't have been."

"Are you wise enough to know what is real and what is not?"

I dropped my gaze. Heat flamed in my face.

Her voice softened. "Korth, you have merely erred in a way that many who claim great wisdom also err. You have no cause for shame."

At her gentle words I raised my head and looked at her. I caught my breath. So lovely was she, and so radiant. Like a goddess.

I dared to ask, "The temples are real?"

The music of her laughter floated over me. "How can I answer that when you don't know the meaning of 'real'?"

"Then tell me why there are two, one on a mountaintop and one in the jungle."

"Temples are the dwellings of gods. Zera dwells in the temple on the high mountain, where she can look down on this world. The jungle temple was built by Makor, her consort. It was abandoned after Molor slew Makor, his twin."

The answer gave me much to think about, but I had no chance to question her further. Saying, "Come, Father is back," she clasped her fingers about my wrist and led me around the screen. I hadn't heard Savnar reenter the tent.

He strode toward us swinging a braided leather cord. "Good work, Lisha. The guards looked right at our friend and didn't see him." He chuckled.

His words deepened my confusion. Savnar implied that I had not left the tent. Yet the guards hadn't seen me.

Wrapped in thought, I jumped when Savnar flung over my head the cord he'd dangled. He and Lisha both laughed at my startled reaction.

"I've given you a fascinum, crafted for you alone," Savnar said. "That should prove you're no slave."

Wide-eyed, I stared down at the charm that hung from the tightly braided leather. A silver cylinder the length and width of my thumb lay against my chest. It was formed like a piece of thorny branch; small silver thorns angled from it. Polished and set into it like gems were the three fragments of Pathfinder Savnar had taken from my hand.

Awed, I lifted the cord and held the charm up for a closer look. Turning it about, I discovered that the side I hadn't seen bore a different design. That side of the charm depicted a burial pillar. Etched into the silver was a bee, wings poised for flight, balanced on the edge of a drooping trumpet flower attached to a broken stem. I studied it, disquieted by a half-memory that refused to become whole. I'd seen the device before and should recognize it, but where I might have seen it I couldn't fathom.

"This fascinum draws on the power of the goddess Zera," Savnar said. "It will serve you well in the lands beyond the Rethe where Zera reigns."

Zera again! I dropped my hand from the amulet and glanced

around fearfully, though no one could have overheard Savnar's words. As a slave I'd paid little homage to any god, but I'd heard of a house servant who'd been severely beaten for a mere mention of the goddess Zera, and I knew a quarry slave who'd been stoned for calling on Zera for help.

"What of the Great One we honor here?" I asked.

Lisha stepped in front of Savnar. Her eyes sparked. "Molor?" She spat the name. "Forget the Twin-Slayer."

I bowed my head. I'd given offense.

Lisha cupped my chin in her hand and lifted my head. She was smiling again, all trace of anger gone. "Korth, here where Molor is honored you've been a slave. Across the Rethe you are free. Doesn't that tell you whom to honor? Trust in Zera's power."

I nodded without raising my head. Already I'd proved myself unworthy of the fascinum.

"I, too, have a gift for you," Lisha continued. "It's in the wagon. I'll get it."

She danced from the tent. My gaze followed her. Savnar cleared his throat.

"Lisha is a many-faceted gem, Korth. A man might devote a lifetime to discovering her aspects and never discern them all."

Why would he make such a statement? Embarrassment and confusion prevented me from voicing my agreement. I was still staring foolishly at the carpet when Lisha returned with a large bundle.

She placed the bundle on the floor and began to unroll the cloth. "I've repaired your shirt."

I hardly recognized the shirt she drew from the wrapper. I'd never seen it so clean, and the tears were mended so I could not see where they'd been. I was still admiring it when she unrolled the wrapper farther and displayed a pair of dark brown leather boots.

"These are plain but well-made and serviceable. Father bartered a fascinum for them."

I accepted them, feeling I must again be dreaming. Although Lisha called them plain, the boots were far finer than I had ever hoped to own. I plopped down onto a pillow and drew them on, terrified they would not fit.

They cradled my feet with comfort. I marched around the tent, grinning with pleasure.

"Father also bartered for this." She handed me a leather belt of the same shade and quality as the boots. "Put it on," she urged.

I held it out and looked at it. Like the boots, it bore no design. Its workmanship was in no way extraordinary, but to a slave who'd never owned a belt it was a marvel. It had a pouch for coins and even boasted a loop for the handle of an axe or mace. I fingered the loop with wonder.

"You must furnish your own weapons," Lisha said.

I opened my mouth to protest that I was not permitted to own a weapon, closed it again. The witness of boots and belt made me believe Savnar when he said I was free.

"Such rich gifts," I murmured. "How can I repay you?"

Savnar's blue eyes twinkled. "If repayment were required, they wouldn't be gifts."

"Korth, thus far I have given you your own shirt and the boots and belt Father exchanged for fascina. You have as yet received nothing new from me."

I stared at Lisha, eager to see what wonder she would produce and stunned at the generosity of these people. I could not believe they would shower me with gifts and ask nothing in return. There would be some price to pay. Did it matter? As a slave I'd been forced to labor without pay. For these riches any service would seem light.

Lisha completed unrolling the cloth from which she'd taken shirt, boots, and belt. From its center she withdrew a ginger jar. She set the jar on the table and lifted off its lid. "You won't need this container. I'll keep it," she said with a smile.

The jar was empty. She must be mocking me.

She returned to the cloth, shook it, and held it up. At the sight of a new poncho my disappointment vanished. Such a poncho! Tightly woven of fine wool, not like the coarse, rough garment I'd ruined, its color, a bright leaf green, would make a lord proud. Woven in brown thread, a design repeated itself in vertical stripes—a branch of thorns.

While I stood paralyzed with amazement, Savnar and Lisha guided my arms into my shirt, tugged it into place, and slipped the poncho over my head onto my shoulders.

Knowing no way to thank them for their kindness, I kept silent. Surely now they'd request some service.

Turning solemn, Savnar said, "Korth, with Manor Guards in the area, it is not safe for you here. These gifts will help you make your way beyond the borders of this land."

My spirits fell; the delight faded. I'd forgotten my intention to leave the land. Savnar's words filled me with sadness and a sense of abandonment.

Lisha took my hand. "We'll take you to the bridge in the wagon and be sure you get past the guards."

Silenced by the sorrow of leaving, I let her lead me outside. The plain daylight seemed drab and alien after the tent's warm golden glow.

Lisha led me to the boxlike wooden wagon, leaped into it, and extended her hand. Stubbornly I grasped the side and pulled myself up, grinding my teeth to stifle an outcry when the movement produced a starburst of pain.

Across the back of the wagon Lisha drew a curtain of the same yellow fabric as the tent. It let in light but shut out all other intrusions.

Cooking gear was stacked on the plank floor next to a small woodstove. Sacks of supplies leaned against a bench littered with the tools of Savnar's craft. Lisha perched on a wooden barrel, and I sat hunched in the only bit of empty floor space.

"The bridge isn't far," she said.

Though the jolting of the wagon would jar my cracked ribs, I'd endure the misery for many hours to stay longer in Lisha's presence.

The wagon shook and lurched. I braced myself.

Lisha rose. "We're here."

I grinned at her joke. We couldn't have moved. I'd heard no clomp of hooves, felt no swaying or bumping.

She swept the curtain back. I expected to see the tent and beyond it the booths of the market. Instead I gaped at empty greensward.

"Where are we? Where's the market?"

Lisha laughed. "We left it far behind. Look, there's the bridge."

My gaze followed her pointing finger. A wide suspension bridge spanned the river. My jaw dropped. "How ... Where ...?"

Ignoring my sputtering, Lisha pulled out from among the stores beside her barrel seat a bulging knapsack. "I've put up provisions so you won't have to stop to forage or work for food until you're two or three days' journey from the bridge."

"I can't lift or carry that," I protested. "My ribs ..."

She frowned. "I've already eased your pain a bit. I'll ease it more, though I can't remove it entirely." She ran her hands lightly down my sides, then helped me slip the straps of the pack over my shoulders and drew them tight. Amazingly I felt only slight discomfort. I'd endured far worse throughout my years as a slave.

Beckoning, she jumped lightly from the wagon. "Come, it's safe."

I clambered down and looked around. Near the bridge in the shade of a drooping willow two Manor Guards lay sleeping, the sound of their snoring borne to us on a fresh easterly wind. Savnar came whistling around the wagon. I pointed a trembling finger at the guards.

He dismissed them with a careless wave of his hand. "They're weary from being overlong at watch. They'll sleep until we're gone."

"How did we come here so fast?" I peered around the corner of the wagon. It stood as I had always seen it, its shafts unhitched to any animal. "What drew the wagon?"

Savnar's eyebrows arched. "Why, my horse." He motioned toward the shafts.

I looked again, blinked, and rubbed my eyes. A massive roan horse stood between the shafts.

"We'd best not tarry here," Savnar said. "Put these decims in your pouch and shoulder your pack." He thrust three copper coins into my hand and led me to the bridge.

Placing his hand on my shoulder, he said, "When you step onto the far bank, you will be out of the jurisdiction of the Manor Guards. They will not pursue you. But you'll face other dangers. We have given you aids to ease the physical transition from slave to free, but the journey of your soul we cannot ease. You must make that way yourself."

I nodded, unable to speak. I looked toward the wagon. The red horse tossed its mane and stomped its hooves. As I stared, it rippled, dissolved into wind-driven flame, and reassembled.

"We must leave you," Savnar said, ignoring the horse. "You and I shall meet again—perhaps often."

The comfort of that promise drew my eyes back to his face. His eyes met mine in a solemn gaze.

"Be warned, Korth. I do not always travel as a fascinator. I have many crafts and many guises. You may not know me when next we meet."

I glanced at Lisha. "I won't forget you so quickly," I said.

"That's not what I meant. And Lisha does not always travel with me."

Disappointment must have shown in my face. Lisha patted my arm. "Father doesn't mean that you won't see me again. Now, go. Hurry, before those guards awake."

Her gentle shove propelled me onto the bridge. It swayed beneath my weight. I trotted forward, gathering speed as I approached the center, slowing as I neared the end. I stopped at the far end. Hand clasped over my fascinum, I turned and looked back.

The wagon was gone. I scanned the riverbank in both directions but spied no trace of it.

The two guards emerged from the shade of the willow. One looked in my direction and gave a shout. They pounded toward me.

I dashed off the bridge and sprinted straight ahead.

I ran until my screaming lungs and aching chest demanded a halt. A glance behind told me my pursuers had not ventured beyond the bridge. I sank down onto a boulder by the roadside. I was free!

Sweat dripped down my face. I wiped it with the fringe of my new poncho and fanned myself with the cloth. I should be carrying the poncho, not wearing it at midday. But I was afraid to slip off my pack, remove the poncho, and try to wriggle back into the pack with no help and my ribs radiating pain. I caught my breath, stood, and trudged on along the hard-packed dirt path.

"You have any idea where we're going?"

I jumped and looked around. The high-pitched voice sounded close. I saw no one along the road. I returned to the boulder and circled it. Someone must be hiding in the tall grass. But no, the grass was thin and offered little hiding place.

All that lay on the far side of the River Rethe was unknown to me and, for all I knew, might be filled with monsters and strange beasts and people very different from those of the Manor Lands. So I steeled myself, supposing I was about to meet one of those peculiar inhabitants.

"Didn't think to ask for a map, I suppose," the voice said from beside my elbow.

I spun around, nerves taut, fingers ready, if only I could find a neck to wrap them around. "Where are you?"

"Right here next to you, you stupid oaf."

"Come out of hiding," I bellowed. "Show yourself."

"I'm not hiding. I'm in plain sight."

Swinging my arms, my fists clenched, I circled, peering all around.

Amid peals of laughter the infuriating voice said, "What a strange dance! What do you call it?"

I stood still, glaring. "Why can't I see you? Or feel you?"

"You're practically senseless, that's why."

"What are you?" A sudden notion chilled my bones despite the midday heat. "Are you Dama Koralie's fiend?"

"I know no Dama Koralie. A pity. She must be a remarkable person, to own a fiend."

"But are you a fiend?" I persisted.

"What foolish questions you ask. If I were such a thing, I would not answer truthfully, so if I say no, will you believe me?"

I rubbed my head, absorbing the truth of that observation. "Who are you?" I asked.

"Ah, that's the question you should've asked first. But before I answer, I think you'd better look up the road. Someone's coming."

I jerked my head toward the bridge, expecting to see the guards.

The road was empty.

"Not that way," the voice barked in my ear. "The other direction."

I whirled around. A juggler strode toward me, dressed in motley and wearing a mask that covered his whole face. A spiky fringe around it and the wide band that secured it to his head hid all but a few strands of dark hair. As he walked, he tossed and caught what I took to be several decorated balls.

He drew nearer. The circling balls took on clearer form. Though small, they appeared to be ... yes! ... human heads.

6

NAMING

The juggler paused, flung the small heads high, twirled them in a ghastly dance, with a flourish plucked them one at a time from their ghoulish circuit, and set them on the boulder.

Seven of them. Each a third the size of a normal human head. The skin, the hair, the staring eyes all looked very real. Only the size showed that they had to be cruel imitations.

I could not tear my eyes from them. I peered at each face, noted each feature. Three of the heads were women's, long hair flung about from the juggling. One had been young, a mere girl, with dark hair and wistful eyes. Another, a bit older, a beauty with hair a coppery red, features fine and even. The third was silver-haired with a long, narrow nose, high cheekbones, and straight-lipped mouth that suggested one who would give orders and have them obeyed.

Of the four men, one had the plain, blunt look of a farmer. The hair of another hung shaggy and shapeless, and his eyes had the feral look of a madman. The last two I judged highborn by their fine features and the fashion of their hair. What most puzzled me was a haunting familiarity about all seven. One I thought bore a resemblance to Savnar, but as I stared at it, the supposed resemblance vanished. I could name none, yet I felt I had known and should recognize them all.

"You like my little beauties?"

I whipped around. In my fascination with the heads, I had forgotten the juggler. He was as much a puzzle as they. Why did he wear a mask covering his entire face, and why was his clothing so odd? Its patchwork of bright colors made it seem that his shirt and trousers had been pieced together with the discarded scraps of garments made for lords and ladies.

In my bafflement I ignored his question. He repeated it, gesturing toward the heads.

I moved nearer the boulder and gazed closely at them. Stifling my revulsion, I said, "They can't be real."

"Ah, can't they?" He caught up two of the heads, held them in his palms, and raised them level with his face. "Are you real, my lovelies?"

He waggled one hand so that the head bobbed about as though speaking and in a high-pitched voice said, "Why, that depends on him."

He waggled the other hand and pitched his voice low. "He will know if he puts names to us."

"How do you expect me to do that?" I demanded, stifling the strange impression that I should be able to name them.

He set the heads back on the boulder and put one finger to his temple in a comic pose. "Let me see," he said. "You've just crossed from the Manor Lands. I wonder why you fled. Could it be because you practiced the rite of Lord's-Kill? And in doing so, received an inheritance—the deathright?"

Fear clamped icy hands around my heart. This stranger knew that I had killed the Manor Lord.

"I don't know what you're talking about." My response was partially true. Though I'd performed the rite of Lord's-Kill as he said, I knew nothing of receiving any inheritance. Nor did I know what he meant by "deathright."

"You're more of a fool than I," he said. "You should have received the spirit and memories of the old lord. You must have received something, for you aren't as ignorant as the slave you were, though neither are you fit to inherit the lordship."

He was making no sense, yet he knew things that made him a danger to me. I flexed my fingers, tempted to wrap them around his throat and squeeze. But although he'd puzzled and irritated me, he hadn't threatened any physical harm.

"What do you mean, inherit the lordship?" I asked.

He leaped onto the boulder with effortless grace. "I'm not surprised that the dama kept you in ignorance, scheming witch that she is," he said, "but I'd have expected your friends to have told you."

"Told me what?" He must mean Savnar and Lisha, though how he knew about them I couldn't imagine. "Answer my questions," I snarled.

He only laughed and balanced on the toes of one foot to spin among the heads.

Furious, I charged toward him. He sprang from the boulder, made an exaggerated bow, and waved toward the circle of heads.

"You hold the answers. They'll come to you if you name my beauties." His hand, palm down, passed above the heads. "Look closely at each face." He pressed his fingers on the head I guessed to be a madman's. "This one, for example. Can you put a name to it?"

I squeezed my brow in concentration, sure I had seen the face before. But no name came to mind. Slowly I shook my head.

"Or this one?" He shifted his fingers to another of the male heads, tilting it upward so its dull eyes stared into mine. "What is he called?"

My mouth tried to form the name. "P ... P ... P ..." The stutter of that single sound was all that came. Again I shook my head.

"And what of this one?" He caught the pretty woman's head by its red hair.

A name danced on the fringes of my memory but would come no closer. "I can't name any. How could I? Why do you ask me to?"

He gathered up the heads and juggled them once more. "To learn what sense you have," he said, and drew a burlap sack from beneath his brightly patterned shirt. He tossed the heads into the sack and pulled the drawstring tight.

"Begone, clown, and take these bits of fakery with you." It was that mysterious voice, back again.

"What trickery is this?" The juggler glared at me. "Have you—"

My bewildered look must have told him I wasn't the voice's source. He broke off and looked around.

"Go, I say," the voice persisted. "Trouble this innocent wayfarer no longer."

Slinging the bag over his shoulder, the juggler said, "It seems you have protection I was not aware of. I'll leave, but we'll meet again— soon." He jogged off toward the bridge without a backward glance.

I stood by the boulder, but I couldn't bring myself to use that resting-place again. I hitched up my pack and stepped onto the roadway.

"Lucky I'm with you. You'd have been easy picking for that trickster."

I stared at the empty boulder. Laughter trilled beside me. "Did you note how quickly he left when I spoke? I was playing a dangerous game, of course, but so was he."

"Who and what are you?" I asked the empty air.

From behind me and to my right the voice answered, "I'm Derli, a fellow-traveler. Nothing more."

I scratched my head. "Nothing more? You seem much less. Only a voice. That's what I don't understand."

A loud yawn blasted my right ear. "It's tiresome being asked to conform to your limitations. I could incorporate, but there's no material for it, and the job's hardly worth the effort. To oblige your stunted senses, why should I put up with the dreariness of being crammed into a clumsy shell? The ginger jar was bad enough. I hate tight places."

"Ginger jar!" I remembered the empty jar Lisha had set on the table while producing my gifts. "You came from *that?*"

A loud and cheerful whistling was the only answer. It grated on my ears. As I walked, my irritation grew, fueled by my aching ribs and the increasing heat of the poncho. I regretted the pride that had made me insist on wearing the garment. Rivulets of sweat poured down my brow and dripped into my eyes, making them sting and burn. I could scarcely see.

My faltering steps propelled me into a massive tree trunk. I staggered back, gasping from the agony of the impact against my injured ribs, forehead smarting from scraping against the rough bark.

"Haven't gone five miles and you're already asleep on your feet. Zera knows I've tried to keep you awake, but you've so little wit to begin with, I can hardly tell whether it's conscious or not. And now I suppose you're going to stand there and wait for the tree to move out of your way."

"Oh, be quiet, will you?"

The nagging voice stilled. I rubbed my skinned forehead and banged nose and glared at the offending tree. I'd failed to see the split where the road forked around the tree and went off in two different directions. I backed out of the tree's shadow and studied the routes.

Cool and shaded, the right path curved among stately oaks, bent sharply to the west, and vanished. The few trees that shaded the beginning of the left path gave way to level farmland through which it ran straight and smooth for as far as I could see. Farmhouses made small by distance nestled on either side of the road until it met the horizon.

"Which one shall I take?"

Silence greeted my question.

"Derli?"

No answer. I'd have to make my own decision.

I considered. The shaded right way offered more protection from the heat, but I couldn't see where it led, and its turnings suggested it might double back toward the river, the one way I did not want to go.

The left led southeast into inhabited country. Here on this side of the river, in a free man's clothes, I had no reason to fear the presence of people. I recalled how Pathfinder had led me to the east when my inclination had been to turn west. In spite of my cruel treatment at the hands of the freedmen, I didn't regret the leading that resulted in my meeting with Lisha and Savnar.

The memory of Savnar and of Pathfinder reminded me of my new fascinum. I placed my hand on it. It gave off a steady warmth.

I turned left, still touching the fascinum. With each step I took, the silver amulet cooled. When I'd gone ten or twelve paces, its icy coldness stung my hand. I pried my numbed fingers off it and turned back toward the fork. I'd gone only a few steps before the fascinum warmed enough to let me hold it comfortably.

I reached the fork and turned right. My hand tingled pleasantly. The fascinum grew hot yet didn't burn. I glanced down, half expecting to see a glow within my fingers, but nothing extraordinary met my gaze.

Convinced I'd been guided away from the left fork, I continued down the right. Although the path made many turnings through the shaded wood, it never long departed from its westerly direction.

In the shade a breeze ruffled my hair and cooled my face and arms. The poncho was still overly warm but no longer unbearable. Small birds chittered from the overhead branches; a carpet of fallen leaves softened the ground. Where the carpet lay thickest, it obscured the path so that several times I nearly missed a turn. There was little underbrush and the trees were evenly spaced throughout the wood, making it easy to wander off the path. But I kept my hand on the fascinum, and each time I strayed its sudden cooling alerted me. Well-being flowed through me. I felt more alive, more complete than I had ever felt.

No mysterious voice disturbed me. Perhaps Derli had taken the other path.

The weather was fair; the world was beautiful. I was at peace. I put behind me the troubling encounter with the juggler and swung along with slow, easy tread, breathing deeply the subtle, spicy scent of the woods.

I stumbled over a stone, thrust out both hands, and caught a branch. Only then I realized I had not for some time had my hand on the fascinum. I touched it. Neither hot nor cold, it was only an inert piece of silver.

I looked at the leaf-strewn ground. No trace of a path. I wasn't alarmed. With the help of the fascinum I could retrace my steps to where I'd wandered from the path.

The stone against which I'd stumbled was on a slope that angled sharply downward into a narrow, deeply shaded ravine through which wound a small brook.

I'd long since walked off the hearty breakfast Lisha had served. Hungry again, I decided to eat in the cool sanctuary of the ravine before hunting the path. It seemed safe enough; I'd encountered no one other than the juggler, nor had I seen houses or other signs of human habitation.

I skidded down the slope and picked my way through a thicket of berry bushes to a bit of bare ground. Here I shrugged off the backpack with only a few twinges of pain and eased it to the ground. I pulled off my poncho, hung it over a limb of a taller bush, and lowered myself beside my pack.

In it I discovered loaves of bread, two large bricks of cheese, a packet of dried fish, and several types of fruit. I stuffed bite after bite into my mouth, eating almost half the rations before recalling with a guilty start that Lisha said she'd packed enough for three days. In this one meal I had consumed more than a day's rations.

Ashamed, I repacked what was left and, although there was a canteen in the pack, I drank water from the brook.

I was more aware of my aching ribs than I had been when walking at a steady pace. The prospect of struggling into my backpack with no one to help me made me postpone the ordeal a little longer.

A large rock provided a backrest. The ground on which I sat was hard-packed clay. Some impulse led me to scoot closer to the stream, lean over, and dip water in my palm to mix with the clay.

I rolled the moistened stuff around in the palm of my hand and began to shape it with my fingers. What prompted me to do such a thing I didn't know. Acting on impulse was not something a slave would do. Now for some peculiar reason it seemed natural to prod and pull and pinch the clay into a shape resembling nothing I'd seen in nature. I formed a creature with a finger-length body to which I attached two rear legs resembling those of a grasshopper and two forelegs like those of a crab that scuttled along the riverbank. The realization that such an odd creature would find movement difficult made me add a third pair of legs midway between the others and configure those in a fashion somewhat intermediate to the other pairs.

Finally I gave my clay creature a large oval head ending in a mouth with protruding lips shaped like a star. The thing made me laugh. I set it down on the ground beside me, scooped up more water and more clay, and shaped a second, trying to improve on my ridiculous design. This activity pleased me, and I soon had over a dozen of these little beasts arrayed beside me, the later ones more skillfully formed than the first, as my new-found talent improved with practice.

I leaned against the rock and surveyed my handiwork, oddly pleased by what I'd made. Relaxed and lulled by the brook's monotonous murmur, I closed my eyes.

The murmur of the brook swelled, took on rhythm, became music of mandolin and flute and drum. Trees became stately pillars.

... I stroll through a huge ballroom among lords and ladies in rich shades of green and blue and lavender and yellow ... flowing robes sewn with jewels ... the men's swirling capes cover silk shirts and satin breeches. Beneath sparkling chandeliers, dancing couples paint an ever-shifting rainbow. I move into their midst, attired as elegantly as they. The couples pause their dance and bow as I pass. I give a distracted nod and scan the crowd, seeking one special face.

I spy her ... pale green gown of rich velvet ... red hair in tight curls around her neck.

I wind through the crowd to reach her side and bow. "My Lady Renata, will you dance?"

She smiles and places her hand on my arm. We slip into the weaving rainbow, part of that living swirl of color. I direct our gliding movement so that when the music stops, we're near an archway leading to an open courtyard. Clasping her delicate fingers, I guide her into the darkened patio.

"My Lady, you haven't spoken. I long to hear your sweet voice speak my name."

I pause, frown. My name ... what is my name? I can't recall. Bewildered, I look deep into her eyes, my hands in her copper curls.

Her body shudders and dissolves, leaving her head hanging by its hair from my paralyzed fingers ...

I awoke and jerked upright.

The head—one of those the juggler had shown me. I could name it now. It was the woman in my dream.

Renata!

Renata. Her sparkling sapphire eyes, the glorious blaze of her red hair, the soft satin of her skin pressed against mine when we made love on the wide lounge in the tower room. I—

What was I thinking? I'd never loved a woman.

I swung my head from side to side, trying to reorder my jumbled thoughts.

What had the juggler said? Something about receiving the memories of the old lord. Could Renata be a memory of his?

Or was it just a leftover remnant of my dream? Perhaps a result of Lisha waking a part of me that slumbered until I heard her voice and breathed her lily scent.

A faint hint of lilies floated on the breeze that played around me now.

Lisha?

Only darkness met my searching gaze.

7

DERLI

Darkness! Full awareness crashed against me. I'd wasted the afternoon forming my useless clay creations and dreaming someone else's dream. By night I had no hope of finding my way out of the ravine and back onto the path.

I might as well go back to sleep and get a fresh start by morning's first light. I stretched out on my rocky bed and listened to the brook, letting its soft song lull me to sleep. I didn't dream, unless a sensation of sinking into unconsciousness deep as death can be called a dream.

From an immeasurable distance a voice summoned me. I couldn't answer. The sound grew closer, loud, insistent.

"Korth! Korth, wake! Wake and move!" The meaningless syllables echoed through the pit into which I was falling. "Korth!" The name formed a hook, snagged my consciousness, and dragged me through swirling dark currents until the sudden and unexpected weight of my body snapped around me like a coffin. My isolation splintered. Something prodded my side. Something shoved my shoulders.

"Korth. Get up."

Whatever the thing was, it was pliant. It rolled me to and fro like a woman's dough-roller under the heel of a giant hand. It molded itself around my body as it pushed. A fetid stench as of long-dead flesh poured into my nostrils. I gagged.

"Korth, for Zera's sake, get up while you still can." I recognized the muffled voice as that of my invisible companion. I groaned.

"Good, you're coming around at last. Come on. You've got to move if you want to live. I can't lift you, and I can't stand this flesh much longer." The words were choked as though with sobs.

I heard the urgency in the plea, but all my muscles seemed turned to water.

The flabby form rolled my body onto its side and cradled me, squeezing me into a jackknife position that caused pain from my ribs such as I hadn't felt since Lisha's healing touch. I tried to pull away from the stifling smell. My hands pushed at the ground and slid.

My eyelids parted. A dim, greenish glow penetrated my blurred vision.

"Move, you great lump, move! My life's forfeit if you die."

Another shove sent me skidding sideways. Searing agony tore at my chest. I pulled myself to hands and knees. Trembling, I focused bleary eyes on a terrifying sight.

Around me, by the early light of dawn, I saw, attached to my exposed flesh and dripping from me, hundreds, perhaps thousands, of swollen black leeches and slimy white grubs.

I yelled and tore at the things. I shook and twisted and rolled, wrenching and scraping the creatures from my skin, but as fast as I dislodged some, others attached themselves.

I did have *some* help. Long-legged insectile creatures were attacking the bloodsuckers. With a start I recognized the things I'd sculpted from clay. They had somehow acquired life and were defending their maker. They were the same size as my attackers but were vastly outnumbered. Already most of them were missing limbs, and some lay broken and as inert as the clay sculptures they had been. It wouldn't be long before all my pitiful creations met that fate. And so would I, if I couldn't get free of the things that were draining my blood.

I hurled myself toward the slope. My feet slipped. The more I tried to pull myself forward, the more I slid back, sobbing and screaming.

A dragging sound made me turn to look behind me. A huge, shapeless white blob oozed toward me, its translucent flesh exuding an eerie glow.

The vile mass nudged my backside. "It's me. Don't be afraid. Let me help you." Derli's voice spoke from the monstrous lump. "You've got to get out of this ravine."

"Can't move," I gasped. "So weak."

"From loss of blood. Move. I'll help you."

The squishy blob pressed against me. I crawled forward. It shifted toward me and pushed me on. I inched up the steep slope of the ravine, prodded and pillowed by the faceless, formless glob of slimy flesh. As we climbed, the slugs shriveled and dropped away. Leeches loosed their suction and fell from my flesh. With flagging strength I dragged myself onto level ground. The amorphous glob that was Derli nudged me toward a tree. I hauled myself to a sitting position and leaned against the trunk.

The ghastly hulk slid away and disappeared back into the ravine. I thought I'd seen the last of it, but I'd scarcely caught my breath when a whiff of its rank scent made me look up to see it undulating toward me. Floating on top of it were my backpack and poncho.

"You'll need these." The thing slithered next to me and toppled its burden into my lap. It glided back to the lip of the ravine, pulled itself into a sphere, and burst into luminescent fragments. Most cascaded into the ravine. The rest landed on the bank and vanished in wisps of steam.

"Pfaugh! Good riddance to that vile mess." Derli's voice spoke from beside me. "That was the worst incorporation I've ever endured."

"You made that ... that thing?" I shuddered.

"Out of the bloodsuckers that crawled out of the mud to attack you. The only things I could use. I clumped several hundred of the varmints together and jumped in. I'd rather bathe in a cesspool."

I fingered my soiled poncho. "The smell will never come out of this."

"Maybe not, but you need its warmth. You lost so much blood ..."

I spread it over my legs. I couldn't bear to bring it any nearer my nose.

"I think we're safe here, but I'll keep watch," Derli continued. "Get some rest so you'll have the strength to walk."

I doubted that the poncho's stink would let me sleep, but I shut my eyes.

Almost immediately a voice called, "Time to wake, Korth."

Sure the creatures of death were attacking again, I opened my eyes and found the wood dappled with the bright light of midday. I sat up. My head swam. My weakness proved the night's horror had not been a dream. I opened my pack and discovered that slime coated the food. I hurled it from me. Fortunately, the metal canteen, tightly closed, had kept the water pure and safe. I wiped the outside with sand and leaves before I opened it and drank.

I folded my poncho and stuffed it and the canteen into the empty pack, squatted and thrust my arms into the straps, and got the straps settled into place.

All the while, Derli kept up the cheerful whistling that had annoyed me the previous day. Now I welcomed the sound for its assurance of companionship and protection.

I lurched to my feet, reeled, and clung to a tree trunk until the dizziness subsided. Then I walked forward, gripping the fascinum. It gave off a faint warmth.

"We must be near the path," I said.

The whistling stopped. After a pause, Derli asked, "Are you sure you know how to use that thing?"

"It kept me on the path yesterday," I said. "I wouldn't have got lost if I'd kept hold of it."

"Maybe." Skepticism colored the single word.

"I'll show you." I walked in one direction, then another, then still another. The fascinum's temperature did not change. I turned in the remaining direction and walked toward the ravine. A burst of heat made me jerk my hand away from the amulet.

"Quite a demonstration," Derli drawled.

I stood at the edge of the ravine and stared into its shaded depths. "It might be safe by day," I said dubiously. "It was night when the grubs and leeches came out. And the brook is shallow enough to wade—I think."

A loud snort expressed Derli's opinion.

I lost patience. "Well, how do *you* say we should go?"

"You should have asked me that yesterday."

"I did. You weren't speaking."

"You'd ordered me to be quiet. I assumed you were talking to yourself—or to your fascinum—when you stood there like a silly fool muttering, 'Which way shall I go?' You seemed satisfied enough with the fascinum's answer."

"It's a reliable guide," I insisted. "Its fashioner was a man of great learning and kindness."

"So you say."

"So I *know*." I felt obligated to defend my benefactor, though in truth I knew little about him.

"Ah, and where did you acquire this astounding knowledge?"

"Why, from being with him. As his guest. He saved my life. He gave me gifts."

"For one so wise, you require a great deal of saving. And if you misuse the fascinum as badly as you have the other gifts, I question how well it can guide you. You've soiled your fine poncho and scratched and scuffed your new boots. Your shirt looks like it was never washed."

I glanced down at the clothes I'd been so proud of. My shame increased my stubbornness. "The fascinum's not harmed. It will lead me well."

"You trust the fascinum because it was Savnar's gift to you. Do you forget that *I* was one of Lisha's gifts? And that *I* saved your life last night?"

I deserved the rebuke. I hadn't forgotten that Derli had saved my life, but I *had* forgotten that my invisible companion had been one of Lisha's gifts. *If* the tale of having been in the ginger jar was true. Could I trust Derli to speak truth?

"So Lisha sent you to be my guide?"

"Savnar gave you the fascinum to protect and guide you. Lisha assigned me those same tasks. You trust the fascinum but you refuse to trust me."

I stepped to the lip of the ravine and looked down. I didn't want to reenter that haunt of death, yet I was curious about my clay creatures. Had I really seen them come to life, or was that a waking dream?

"The fascinum's heat indicates that we should go this way," I insisted. "I haven't heard you offer guidance."

"Because you don't ask for it. For one so recently a slave, you have a great deal of stubborn pride. It ill suits you."

"If I could see you, I'd be more inclined to trust you. I don't know what you are. I only hear your voice, and it's always carping and criticizing." So saying, I clambered down the slope to the edge of the brook. Loud sighs from Derli accompanied me. I took a quick look around for remnants of my clay creatures, found nothing but a few shapeless bits of dried clay. I must have dreamed their coming to life.

A touch found the fascinum cooler than it had been at the top of the slope. Alarmed, I took my hand from it. I was about to ask for advice, when Derli spoke.

"You're still a slave, Korth, for all that Savnar and Lisha told you that you were free."

Angered, I said nothing, but I resolved to ford the brook to prove myself to this invisible companion.

A row of sizable stones seemed to offer a crossing. I stepped out onto them.

Slime coated the rocks. Halfway across I slipped and tumbled into the icy water. Leeches fastened onto my hands. Something wrapped a tentacle around my ankle. I tore free of the mire, pulled away from the clutching tentacle, and scrambled up onto the opposite bank, my clothing dripping mud. Shaking, I plucked the noisome leeches off my arms and legs, and tried to climb the slope. A thick tangle of thorn-bushes barred the way. I was forced to pick my way along the side of the brook, keeping a fearful watch for its mud-dwellers.

The narrow strip of bare ground dwindled to nothing. I had either to reenter the brook or brave the thorns. Too frightened to attempt the brook, I crashed into the thorn-bushes. Gasping and coughing, I reached the top, hands bleeding, pack askew, trousers and shirt muddy and ripped. I was Tatterman again.

A loud throat-clearing proclaimed Derli's presence and made me look up. A few meters away a stone bridge spanned the ravine. "Had you asked, I would have advised you to take that way," said the voice.

I didn't answer, this time from shame rather than from anger.

On the path leading from the bridge an old man in baggy trousers and an ill-fitting brown tunic leaned on a gnarled staff and gawked as I wound my way toward him.

"You and the lady have chosen a difficult path, good sir," he said when I reached him.

"We felt the exercise would be of benefit," Derli said while I puzzled over what he meant by "the lady."

The old man showed no surprise at being addressed by a disembodied voice. His rheumy blue eyes fixed on a point to my right. "Those who choose hard paths do benefit, I've heard." He turned toward me and stroked his shaggy beard. "Your garments have fared ill. There's a refuge up ahead where you may cleanse and refresh yourself."

"Do you go that way, Sighted One?" Derli spoke in a respectful tone.

"No, Lady. I'm a nut gatherer and must be about my business." A veined hand held a burlap bag out toward the space beside me. I squinted at the point toward which his hand reached, saw only rippling sunlight.

"Can you tell me where this path leads?" I asked, concealing my amazement that this humble nut gatherer could see the companion invisible to me.

The old man's lips parted in a grin that exposed nearly toothless gums. "Why, to the Temple of Zera, of course."

The temple! My heart soared. "My fascinum hasn't led me wrong. I *am* on the right path."

The nut gatherer chuckled. "I couldn't say. *All* roads lead to the temple. Some are long and fraught with dangers, and all have many turnings before they reach their end."

Frowning, I asked, "Is this path a safe or a dangerous one?"

His eyes swept my torn and muddy clothing, my scratched boots, and my pale and bloodied skin. "I should think you'd already found that out." He hobbled off the lane toward a thick clump of trees, but he'd gone only a few steps before he turned and peered at us. "Lady, beware the trapper."

With that warning, he shuffled off and disappeared among the trees.

"What did he mean?" I asked. "And why didn't you tell me you were a woman?"

"If you weren't so dense, it would have been plain to you." I thought she was answering my first question until she added, "As to what his warning meant, I suppose we'll find out soon enough."

I set off at a slow, easy stride. The fascinum exuded the same tingling warmth I'd felt yesterday, assuring me we were back on the right path. I told Derli, but beyond that we spoke little. Now that I knew her gender, I felt awkward in her unseen presence. Weakness and hunger concentrated my thoughts on the refuge the nut gatherer had told us of.

She, too, was quiet, her whistling stilled. Perhaps the old man's warning had dampened her spirits. But her silence no longer made me doubt her continued presence at my side. She'd saved my life, accompanied me in my foolhardy return to the ravine—though the place must have been as hateful to her as to me—and, contrary to my expectations, had not made fun of me when we discovered how unnecessary that painful trek had been.

The trees thinned, letting in more light. A cool wind chilled me in my wet clothes, and my poncho was in my pack.

I rounded a curve and came on a clearing in which stood a log cabin. I stopped. This could be the refuge.

"There's a well," Derli said, calling my attention to a stone circle in front of the cabin. Smoke curled from a stovepipe chimney, and I caught a whiff of salt-pork frying. My stomach urged me toward the cabin door.

I halted.

"What's the matter?"

In answer to Derli's question I pointed to a tanned hide spread out and nailed up beside the door. "That's a fox pelt."

"So?"

I backed into the shadow of a tree. "This must be the cabin of the trapper you were warned about."

"I don't think—"

"I may not know much, but I *do* know a trapper's cabin when I see one. Look there." I pointed to frames where pelts were stretched to dry.

I heard loud sniffs. "The place smells safe."

"He's probably not curing any hides at the moment."

"I wasn't talking about that kind of smell. I was talking about the smell of evil. The ravine reeked of it."

"The ravine reeked of slime and vermin. Evil has no odor," I said.

Derli snorted. "How would you, with your feeble senses, know what odor it has?"

"I have the sense to know this is a trapper's cabin. You're at risk here if the nut gatherer is to be believed, and you made it clear that you respected his advice. We should go on and find the refuge he spoke of." I headed back to the lane and marched resolutely past the cabin and clearing. Derli's loud sigh told me she'd come with me.

A short distance beyond the cabin our path left the woods and shot due west across level fields. Ahead, on the left side of the road, was a cheerful high-eaved, flower-bordered building. The horse and wagon painted on the sign in front of it identified it as an inn.

"The refuge." My weary steps acquired a bounce as I hurried from the lane to the inn's open door.

As I approached the door, I heard several loud sniffs.

"Don't tell me this place doesn't smell right," I snapped.

Derli sighed. "How do you hope to learn anything if you tell people what they may or may not say to you?"

Before I could answer, a plump, balding man opened the door. Smiling and bobbing, he wiped greasy hands on a long, gray apron smeared with food stains.

"Welcome, journeyer. By the looks of you, the road has been unkind. Here you'll find food and rest—mending for your body and your clothes."

The unexpected warmth of the innkeeper's welcome delighted me. "I'm in need of both." Remembering the three decims Savnar had given me, I added the cautious question, "What are your rates?"

"A decim a day, the first payable in advance. If you stay longer than one day with us, you pay the balance when you leave."

"I'll be here no more than one day." I fumbled with the flap of the pouch, extracted a coin, wiped it on my shirt, and handed it to the innkeeper.

He squinted at it and thrust it into a pocket beneath his apron. He led me to a desk from which he dug out a worn ledger and a tarnished brass key. He made a great show of recording something in the ledger, but I had no idea what he wrote, being ignorant of letters. "Fifth room down the hall," he announced, handing me the key with a flourish. "Meeda will take you there and see to your clothes and your bath."

The innkeeper clapped his hands. A woman of great girth came out from what I guessed to be the kitchen area. She waddled past elaborately scrolled double doors and into a dark hallway. I trailed behind her. She stopped before the last of several closed doors. "Room five," she said.

I fit the key into the lock, turned the handle, and swung open the door. The room was of comfortable size and boasted a white-curtained window, a wardrobe, and a bed.

Meeda pushed past me and lumbered toward an unpainted screen. "I'll pour your bath. Strip, bathe, and get into bed. I'll take your clothes to be washed and mended. You'll have them back by suppertime." While I stood gaping, she squeezed behind the screen. The clang of metal buckets and the gurgle of water being poured from one container to another told me she was filling a tub. The screen swayed and shook from the movements of so large a body in so small a space.

"What do you think of this place?" I whispered to Derli.

"Why should I answer that when you don't want to hear my answer?" came the acerbic reply.

"Seems fine enough to me." I pressed down on the bed. It protested with a loud squeak. "Anyway, we can't complain. We have lodging for two for the price of one."

I unbuttoned and stripped off my shirt, unfastened my trousers, started to lower them, and stopped with a flush of embarrassment.

"You needn't worry. I'm not looking."

Derli's assurance did little to relieve me. "How do I know that?"

"You'll have to take my word for it, though you're not very good about doing that."

"I'm sorry. I'll try to trust you more." I stepped out of my trousers and surveyed my grime-caked body.

"Wrap up in the spread," Derli suggested. "That way you won't get the sheets dirty—if they happen to be clean."

I stripped the heavy beige coverlet off the bed and wrapped it around me. In that cocoon I'd just settled onto the bed when Meeda backed out from behind the screen.

"Water's ready," she announced. "Will you want food before the evening meal?"

"If it's not too much trouble. I've had no breakfast this morning."

"I'll have a bowl of soup on your dresser when you're done your bath."

She gathered my discarded clothing, including the poncho I'd taken from my pack. Carrying them at arm's length, her round face squeezed into an expression of distaste, she took her leave, letting the door swing shut behind her.

I went behind the screen trailing the beige wrapping and found a metal tub filled with water kept warm by hot stones placed in it. More stones baked on a small brazier and a pair of tongs for transferring them from brazier to tub hung on the wall.

I sank into the steaming water and scrubbed away the filth of the ravine. By the time I was done, my body was a bright pink and the water a muddy gray. I dried with a large towel Meeda had left on the floor beside the tub, wrapped it around me, and returned to the bedroom.

I hadn't heard Meeda come or go but, true to her word, a brimming bowl of barley soup waited on the dresser. I secured my towel, grabbed up the bowl in both hands, and gulped down the soup.

"Humph," Derli snorted. "Manners of a slave. I'll have to teach you about spoons."

I set the bowl down and saw the spoon placed beside it. Not caring to admit to Derli that I'd never used one, I shrugged and crossed to the bed. I stared at it and rubbed my chin.

"There are two sheets. Get between them."

Derli's instructions saved me from another blunder. I drew back the top sheet and lowered myself onto the side of the bed. The frame creaked. I stretched out stiffly over the mattress's humps and lumps. The bed was cold and comfortless; it didn't gather me in like my hammock. Scarcely daring to move, I groped for the top sheet, pulled it over me, and attempted to unwind and remove the towel. The twist of my body carried me too close to the edge of the bed. I tumbled out and sprawled across the floor, entangled in the sheet.

A muffled giggle exploded into a burst of laughter. "I'm sorry, Korth," Derli shrieked. "You look like a beached fish."

Furious, I scrambled to my feet, threw myself crosswise across the bed, pulled the sheet over me, and wished for my comfortable, safe hammock.

"I'm sorry I laughed, Korth." Derli's voice was low, contrite. Close by my ear she began humming a sweet, soothing melody. I relaxed and drifted into sleep.

A pounding on the door awakened me. "Your clothes are ready," Meeda announced. "It's time for the evening meal."

I arose, wrapped the sheet around me, and accepted the clothes from the pudgy hand Meeda thrust in through the partly open door.

The shirt and breeches were clean and mended, though the repairs were not invisible like those Lisha had made. Even the poncho was clean except for a faint lingering trace of fetid odor. I hung it over a bedpost to air.

After dressing, I left the room in search of supper. The bowl of soup had been tasty but hadn't dimmed my hunger. The double doors we'd passed earlier stood open, allowing tantalizing aromas to drift into the hall. I entered.

A long table piled high with food and lit by candles in tall candlesticks captured my gaze. A roast pig, plump and juicy, sat in the center, surrounded by fried fish; a selection of vegetables and fruits, baked, stewed, fried, and raw; breads and pastries; flagons of wine, and pitchers of milk. The innkeeper sat at one end and the lardy Meeda at the other. The whole scene was repeated in a mirror that covered the room's far wall, making the room appear much larger than it was and by reflecting the table and those who sat at it, doubling my hunger as it doubled the appearance of the feast.

The innkeeper looked up and beckoned me in. "Come, sir, you're just in time. Take a seat and let the feast begin."

Meeda gave me no greeting. Her eyes were fixed on the food. She licked her lips and grasped a knife and fork as if barely able to restrain herself from attacking the roasted pig. As eager as she, I hurried toward a chair.

"Ssst, Korth," Derli's voice hissed in my ear. "Look who's here."

No other guests sat at the table. I looked around. Through a door behind the innkeeper pranced the juggler. The large mirror captured his image, multiplying my unease. I should have listened to the warning Derli had tried to give me about this place.

In one hand the juggler carried a tall staff ending in curved prongs from which dangled six small heads. Shaking the staff, he capered in front of the mirror.

The innkeeper and Meeda paid no attention but stared at the array of food as though mesmerized. But the juggler drew me like a lodestone. I had to have a closer look at the heads. I sucked in my breath and squeezed behind the innkeeper to get around the table.

I halted before the smirking juggler. I hardly needed to look at the six heads hanging by their hair from the staff to know which of the original seven was missing—Renata's head was no longer among them.

"Well met again, wayfarer," the juggler sang out. "Do you wish to name another of my lovelies?" He shook the staff and set the heads swinging.

From nowhere a name popped onto my tongue. I pointed to the head of the older woman. "Brinabeth."

I stared at the head, expecting some transformation, but the set grimace did not alter, and the head went on bobbling among its fellows.

An anguished shriek rang out. The mirror clouded.

"Korth, help me! I'm trapped. I'm …" Derli's voice, distinct at first, trailed off into some mysterious distance.

A peal of maniacal laughter burst from the juggler.

8

TREACHERY

I lunged at the juggler. My hands gripped his throat. His staff toppled to the floor. "Let me go," he rasped. His face purpled.

"What have you done with Derli?" I demanded, loosening my grip enough to let him speak.

"I've done nothing," he gasped.

"She said she was trapped. Set her free."

"She was not trapped by me. Who knows—where she's gone she may find freedom."

The nut gatherer had warned Derli of a trapper, and now she was trapped. Who could have done it but this juggler? He'd free her or die. My fingers tightened. His knee smashed into my chest, breaking my grip. I staggered against the table. My elbow hit a tureen. The soup slopped over the rocking table. The roast pig slid toward me, sending hot grease splattering across my shirt. My chest burned. Steaming tomatoes splashed on me. I screamed, lost my balance, and fell.

The juggler leaned against the wall, pointed at me, and laughed until tears streamed down his cheeks. I staggered to my feet and charged him.

He dodged, caught up his staff, and thrust the dangling heads in my face. I grabbed the staff and swung it toward the mirror. The heads crashed against the clouded glass. One of them passed into the glass and disappeared.

The juggler dangled the remaining heads in my face. Missing was the one I'd identified as Brinabeth.

I walked to the mirror and reached out to place my hands against the glass. My arms plunged into what felt like wet wool, drawing me forward. My body banged into unyielding glass.

I pulled my arms free and stepped back. "What is that?" I whispered, staring at the mirror.

"A gateway to the past."

"I don't understand."

"Not surprising." He laughed. "You understand very little."

"I might understand more if you explained. What do you mean by 'a gateway to the past'?" I needed to help Derli, and this madman kept spouting nonsense.

The juggler twirled his pole, sending the heads dancing. "How about it, my beauties?" he addressed them. "Shall I explain?"

I reached for his throat. "Stop wasting time. Where has Derli gone?"

He easily dodged my grasp. "I have no idea. This gateway leads to many times and to no time."

"No time? You mean she might be dead?"

"I mean that the gateway leads to the past, but also to that place where time does not exist."

I shook my head. I would not admit again that I didn't understand. "But she did pass through the gateway."

"She did."

"And I can't?" Gingerly I reached through the mystifying surface.

"You can if you remove the charm you wear around your neck."

"My fascinum?" I removed my hand from the cold wet substance and touched the silver amulet. My fingers burned. I jerked away from the hot metal.

The juggler grinned. "Zera's power can't serve you where this gate leads. Leave the charm behind." He stretched out his hand.

I ignored it. "Will the gate take me to wherever she's gone?"

"I can't say." He did a little dance and sang, "The past is vast. Vast is the past." Laughing, he said, "You must go through the gate to find where it takes you."

Again I tried to push myself into the mirror. My head entered something like a dense fog, but my shoulders pressed against glass.

I eased back. The juggler stood with outstretched hand. "Give up your fascinum. Otherwise you will not rescue your friend."

Derli was not exactly my friend, yet she had saved my life. I heard again her anguished scream when she had been drawn through the glass. And I remembered that we were here because of my stubborn refusal to follow her instincts.

I couldn't desert her. But neither would I entrust my fascinum to the juggler. I turned toward the table. The innkeeper and Meeda had not moved. Like statues they stared at one another across the wreckage of the feast. The juggler must have placed a spell on them.

Tomatoes squished beneath my boots as I walked to the end of the table where Meeda sat. I lifted off my fascinum and slipped its cord over her head. The amulet dropped against her chest.

Meeda shuddered. Her eyes blinked and focused on me.

"Take care of my fascinum," I said. "I'll take it back when I return."

Her hand crept to her breast. Her fat fist swallowed the amulet. I could see by her befuddled look that she understood little of what had happened or what I'd said. Why I trusted her with the fascinum I couldn't say. She'd been kind to me, but it was more than that. Some instinct made me trust her. She fell back into the stupor from which the fascinum had roused her, and I had no assurance that the juggler would not seize the fascinum as soon as I had passed through the mirror. But I had to take the risk if I had any hope of saving Derli. I turned toward the mirror. The juggler stood in front of it, sentinel stiff, holding his staff like a pike. I brushed past him and walked through the mirror. With dreamlike slowness I stumbled through dark, swirling clouds that gave way to a long hallway lit by sweet-scented tapers in gilded niches.

Thick carpet cushioned my feet, reddish-brown velvet lined the walls, and on the ceiling a mosaic of polished woods reflected the tapers' dancing light. I stared at the rich surroundings. They were vaguely familiar. I recognized the design on the carpet: green vines and brown ones twisted together—life and death. I'd seen it in the Manor House, studied it while waiting for Dama Koralie's servant to verify the old lord's death. I must have been transported back there, back to the danger from which I'd fled.

"You've come!" A dark-gowned, dark-haired wisp of a girl darted from an open doorway, grabbed my arm, and tugged at me. "Hurry. *She* mustn't see you."

Bewildered, I let the girl draw me into the room and watched her latch the door behind us.

We were in a bedchamber, but not the one where I'd slain the old lord. Heavy curtains drawn across the room's single window prevented any outside light from entering. An oil lamp glowed on the table beside the canopied bed, illuminating a dressing table with a scrolled mirror and an ornately carved highboy standing against the room's rear wall.

The girl picked up the lamp. Its light played on the rich purple of her gown. She caught my wrist and pulled me around the bed to the highboy. Slender and frail though she looked, when she grabbed the sides and pulled, the highboy grated away from the wall to reveal a narrow passage. Holding the lamp high, she squeezed through the opening. I followed. "Pull it closed," she ordered.

I tugged at a handle on the back of the highboy that she had moved so easily. Grunting, I used all my strength to slowly slide the heavy piece of furniture over the opening.

"She won't find us now." The girl headed briskly down the narrow, winding passage. I had to trot after her or be left in inky darkness.

"Who is *she*?" I called.

She cast an amused glance over her shoulder. "Dama Brinabeth, of course."

Brinabeth. A parade of chills marched up and down my spine. The head—how had I known its name? And—*Dama* Brinabeth? What happened to Dama Koralie?

The juggler had called the mirror a gateway to the past. I must have gone back before Dama Koralie's time.

More chills accompanied the recollection that Derli had been trapped when I identified the head. "I came here searching for someone," I told the girl. "Derli. Do you know where she is?"

The girl turned toward me, brows drawn together. "Derli?" The lamplight kindled twin fires in her dark eyes. "I don't know that name. I don't like its sound."

Afraid to ask why she didn't like it, I said merely, "She's a ... a friend. She's in danger. I came to rescue her."

The flame in her eyes leapt up, independent of its source. "You came because I sent for you." Her voice was sharp. "You have no friend here but me." With that ominous declaration, she turned and marched forward, holding the lantern high. I trailed after her.

The passageway ended in a curtained arch so low my guide had to bend to pass through it. I dropped to my knees and crawled through. I emerged in a tiny, windowless cell containing a cot, a plain wooden chair, and a small table, on which the girl placed the lamp. On the cot's bare mattress lay a young man, arms at his side, face waxen beneath a stubbly growth of whiskers. His clothes were those of a slave.

I stared at the face, haunted by a sense of familiarity even greater than that which I'd experienced with the juggler's little heads. The strong features, straight nose, and deep cleft of the chin were all familiar, yet I could put no name to him.

"Who is he?" I strained to get the words out through a throat grown tight with a terror I did not understand.

"He is Brid." She stroked the high, pale brow, brushed back the dark curls, and touched the colorless, partly open lips.

Brid Lord Terral was the lord I'd slain! But he'd been ancient. This was scarcely more than a boy.

The gate must have taken me back to the time of the old lord's youth. But if so, why was he lying hidden? "Is he ... is he dead?"

She gave me a brief, amused glance. "No. He is ensorcelled."

I lifted my hand to my chest, pressed my fingers on the empty space where the fascinum had hung. Lacking its protection, I traced a warding sign in the air before my face.

She laughed. "That will have no effect. But I have the power to protect you. We must hurry. Time spreads." She took neatly folded garments from the seat of the chair and thrust them into my hands. "Change into these. Quickly."

I stared at her.

"You can't go out of here dressed as you are. You—" her eyes fell on the crimson stains on my shirt. "You're hurt?" Alarm sharpened her voice.

"No." I fingered the red blotch left by the tomatoes.

Her eyes narrowed. She sniffed. Her nose crinkled. "Filth," she said. "Change clothes. Hurry."

Such was the power of her presence that even as she watched, I stripped off my stained garments and dressed in the clothes she'd given me—doeskin breeches and a shirt of pale green silk, the attire of a lord.

She caught up the clothes I'd removed, wadded them into a ball, and tossed them into a corner. "Sit down." She pointed at the chair.

I sat.

"I'll return shortly." She snatched up the lamp, bent low, and disappeared into the passage, plunging the room into darkness.

I remained seated, uneasy but afraid to get up and try to find a way out with no light. Time passed and my unease increased.

Finally I could stay still no longer. I fumbled my way toward where I believed the arch was but crashed into solid stone. I groped for the opening, found nothing. Moving blindly about the room, I stumbled into the cot and felt the cold, clammy skin of its occupant. It startled me so that without realizing what I did my fingers found the throat and curved around it.

A light fell across the bed. I started and jerked my hands away, horrified by what I'd been about to do.

The girl was back, the curtained arch clearly visible behind her. She must have seen me with my hands at Brid's throat. I could face a terrible death.

But she spoke calmly. "Not yet, Korth. He must indeed die by your hand, but not yet." Her voice softened as she shifted her gaze to the man on the bed. "He's safe here, and it pleases me to look at him. He's very fair, is he not?"

"Help me. Please, help me." The plaintive whisper startled me. The young man's eyes had opened, and in their depths I read a soul-wrenching appeal.

I reached out involuntarily, not to kill this time but to give what aid I could. The girl quickly interposed herself between me and the bed, and I lacked the will to oppose her.

In one hand she held the lamp, the other gripped an amber flask. This she placed to the lips of the man she called Brid. The man who must be destined to become the old lord I would kill in my own time.

"Drink," she urged Brid. Her voice was gentle, soothing. She tipped the flask and spilled a few drops of liquid between his lips. He swallowed. His mouth opened wider. She set the lamp on the table and slipped her hand beneath his head, cradling it. She held the flask to his mouth and gave him several more swallows. His eyelids drifted shut. Drops of pearly liquid dribbled down his chin.

She lowered his head and stroked his cheek. "Sleep on, Brid," she whispered. "Dream of me."

She set the flask on the table by the lamp. From beneath her bodice she drew a small packet and opened it, cupped her hand like a funnel around the chimney of the lamp, and shook a gray powder onto the flame. A heavy, too-sweet scent filled the tiny room. I gasped for breath. My head swam.

She pushed me onto the chair. "Breathe deeply, Korth," her soft voice urged. "Don't resist."

My hands gripped the edges of the seat in a futile effort to slow the spinning room and rise. I had no strength. My head lolled against the chair's hard back.

"Hear me, Korth," her voice caressed. "You are my creature. You will obey me. Do you understand? In all things you will obey me."

"I will obey," my thick tongue echoed the words against my will.

"I am your mistress. I am Koralie."

"Mistress Koralie," I mumbled—a slave once more.

"Good. You will no longer answer to the name of Korth. Your name is Terral."

"Terral," I repeated.

"Now I will instruct you as to what you must do."

9

TESTED

"I am Terral," I said, following Koralie's order to claim the name of the first manor lord, founder of the line, whose name became a title used by all subsequent manor lords. Koralie's hold over me kept me from being intimidated by the three lord councilors sitting by the water sculpture in the center of the Manor House's marble-floored Great Room. She had explained exactly what I would face and described each man so well that I recognized them with no difficulty.

Senior Councilor Hulsin twirled the circlet of braided hair hung on a silver chain around his neck. "That claim is easily disproved." He let the circlet fall against his blue brocade robe and peered at me over his hawk-billed nose.

I did not waver. "I am willing to meet the test."

Councilor Boral yawned and folded his pudgy hands over his protruding belly. "I see no need for any test. Dama Brinabeth has declared the lordslayer the Inheritor."

"Produce him," I challenged. "Let's see whose claim is valid."

Councilor Kast grasped the jeweled hilt of the dagger thrust into his belt. "You discredit the word of Dama Brinabeth?"

I met the steady gaze of his flint-gray eyes. "I speak no ill of the dama. I merely affirm my willingness to prove my claim. I believe I can satisfy the dama."

Koralie had explained that a dama has the final authority to find the one who must perform the rite of Lord's-Kill. It is she who determines whether, in the performance of that rite, the dying lord's spirit enters his slayer, as it should. If it has, the slayer receives with it the memories of that lord and his predecessors, and the dama declares the lord's slayer his successor. In this time, some sixty years before my own, Koralie had further explained, Brid had performed the rite of Lord's-Kill for the previous manor lord, Lord Stamsel, and had received the deathright, and thus should succeed him. But she had other plans and meant to use me to carry out those plans.

Boral's heavy-lidded eyes flickered open. He awarded me a brief glance and looked back at the water sculpture. His hand swept idly through its jets, altering the intricate pattern formed by the interweaving streams. "It is unprecedented for a rival claimant to appear and challenge a lordslayer. Only when the lord dies unslain is the new lord revealed by testing."

Kast's hand did not release his dagger hilt. His body was rigid, his long legs tensed, ready to spring from his chair.

"This is some mischief of the Zerans," Hulsin muttered.

Kast's fingers caressed the carved bird that formed the pommel of the dagger hilt. Boral pulled from beneath his robe a fascinum of clear crystal twisted into a convoluted form. He thrust it toward me. It shimmered with reflected light. Blinded, I stepped back.

Kast drew his dagger and leaped to his feet, sending his chair tumbling backward. The point of his dagger pressed against my throat.

"Send for Brinabeth," Hulsin bellowed.

"Brinabeth has come," a crisp voice spoke.

I turned. A woman clad all in white—straight, white gown, white kirtle, a white mantilla over her white hair—leaned on a staff of white wood. I recognized her from the head I had seen on the juggler's staff and stared to be sure her head rested securely on her shoulders.

"Why am I sent for?" Her gaze turned toward each of the lords, lingered longest on Kast. My presence she ignored.

Boral waved his hand toward me. "This one calls himself Terral, Dama. He asks for the test."

"Brid has inherited. This is an impostor." Her wintry voice chilled my blood. My courage failed.

A purple shadow glided into the room. My mistress Koralie halted against the windowed wall, her slender figure half hidden in the shadows of the heavy blue draperies. Hulsin wrinkled his nose, reminding me painfully of Derli's claim to smell evil. How I wished I'd believed her.

To steady myself I took several deep breaths. I could not disobey my lady. I said the words she had drilled into me: "If Brid confronts me and declares in my presence that he is Terral, I will renounce my claim to that title."

Dama Brinabeth shifted slowly toward me. She lifted her staff. It was straight, its top carved into a white owl with silver eyes. Dama Brinabeth's eyes were silver, too. They scanned my face.

"Koralie," she called without turning. "Fetch Brid."

My mistress stepped forth from the shadows and curtsied to the councilors. "Dama," she said to Brinabeth's back, "Brid is not with his tutors. I went there a short time ago."

"Find him." Brinabeth issued the curt command without taking her gaze from my face. Koralie glided from the room.

"Who gave you the name of Terral?" Her abrupt question pulled my mind from Koralie. It was a moment before I could recover and get out the answer Koralie had taught. "No one, Dama. It came to me. It is my name."

"What is your given name?"

"Terral is the only name I know," I lied, for my mistress had warned me not to reveal the name Korth.

"You have presented an enigma that I must solve. Kast, your dagger." She held out her hand.

Kast laid the hilt of the dagger in her open palm, and her fingers closed around it. She turned the blade upward and raised her arm until the point was level with my eyes. I did not flinch but focused my gaze on the point as it moved toward me. My vision blurred.

With the suddenness of a wasp sting the blade darted in, pricked the skin of my forehead, and withdrew. Although Koralie had warned me to expect this, I couldn't keep my head from jerking back. A warm trickle of blood coursed down the bridge of my nose.

Brinabeth backed away, holding the dagger upright like a candle. She lowered herself into the seat that had been Kast's and stared at the spot of blood on the dagger's point.

Boral sank back into his seat. Kast and Hulsin stood together on the other side of the water sculpture. Hulsin propped a velvet-booted foot on the circular tile border. I stooped, dipped my hand into the pool beneath the water sculpture, and washed the blood from my face.

We waited like floaters on time's ocean. Brinabeth stared at the crimson point. Hulsin ran his finger round and round the braided circlet of hair. Kast gazed at the water sculpture. Boral seemed asleep.

Some time later Koralie returned. A thin, whey-faced man followed her and groveled before Dama Brinabeth. Koralie launched into a breathless recital. "Dama, I have had the Manor House searched," Koralie said. "Brid is not to be found. This witless one confesses that for two days Brid did not appear for the genealogy lesson and it did not occur to him to report it." She nudged the hapless man with the toe of one tiny foot.

Brinabeth gave the girl a sharp look. "Enough, Koralie. Rugyar, you may go. I'll speak with you later."

The man backed away and scuttled from the room like a frightened crab.

"I've ordered a search of the grounds," Koralie continued. "Overseer Tayya has been notified in case Brid returns to the longhouse."

Brinabeth shook her head. "He has not gone back to the longhouse. There is some knavery at work."

Knavery indeed. I thought with pity of the pale young man who lay unconscious in a hidden room, drugged by Koralie for reasons I didn't yet understand. My understanding was not required. I was under her power, and I had no choice but to follow all her instructions. I stepped to Koralie's side. "Could it not be that he fled rather than be unmasked as an impostor?"

Dama Brinabeth gripped her staff in one hand and drew herself to her feet. "He is no impostor. He *will* be found. I have ways of searching my apprentice has not learned." She directed a hard look at Koralie.

"I suppose this means the test will be administered after all," Boral drawled.

Brinabeth marched to the fountaining water, dipped the blade of Kast's dagger into the spray, and handed the weapon back to its owner. "His blood does call to the past lords," she declared. "I cannot withhold the test."

Kast nudged Hulsin and muttered something I couldn't hear.

Two servants in gray robes entered with lighted tapers. They drew the draperies across the windows and lit the candles in three large candelabra standing like silver trees at points equidistant from the water sculpture. The sculpture's jets intertwined, separated, and rejoined, forming whorls, loops, and braids in ever-changing patterns that shimmered hypnotically with the candles' reflections.

The lord councilors arranged their chairs at wide intervals around the water sculpture. Servants brought a heavy armchair for Brinabeth and set a low stool beside it for Koralie. They brought me a cushioned chair like those the councilors sat in and placed it alongside the water sculpture facing the dama. I sank into the chair, alert to the danger my mistress Koralie had warned me of.

Brinabeth nodded to Hulsin, who came and stood in front of me.

"Look at this fascinum," he ordered, swinging the chain between his fingers. The hiss and splash of the water swelled to fill the silence in the Great Room.

Koralie had instructed me to guard my mind and not let myself be drawn into a trance but to pretend that I was spellbound. She'd supplied me with answers to questions that might be asked while I was in the supposed trance. I tried to do as she had bidden, but I found it impossible not to stare at the twirling circlet. The spinning circlet became an expanding globe. Powerless to resist, I entered its orbit and it encompassed me and I spun inside it, a solitary universe in a dark sea.

"Terral," a low voice filled the void. "Terral, do you hear me?"

"I hear you, Dama." My own voice came faintly to my ears, speaking as though from a great distance.

"You are Terral?"

"I am."

"You are the Inheritor?"

"I am," I repeated, the answers familiar because they were the same as those supplied me by Koralie. Yet they did not come from my recall of her instructions but from some inner voice over which I had no control.

"You are the confluence of many waters. Can you trace to their source the streams that join in you?"

"I can," that inner voice responded against my will and over the doubt that filled what little remained of my conscious mind.

"Follow the waters to their fount."

I felt myself drawn into a maelstrom, spiraling inward in tighter and tighter circles until the motion slowed, stopped in a shower of golden rays. I stood newly made in the blazing light. "We are Terral," I said. "Who summons us?"

"Dama Brinabeth." The voice was distant, faint. "I summon you and each of your heirs."

"We are one."

"Still, I would speak to each in turn. I summon the First Inheritor."

A presence joined me. "I am here," said a rich and vibrant voice.

"Identify yourself."

The voice hesitated, said slowly, "I am Treden Lord Terral."

"As the second Lord Terral you built this Manor House. Tell us, Lord, under which sun-cycle you laid the first stone."

This time the answer came promptly. "The twenty-third from the founding of the lord line."

"And do you claim as heir this one through whom you speak? Would you have him rule this house and all its vast holdings?"

"I claim him. He shall rule."

"Who was your slayer?"

"Lonness."

"Let him speak."

"Lonness is here." The new voice was slow and sad.

"Lonness of the many battles?"

"Aye. I won that title by surviving nine battles with the Dunesmen of Labon. But in the war I lost all my sons."

"Yet you survived until the rite of Lord's-Kill."

"Aye, the inheritance passed, as it should, to my slayer."

"Has it now passed rightfully to the one who gives you voice?"

"Aye, it has."

"I summon Galor, the fourth Lord Terral."

More vague forms gathered around me. Their voices spoke through my mouth. I was but another listener, understanding little of what they said.

"Galor is present." A dry, brittle voice answered the summons.

"You were a man of peace and great learning."

"Say not 'were.' As Terral I live on."

"In this one who gives you voice?"

"He is the Inheritor."

"To prove he speaks true, tell me: you devoted your life to accumulating a library of rare and valued knowledge. What number of volumes did you acquire for the Manor?"

"Two thousand eleven." The voice crackled with pride.

"You passed the love of learning if not of peace to your Inheritor. I call Ordred."

"Ordred Lord Terral answers," a deep voice boomed.

"From your predecessor's books you learned the art of war. How many years did you require to conquer Labon?"

"Eight years, Dama. I defeated the Dunesmen, but the wound I received in the final battle cost my life. A high price for victory. Slain by my enemy, who became my Inheritor."

"A Labonite outcast."

"The ways of Molor are unfathomable. I had to merge with the soul of my enemy or wander forever that desert where time does not flow."

"Your Inheritor was …?"

"Mett." The name was spoken in a husky whisper. Like a hot, dry wind, the voice continued. "I did not wish the lordship. It was forced on me, but through it I redeemed my people."

"And passed the deathright early to your Inheritor."

"To me, Kadry, seventh Lord Terral," a laughing voice broke in, not waiting to be summoned. "To one who knew the secret of life is not to take it seriously. I brought to this house mirth and music, feasting and merriment, good women and good wine."

"And died in a drunken stupor, I've heard."

Brinabeth's caustic comment evoked a hearty laugh. "A gross exaggeration, Dama. I died as I lived, enjoying myself to the utmost, full of good wine, it's true, but hardly in a stupor. I was, in fact, engaged in a …" the voice hesitated "ah, a liaison with a lady of such exquisite talent that my heart burst from excitement. One could not wish a more pleasant exit." He chuckled. "And I alone found the means of transferring the inheritance to my son."

A whiny nasal voice took up the tale. "I am Chevor. Because my father died at the moment of my conception, the deathright passed to me. But I endured long years of hardship and deprivation before I was able to assert my claim. Even after I won the right to bear the name Terral, the councilors treated me like an interloper. Often I caught the servants sniggering behind my back. I taught them a lesson. I forced most of them into slavery. Why pay the lazy louts, and why limit slavery to prisoners of war? Dama Chevaise did not support me in this decision as she should have, though I prevailed, and slaves still provide the Manor Lands with free labor, I'm proud to see. It did the dama no good to object.

"Too many times Dama Chevaise sided with the councilors in disputes between us. The final insult came when I was struck with an illness from which I could certainly have recovered, but they gave me a sleeping potion and sent for the lordslayer. I was forced to cede the inheritance before my proper time."

"You neglect to mention what happened to Dama Chevaise." Brinabeth's voice was icy.

"She deserved her fate," came the petulant reply.

"To die a slow and agonizing death, screaming in pain while the poison you put in her wine burned its way through her body?"

Chevor sniffed. "She should not have mocked me."

"Be silent. Let your successor speak."

"I am Ladin Lordslayer," a proud voice said. "As the ninth Lord Terral I avenged the death of Chevaise and righted the wrongs of my predecessor. And when the famine that fell across the land was blamed on me for the blood I'd shed, I willingly surrendered to the next lordslayer so the land might be cleansed."

"By his sacrifice the noble Ladin opened the way for the peace and prosperity of my long tenure." The next voice cracked with age. "I dandled my grandchildren on my knees; great grandchildren were placed in my arms to receive my blessing before the lordslayer received my final breath."

"Many of those you held still grace this house, Maxin," Dama Brinabeth said. "But where is Stamsel, your Inheritor?"

A brief silence was broken by a loud yawn. A voice thick with sleep said, "Your pardon, Dama Brinabeth. So recent was my passing, I'm not fully awakened."

"You were ever a late riser." Brinabeth chuckled. "I am sorry to disturb your slumber, Lord. Dama Stamsine used to say—but I forget myself. For you I have the most important question of the test. I would know, Lord, how it happened that the deathright failed to pass from you to the lordslayer."

"I do not understand, Dama," the groggy voice said. "We passed into the lordslayer as we should."

"Then who is this? Why have the others affirmed him? Where is Brid? It is he who should be the twelfth Lord Terral."

A groan answered Brinabeth's sharp questions.

Brinabeth gasped. "Brid?"

"Here, Dama," a low voice moaned. "And not here. Help me. I'm torn in half. Oh, gods, the pain." The words ended in a tortured groan.

"Brid. What treachery is this?" Brinabeth's voice shook. "Who is this who wrests his inheritance from one not dead?"

I couldn't tell whether the dama's question was addressed to Brid or to me. Brid did not answer. I battled the compulsion to speak.

"You who call yourself Terral, who are you? Speak your name."

"I cannot," I said. "I'm forbidden."

"Who forbade you?" Rage quivered in Brinabeth's voice. The rat-a-tat-tat of her staff pounding the floor broke my trance. My eyes blinked open.

The dama stood over me, her face livid; her eyes like molten silver.

I cringed and my gaze flickered to Koralie, seated on her stool, head lowered, fingers tracing invisible symbols on the pale blue marble floor.

"Speak!" The dama lifted high her staff and slammed it down.

The staff splintered from bottom to top and buckled beneath her weight. Brinabeth pitched forward. Her head struck the arm of my chair. She crumpled beside my feet.

Koralie leaped to the dama's side. She knelt and enfolded the dama in her arms, bent her body low over her fallen mistress.

Hulsin and Kast sped toward me. Hulsin bent over Koralie and tore her away from the fallen dama.

Powerful hands gripped my shoulders and pinned me against the back of the chair. I raised my head and peered into Kast's hostile glare.

While Hulsin held the struggling Koralie, Boral dropped beside Brinabeth. Gently he straightened her body. His fingers probed her head.

"Let me go to her." Koralie writhed in Hulsin's grasp. "She's hurt. Let me help her."

Boral looked up. Awe and grief sharpened his bland features. "You can't help her. She's dead."

10

VOICES

Boral's announcement stunned me. It must have had the same effect on Hulsin because Koralie easily tore free of his grasp. She fell to her knees beside Brinabeth and stroked the dama's pallid cheek. Hugging her arms to her breast, she rocked back and forth, keening.

Kast poised his dagger to sever my throat. "You sent the dama to her death. I send you after her."

"Hold!" Hulsin's shout stopped Kast's hand. "If you slay him, we may never learn Brid's fate."

Kast frowned but pulled back his knife.

"Hulsin's right." Boral stretched out his hands in appeal to Kast. "The test showed two things. The first is that something very peculiar has happened to Brid. The second is that this man has, in some manner, inherited. Who he was or how he managed it we do not know, but he *is* Lord Terral."

"I will never accord him that title," Kast growled. His fingers gouged my shoulders.

Koralie hushed her keening, raised her head, and peered at Hulsin through red-rimmed eyes. With both hands she brushed her hair back from her face. "I did not wish such responsibility thrust on me so soon." She sighed. "Councilor Boral, will you help me to rise?"

She lifted a dainty hand. Boral grasped it and drew her to her feet. "Of what responsibility do you speak, girl?"

Koralie met Boral's gaze. "As apprentice to Dama Brinabeth, I must fill her place."

Hulsin shook his head. "You're too young and inexperienced. No doubt Dama Brinabeth was pleased with your progress, but you are not ready to claim—"

"The right to be called Dama," Koralie broke in. "I do claim it." Her voice was intense. Her eyes glittered. "You admit this man has received the deathright. He *is* Lord Terral. You ask how he inherited. I do not know the how of it, Lord Councilors. Molor works in ways we cannot fathom." She turned slowly, gazing at each of the lords. "Molor opened the way for this new lord to come to us at the time of his calling Brinabeth to himself. By Molor's power I am dama." She fixed her gaze on me. "My Lord, you must speak your slave name."

I stared into the depths of those deep, dark eyes and fell completely under her spell once more. "I am Korth," I said.

Kast's fingers jerked away from me. I leaned forward and massaged my aching shoulders. Boral moved around the chair and stood in front of me, hands on his crystal fascinum. Candlelight shimmered on the amulet's twisting surfaces. "Speak that name again." He held the fascinum before my lips.

"Korth," I repeated.

The fascinum vibrated with a single bell-like note.

"And your lord-name," Boral said.

"Terral."

Again the crystal sang the single note.

"The names are his." With the grudging admission, Boral dropped the fascinum beneath his robe and turned, grim-faced, to the other two. "It seems we have little choice but to acknowledge both lord and dama."

Hulsin flung himself into a chair. "If, as Koralie says, Molor has done this thing, I must accede to his will."

Kast sheathed his dagger. "I refuse. Brid's disappearance and the dama's death can't be the work of Molor. I will not acknowledge this man as lord." He spun on his heel and stalked from the room.

Hulsin broke the silence Kast left behind. "Koralie, we will hold four days of mourning for the dama. For those four days you will see to this man's lessoning. If by nightfall of the fourth day, Brid has not been found alive, you will be dama and he Lord Terral."

Hands clasped demurely in front of her, Koralie bowed her head.

"I'm sorry, Duenna." I kneaded my head with my fists. "It's all too new."

"You'll make a fool of yourself tonight and the new dama will have me beaten." With a sigh, the old woman tucked stray wisps of white hair beneath her lace cap. "How will you learn if you don't attend?"

"I'm trying," I said, staring in despair at the bewildering array of utensils spread on the gleaming white linen. I wondered again why these people reckoned transporting food from plate to mouth a process so complicated it required a table full of tools. Until a few days ago I'd used nothing but my two hands and a hunk of bread, and I'd never gone hungry. "My head aches and I can't think."

"Why didn't you say so? I'll fetch you a cup of tea brewed with healing herbs." The duenna bustled off toward the kitchen.

Again I pressed the heels of my hands against my aching forehead. It had been only nine days since I fled the longhouse. But this was decades before that fateful day. When I killed the old lord, Dama Koralie had been old too. Here she was young and powerful, and although I tried, I could not break her control over me.

You should go back.

I groaned. Brinabeth's test had given voice to the Lords Terral who preceded me. They carried on a continuing debate in my mind. "I don't know how. Leave me alone."

That first night after Brinabeth's death, when Koralie led me to my bedchamber, I'd complained to her of the voices. She became agitated and demanded to be told all they were saying. "They argue about my right to be in this time and to accept the lordship," I'd answered.

"You must not listen. You must obey no voice but mine." Her black eyes cast their darkness into my soul.

"I obey you, Mistress, but I cannot stop the voices."

"A good rest will quiet them. I will give you a sleeping potion. As you study your heritage and know the rightness of your place, they will disturb you less."

She mixed some herbs in wine and had me drink it down. My limbs grew heavy and my eyelids drooped.

"I leave you, Korth. Sleep well."

She locked the door behind her. I staggered to the bed, tumbled across it, and fell into a dreamless sleep. But in the morning when Koralie awakened me, the voices began again. I told her.

"I forbid you to listen to them," she said as though the fault were mine. She dragged me off to begin my lessons in lordship.

For four days now the duenna had given me lessons in etiquette and proper table manners. She returned to me carrying a steaming cup of pale orange tea in which floated flecks of green. "This will soothe you." She placed the cup in my hands.

I drank the tea as rapidly as its heat allowed. It eased the pain in my head but did not still the voices.

Have you forgotten why you came? You've done nothing at all about finding Derli.

It was Mett's voice. How did he know about Derli? *No, I haven't forgotten*, I thought back to him. *I asked Koralie about her. How can I search for her when I can't see her?*

"Look, Korth," the duenna called me to attention. "This fork you use for spearing shellfish. And when the fork is not sufficient to persuade it from its shell, which knife assists you?"

"That one?" I pointed to a small knife with a curving blade.

"No, no. That one is for coring fruit." The duenna tugged at her lace cap, allowing more hair to slip from its confines. "The small straight-bladed one is for shellfish."

Kadry's boisterous voice distracted me. *When you learn all this nonsense, you'll have such fun scandalizing the nobles by breaking the rules. Use the meat knife to spread butter on your roll, sop the buttered roll into the gravy, spear it with a knife, and pop it into your mouth. Drives them crazy.*

"Repeat the uses of the knives." The duenna folded her arms and leaned back.

"You use the meat knife to spread butter—" The horrified lift of her eyebrows stopped me. "No. I ... I don't know." I shook my head.

See how you've confused him, Maxin reproved.

Kadry roared with laughter. *He doesn't need to learn this. We'll help him at the feast.*

I don't know why you insist on encouraging him, Father. He has no right to be here, Chevor whined.

He is here. Mett's husky whisper contradicted Chevor. *He received our spirits through the rite of Lord's-Kill. Even though it was in another time, that fact accords him the right.*

"You must get them right." The duenna pointed a finger at the line of knives.

You must defy Koralie and rescue Brid, Ordred's gruff voice urged.

Time for that later. Let him gather a taste for learning. Galor's voice rustled like leaves of parchment.

The duenna threw up her hands at my befuddled stare. "You've little taste for this, it's clear. I don't know how you'll manage at tonight's feast."

The session in the library with don Lorgio fared no better. The musty smell of old books made me sneeze. The yellowed charts with their interminable columns of statistics meant nothing. The don spread them over the polished mahogany tables and, though I'd told him I couldn't read, took perverse pleasure in pointing to the cryptic scrawls and squiggles while he recited statistics he expected me to memorize. The strange thing was that those squiggles and scrawls were beginning to resolve themselves into letters, the letters into words. Intelligible words.

Thanks to the past lords, I *could* read. But I didn't reveal that discovery to don Lorgio. He'd only present me with more records filled with dry statistics. I sneezed again.

"The Lord Terral's estate consists of four thousand one hundred and fifty-three hectares, of which one thousand three hundred and eighty-five are in cultivation, the major crops being ..."

This library has been shamefully neglected. We'll have to correct that.

How can you concern yourself with the condition of soulless books and not protest the wrong being done our Twelfth Inheritor?

"Two hundred thirty-nine lie fallow, eight hundred and seventy are used for grazing, six hundred and fifty-eight are forested ..."

How can anyone be expected to stay awake for this drivel?

You don't stay awake for anything, Stamsel. A lord must know the workings of his estate.

"Nine hundred ninety hectares are set aside for the farms and villages of the freedmen, and from them the nobles collect rents. This column shows the amounts exacted of each village. If you will note ..."

Help me! Free me from this torment. Brid's desperate plea drove me to the edge of insanity. I groaned loudly and tore at my hair.

Roused from his columns of statistics by my distress, don Lorgio asked, "Are you ill? You're pale and trembling. Shall I call Koralie?"

"No, no. I need fresh air, that's all." I pushed away from the table and stumbled from the room. I dashed through the halls shouting Derli's name. Startled servants and house slaves fled before me.

A sweet, soothing music penetrated my fevered brain. I slowed my mad pace and listened. Mandolin chords blended with the high clear melody of a flute. I traced the sound to its source in the Great Room. Beyond the water sculpture the lord councilors listened to musicians, and as I observed I learned the musicians were vying to play for the evening's feast.

A soft rose light filtered through the windows, bathing the Great Room in splendor. Sweet music of mandolin and flute drifted over me, bringing the only peace I had known that day. I craned my neck to see past the lords to the players.

While other musicians, awaiting their turns, clustered in the shadows by the far wall, an older man and a young woman performed in a circle of light before the three lords. He stood, eyes closed, pouring his breath into the flute and drawing it forth as clear, high melody. Seated beside him, red hair shimmering, she plucked the mandolin strings and her music played in my heart.

The music stopped. The slender, silver-haired flutist bowed and gave his hand to the mandolin player. Flushing prettily, she rose and curtsied. Still caught in the spell of the music, I clapped my hands in loud applause.

Kast's voice cut through my trance. "Have you never seen a woman before, Pretender?"

I lowered my gaze, snapped it up again. I was no slave. I was Terral, soon-to-be Lord of the Manor. "Forgive my ill manners, My Lady," I called to her. "I was dazzled by your beauty. What is your name?"

"Renata, My Lord." She favored me with a shy smile, curtsied again, picked up her mandolin, and bent over it. Waves of copper hair cascaded over the instrument. Slender fingers plucked the strings, producing ripples of music that danced like laughter. I stood open-mouthed, drinking in the loveliness of music and musician. The notes died away; the musician raised her head; brilliant blue eyes smiled into mine.

"My thanks, My Lady." I bowed.

Kast snorted. "If you *were* Terral, you'd know she's only a hireling musician, not a lady. Those two are freedmen."

I glared at him. "Whatever her rank at this moment, when I am named Lord Terral she shall be the Lady Renata."

Kast's brows furrowed in an angry frown. His hand pressed the sheath of his dagger.

Koralie strode into the room, scowling. Ignoring the councilors and musicians, she halted in front of me. "Where have you been? I've been looking all over for you. We've but three hours before you are named lord. I must take you to the fascinator and have him craft you a fascinum before time to dress for the ceremony."

Clutching my arm, she dragged me away. I cast a last, wondering look at Renata.

Koralie led me away from the Manor House. The prospect of a new fascinum distracted me. Savnar had promised I'd see him again. Could he be here? He could break Koralie's power over me and set me free.

We passed through gardens to a small workshop. The fascinator came to greet us. I could scarcely conceal my disappointment. This man was cadaverously thin with hunched shoulders, long, narrow hands, and eyes so deep-set I couldn't tell their color.

"Joal, this is the Inheritor," Koralie said. "You must fashion a fascinum he may wear as lord."

The man nodded, beckoned me in, and motioned me to a high stool. While Koralie waited in the shadows by the door, Joal clasped his hands behind his back and walked round me several times. Occasionally he slowed in his circling and sniffed. The sniffs reminded me of Derli and filled me with such sadness and guilt that I could not speak, and he showed no inclination to do so.

Abruptly he halted and leaped to his workbench. From a metal box he drew out a lump of gold, heated it to a fiery orange in a small forge, and hunched over it, hammering and twisting. In a surprisingly short time he brought for my inspection the completed amulet. I frowned, disappointed by the simple almond-shaped ring of gold.

"It is a mandorla," he said, breaking his silence. "It is formed of the arcs of two intersecting circles representing life and death." He returned to his workbench, rummaged through the metal box, drew out a slender gold chain, and slipped it through the oval. Koralie stepped forward, and he handed it to her.

She clasped it around my neck. "You have your link to Molor. Come and dress for the feast."

Brid had not been found. Koralie led me into the Great Room for the ceremony. The robes of state hung on me, heavy and hot. I was blinded by the sharp pain brought on by the voices shouting in my head. My new fascinum failed to still them, and only Koralie's presence at my side kept me from running berserk a second time.

Nobles in flowing robes filled the Great Room. Liveried servants lined the walls. Koralie led me to an open space beside the water sculpture where Councilors Hulsin and Boral waited. Kast did not appear.

The loud, clear blast of a trumpet stabbed barbs of agony through my head. Hulsin read from a large, leather-bound volume. I believe the reading had to do with the founding of the lord line, but the shouting in my brain drowned out his words. The heavy scent of burning candles nauseated me. I sweated profusely in the suffocating robes.

Boral's speech was mercifully short. I have no idea what he said except that once I heard him mention Brid. I swayed and nearly fainted. Koralie cupped her hand under my elbow and supported me.

Through slitted eyes I watched Hulsin step before me. In a flat voice he proclaimed me Lord Terral and charged me to be true to my inheritance. Each word was a hammer pounding my brain. I wanted none of this, wanted to shout that I was an impostor, an interloper from another time. With Koralie at my side I was helpless to do anything other than her will.

Boral settled a rich gold cloak over my shoulders.

The voices stilled. The pain winked out like a snuffed candle. I took a deep breath and opened my eyes.

The gathered nobles in their jeweled robes presented a garden of color, and the air was a fragrant blend of sweet perfumes. I *could* get through this. What up to now had felt wrong suddenly felt right and fitting. I smiled.

"Now to the feast." Koralie's smile answered mine. She and I walked side by side to the banquet hall, flanked by the councilors.

I took my place at the head of the long table. Hulsin sat at my right, Koralie at my left. Boral sat beside Koralie. After them filed so many noble lords and ladies that by the time all were seated, my appetite was fully recovered. My mouth salivated at the sight and smell of the steaming trays of meats and vegetables the servants placed on the table.

When I viewed the array of plates and utensils spread before me, I sent a desperate mental plea: *Lords, where are you? Lord Kadry, help me.*

Relax, lad, I'm here, the familiar booming voice resounded in my mind. *Now that you have attained the lordship we may come only when you summon us.*

That was a relief! *Guide me,* I bade the jovial lord. *Make the duenna proud of me.*

Kadry guided my hands to the proper fork, taught my clumsy fingers how to grasp the stemmed wineglass, and reminded me to use the gleaming white linen napkin to blot my lips and wipe my fingers clean. Most important, he placed in my mind the proper greeting for each guest and the witty small talk that kept the conversation flowing smoothly throughout the meal.

As lord, I was served first from each platter and was obliged to sample every dish. A different wine was served with each new course, and each time I took a sip, an alert servitor refilled my glass.

I soon forgot my worries about which fork or knife to use, and under Kadry's expert tutelage I relished the food and drink.

"It's a pity that Kast, from stubbornness, missed such a fine feast," I remarked to Hulsin.

"It is indeed, My Lord," he said with unexpected deference

Never had I eaten so many delicacies nor drunk so much wine. When I thought the meal had ended and wondered whether I would ever need another, a parade of servants filed in bearing silver bowls of cherries alight in flaming brandy. The blazing spectacle so delighted me I lifted my hands and applauded.

As though I had given the cue, musicians in robes of black and silver strolled into the hall playing a lively air. Renata was among them. My heart leaped.

I rose unsteadily to my feet. A servant pulled back my chair. Weaving a bit, I made my way to the cluster of musicians and caught Renata's hand. "Now, My Lady, you shall see I keep my promises."

She drew back and looked around like a frightened rabbit. "My Lord, please don't call attention to me."

"But you are worthy of attention," I insisted, the wine making me reckless. "Or do you have a jealous husband? Or lover?"

She colored prettily. "No, My Lord. No one. It isn't that. It's—"

I didn't let her finish. "Come with me," I ordered. She set the mandolin down carefully, and I drew her back to my place at the table. I chimed a dessert spoon against a crystal wineglass. Conversation ceased. All heads turned toward me.

"Lords and Ladies," I called, "I present the Lady Renata."

11

RENATA

I motioned to a servant to bring a chair and seat Renata beside me at the head of the table. A rose flush suffused her ivory skin. She bent toward me. "My Lord, I thank you for honoring me, but I fear you should not."

With a careless wave of my hand I dismissed her anxious murmur and signaled another servant. "Wine for my lady." I was somewhat aware of the scandalized gazes of my table companions, but my attention was focused on Renata and I could think of no one and nothing else.

A sudden realization struck me with horror. "Lady, you entered at the feast's end. You have not eaten."

She shook her head. "I ate before you did, My Lord. They served us in the kitchen."

"The kitchen! Never again, Lady Renata, will you be served in a kitchen."

Her sapphire eyes sparkled with more than a hint of anger. "My Lord Terral, the food is as tasty there and warmer than when it reaches your table. I was not deprived."

"But I was deprived of your company throughout the feast." I placed my hand over hers.

She drew her hand away and curved her fingers around the stem of her wineglass. She said dryly, "And could not eat for grief?"

Kadry, who had been prompting my rash actions, supplied the proper words. "Ah, Lady, I ate, but I would have savored it more with you beside me."

She raised her goblet to her lips, the wine casting its ruddy reflection on her cheeks. I raised my own glass and drank in great gulps, imbibing her beauty with the wine. My eyes caressed her face, rejoiced in the copper sheen of her hair, traced the alabaster lines of her neck and shoulders, and lingered on the soft rise of her breasts beneath their sheath of black and silver.

"Lord Terral, you neglect your guests." Koralie's barbed words snagged my attention. I turned to her. Her lips smiled but her eyes smoldered. The sight of them sobered me. Instinctively I raised my hand to my fascinum.

The gold oval lacked the comfort of the silver charm I'd given up. I missed the reassuring feel of Pathfinder's polished fragments. My fingers traced the outline of the mandorla. "What would you have me do?"

"Attend to the conversations around you, smile at your guests, and drink no more wine."

Gravely I bowed my head. I attempted to do her bidding. My guests, though, were managing well on their own, and my effort to unravel the mingled threads of conversation made my head whirl. I turned back to Renata and found her gazing wistfully at the musicians.

"The music suffers from my absence, Lord," she said quietly. "Please allow me to return to my place."

I caught her hand and enfolded it in mine. "My Lady, I don't doubt that the music suffers without you, but the guests are paying it no heed, and I would suffer if you were to leave my side." The words were more Kadry's than mine, but in my wine-addled state they seemed appropriate.

She blushed and looked away. This time when she attempted to withdraw her hand from mine I grasped it more tightly, lifted her hand, and pressed it to my lips.

Boral leaned toward me. "My Lord, I see you've acquired a fascinum."

I raised my amulet. "Joal made it for me this afternoon," I said. "I'm not yet accustomed to it."

"Its simplicity suits you, Lord." Hulsin said.

I frowned, suspecting an insult.

"Don't be deceived by the simplicity of a fascinum's design." Koralie smoothly recaptured my attention. "The most unassuming may hold great power." She turned toward my lovely companion. "And you, Lady Renata," she purred. "What fascinum do you wear?"

The color drained from Renata's face. Panic clouded her eyes. Her hand fluttered to her neck. "I ... I've never acquired one, Dama."

Koralie, her voice silky, said, "I'm told that Zerans wear no fascina on this side of the Rethe. But you, I'm sure, are a true follower of Molor."

"She is as true as I," I said hotly, before Renata could speak.

Hulsin snorted. "In truth, Lord, we've seen little evidence of your devotion to the Winged One."

I placed my hand over my fascinum. My fingers traced its form. I recalled the words of Joal. "I wear a mandorla, sign of life and death," I said. "Is that not a fitting tribute to Molor Twin-Slayer?"

"Twin-Slayer!" Hulsin rose from his seat with a growl. "That's a Zeran term."

This is not my province. Kadry's voice grew faint. *Summon Galor.*

I thought the name and the dry voice of the studious lord whispered words in my mind. I repeated them aloud. "Councilor Hulsin, I know little of such distinctions. Does it dishonor Molor to speak the truth about him?"

A trembling hand pressed my arm. Renata whispered, "My Lord, I must rejoin the musicians. My father—the flutist—has signaled me."

Now that Kadry had retired from my mind I sobered enough to be horrified at my boorish behavior.

"Yes, go." I squeezed her fingers as she rose and returned to her place with the musicians. Then as Galor urged, I gave my full attention to the discussion.

"You speak heresy!" Boral slammed a fist on the table, knocking over his empty wineglass. A servant snatched it up and replaced it with a full one.

An ominous silence surrounded us as guests hushed their conversations to listen.

"Why is it heresy"—I repeated Galor's words—"to affirm that

Molor had the power to slay his twin? Did he not thus break the power of Zera, Makor's consort? My Lords, why do you question my devotion to Molor? Dama Koralie has told you I'm here by his power."

"It is the custom," Hulsin said, "for each new Lord Terral to swear fealty to Molor and opposition to Zera."

"Strange that only now am I told of this custom," I spoke words given me by Galor. "Still, I will honor it." I stood and looked from Hulsin to Boral and spoke words that did not come from Galor but from some other source. Not any of the past lords, but something— someone—within me, a presence I didn't recognize. "With the power Molor gathered from Makor when he slew his twin was this land and its lord line established," I said, the words flowing freely. "To that power, which has granted me the deathright, I swear fealty, and I vow to resist all efforts of Zera to avenge herself on Molor for Makor's death."

Hulsin scowled, Boral looked puzzled, and Koralie, with a startled stare, yanked me into my seat. But the crowd, befuddled by wine, failed to notice the ambiguities of my oath.

"Hear, hear!" someone cried. Others took up the cheer, accompanying it with fervent applause.

Boral swayed to his feet and lifted high his refilled wineglass. "Lords and Ladies," he shouted. "I propose a toast to the new Lord Terral, faithful servant to the Winged One."

Koralie, regarding me with a speculative gaze, did not join in the applause.

The strange voice had unnerved me. I pushed myself to my feet. "Lords and Ladies," I called, gathering my wits as best I could. All eyes turned toward me. "I thank you for the toast and for your presence here. I conclude the evening's festivities by offering a toast to Dama Koralie, the youngest and loveliest of all damas." I saluted Koralie with my glass, raised it to my lips, and drained the wine.

Koralie forced a smile and, rising, acknowledged the applause. Unsteady on my feet, I clutched her arm. The room had not yet quieted when I called out again.

"My Lords and Ladies, stay and enjoy the music as long as you will." I waved so expansively toward the musicians, I nearly lost my balance. "I beg your leave to depart. The wine has made me light-headed." I stumbled against Koralie.

"You need fresh air, Lord Terral," Hulsin said, his voice feigning concern. "A turn through the garden will restore you."

"Excellent idea, Councilor Hulsin. My Lady, will you attend me?"

Koralie steadied me. I'd thought I was exaggerating my drunkenness, but the floor pitched and rolled beneath my feet, and I clung to Koralie in earnest. A short stroll down a torch-lit corridor brought us to double doors that opened into the night-shrouded garden.

We stepped outside, but Koralie stopped within the block of light that spilled from the corridor. "Korth, your behavior this evening has been heinous," she said. "You embarrassed yourself with that ridiculous oath. Not to mention taking up with that mandolin player. Calling her a lady. Scandalous!"

Her rebuke stung. The wine gave me a false courage and, in my drunken state, a bit more freedom to resist her.

"I far prefer Renata's company to yours," I said rashly.

She glared at me for a long moment, her dark eyes smoldering. "Very well," she said in a voice dangerously calm. "You shall have the company of your lovely lady."

She released my arm and left me staring at her retreating back as she returned to the banquet hall.

I dared not accompany her, but I did step back into the corridor and waited to see what Koralie would do. It was only a few moments before Renata came toward me. I stepped forward to greet her.

She paused. "My Lord, it was not my wish to come here. The dama ordered it. At your request, she said."

"It was her suggestion, but now that you're here, will you accompany me into the garden?" I threw open the doors and stepped out onto a path. Gravel crunched beneath my boots. I drew Renata after me and closed the doors behind us. A cool wind brought the scent of night blossoms and the soft whisper of leaves.

"Is it so unpleasant to be here with me?" I asked.

"It is not unpleasant, Lord, but it is dangerous to me, and, I fear, unwise of you." She spoke in a low voice as I led the way through the darkness, Maxin guiding my uncertain steps.

"I guessed from your demeanor during my exchange with Boral that your allegiance is not to Molor. Is that why you fear danger?"

"It is, My Lord."

I stopped and drew her to me. "Call me Terral." I entwined my fingers in her soft hair. "I don't care if you are a Zeran. Such matters mean nothing to me."

She reached up, disengaged my fingers, and stepped back, out of my reach. "My Lord, please—"

"Call me Terral," I urged again. Though she resisted, my arms encircled her. I brushed my lips across her hair. "Renata, you are so beautiful," I murmured. "I swear you have no reason to fear me."

"It is not you I fear, Lord Terral."

At the scuff of a boot over gravel, Renata jerked free of my arms. Unbalanced, I pitched forward just as a dark shape lunged toward me. My hands scraped over the gravel.

Renata screamed. I staggered to my feet. My flailing hands caught hold of cloth. I hung on and felt for the owner's throat. The material tugged against my hand and went limp. I held an empty cloak.

Cold steel, razor-sharp, pressed against my neck. "Now, usurper, you die," a voice blew hot breath against my cheek.

I ducked beneath his arm, butted my head into his stomach, grabbed his legs, and hurled him to the ground.

"Renata!" I ran to where she stood hugging herself. I grabbed her and pulled her with me toward the house. Snapping branches accompanied a muttered oath as behind us my unknown foe regained his feet.

I hurled open the door, and with Renata in tow I pounded down a dimly lighted corridor. I heard the would-be assassin enter and come after us.

Dizzy with wine and weighted by my heavy robes, I had no hope of outrunning our pursuer. I scanned the hall for an open door. All were shut. No time to try them. Footsteps thundered behind us.

Out of the darkness two figures ran toward us. A shadowy third form loomed behind them. I faltered. Renata clung to my arm.

"It's a mirror," she gasped.

I thrust out my hand, struck glass. We faced a dead end. Renata sagged against me. I held her and turned to face the attacker.

I stared into Kast's grinning face.

"You evaded my dagger in the garden, but you won't get away this time, false one!"

"Kill me, but don't hurt Renata."

"My quarrel is with you, but she blocked my way when you fell in the garden, and my dagger found her."

I looked down at Renata, saw and felt the warm, dark blood seeping through my fingers where I clasped her shoulder.

"Renata, no!"

A low moan answered my horrified whisper. She slumped to the floor.

In a blind rage I threw myself at Kast. He sidestepped, and my rush carried me several paces past him. I swung around and raised my arms to ward off his attack.

A white blur in the mirror caught my eye. I stared at what took shape there. Kast planted himself in front of me and raised his dagger.

"Hold, Kast."

He whirled around at the sharp command and backed away, open-mouthed. Shimmering white, Dama Brinabeth stepped from the mirror.

12

DOORS

Bathed in a soft white glow, the dama stood over Renata. The eldritch light revealed the crimson stain spreading over Renata's shoulder and breast. I wanted to go to her but didn't out of fear of approaching Brinabeth.

Kast's dagger clattered to the floor. He slumped to his knees. "Dama. You live!" His awed whisper hung in the breathless air.

She shook her head. "No. I have found a way to return very briefly to try to right a wrong. I cannot stay."

From Kast she turned her cold, silver eyes to me. "I know you now," she said. "You don't belong in this time. What you came for is not here."

My fear of this dead woman kept me from uttering a word. I put my hand against the wall to steady myself.

"You have done Koralie's bidding without reasoning the consequences. If you claim the lordship now, from whom do you inherit the deathright?"

Like shards of ice her words splintered the seal Koralie had placed on my thoughts. I understood that Koralie's action could redirect the currents of time. If Brid died in Koralie's captivity, I could cease to exist.

"You see you must free Brid," Brinabeth said.

I nodded.

"I offer you what protection I am able to provide. You must act quickly, before time's waves disperse the power Molor has placed at my command."

She leaned forward and breathed on my fascinum. Light flared from it and died away, leaving it dull and tarnished. "I have cleansed it of Koralie's curse," she said. "It is well made. You may draw on its power. Go."

"Dama," I found my voice. "How can I leave the Lady Renata? She is wounded and may be dying."

With an air of impatience, the dama waved her hand over Renata's inert form. "I have halted the ebb of her life," she said. "She exists in the same state of half-life as Brid. Kast will carry her to a bedchamber and guard her until you return. If Brid recovers, she will recover. If you fail to release Brid and reestablish him as lord, Renata will perish."

I felt numb. "Dama, I'm not clever or skilled in sorcery. How can I do this thing?"

"You can. You must. What the dama has done only the Lord of the Manor can undo."

"But you are dama."

She shook her head. "Koralie's power has banished me from this shore of time." She pointed at the mirror and added, "This door will not open for me again."

She stepped backward and disappeared. The "door" was a mirror once more.

Like one waking from a dream, Kast rubbed his eyes and rose slowly to his feet. I squatted beside Renata and rubbed her cold hands, anxiously searching for some sign of life.

Kast shoved me aside, stooped, and gathered her into his arms. "Get on with your task," he snapped. "I'll guard her as the dama ordered."

Carrying Renata, he stalked off. Reluctant to let Renata out of my sight and having no idea where I was, I stumbled after him. He turned into another hall without glancing behind him and passed through an archway, ascended a short flight of stairs, and carried Renata into a spacious suite of rooms. I stood uncertainly in the doorway as Kast lowered her onto a lounge and tossed a lap robe over her.

He turned, noticed me, and scowled. "What are you doing? You won't find Brid here."

I leaned against the doorframe. "I don't have any idea how to find Brid. I wanted to be sure Renata was safe."

"I won't harm her. You have my word as a lord councilor. But she won't be safe until Brid is restored." His fingers caressed the hilt of his dagger.

I shuffled into the hall, reeling from weariness. My stomach churned from the wine I'd drunk. I was no match for Koralie. What could I do? I dragged myself through the maze of halls searching for the corridor I'd entered when I came through the time gate. I had not seen it again since that fateful night.

"This house holds too many secrets," I muttered. "How did Brinabeth come back from the dead? Not the time gate. That opened onto a carpeted hall. A death gate?"

I shuddered. My hands flattened against the wall, and I rested my face on its velvety surface, feeling weak and ill, in no condition to undertake the quest.

"Where are you hiding now that I need you?" I asked the silent lords.

Clinging to the wall, I pulled myself along until I reached a bathing chamber, found the basin, hugged it, and gave up to its painted interior the rich food and abundant wine I had consumed. I might bear a lord's name but I had a slave's stomach. Drained and shaken but with my mind a little clearer, I pulled myself up onto wobbly legs and resumed my search.

At this late hour many of the wings were plunged in darkness, and in those areas where candles flickered or torches guttered in sconces, only shadows moved. I passed through a parlor where guests sprawled snoring on sofas and envied them their sodden sleep.

I found the Great Room. From here I knew my way to the major areas, including, I thought longingly, my own lavish bedchamber.

Candles sputtered in the candelabra, sprinkling islands of light among the restless shadows. I was fortunate to have that meager illumination. The servants whose job it was to snuff out the candles must have celebrated too heartily to perform their task. I located the water sculpture by the tinkling of the spray, splashed its cool water on my face, and bathed my clammy hands. On an impulse I thrust my fascinum into a jet. A cascade of droplets showered my clothing.

I stepped back and wiped the fascinum on my embroidered collar. It sparkled with reflected candlelight. "I need strength and a guide to lead me to Brid," I said aloud to the amulet.

A guide you have, the voice of Maxin spoke in my mind. *Summon Treden, the builder of this house. He knows its secret ways. Ask Lonness, the strongest of us, to lend you strength.*

He faded back into obscurity. Pressing my fascinum, I summoned Treden. "Lead me to the hidden chamber where Brid lies ensorcelled."

You will need a lamp.

I took a candle, shielded its flame with my cupped hand, and hunted until I found a lamp, which I lit from the candle's waning flame. With a plea to Lonness to lend me vigor, I urged my weary feet to follow Treden's guidance.

He led me through the twisting hallways, down a carpeted stair, across a starlit patio, beneath a low archway, into another hallway, down a winding stairway, up a sloping corridor and into a magnificent hall with a mirrored wall at its end. I cast a nervous glance at the mirror before searching for the door I wanted.

My feet whispered across the thick pile, my hand held the latch and twisted slowly. The door was locked. I studied the aged wood. I could kick it in, but the noise might alert the servants and warn Koralie. I set the lamp on the floor, grasped the latch in both hands, pressed my shoulder against the door, and shoved with all my strength while I wrenched the handle. The lock shattered and the door burst open. I stumbled inside.

Grabbing hold of the end of the bed to regain my balance, I waited until the frantic pounding of my heart calmed, fetched my lamp, and hurried to the highboy in the corner. I tugged and yanked, grunting with the effort. Koralie had pulled it forward easily, but for me it yielded grudgingly, squealing its protest. If Lonness had not renewed my strength I could never have moved it. Sweat poured down my face and arms by the time I pried it far enough to wedge my body into the dark opening behind it.

The lamp enclosed me in a bubble of light against whose fragile skin the darkness pressed. I took three or four hesitant steps along the narrow passage. My bubble expanded to engulf a purple-clad figure.

Koralie blocked the passage. In her hand she held a plain wooden staff. "You are up late and far from your chamber, Lord Terral. What do you seek here?" Her voice was soft and gentle.

"You know whom I seek, Mistress. I can no longer do your bidding. Brid must be restored to the lordship." Afraid to meet her eyes and fall prey to her hypnotic gaze, I focused on her staff.

"Brid is not here. You have discovered my place of meditation, nothing more."

"I think not. I was here before, as you know well."

Her lips formed a tight little smile. "I'm surprised you remember. I brought you here to recover from the confusion of your passage through the time gate. You were badly disoriented. Perhaps you dreamed—"

"It was no dream. Brid lies in the room at the end of this passage." I pointed at the darkness behind her.

"This passage is only a hideaway. It goes nowhere. Its end is closed by the house's foundation stones. See for yourself." She stepped aside and let me pass.

I edged warily past and hurried forward but didn't get far. A wall of massive stones reeking of age and dust sealed the passage. Holding my lamp high, I examined the rough-hewn stones. My fingers probed each crevice, found only the crumbling shell of a long-dead spider.

"You see?" Koralie said. "If you expected to find a room and Brid hidden in it, you were suffering a delusion."

Could it be? I *had* been confused after coming through the mirror. Had I hallucinated the room and Brid?

She lies. Treden's voice cracked like a whip across my disordered thoughts. *A chamber is cut into the stones of the foundation. Her sorcery has hidden it.*

How can I find it?

Lonness's brusque voice answered my mental plea. *Force her to break the spell.*

With Lonness guiding my movements I leaped at Koralie, grabbed her arms, spun her around, and pressed her wrists against her spine.

"How brave you are with a defenseless woman, Korth." She spat the words. "I can't match your strength. Release me and I'll open the chamber."

The surrender was too easy. "Open it first. Then I'll release you." I lifted her wrists high between her shoulders.

She shrieked. "Stop! You're breaking my arms. Let me go. My hands must be free to use my staff."

"Do you swear to keep your word if I release you?"

"I swear by Molor that I will open the hidden door."

Reluctantly I opened my hands. She pulled her arms free, held out her staff, and pointed it, not at the foundation stones but at the passage's side wall. Muttering words I could not understand, she marked a door with the end of the staff. A purple flame shot out and inscribed a glowing rectangle. Koralie made another pass with her staff. The wall within the rectangle wavered and vanished.

"There. There's your chamber. Go in." Koralie pointed the staff at me.

The opening didn't look like the one I remembered. I was sure it had not opened off the side wall as this one did. I fought it, but the power of her staff dragged me against my will toward the glowing doorway.

Was I to be trapped like Derli? My hand around my fascinum, I shouted Derli's name as I stumbled through the flame-rimmed door.

13

MEDARA

I blinked in the unexpected glare of sunlight. Wherever I was, it was not Brid's cell. I stood on a wooden floor strewn with rushes in the manner of earlier times. They gave the room the scent of drying grass.

My gaze traveled to the center of the room where the rushes were brushed aside and a crude circle drawn on the floor with yellow chalk. At the circle's center stood a slim figure in a long gown of beige homespun caught around the waist with a braided rope sash.

A slave, I guessed, until my gaze reached her face. Light streaming from a round window behind and above her crowned her tawny hair with a blazing glory. From that corona of light, as from a miniature sun, radiant beams streaked in every direction. I squeezed my eyelids shut to protect my vision.

A crackling of rushes made me open them. The woman had stepped out of the circle. The halo had vanished. An ordinary woman hurried toward me with a smile of greeting.

"You've come, Molor be praised. I'd hardly dared hope ... But there, that's the way of it, isn't it? You ask a boon of the Winged One, and when he grants it, you're surprised, though you know he's pleased to reward his servants. I asked for a protector, but I never dared hope for such a noble lord."

She halted in front of me. Wide brown eyes lit with flecks of gold examined my elaborate robes and studied my face. Slender fingers toyed with the fringe of her sash. I watched her, still too stunned by the sudden transition to speak.

I was at a loss for words, but she certainly was not. "See now," she continued, "here I was, singing the sun-song at just the proper light to bind its strength and send it off to fetch the protector I beseeched the Winged One for, and didn't it find you and haul you in, and when you pop out of nowhere, I'm that shocked, I can't move. Of course, I'd never done it before, but Dama Ordell said I had the power, and she taught me all the songs, and she herself said the sun was at its nearest and there'd never be a better chance to tap its power, but I wasn't sure I'd get it right. In fact, I'm sure I mixed up some of the words but I guess Molor understood what I meant even if it didn't come out quite right, and ..." The torrent of words ceased. The girl's nostrils flared, her turned-up nose crinkled, and her head swung from side to side. Her face broke into a wide smile and she clapped her hands. "How small was my faith. I asked for one protector, and Molor sent me two. Welcome to you both."

I twisted my head. Had Koralie followed me?

A familiar laugh burst out beside me. "She means me, Korth. Her senses are better than yours."

"Derli!" My arms flung out to embrace the air. "How did you get free? I couldn't find you."

"Your shout loosed me and pulled me here. Though that witch tried hard to close the door on me."

"Witch?" At our unknown hostess's puzzled question I fell silent, but Derli answered readily.

"An evil woman. She intended to seal Korth in a time bubble where I was already caught, and had you not summoned him when you did, she would have left us both trapped."

I scowled, struck by a sudden suspicion. "How do you know about her if you weren't there until I shouted your name? Are you telling the truth about being trapped the whole time?"

"If you were wise enough to sense my presence, you wouldn't have to ask such a foolish question."

Derli's sharp retort ignited my temper. "I'm wise enough to notice you haven't answered." I glared at the empty air. "Have you been playing a trick on me?"

"A trick!" Derli's voice grew shrill. "You think I'd play silly games when that witch was twisting time?"

"Don't quarrel, please. We can't delay. I must take you to Dama Ordell, and after that we must ready ourselves for our journey."

"Journey?" Dismay cooled my anger. Whatever this rough-clad girl intended, I must make her understand I couldn't serve her purpose. I had to wrest Brid from Koralie's spell and save Renata.

"Can it be you've come without knowing why?"

"I only know that I am not whatever or whomever you summoned," I said. "I was yanked here from another time, where I have an urgent duty to fulfill."

The girl's brow wrinkled; her lips pursed. "But you did answer the summons. I'm sure Molor sent you. I don't know why … But what do I know of his ways? The Winged One's wisdom is not mine. You don't know the purpose of my summoning, I can see. I asked for a protector on my journey to find the Inheritor."

"Inheritor?" I blinked stupidly.

"To Ordred Lord Terral. I'm Medara, apprentice to Dama Ordell. The dama has been ill since the lord was slain in battle without passing the deathright to a successor. The councilors withhold from me the title of dama, though Ordell has named me so. They champion the cause of Ordred's brother, Ordrain. Dama Ordell refuses to cede him the title, though it would be an honor for her to be dama to two lords. But she can't be, because Ordrain hasn't inherited, so he won't pass the test. Unless, of course, the lord councilors play false and feign the responses, as they're capable of doing."

"Hold on." I raised my hands to fend off the flood of words. "This is the Manor House, then?"

"Of course. Where else would we be?"

"And you say *Ordred* is—or was—lord?"

She gave a vigorous nod, took a deep breath, and started in again. "He was killed battling the Labonites, the Dunesmen, you know, over a year ago now, and—"

"Ordred, the fifth Lord Terral?" I shot my question across her barrage. Ordred lived two hundred and ten years before the young Brid's time plus another sixty before mine.

"Yes, and Dama Ordell is calling into herself the curse that has settled on the land because there was no rite of Lord's-Kill, and she grows weaker every day. She can't hold on much longer. I must find an Inheritor, or war and plague will strike the land, and we'll all be doomed. I'll go to the battlefield where Ordred died to begin my search, but I've needed a protector to go with me because Ordrain is sure to try to stop me, and he—"

"Then you don't want me. I'm no protector. You need someone skilled at arms. I'm no soldier, no fighter. I'd be useless to you." I grasped her shoulders. "And you don't need me. You'll find the Inheritor. His name is Mett. He's a Labonite, but—"

"You know the Inheritor?" Her face gleamed. "Then you *are* the one. Oh, what a boon the Great One has granted in sending you." Medara hopped up and down. "Hurry. Ordell must know."

She caught my arm and dragged me toward the door.

I resisted. "I can't go with you, Medara. I have to go back to the place you called me from. Lives depend on it. And I don't know where to find Mett. I only know he is—will be—the lord who follows Ordred."

"But that knowledge is invaluable," she insisted with infuriating stubbornness. I suspected she heard only as much of what I said as fit her conviction that I was here in answer to her summons. "It has been revealed to Dama Ordell in a vision that when Ordred died in battle, the deathright passed to his slayer. So we know in general where to look—among the Dunesmen's forces. But until now I had no idea who I was looking for. Only that he is one of our sworn enemies. I don't see how such a one can be the Inheritor, but Dama Ordell's visions are true, so I have to go find him, and as if hunting among the Labonites isn't dangerous enough, and how I'll persuade a Dunesman to become Lord of the Manor Lands I don't know, but now Ordrain has claimed the inheritance, and he'll try to stop me. That's why I need a protector."

"I understand your problem," I said, "but I've told you I'm no protector. You have to send me back to—"

"Don't be silly, Korth," Derli interrupted. "She can't send you back. You have to help her. If Mett isn't found and Ordrain is named lord, there'll be no Brid to rescue."

My mind whirled. I felt helpless and unutterably weary after all I'd been through this interminable day. "But there isn't time." Even to my own ears my objection sounded plaintive and whiny.

"There are too many times," Derli corrected me. "It's up to you to sort them out."

"I wouldn't know how to send you back." Medara's gold-flecked eyes were wide and worried. "Only the Winged One can call you back to wherever he took you from. I only know the summoning, and I'd never done that before today. You saw how startled I was when you came. I suppose I shouldn't have been, but it's always a shock the first time you get a thing right."

With a sigh I let her lead me from the room. Perhaps I could persuade Dama Ordell to send me back to Brid.

Medara led us through ways much less ornate but no less confusing than those of the Manor House of Brid's time. Gone were the carpeted floors and velvet walls; gone the ornate candelabra; gone, too, the mirrored corridors. I saw patios where I did not expect them, and many places where I expected doors or stairs I saw only bare walls.

Medara ushered us into a large bedchamber. Looking lost in the wide bed, a frail woman lay propped on a pile of pillows. Medara hurried to her side and bent low to speak into the woman's ear. "Dama, it's Medara, back from the sun spell. It worked. Molor sent a protector, as you said he would. And the protector brought a fala with him."

The woman's lips opened. A murmur, faint and indistinct, drifted to me. Medara motioned me closer.

Faded eyes that might once have been green peered from beneath drooping lids. A gnarled and tremulous hand fluttered toward me; a knobby finger grazed my fascinum. I had to place my ear directly above the papery lips to catch the whispered words.

"Danger. Be strong. Time is in your hands ... to disrupt or restore." She fell silent, clearly exhausted by the effort of forming those few sentences. It would be useless to press for an explanation. And by her puzzled expression I guessed Medara understood no more of the dama's words than I did. Though I'd question her later.

"I'm sent to be with him when the times turn, Dama." Derli's voice spoke from the narrow space between my head and the dama's. I jerked my head back and nearly missed the dama's soft-sighed words.

"Your pain ... is worse ... than mine."

Medara pressed the dama's hand. The faint voice breathed a final command. "Find the Inheritor."

Medara grabbed my elbow and steered me from the room. Silent for once, she led me to a chamber a few doors from the dama's. Only when we were inside with the door shut did she speak. "Dama Ordell was greatly pleased by your coming. I don't understand what she told you. She knows you, I think, and if she had done the sun-singing, she wouldn't have been surprised when you came, and she could have answered all your questions, but she's too little breath left now. She approves you as the protector, that's certain, and that will have to do. We'll leave on the search after dark. We have to travel by night to hide from Ordrain. I hope we can get far from the Manor House before he discovers I'm gone. He mustn't learn you're here. I'll make the final preparations. You stay in this room until I come for you. The servants in this wing are loyal to the dama, but even here there may be spies. Rest if you can. I must rest, too, before we start. The sun spell has worn me out. When I return, I'll bring you food and clothes."

She left before I could raise my questions. With no way to return, I had no choice but to postpone the attempt to rescue Brid and revive Renata. My only consolation was that they would not even be born for another two centuries. Whatever happened here, it need not delay my action there—if I could find a way to get back to the same moment when Koralie had sent me away. A big *if.*

Derli had apparently understood the dama's cryptic remarks. Perhaps I could pry information from her, though I knew too well how difficult she could be.

I sank onto the edge of the bed, tugged off my boots, and lay back. "Derli?"

"Here, Korth."

Her presence comforted me. I closed my eyes, but, exhausted as I was, I wasn't ready to sleep. "Derli, what is a fala?"

"I am." A chuckle accompanied the words.

"That doesn't tell me anything."

Tinkling laughter rang in my ear. "It will."

"When? Why can't I see you? Why do you tell me so little?"

"Haven't you already learned much about me?"

I considered. I'd come to accept her presence, even welcome it. But I didn't understand her at all. I tried a different tack. "What did Dama Ordell mean when she said your pain was worse than hers?"

The laughter ceased, replaced by a long pause. At last in a low, flat voice she said, "One day you'll understand that, too."

"How can I, when you explain nothing? Tell me what you meant when you told the dama you were sent to be with me when the times turn. You know so much more than I about all this that is happening to me. I want an explanation."

"I'm forbidden to give you one."

"Forbidden by whom?"

"I'm forbidden to tell you that."

"You were a gift to me from Lisha. Did she forbid you? But why?"

"I was a gift from her, it's true, but I do not answer only to her."

"To whom, then?"

"I can't tell you."

I couldn't pry more from her. But something else bothered me—a thing I found hard to say. "Derli, I tried to find you after you shouted that you were trapped. I followed you through the time gate. But everything was so confusing. Koralie put a spell on me. I didn't know how or where to hunt for you. I called you several times, but you didn't answer." My words trailed off. The excuse seemed weak and inadequate now. I dredged up the courage to add, "I'm sorry it took me so long."

Her voice turned soft and gentle. "In truth, Korth, it didn't take you long. You found me more quickly than I'd expected."

In my weariness I could make no sense of her answer. I yawned. "Derli, sing me to sleep as you did in the inn."

A sweet melody arose around me. Enclosed in its soothing cocoon, I drifted into slumber.

All too soon Medara woke me. "I've brought journey clothes and a snack," she said. "Dress quickly and eat as we go. I was right about the spies. Ordrain is missing. He must have found out about you and about our plans, and I'm afraid he's well ahead of us on the road. He'll set an ambush to stop us. Or if he knows everything, he'll try to find the Inheritor before we do and kill him. Dama Ordell is too weak to give me any more help. I have a few tricks of my own, not many, but they'll have to do. He may not know about you or the fala. That would give us some advantage. We'll have to hurry, if we hope to outwit him."

I tried to protest again that I had no experience with weapons and could not possibly be the protector she'd expected. To no avail. She insisted that Molor had sent me in response to her summoning, and, inexplicably, Derli backed her up. I had no choice but to set out with her on what seemed to me an impossible mission.

I could be of no help with finding the location of the battlefield where Ordred was slain and his spirit passed to Mett. The battle against the Dunesmen took place beyond the Manor Lands' northern border, with the Dunesmen dwelling still farther north, in the Desert of Labon. There Medara hoped I could locate and identify the Inheritor, something that neither she nor Ordrain had any means of doing. I doubted that I could, either. I knew his voice, but not his appearance.

We toiled up a steep and rocky hillside, Medara in the lead. I followed. Abbi, Medara's personal servant, trailed behind me, and Pik, a husky guard, brought up the rear. I wondered anew why Medara insisted that I was the protector. Pik had to be a better protector than I'd be.

Where Derli was, I had no idea; she'd fallen silent since we reached the hills. Perhaps she was scouting ahead. She had no need of the spirit lights the rest of us carried—narrow glass cylinders filled with glowing grubs. The luminous creatures provided a dim but reliable bluish light. The grubs would survive for from ten to twelve days so long as we kept them supplied with small amounts of the leaf mulch they fed on.

We'd traveled safely and uneventfully through the level fields and pastures beyond the Manor House. Medara was pleased. We detected no sign of pursuit and we covered a considerable distance on our first night's trek. In the hills we'd more easily find shelter for our day's rest.

Medara disappeared over the crest of the hill. I rounded the crest and collided with her. She pushed me down and motioned for me to mask my spirit light. Hers already wore a black cloth cover. She pointed.

A plume of smoke rose gray against the dark shadows of trees. I traced it downward and made out the pale outlines of tents and the moving shadows of men and horses. Even in the darkness my form would present a visible target on the bare hilltop. I flattened myself against the ground. Medara slipped back to warn Abbi and Pik; I edged slowly after her.

"Who are they?" I whispered when I reached her.

"I sent Derli to spy, but I'm certain it's Ordrain and his men. Ordrain's clever and commands great loyalty among his men. I'm not surprised they've anticipated our route."

"They're breaking camp. Maybe they haven't seen us."

"If they're that close, they'll find us," Medara said grimly. "They'll have a nezzi with them."

"What's that?"

"A small creature with a big nose," Derli's voice startled us. "It sniffs out anything and anyone it's set to find. And, yes, they have one. They know we're in the area. Their watchers spotted us."

Abbi whimpered with fear. Why had Medara brought the girl on such a dangerous trek?

"Hush!" Medara jabbed a finger into her maid's back. "We can't panic. We have to think what to do."

I was familiar with the hills but knew nothing of the land to their north. In my day these hills would be quarried. As a slave I'd toiled in those quarries. "We'd better head back the way we came," I suggested. "We can take a more easterly route through the hills."

"That would take us into the Badlands. They're impassable." Medara started back down the trail.

"West, then."

She shook her head. "There the hills curve away from the desert.

We'd add several days to our journey. And the paths are more open. There's nowhere to hide. This path we're on is the safest and most direct way."

I slid down a sharp incline to reach her side. "It's not safe any longer."

She unmasked her light and motioned for the rest of us to do the same. "We may be able to open it. If we confuse them and send them off on a false trail …" Leaving the sentence unfinished, she led us on down the slope.

Abbi was weeping. Medara dropped back, to comfort her, I supposed, and I took the lead. Slipping and sliding, we threaded down the twisting path. I felt something streak past my ankles, heard it swish around us, snuffling.

Medara shined her light toward the sound. "The nezzi." A tiny dark creature streaked away. "He'll lead them straight to us."

"Maybe not," Derli said. "Korth, use your fascinum to call the thing back."

"My fascinum! Can it do that?"

"Possibly. Try."

I clamped my hand on the golden oval. "Nezzi," I called softly, feeling foolish. "Come to me."

Something rustled over the dry ground. A dark thing little longer than a man's hand crept toward me over the rocky path. I held my breath. When it came near my foot, foolishly I grabbed at it.

Sharp teeth crunched my palm. I yelped and tried to shake the thing loose. It dangled from my hand, its teeth scraping the bones. With my other hand I grasped the wriggling creature and squeezed until it went limp. Medara pried its mouth open and eased its teeth from my flesh. I bit my lips to stifle a scream. Medara flung the dead creature to the ground, and Pik piled rocks over it. Blood spouted from the deep punctures in my palm.

"Is it poisonous?" I asked between clenched teeth.

"I don't know." Medara ripped a piece of cloth from her dress and bound my palm. "No one's ever caught one that way before. I didn't know you had that power."

"It didn't do us any good." Pik pointed below. Shadows clambered over rocks at the base of the hill.

"Quick. Follow me." Medara headed back up the hill, but ducked behind the first large outcropping of rock we passed. She placed the trembling Abbi against the rock and motioned Pik beside her.

"We have only one chance left." Medara was breathing hard. "I'm going to try a transformation spell."

A deathly quiet followed her words. Medara's eyes closed; her body swayed back and forth, her fingers inscribed symbols in the air. A low hum blended with the moan of the night wind. Her body blurred. I squeezed my eyes shut to clear my vision. When I opened them, Abbi stood where Medara had been and Medara cringed against the rock.

The new Abbi frowned and said in Medara's voice, "Why didn't it work for you?" She gasped. "The amulet you wear. Give it to Pik. Hurry."

Grunts and the scuff of boots over rock removed my hesitation. I pulled the chain over my head and tossed it to Pik. He slipped it on, and we froze again while Medara-as-Abbi repeated her conjuring.

A wave of intense nausea swept over me. A shudder wracked my body. When the attack passed, I saw against the rock next to Medara not Pik but myself.

"It will buy us a little time," the real Medara whispered.

Around our hiding place black-garbed figures materialized out of the night. We tried to run. Swords barred our way.

14

EXCHANGE

Our captors herded us at sword's point into the center of the enemy camp. The sun had risen. Dying embers marked the site of the blaze we'd viewed earlier. Most of the tents had been taken down, leaving just one large one and two small ones in place. A tall, spare man stepped from the large tent and glared from beneath beetled brows. High cheekbones accentuated the thinness of his face. His haughty gaze raked the company. Such was the force of his presence that I reverted instinctively to slave status, lowering my eyes. My feet scuffed the ground.

"We have her, Lord Ordrain." His men dragged forward Abbi in the semblance of Medara and thrust her to her knees before him.

Overcome with a feeling of helpless resignation, I cringed as a swordsman kicked the trembling girl. Without raising my head, I cast an upward glance at Pik. Why did the Protector make no attempt to defend our lady?

My senses blurred. Medara clutched my arm. I pulled free of her grasp and, ignoring the throbbing ache in my injured hand, let both arms fall limply by my side. My shoulders hunched in the old familiar slave stance. We were no more than a few paces from where Ordrain stood over the cowering Abbi, but his voice came to me as though from a great distance.

"You were warned what would happen if you left the Manor House to attempt this journey."

The girl moaned and rocked back and forth, her arms locked tightly about her body.

Ordrain leaned over her. "It's too late for regrets. You'll never be dama. I am the Inheritor. I give you to my men." He shoved her into the arms of the nearest man.

My hand throbbed. Its painful beat pulsed through my body, reducing Ordrain's harsh words to a hollow echo. Dimly, through a sudden haze, I watched men drag Abbi into a tent. Their laughter and her screams reached me filtered through the pounding of my heart. They were raping her! But I was only an injured slave. I couldn't help her. My bitten palm, purpled and hot, had swollen to twice its normal size. My arm, too, was swelling. The coarse material of my shirtsleeve grated against my skin.

"Lord, this is the one the girl calls her 'protector.' What use he is, I can't guess." One black-clad minion pushed Pik forward while the others guffawed.

The sight of my face, my form, standing defiantly before the usurper lord dizzied me. My knees buckled. The stony ground rose and crashed against my face.

I claw at the vines wrapped around my arm. A deadly viper slithers away into the thick undergrowth; its poison courses through my body. Brilliant birds swoop down with raucous cries and stab me with their beaks. I try to fend them off with my free arm, but each time I lower my arm to tug off the vines, more of the feathered missiles plummet toward me. I wrench myself from the vines and stumble toward the temple, blood pouring down my head.

The façade has fallen into ruin. Large chunks of masonry have crumbled to dust. Roots and runners have found, filled, and enlarged the gaps.

The door is barred. I slam my body against it again and again. The carved surface gouges my flesh. Finally the aged wood splinters and the door breaks away from its hinges and crashes inward. I lurch over it, bruised and racked with pain.

The interior of the temple is dark and dank. Spiderwebs veil its inner chambers; thick mold obscures its painted walls. I stumble through the gloomy recesses. "Lisha," I call, "where are you? I've come."

My shouts wake a ceiling full of slumbering bats. With shrill squeaks they dart around me, their leathery wings fanning my face.

Dust-filled light falls through a chink in the wall. By its rays I see Lisha standing motionless on a pedestal. I rush to her. She smiles down on me, her thick hair a mantle of night about her shoulders. I clasp my arms around her ankles beneath her full red skirt.

My arms embrace cold stone. I lean my feverish head against the carved feet and weep tears filled with the venom of the viper. The stone warms in my embrace. The carved ankles soften, acquire the feel of flesh. The scent of lilies washes over me.

A gentle voice says, "Korth, why are you here so soon? You do not honor the goddess by breaking down the doors of her temple. Go, repair the damage. When you come by the true path, the doors will open for you."

"Repair the doors of a ruined temple?"

She must have stooped; her hand rests on my head. "The temple will be restored if the doors hold firm. But if you destroy the doors, the jungle will creep inside and tear the stones apart past all rebuilding."

I want to ask her how she expects me to repair the shattered, rotting wood and with what. But she straightens and I gaze at a statue of painted granite. A spider scampers across the stone face.

I slog through bat guano to the splintered doors, lift them, and try to prop them in place. The wood crumbles in my hands. A rush of jungle growth bursts toward the temple. I brace myself in the doorway. I cannot move. Roots creep over my feet; tendrils wind around my ankles. Vines spread up my body. The frond of a leaf fern wraps around my palm.

"**K**orth, wake up. I've stuck my finger and used my own blood to drive the nezzi's poison from your body. Hurry. You must wake."

The low, urgent voice swept through the jungle like a hot wind. The creeping vines halted, the trees and ferns shriveled, the flowers dissolved into ashes. The temple sank into the earth. I sank with it, but the earth did not receive me. I remained, lying on the barren ground.

My eyes struggled open. Medara leaned over me, her face grave.

"Korth, you must wake. It's night. We have to escape." Medara gave my hand a hard squeeze. "I thought we'd lost you. That vile beast *was* poisonous. And I had all I could do to hold the transformation spell in place. I couldn't relax it to draw healing power. The power for the transformation doesn't come from the same source. It's sky power and the other's earth power, and I can't use them both at the same time. Derli's been after me all day to drop the transformation, but I couldn't, you know, because they were watching us, and they'd've seen me and done to me what they've done to poor Abbi, and then, of course, I'd have no power at all and our search would be useless—"

"Don't wear him out as soon as you've brought him around." Derli's sharp voice brought me back to full awareness.

My eyes opened wider. A spirit lamp tied to the center pole illuminated the tent in which we huddled. Even without Pik and Abbi, we were cramped in the small space.

"Someone's coming," Derli warned.

"My warding spell must have failed. And me too tired and weak to restore the transformation." Medara groaned and curled herself up, concealing her face with her arms. "Hide your face, Korth."

I obeyed her whispered command. Heavy footsteps thudded in my ear.

"Zera!"

At Derli's exclamation my head snapped up and Medara uncurled. Pik ducked through the tent flap, Abbi's limp form in his arms. He wore his own shape, but my fascinum still hung against his bare chest. He bent and lowered his burden to the tent floor. On his shoulders flayed skin hung in loose strips. I gasped at the raw ruin of his back.

Abbi lay still, her naked body a mass of bruises, her thighs stained with blood.

"They took turns with her." Pik's voice trembled with anger. His venomous gaze shifted back and forth between Medara and me. "All day. Not Ordrain. All his men. After they scourged me, they took me in and made me watch."

His voice trailed off. He sank to his knees beside her and with bloody fingers touched her tangled hair.

"She trusted you." Eyes dark with pain, he looked at Medara. "She obeyed you. So did I. Where was the protection you promised?"

Medara twisted the frayed end of her rope sash and did not meet Pik's eyes. "I couldn't ward you and us, too. Not and keep the transformation spell in place. I'm only an apprentice yet. I haven't got the power of a dama."

"You had power enough to save yourself."

Medara shrugged.

"Heal them, woman." Derli shrilled.

"I can't, I tell you." Medara glared at the empty air. "I'm worn out from holding the transformation spell all day. That wouldn't be an easy thing even for the dama. I did heal Korth, and you don't know what that took, and I have to leave myself strength to escape."

"You have enough for talking," Derli snapped. "Use that to heal them."

Medara rose and edged past Pik and Abbi to peer out of the tent flap into the inky blackness. "How did you get here without being seen?"

"I sneaked around through the shadows." Pik fingered the fascinum hanging against his bare and blood-streaked chest. "This thing led me to you."

"They'll be looking for you. I can't stay here." Medara unfastened the spirit light from the tent pole. "I'll have to try to restore the transformation."

"Haven't you done them enough harm?" Derli's voice seethed with anger. "You've already saved yourself at Abbi's expense."

"That's why I brought her with me."

Pik rocked back onto his heels and glared up at Medara. "You sent her to be raped."

Medara backed away from the rage in Pik's accusation and stood behind me. "I knew what they'd do to me if they caught me. A dama has to protect herself. Abbi understood."

"Korth, do something," Derli pled.

"I? What can I do?"

Use the fascinum. The voice of Treden startled me. The lords had been silent since I was thrown into this time.

I stood and reached for my fascinum. Pik's eyes rounded. He stepped back and raised his hands, fending me off. "Leave it. It's mine."

I knocked his hands aside and clasped the oval. "I won't take it from you. Only let me hold it."

He tried to shove me back, but I kept a firm hold on the fascinum. "Now what do I do?" I mumbled to Treden.

Follow your instincts.

Instincts? I had none. I was no healer—I was a slave.

No, not a slave. Not since receiving the deathright when I slew the old lord. I hadn't been named lord in his place, but whatever I was, I was *not* a slave.

In the young Brid's time I'd been named Lord Terral. Perhaps that conferred on me the ability to heal. No harm in trying. With a sudden burst of confidence, I concentrated on Pik's condition, willing him to heal.

Pik's hands fell to his sides, his face took on a slack, vacant expression. His memories opened to me.

With a crack like thunder the lash sliced through my flesh. A second sharp crack. A second blow cut deep across my back. A third stripe tore across the first two. Searing pain raked my back and shoulders.

"Why are they doing this?" I moaned. "I'm only a servant. I—"

The lash fell again. I screamed.

"Silence!" Medara clapped her hands over my mouth.

"Courage, Korth." Derli's whisper brought me back to the present. I stared at Pik in amazement. The red welts on his shoulders had closed. I'd done it! I'd healed him!

"His back's healed, too," Derli said. "Now help Abbi."

I looked at the crumpled form at my feet. Was she still alive? And could I bear to take into myself the pain she'd endured?

"For Zera's sake, Korth, hurry!" Derli hissed.

I pulled Pik toward me. He seemed in a trance. I kept one hand on the fascinum and placed the other on Abbi's side. Waves of fear and nausea swept over me. Fiery torment gripped my vitals. I writhed in agony, fighting the instinct to pull my hand free of the fascinum.

The tent flap was swept aside. Two black-clad men pushed into the tent. One shoved Pik, and the other kicked Abbi and lunged at me. I twisted away. Medara hurled the spirit light to the ground. Glass shattered.

A hand grabbed my shirt and hauled me to my feet. "Bring light," a voice bellowed.

A tenuous, wavering form crept up the tent pole and launched itself into the air. An eerie blue mist drifted slowly downward before the startled faces of Ordrain's men. "You disturb the vigil of the dead," a hollow voice intoned. "You will join our ranks."

One man ran howling from the tent. The other tried to follow and collided with me. My hands found his throat, tightened, and the ghostly threat became fact.

"Take his sword, Korth," Derli instructed in her normal voice.

By the luminescent flesh of the grubs Derli wore, I found the sword. With a dazed expression, Pik lumbered to his feet and lifted the still unconscious Abbi.

"Leave her," Medara said. "We'll have to fight our way out."

"I'm her Protector. I won't leave her." Pik clutched the frail body to his chest.

Medara cast him an angry glance and turned to me. "Stay by me."

"Pssst, Korth. Take me with you." Derli was wrapped around the tent pole, the grub-flesh she'd assumed stretched to a thin transparency. I held out my hand, and she slid onto it and spread herself across my shoulders, a glowing cloak.

We burst from the tent. A brisk wind caught us and propelled us toward Ordrain's men. Swords drawn, faces set, they fanned out in a broad semicircle and stood waiting, stiff as a row of fence stakes.

I gripped the sword. "Lonness, show me how to use this," I muttered.

I felt the old lord's ability infuse me. And something else: a shadowy presence, incomplete, not one of the past lords. It, too, was directing my hand.

The fence stakes separated. Ordrain stepped into the center of the semicircle. As I headed toward him, Derli slipped off my shoulders. The wind caught her and hurled her in front of me. Spread out into a thin sail, she swept toward Ordrain. He hacked at the pale wraith with his sword, sending bits of blue phosphorescence flying like sparks. The fragments swirled around him and reformed, gauze thin.

"You cannot kill the dead, but you can join us," the ghostly voice intoned.

Ordrain snorted and looked at Medara. "Your tricks don't frighten me." Sword drawn, he strode toward her.

I stepped in front of him. He thrust at me. I parried his thrust with an awkward turn. A grim smile played on his lips. He jabbed at my chest. I swung my sword, blocking him. We fought for several minutes, Lonness and that other shadowy presence guiding my moves. I aimed my sword at his chest and lunged. He dipped his blade beneath mine and flicked it upward, knocking the sword from my hand.

Derli wrapped her thin drapery of flesh around Ordrain's face. He dropped his sword and clawed at the tightening envelope.

I leaped for his throat. Gasping through the blue membrane, he tore at my hands, but my grip held. The lessons preparing me for the rite of Lord's-Kill again served me well. His body went limp. I squeezed until I was sure he was dead.

I looked around. Pik had grabbed up a sword and with one hand was fending off Ordrain's men. I snatched up the other sword and plunged into the fray.

Our opponents backed off. With Ordrain dead, his men had no stomach for fighting. Most broke ranks and ran for their horses. I battled the few who remained with a ferocity that made up for my lack of skill. Horses thundered off into the night. Our foes scattered.

A riderless horse stood alone at the edge of the camp. I darted to it and grabbed the reins, intending to give chase. It neighed and pawed the ground. I backed off. I'd never ridden a horse.

"Korth. Come back."

Medara's call resolved my dilemma. Relieved, I loped back to the center of the camp.

Medara threw her arms around my waist and gave me a warm hug. "There, I knew you'd prove a good protector. You've killed Ordrain. Now I know we'll succeed. We're not far from the desert, and there's nobody left to stop us. We'll find the Inheritor. There's no point in going after those cowards, but we need to get away before they come sneaking back to take revenge."

Embarrassed, I interrupted the verbal stream. "Where's Derli? She's the one who saved us. I hope she wasn't hurt."

"Of course she wasn't. A fala can't be hurt." Medara waved toward the tents. "Look for supplies. We need lights. And water. Try to find our packs." She turned to Pik. "Put Abbi down and help Korth. I'll care for her."

The big man hugged his burden tighter. "You won't touch her again."

Medara tossed her head. "Fine. We'll save our strength for our journey."

She clutched my arm and drew me away. "The transformation's affected his mind," she whispered. "It happens sometimes. The effect will wear off, but we'll have to keep a close watch on him until it does."

"Shouldn't I force him to let me heal her?"

"If you try, he could become violent. Wait until he tires of carrying her."

I nodded, thinking of the pain I'd have to endure when I attempted the healing.

In the tent that had been Ordrain's I found a torch and a blanket. I took the torch to Medara, helped Pik wrap Abbi in the blanket, and hurried off to search the other tents.

I found our packs, gathered extra rations, and returned to Medara. "Here's another torch and a canteen full of water. I couldn't find Derli. Do you see or sense her?"

"No. Don't worry about her. When we leave, she'll join us." Medara pointed northward. "The edge of the desert lies beyond these hills. We can't be far from the battlefield where Lord Ordred was killed. With luck we'll reach it by daybreak."

With a glance at Pik, she led off on a westerly course. I urged Pik after her and followed behind him. When we were out of sight of the camp, I shouted for Derli.

"Be quiet, Korth." Medara raised the torch so its light shone on my face. "She'll find us."

I pursed my lips and marched on in worried silence.

"Pssst. I'm here, Korth."

The whisper relieved my mind, but what was Derli up to, that she was hiding her presence from the others?

The trail twisted, and I lost all sense of direction. We trudged on for hours. Pik grunted occasionally and shifted his burden. When he lagged behind, I offered to take Abbi from him. He only shook his head and plodded on. Sunrise found us still in the hills. Medara called a halt and sank down on a grassy slope. Pik set Abbi down away from us and crouched over her. I approached him.

"Leave her alone," he growled.

"He only wants to help her," Medara said, her voice stern. "He helped you."

"I didn't ask for his help." Pik glared at me and rubbed his arms. I could imagine how his muscles ached.

"I'll try again to heal her. Give me my fascinum."

"No." His eyes were wild. He clamped his hand over the gold oval. "It's mine now."

"Pik, hand it to him at once." Medara stamped her foot. An angry frown creased her forehead.

Pik stalked toward her. "I'll take no more orders from you."

I jumped between them. "Calm down, man. You're denying Abbi the help she needs."

He broke into crazed laughter. "Help her, then, Protector. Let's see you raise the dead."

I bent and touched Abbi. Her flesh was cold, rigid. Pik had carried a dead woman through the rocky hills.

Pik lunged at me. We grappled, arms locked. He fought with a madman's strength. I strained against his grip. He slammed a knee into my groin. I gasped and doubled over. His fists crashed down on my head, and I toppled to the ground. He dropped too, pinning me. My head reeled. He lifted me and slammed me against the ground.

Consciousness returned. Ropes cut into my wrists and ankles. I lay unable to move, sharp stones stabbing my flesh. Shouts and scuffling noises made me turn my head.

Pik dragged the struggling Medara around a bend in the path. Her cries and curses faded into the distance. I twisted and writhed. The rope cut into my arms. I cursed my helplessness.

"Lie still, Korth. I'll untie you."

I turned my head. Abbi stood beside me.

15

THE BADLANDS

I stared at the slender figure wrapped in the dark green blanket.

"I waited until they got out of sight. Couldn't tell how Pik would react to Abbi's resurrection." She dropped to her knees and tugged at the knotted cord binding my wrist. "I'm not much good at this. It'll take a while."

"Derli! I thought you really were Abbi."

"Your mind's in a muddle. You know Abbi's dead." Her angry yank on my wrist tightened the rope instead of loosening it. I let out a yelp of pain. With no sympathy in her voice she said, "You waited too long before you insisted on healing her."

I winced and squeezed my eyes shut. "I didn't know she was dying." It was a weak excuse.

Derli gave my wrist another savage twist and the rope fell away. "Medara knew. She found it easier to let Abbi die than to face her."

I sat up and rubbed my wrists while she worked on my ankles. When I regained sufficient feeling in my wrists, I leaned forward and helped with the ankle ropes. "I can't believe Medara would be so cruel."

Derli snorted. "She's a selfish little windbag. I guess we'll have to rescue her though." She rose to her feet and helped me stand.

I nodded. "She has to find Mett." I left unvoiced the conviction that I dared not fail here as I had with Brid.

We started along the trail. Still shaky, I leaned on the shoulder Derli offered. The body she wore had regained its warmth. A sudden awareness of its closeness made me feel awkward and self-conscious. I drew away, let her precede me, and hobbled behind her.

She spun around, gray eyes sparking. "What's the matter with you, Korth?"

I stared at the path and mumbled an apology.

"Look at me." She grabbed my arm. "You're acting like a slave again."

My eyes snapped to her face. She had sounded so like Lisha I half expected to see the intense blue eyes and night-black hair I had seen in my vision.

Abbi's face was plain and unremarkable. Her mud-brown hair badly needed combing. The new intensity of her gray eyes lent interest but not beauty to her face.

Her thin brows drew together in a frown. "Medara's transformation spell scrambled you and Pik a bit, I'd guess. No wonder poor Pik's gone mad." She kept her hold on my arm and pulled me along the path. "We've got to find them and undo the damage."

I ran stumbling after her. She released my arm as the path grew rougher and steeper. We jogged around frequent rockslides and scrambled over tumbled boulders.

Panting, I pled with Derli to stop and flung myself down on a flat-topped rock. Its sun-baked surface burned my skin. Too tired to rise, I rolled off it and huddled in its scanty shade. The sun blazed down not far from the zenith. I dried sweat off my face with my sleeve; my shirt stuck to my back. "Are you sure we're on the right track?" I asked. "Medara said we'd be in the desert by daybreak. It's nearly noon, and we're still in the hills."

Derli eased herself down beside me and adjusted her blanket, tightening the rope she'd tied around her to secure it. She seemed not to feel the heat. "This is the way they came, but it doesn't lead to the desert. We're entering the badlands."

I groaned at the thought of tracking our quarry through unknown ways. My cracked lips and parched throat ached for water, but Pik had the canteen we'd brought, as well as the other rations. "Can they be far ahead of us?"

"No, but—" Derli sniffed the air and jumped to her feet. "I sense something … someone … between us and them. The place reeks of evil." She clasped her blanket firmly and ran forward, calling back over her shoulder, "Hurry. Danger."

I scrambled to my feet and straggled after her. She disappeared among the craggy rocks that lined the twisting path. When the thud of her pounding feet faded away, I halted. Boulders strewn as though by some fearful upheaval of the earth hid the path.

A single, agonized scream jolted me into motion. Its echoes bounced off the rugged hills. Derli? Or Medara? I raced in what I hoped was the right direction.

The path veered to the left and dipped into a caldera filled with spires and buttes twisted into tormented forms by the force of a malign nature. I descended the steep path cautiously, avoiding fallen rocks and crumbling soil.

A rock-brown figure dropped before me. His upraised blade caught the sun. Blinded by the reflected gleam, I stepped back. He lowered the knife. Tall and sinewy, his hair and skin the color of dry earth, he stared at me, cold-eyed, brows lifted in a quizzical arch, as though daring me to say or do something. Behind him the crags and tors suddenly swarmed with brown-garbed men.

I tried to rush past him before his companions blocked my escape route, but they were too swift. Like lizards they scuttled down the cliffs and dropped onto the path.

All were hideously disfigured, their faces crisscrossed with jagged scars, several with ugly red lesions where an ear should be, some with a gaping hole in place of an eye or nose. Many were missing hands or even an entire arm, and one hopped around on one leg. The ghastly crowd surrounded me. None but the leader held a weapon, yet Ordrain's men with their swords hadn't terrified me like these did.

The man in front of me stared and spoke words in a language I didn't understand. I shook my head, wishing again that I knew where Derli was.

"I asked why you come here." His voice was hoarse and low. The other men scowled and muttered.

I grasped the significance of the foreign speech, the maimed bodies. "You're Dunesmen of Labon!" Battle-scarred refugees from the long war between the Manor Lands and the dwellers in the Desert of Labon, they had nothing more to lose. They'd kill on a whim.

The man shook his head. "We have no homeland. We're outcasts—escaped slaves, dispossessed victims of war, Zerans, madmen." He gave me a shrewd look as he named the last category. "Have you come to join us?"

I repressed a shudder. I was defenseless against these men. "I've come in search of one who may dwell among you. He's called Mett."

The man's lips twisted into a wry grin. "You've found him."

"You!" My mouth dropped open. Why hadn't I recognized him? I should have felt immediately the bond between us. "You—the Lordslayer?"

The muscles of his bare arm tightened until they stood out like thick cords. "For the second time today I hear that title."

Medara! She must have spoken to him. "Where is she—the one who called you that?"

He flashed a twisted smile at his men.

One, tall and scarecrow thin, stepped forward. With a leer on his pockmarked face he said, "Do you come as her rescuer?" An inhuman light smoldered in his eyes.

I drew back from the gangling figure and fixed my gaze on Mett. "I come as her companion."

The scarecrow interposed himself between Mett and me. His grin widened, exposing crooked and chipped teeth. "She had a companion. He gave her to us."

"Pik!" My anger flared. "He had no right—"

Mett pushed his confederate aside. "He offered the woman to me as a token of good faith. But if you would be her champion …"

The mutilated faces around me wore dangerous smirks. The one-armed man danced a weird jig, stirring up a cloud of dust. A man with no ears clapped his hands in rhythm with the dancer's frenetic movements. The clapping grew louder. Others joined the dance, one whirling on one leg, another beating time with stumps of wrists.

The tall man towered over me like a kite on a string. "Perhaps you'll champion both women. That would be great sport." His laughter blasted me with fetid breath.

Derli! They had her as well as Medara! I swung toward Mett. "You haven't hurt them?"

"They're safe and untouched." Mett placed his knife against my back. "Come and see." He thrust me forward.

His men ceased their capering, closed in, and drove me along at a trot. On our wild descent we wove around jagged spires of rock. As we approached the center of the vast basin, we dodged fissures venting hot steam. Sulfur fumes dizzied me. Overhead the sun's red eye blazed.

We halted so abruptly I nearly lost my balance. Before us a stone archway gave access to a bubbling lake of molten lava. Waves of heat poured off it. My knees wobbled, forcing me to sag against the stone pillar that supported one side of the arch.

The heat and fumes had no apparent effect on the band of maniacs. They cavorted around us as Mett drew me with him under the arch to the brink of the fiery lake. He clasped my arm with one hand and with the other he pointed. "See, there they are."

A rocky island rose out of the pool of bubbling lava. Through the smoke and mist a still figure was visible lying on the rocks. Another crouched beside her.

"How did they get there?"

"At intervals the ground shakes, the level of the lava pool lowers, and a walkway appears. If you are quick and sure-footed, you can cross to the island and back before the walk recedes below the lava. When the pathway rises, you may try your skill."

The tall one detached himself from the crowd and thrust his spindly frame between us. "Shall he not win that right? The one who brought the girl is eager for battle."

"Where is he, then?" Mett glared at the man. "Fetch him, Scrug."

The tall man melted into the crowd.

Pik! I had no desire to fight that madman. If only the walkway would appear before he got here. I turned back toward the lava lake and the island in its midst.

The crouching figure had risen and walked to the edge of the island. It was Derli in Abbi's body. She seemed to be looking at me. Unexpectedly she stepped into the fiery lake and waded toward me.

"No!" I dashed to the brink of the lake. "Go back!"

She paid no heed but staggered on. Mett gasped. His men stopped their mad dancing and gathered around, watching in awed silence.

Her steps dragged through the thick brew. Her legs blackened more each time she plucked up a foot and set it down an agonizing pace nearer her goal. I expected to see her fall, but she kept on, feet reduced to charred and shapeless stumps. I leaned forward and stretched my arm as far as I could reach. A final tottering step and her hand clasped mine. I pulled her nearer, grasped her arms, lifted, and swung her out of the liquid fire. The stench of scorched flesh gagged me.

I lifted her into my arms and winced when through my clothes I felt the heat from her seared legs. "For Zera's sake, Derli, dematerialize. Get out of that body."

"Had to tell you," she wheezed through clenched teeth. Tears streamed down her cheeks, blood oozed from her bitten lips. "Flux fiends. Here. Mett's man, Scrug. And Pik. He's possessed."

Fiends from the Flux of Time, here? "I don't understand." I carried Derli away from the lava lake and lowered her gently to the ground.

She groaned. "Here to kill you. Trapped me, but not for long. Take care." Her face spasmed. "We'll meet at time's next bend."

A shudder wracked Abbi's body, and I looked at an untenanted corpse.

Like a company of magicians, the desert men melted into the scarred landscape. Though I couldn't see them, I had no doubt they watched my every move.

Why would Flux fiends gather to kill *me*?

An angry yowl jerked me around in time to see Pik leap toward me. He bounded across the space between us, my fascinum bouncing up and down on his bare chest. I veered, but he swerved to block me. I jumped out of the way.

"Abbi!" he roared. "You've killed her again!" With another roar of rage he charged me.

I ran and Pik gave chase.

Around pillars of slag I dodged and he followed. Panting, heart thudding, I leaped over smoldering coals, zigzagged around vents belching steam, skirted small pools of hissing lava, and careened past cinder cones and rock cairns. I couldn't lose him. The ground rumbled and shuddered beneath us, and over the rim of the caldera the sun glowered through a yellow haze.

Pik hurtled toward me. For just a moment his figure flickered, changed, took on bat wings and beaked visage. It was the fiend from my dream on the night I killed Overseer Vicca. My blood froze. I shrank back.

His head crashed against my chest. I fell, breathless. Pik straddled me, no demon but a crazed, enraged man. His fists pummeled my head. Dazed, defenseless, I waited for death.

The rain of blows stopped. Sitting astride my waist, Pik lifted his head toward the sun's red disk and howled. The sound awoke my reflexes. My hands lifted, circled his throat. My fingers tightened.

He clutched my arms, tore my hands loose, shoved me back, and hurled himself on top of me again. Grunting and puffing, we rolled down a rocky slope.

We skidded to a halt on the edge of a rent. The ground shook. Pushed back by a blast of intense heat, we leaped to our feet. A fountain of molten rock jetted from the fissure and arced toward us.

Pik shoved me toward the rain of fire. I sprang away. With Pik at my heels, I ran from the inferno. Out of range of the fiery fountain, he tackled me, and we crashed to the stony ground. I lay still, pretending to be stunned, and let him turn me over and grab my shoulders. My knees slammed into him, I threw him backward, rolled around, caught him, and pounded him against the rocky surface. His arms clutched at me, flailed the air, grabbed at the fascinum. My fingers tightened around his throat. His face purpled, and his body fell limp. I released my grip and pried the mandorla from his fingers, not checking to see whether he was breathing.

I slipped the chain around my neck and drew comfort from the feel of the charm lying against my chest. I stood, stumbled to a nearby spire of rock, and leaned against it, panting. If Pik still lived, I had to get away before he regained consciousness. I scanned the basin for some landmark to guide me to the lava lake. The mounds and pillars created a maze shot through with red flares where tongues of lava licked hungrily at the blackened earth. The similarity of this fiendish place to that of my dream on my last night in the longhouse must have been what made Pik appear for a moment to be the fiend from my dream.

The earth shook. The rock beneath my feet cracked and split with a terrifying roar. I scrambled to more solid ground. With horror I saw Pik topple into the gaping maw. A second powerful tremor threw me to the ground. It rocked and buckled. I clawed at the stony surface, expecting to follow Pik into the bowels of the earth.

The rumbling died away. I lifted my head and looked for the fissure that had opened to receive Pik. It was gone. The ground was whole and still. No trace of the fissure remained.

I struggled to my feet and lurched forward, wanting only to get away from that place. Mett found me wandering among the fumaroles and slag piles and guided me back to the stone arch.

He gazed at me with a new respect. "Who are you," he asked, "that the earth and the rocks fight for you?"

I had no answer, but a low rumble answered for me, stirring the thick air. The sound sent claws of dread scratching along my spine. With a buzzing and hissing as of swarms of insects, the pool of lava shrank and a walkway of slick obsidian appeared, leading to the island.

"It's time. You've won the right to rescue the lady. But you'll have to hurry." Mett's rough hands grabbed my arms and shoved me forward. I stumbled onto the walkway.

Heat penetrated the thick soles of my boots. Through the sulfur fumes I could smell the stench of scorched leather. I leaped back.

"Lost your nerve?" Scrug, the tall one, materialized beside Mett, while the other men hovered in the background. Scrug sneered. "Decide she isn't worth the risk?"

I ignored him and turned to Mett. "If I rescue Medara and bring her to you, will you go with her to the Manor Lands and accept the lordship?"

Scrug thrust his pockmarked face close to mine. "Our leader doesn't bargain with fools."

"Quiet, Scrug." Mett motioned him away and returned my stare, unblinking. "You've delayed too long. I think you've lost your chance. But, yes, I'll wager my freedom against your prowess. Get the lady and bring her here on this same rise of the walkway, and I'll go with her to the land of my enemies."

"They'll no longer be enemies but your loyal subjects." With that promise I turned and ran out onto the trembling walkway.

With my arms outspread for balance, I fairly flew over the slick surface. Even through my boots my feet burned where they touched the hot rock. With the lava licking at my heels I bounded up onto the strange, dark island.

The heat drained me. I staggered toward the crumpled figure on the rocks. Coughing and choking from the sulfur fumes, I clawed my way to her with hands slippery with sweat.

A weak cough told me she lived. I dropped onto my knees beside her and lifted her head. Her eyelids crept open; she gazed at me. Her lips moved but no sound came forth. I picked her up and eased myself down the rocks toward the treacherous lava.

The causeway speared across the steaming pool. Poised to step into its slick surface, I hesitated, tore my gaze from the hissing, gurgling lava to peer at the opposite shore. Mett stood alone within the stone archway.

I stepped onto the obsidian strip, staggered and nearly fell. Teeth clenched, I teetered along the narrow path, the soles of my feet a blaze of pain. The walkway trembled. Lava splashed over it. I felt Medara slipping from my grasp. I lurched forward and heaved her toward the bank. Mett caught her and pulled her to safety.

The lava sucked at my smoldering boots. I dragged my feet forward and toppled onto the shore. Mett set Medara down in the shade of the arch and returned to me.

"Against all odds, you've won the wager," he said.

"You … you'll keep your word?" I got the words out through cracked lips.

"I always keep my word." He took a canteen from his belt and held it to my mouth.

He helped me to my feet. I limped after him to Medara's resting place. He lifted her and strode away. I staggered after him, each step agony. Mist and smoke curled about him, threatening to cut him off from my sight. I opened my mouth to shout for him to wait, but other, wilder shouts drove mine back down my throat. His men materialized out of the mist and danced around him, laughing and shrieking. Scrug plucked Medara from his grasp and lifted her high above his head, supporting her body with his hands while her arms, legs, and head dangled like a child's rag doll.

Betrayed! Mett had broken his word and delivered her to his men. I had to save her. I tottered toward them. Laughing evilly, Scrug tossed Medara to Mett and shouted a foul-sounding word that seemed to hang in the air like fiery mist.

With a thunderous crack, a fissure like the one that had swallowed Pik opened before me. My knees buckled. My frantic fingers clutched empty air. I toppled into utter blackness.

I pushed against the dark. My hands plunged through something like cold, wet wool. Like a swimmer battling a treacherous current, I fought through the smothering stuff. My outstretched hand contacted what felt like a curved metal rod. I grabbed it and hauled myself toward it.

With a suddenness that threw me off balance, I plunged into a lighted room. I lost my hold on my anchor and slid on a slimy surface. Arms swinging, I fought to right myself. The heels of my hands struck a hard edge. I clutched it and pulled myself upright. My eyes blinked, trying to adjust to the sudden light.

I stood at the edge of a wide table filled with rotting food. Flies buzzed and maggots crawled in and out of reeking green meat and moldy vegetables. I gagged at the putrid stench. At each end of the vile table sat a motionless figure. I recognized this place—the dining room of the inn. The innkeeper and Meeda still presided over the decomposed feast. Someone had placed fresh candles in the candlesticks to illuminate the disgusting scene.

A peal of laughter drew my eyes to the hall door. Framed in the doorway, the juggler grinned and shook his pole. From it he plucked two of the five remaining heads, tossed them toward me, and ran from the room. The heads landed on the table on either side of the rotted roast.

Amid the wreckage two faces stared up at me. One was Pik's and the other Ordrain's.

16

MEEDA

I started after the juggler, but my burned feet made a chase hopeless. Instead I shuffled across the slippery floor to the mirror, hoping to pass through to the Manor House of Brid's time to rescue Brid and Renata. I thrust my hands forward. They slammed against solid glass.

My fascinum had prevented my passage through the time channel the first time. I made my way to Meeda and touched her shoulder. Her flesh was warm, but she sat motionless, the fascinum Savnar had made resting on her ample bosom. I removed my second fascinum, drew the chain over her head, and dropped the golden oval against the silver cylinder.

A flash of brilliant light burst from the two fascina and ebbed to a warm glow. Meeda's breathing quickened. Her nose twitched. The combined power of the fascina seemed to be breaking the trance.

Not waiting for that to happen, I skidded back to the mirror—and crashed against a surface as hard as before.

"Closed ... the gate ... closed forever."

I spun around. The innkeeper blinked and repeated the words in the deep, slow monotone of one talking in his sleep.

"No! That can't be true!" I pounded the mirror.

The glass splintered. I leaped back. A rain of shards clattered to the floor, exposing behind the mirror a dingy gray plastered wall no different from the room's other walls. I picked slivers of glass from my bleeding hands and crunched through the fragments to reclaim my fascina.

Meeda's chins quivered; her eyes stretched wide. She placed a protective hand over the glowing charms.

"I'm sorry." I pushed the pudgy fingers aside. "I have to take them now."

Tears glistened in her eyes as I lifted the chain and cord over her head. They held a single fascinum. The original charm had absorbed the mandorla. The cylinder was no longer silver but the pale gold of electrum.

I slipped the chain with its fused fascina around my neck; I'd worry later about why they'd fused. I looked for a way around the table.

The carved back of Meeda's chair pressed against the plaster wall— no exit there. I picked my way back to the opposite end of the table, where the innkeeper stared at the rotted feast as though waking from a nightmare. He shoved his chair against the wall, jumped up, grabbed a candle, swept its flame across the refuse on the table, and rushed from the room.

The grease around the rotted meat caught fire. In seconds the table was blazing. I slammed the innkeeper's empty chair out of my way and moved past it, ignoring the throbbing pain in my feet.

Meeda pushed herself from her chair and headed for the door. I reached it first, and sped into the hall, with Meeda lumbering behind me. Flames filled the room we'd left and spread toward us. I raced to my room, knowing there was nothing I could do to help Meeda. I had to hope she could escape on her own.

My poncho and pack lay where I'd left them. I grabbed the pack, snatched the poncho from the bedpost, and ran to the door. When I opened it, I choked on smoke. I turned back and hurried to the open window, climbed over the sill, and dropped into the flowerbed beneath the window.

I landed on my hands and knees. For several minutes I stayed there, drawing in deep breaths of cool, fresh air.

Smoke and the crackling of flames brought me to my feet. Pack and poncho dangling from my hand, I raced around the burning inn to the road and ran until I had to catch my breath.

Gasping, I looked behind me. Flames shot skyward. Silhouetted against the blazing backdrop, a wide figure jogged toward me. Meeda *had* escaped. I didn't welcome her company, but I was relieved that she hadn't died in the burning inn.

She trotted up, breasts bouncing, rivers of sweat coursing through the canyons between rolls of fat, and wiped her hands across her tentlike cotton dress.

"Take me with you," she wheezed, hitching the garment higher up her wide shoulder. With her other hand she mopped her brow and pushed sweat-soaked strands of tawny hair from her face.

I frowned and nodded, concerned with how far the fire was spreading. The wind was blowing it away from us, across the fields behind it. We were safe for now, but the wind could shift. We needed to keep moving.

I forced my feet to move. My run had made them even worse. To keep from thinking about my pain and weariness, I asked, "What happened to the innkeeper?"

"I don't know. I had no time to look for him."

I shuddered. "Was he your husband?"

Meeda snorted. "Him? No. I worked at the inn for my food and lodging."

"You have no family?"

"Not anymore."

"I'll be of no help to you. I don't know where I'm going." I jiggled the empty pack. "I don't have food or money." I settled my poncho over my shoulders, took up my pack, and limped toward the remaining patch of light that marked the sun's descent.

She said nothing, but her heavy footsteps thudded behind me. I didn't order her away, though she was not the company I wanted.

Derli had said we'd meet at time's next bend. Did that mean here? "Derli?" I felt foolish shouting the name to the vacant fields. Meeda made no comment on my peculiar behavior.

Meeda's presence did nothing to relieve my loneliness and sense of failure. I glanced up at the sky, where stars sparkled now that the smoke no longer hid them.

"The town of Diakos is about three hours' walk along the road," Meeda said. "If we enter it in the middle of the night, they'll take us for thieves. We'd best stop and sleep in a field for a few hours and enter town after daybreak. I could probably find work, cleaning or cooking, and earn us some money for food."

"I'll earn my own way." I plodded on, irrationally unwilling to take Meeda's advice. I hoped she'd get discouraged or frightened or simply too tired to go on, and I'd be rid of her.

I pushed onward as if in a dream. My burned and blistered feet grew completely numb. I felt no pain as they moved up and down, no sensation of road beneath them. My only link to reality was the sound of Meeda puffing and panting behind me.

Questions filled my mind. Who was the juggler? Why had I been bounced to two past times and back to the present? Traveling back and forth in time ought to be impossible. Whoever heard of anybody doing it? I never had. People didn't. Gods did maybe. Molor. Zera. Not people, especially people like me.

The heads he taunted me with. I was supposed to be able to name them. Why? I had named two somehow. Didn't make sense. And now I could name four. What did it mean?

Derli. A fala. Falas were in the stories about the gods. Molor and Makor fought over falas. Can't remember the details. Who was right? Maybe both. Maybe neither.

Medara had seen Derli. The old nut-gatherer, too. Why couldn't *I* see her? Lisha gave her to *me*. To protect me. Medara said *I* was a protector. Didn't protect her. Or Abbi. Not anybody. Found Mett though. Wonder how that turned out. Couldn't even protect Derli. She needed my protection. Supposed to protect me, but I should've protected her. Didn't protect Renata. Or Brid. What good am I?

Better at killing than protecting. Killed the old lord. Just the way I was supposed to. Killed Overseer Vicca. Killed Ordrain. Guess I killed Pik. And Abbi, by neglect.

Weird that I could heal Pik. Where did that come from? The old lords helped me with lots of things, but not that. They weren't healers. Don't think so, anyway. I'd ask them, but they don't answer me. Maybe they're not in my mind anymore.

Something or someone else is—that odd, alien presence I'd felt when I was fighting Ordrain. It didn't speak. Maybe it had no voice. Had power, though. It was keeping my legs moving when all I wanted was to collapse right here and sleep.

What was it? Who was it? Derli? No, she'd make herself known.

Molor? Medara had a lot of faith in Molor. Said he was the source of her power. Koralie's stronger than Medara, and no matter what she professes, I don't think she has faith in Molor. Or anything else outside of herself. She's evil.

Medara's not evil. Even so, Derli's right about Medara. She is a selfish little windbag. Smart, though. Knows a lot of spells. Had a good teacher in Dama Ordell. Good woman. Must be dead by now.

'Course she is. It's almost 300 years later. I'm getting mixed up. Don't know what time I'm in anymore. It's like I'm outside of time now. Can't be. That's silly.

"Korth. Korth." Meeda's voice threaded through my jumbled thoughts. "You've been walking in your sleep. We're here. We've reached Diakos."

Had I really been walking for three hours? It seemed impossible.

Somewhere in that time Meeda had taken the lead and let me trudge along in her wake.

The town slept. I stumbled over rough cobblestones past shuttered buildings. Diakos was not a large town. An open square marked its center. Scrawny trees presented dark outlines against the night sky. For want of a better shelter, I threw myself beneath a tree, wrapped my poncho around me, and fell asleep on the damp grass.

Shouts and cries awakened me. I struggled to sit, rubbed my aching legs, and looked around. My first impression in the dim light of dawn was that I had slept beside a small hill.

The hill stirred, producing a mild earthquake, stretched, and sprouted a head, which gazed off in the direction of the shouts. I had not lost Meeda after all.

Clutching a length of sausage and a loaf of bread, a slender boy darted out of a narrow arcade and dashed toward us. He zigzagged around Meeda.

"Behind me," she snapped. "Lie flat."

A man and a woman erupted from the arcade. Yelling, "Thief! Stop!" and brandishing sticks, they raced toward us.

"He ran in there." Meeda pointed to a dark alleyway between two buildings of age-pocked stone.

The pursuers scoured us with suspicious looks but tore off into the alley. The young miscreant emerged from his hiding place. Meeda's fingers clamped around his wrist.

"They'll be back!" He twisted and jerked his arm, feet dancing, ready to fly.

"We'll take half that bread and most of the sausage. That's your payment for our protection."

The boy frowned and yanked harder. He aimed a kick at Meeda's leg. She gave his arm a violent twist. "They're coming back."

"Here, then." He thrust the bread and sausage toward her. With her free hand she broke off half the loaf of bread and dropped it into her capacious lap. With one motion, she released his wrist, grabbed hold of the sausage, and tore off a good two-thirds of its length. The lad glared and shot away. He was out of sight by the time his luckless pursuers emerged from the alley.

The woman stalked across the square and disappeared into the arcade from which they'd come. The man bore down on Meeda and me. Meeda dropped the sausage beside the bread. Her thick arms covered her prizes.

"Young cur got away." The man's flushed face twisted into a scowl. "Don't know how he disappeared so fast. You sure he ran up that alley?"

Meeda squinted toward the shadowy passageway. "I thought that's where he went. But if you didn't find him there, maybe he dodged into one of those buildings."

The man followed her glance with his eyes. "Mmm. Well, he'll turn up. And when he does, I'll take that breakfast he stole out of his hide."

He frowned and wrinkled his nose. A gesture of disgust? Or had he smelled the sausage buried in Meeda's lap?

"What are you doing in the square at this hour? Today's not market day."

"We arrived during the night," I said, not wanting to leave all the talking to Meeda. "It was too late to find the inn. We're looking for work."

His flinty gaze studied my unkempt hair and ragged beard, inspected my soiled journey clothes, lingered on my scorched boots. "I don't know who'd hire you. Here we do our own work. I took in that scamp Divian as an apprentice, and you see how he repaid me—stole my breakfast right off my table. My wife and I are good, honest folk. We want no truck with scoundrels. We agreed to take the lad only because the Zeran priest paid—uh—persuaded us. When the neighbors hear how I've been served, they won't likely hire another stranger. You'd best be on your way."

Zeran priest! "Is there … is there a Zeran temple here?"

He folded his arms across his chest and raked me with another close look. "There is. Finest building in Diakos, and rightly so, of course. But you don't look fit to go there."

He shifted his gaze back to Meeda. "There's an inn near the temple. You might find work in its kitchen."

"Thanks, I'll try there." The edges of Meeda's smile vanished into her full cheeks. "I hope you find your apprentice. What's your trade?"

"A cooper." His eyes roved over Meeda's girth as if measuring her for the hoops of his craft. "My shop's in the fourth archway of the temple walk. I'd best get back to it. If you should catch sight of young Divian, send someone to fetch me." He bustled off into the arcade.

The temple. I could think of nothing else. The temple of Zera. If I could reach it, I might find Lisha there.

The square was no longer deserted. Morning's light had spawned life: sounds and scents poured from the buildings—the clutter of pots and pails, the tantalizing smell of frying bacon and baking bread, the wails of infants, the cries of vendors.

I should get up, but I could not force myself onto my still-numb feet. I sat and watched the activity. Milkmaids carried pails of milk into and out of doorways. Two young boys bore on their heads huge trays piled high with bread. Its just-baked smell made my mouth water. Shutters clattered open against the wooden walls. Women in freshly starched bonnets poked their heads out of windows and called out cheery greetings to each other and orders to the bread boys. Wheels rumbling and clacking, wagons bumped over the cobblestone streets carrying teams of young men out to work the fields. Doors flew open and the anonymous buildings acquired their distinctive daytime personalities.

Opposite us, a bald man trundled out a table draped with bright bolts of cloth. Next door a rosy-cheeked woman in a white, lace-trimmed apron wheeled out a heavy rack of candles. A man in a leather apron hung a sword above his door, stood in his doorway, and with a chamois skin polished the curved blade of a knife. From the open door behind him came the grunt of a bellows and the clang of iron on steel. From another door came sounds of sawing and hammering and the fresh, piney scent of sawdust.

We were the only idlers in the midst of all the activity. "We'd better move before someone gets curious about us," I said.

Meeda shook her head. "I'm known to many of the people here. I come here on market days to buy supplies for the inn. I'm not sure the cooper didn't recognize me even though I've not had any dealings with him. He's a surly fellow. Here, have some breakfast." With a grin she tossed me half the confiscated bread and stuffed most of the remainder into her mouth.

She held up the sausages, a chain of five plump links, tore off two for me, and kept three for herself. Hungry as I was, my dry throat made it difficult to swallow. Only the greasiness of the sausage and the softness of the fresh bread made me able to get them down.

"Not bad." Meeda wiped her hand across her mouth and pulled herself to her feet. "Needs something to wash it down."

I nodded, still trying to swallow the last bite of sausage.

"I'll see what I can find." She swung off toward the chandlery.

I cleaned my hands on the grass, stretched, and tried to stand. Pain shot through my legs. Sinking back to the ground, I examined my feet. Above my boot tops my calves were puffed and red. I tugged at my boots. They seemed glued on. I had to rip the charred leather and peel it from my raw, bleeding, and no longer numb feet.

Teeth clenched to keep from screaming from pain and gagging at the stench, I swatted the flies that came buzzing around the oozing flesh. I'd do no walking for some time.

Helpless, hurting, without money, without shelter, I'd fallen far lower than the slave I had been. As a slave I'd had regular meals and a warm place to sleep. I'd worked hard, but I was strong and healthy, and if I had no dreams, neither had I known the pain of seeing my dreams crumble to dust. I'd known neither love nor loss. I'd been content. If only my time traveling could take me back before I'd slain the old lord and so set in motion the events that had brought me here. I hid my face in my poncho and wept.

Something jabbed me in the side. "Temple's the place for beggars, son. He-he-he. They'll run you out of the square, they will. He-he-he."

I dropped my poncho and glared up into a wrinkled face adorned with a twisted and flattened nose that must have been broken more than once. On either side of it, beady blue eyes glittered. Cracked lips spread wide in a toothless grin framed by a scraggly beard. Wrapped like a sack of turnips in dirty burlap, the old man supported himself on one leg and a rough wooden crutch. The rag-bound stump of his other leg dangled from his wrapper. The second crutch jabbed my side again.

"We'll meet on the temple stairs." A crinkly eyelid descended over one eye and lifted again in an exaggerated wink. "I'll be your sponsor. He-he-he." He gave me a parting jab and hobbled off, chortling.

I had to get to the temple. Had to find Lisha. She'd heal my feet.

Meeda clomped across the square, a cup cradled in one hand. "What'd that beggar want?" She scowled at the cripple's retreating back.

"He wanted me to join his guild." With a rueful grin I pointed to my feet. "I guess those qualify me."

She gasped, thrust the cup into my hand, and bent to examine the festering wounds. "You walked on these all night!"

I nodded and gulped down the cup of sweet cider. Its coolness brought my parched throat a measure of ease and a strong desire for more.

"Why didn't you tell me your feet were burned?" Meeda probed my swollen ankles.

"I didn't know they were so bad. Can you get more of this cider?"

"Maybe later. I had to lift racks of candles out of hot wax to get that cup and the cup I drank. The chandler's wife's a good sort, but she drives a hard bargain."

I licked my lips in search of a lingering drop of the life-giving liquid. "So thirsty," I muttered.

"You have a fever." Meeda sat back and peered at me. "The evil in your feet is spreading through your body. It will kill you if we don't stop it."

She spoke truth, I knew, but it didn't seem to matter. I'd failed at everything I had attempted. Brid and Renata still lay in deathlike sleep. I didn't know whether Medara had survived, but her plight had looked desperate when I was caught away. If Mett had not inherited, all history would be changed. I still lived, but for what? All might have changed so that I had not inherited the deathright. If I had, better I should die and let the deathright pass to someone more worthy.

"Korth, your fascinum. Use it. Drive the evil from you."

I fumbled for the amulet. The transmuted metal was cold against my palm. I pressed it to my chest. An icy finger twisted toward my heart. With a sigh I lay back on the grass, my hand covering the fascinum, sending its cold into my weakening body. I began to shiver.

"That's no good." Meeda heaved herself to her feet. "I'll have to get help." Her heavy footfalls receded into the distance. I heard her shout, "Here, you. Come here, lad."

The ground shuddered. The pounding steps returned, accompanied by a lighter tread. I squinted upward through a frosty haze. Meeda hove into view, her hand clasped tight around the boy Divian's wrist.

"You'll help me carry him to shelter, or I'll take you straight to your master." She pushed him toward me. "Take his shoulders. I'll take his feet."

I wondered that the boy didn't dash away when she released him. He could easily have eluded Meeda, but he bent over me as though to do her bidding.

Gleaming, his eyes gazed into mine. I felt his fingers close around my throat. I understood.

"Lordslayer." My lips shaped the word and relaxed into a smile. Gratefully I slipped into unconsciousness.

17

DIVIAN

I stand, dazed, at the fork in the road. In front of me looms the dark shape of a tree with bare branches extended outward like long arms, pointing. I peer into the gray mist. On the road's eastern branch a lone figure stands wrapped in a dark, hooded cloak. Its sleeved arm beckons me. The branches of the tree shake as though stirred by a powerful wind, though I feel no breath of air. I feel nothing—no dampness despite the mist, no chill despite the dreary gloom of the … day or night? The dull, diffused light gives no clue. A scent of lilies hovers around me, the only sensation of which I am aware. I step toward the cloaked figure.

The tree shudders and its branches quake. I hesitate and glance at the alternate road. A silver-winged being descends like a falling star. The scent of lilies fades, lost in the sharp, clear odor of a thunderbolt. The Winged One furls his wings and extends powerful arms toward me. One hand holds a spear. About him the mist falls away, and a blaze of rainbow-hued light touches the road with color.

Blinded by the radiance, I stumble back to the fork.

"Will you walk this way with me?" The ground shakes at the words of the Winged One.

I take one hesitant step toward him. And another. I cast a wary glance at the other fork.

The cloaked figure has stopped and turned toward me. In the increased light I see the face, beautiful and powerful. Lisha?

Not Lisha. It is no mortal woman who smiles and holds out her hands toward me but a goddess. Zera! Drawn by her loveliness, I turn from the Winged One.

"Fool! Betrayer." He raises his spear and casts it.

A searing pain tears through my heart. I crash to the ground. The mist closes in around me. My life flows into a realm of darkness. Small flames flicker like a constellation of glow-grubs but do not lessen the dark in which they dance.

A bright flame darts past my eyes. "Korth, hear me. I ordered you to save Brid." I quail at the cold voice of Dama Brinabeth.

"Help me." The moaning plea of Brid comes from a faint, guttering spark.

"Save me, Korth." Renata's sweet voice wrenches my heart. I reach out, but the flames scatter, vanish.

Two soft arms cradle me like a babe. My fatal wound is healed.

I open my eyes. I lie in the arms of the goddess. The scent of lilies drips from the hands that stroke my brow. "You've come too far to die again," Zera says, and then her sweet voice sings a binding spell.

"He'll live only if he's gained wisdom." With that cry, the Winged One swoops over us, snatches me from her arms, and sets me on my feet. He points along the westward road. My gaze follows the direction indicated.

Spread before me is a beautiful land, green, blessed with fruited trees and flowering fields. Its sweet odor rises and fills my nostrils. But as I feast my eyes on the loveliness, men clad in desert brown march in from the north. Like locusts they swarm over the land, torching fields, axing trees, damming the free-running streams.

"Go." He pushes me forward. I'm whole again, strong. "Run," he says. "Save the land—if you can."

"No. Stay with me." The goddess stretches her lovely arms toward me. "He claims the land as his. Let him save it."

I take a step toward her.

"Refuse and you forfeit your claim," says the Winged One, crossing his arms over his chest.

"Claim? What claim?" I ask, confused.

"Why, to the Manor Lands. To the lordship," the Winged One answers. "Have you not claimed the name and title of Terral?"

"Give it up, Korth," the goddess urges. "Stay with me. Learn your true name. Break the circle."

I recognize now the land before me. As from a great height I look down on the entire Manor Lands. The geographical features are plain to see, but where is the Manor House, where the worked fields, where the villages of the freedmen?

Still, it is the Manor Lands, and I am the Inheritor.

I tear down the road into the valley. The destruction has to be halted.

"Come to the temple, Korth. Meet me there." Zera's call fades into the distance.

The call of the Manor Lands is stronger. With the strength of Molor infusing me, I run.

Divian ran. Shaking off my troubling dream, I struggled to a sitting position and watched the boy's pounding feet raise clouds of dust until he vanished between two old buildings on the far side of the square.

Meeda glared after him, clenched hands pressing into her bulging hips. "Little rat," she shouted, "if you've killed him, I'll come after you and find you no matter where you hide." She turned toward me.

She blinked. Her eyebrows flowed upward toward her hairline.

"You ... you weren't breathing. I snatched him off you and tossed him as far and hard as I could. He picked himself up and bolted. I wanted to chase him, but I was afraid to leave you. And now you're sitting up, looking alert, and he's got away."

Still trying to sort dream from reality, I massaged my bruised neck and stared off at the alley into which Divian had vanished.

And yet had not vanished. My eyes could not see into the dark passage, but with another vision I raced with Divian through the tight space, felt his elbows scrape the damp stone walls, knew his laughter at the image of Meeda trying to squeeze into the passage to follow him. I sensed his exultation when he burst from the dark space into the warm sunlight beyond.

He was sure he'd killed me. He'd breathed in my dying breath and with it the deathright—or so he believed.

He *had* received something. I shared his thoughts, looked out through his eyes, and received the impressions of his senses. Yet I was here in the park with Meeda, listening to her voice.

The effect confused and dizzied me. My head swam. I lay back, half fainting, and tried to withdraw from Divian, but a portion of his thoughts clung stubbornly to mine.

I envied him his excitement, his eager confidence. If I had understood, when I slew the old lord, the gift I received with his dying breath, how different my story might have been. But I'd known nothing, and it suited Dama Koralie's purpose to tell me nothing.

From somewhere Divian had gained the knowledge of the lord line. Where or how I couldn't imagine. Here on this side of the Rethe, I didn't think the custom of deathright was even known. Yet this young lad knew. He wanted a place in the lord line. Even stranger, more incomprehensible: his resolve was not to succeed me in the present but to go back in time and wrest the place of an early lord.

Just as I, under Koralie's tutelage, had done with Brid.

I hadn't saved Brid. I had to stop Divian. I grasped Meeda's wrist and tried to pull myself up.

"Don't be foolish, Korth." She pushed me down. "You can't stand on those feet."

"Have to. Have to reach the temple." I tried again to rise.

She held me down by leaning on my shoulders.

"Meeda, I must—*we* must—stop Divian." I tried to squirm out of her grasp.

She tightened her grip. "What makes you think he's gone to the temple?"

I had no time to explain my double vision. "The cooper told us a temple priest paid him to take the lad as apprentice. I'm guessing he'll go there for protection."

"Well, we'll have no protection there—not in a Zeran temple."

"What makes you say that?"

Her fat cheeks reddened. She released her grip and stepped backward so that I could no longer see her face. "I'm sworn to the service of Molor."

I shrugged. "I have to go to the temple. You can do as you wish. I'll crawl there on my hands and knees if I must." I scrambled onto my knees and crept forward on all fours.

"Here. That won't do. You'll never make it." Meeda squatted in front of me. "I'll carry you pickaback. Put your arms around my neck."

She hoisted me onto her back and staggered to her feet, her arms supporting my legs. Bending so that her back bore my weight, she stumped from the square into the arcade. People in the streets stopped and gaped; even some shopkeepers stared at us from their doorways. The raw and running sores on my feet were plain to see and no doubt explained the need for my novel method of transport, but I was embarrassed, nonetheless. To forget my humiliation, while my body sagged on Meeda's wide back I concentrated on Divian, focusing my consciousness into him.

It worked! I was with Divian as he edged around one of the twin pillars of the portico, keeping hidden from the group of worshippers entering the temple. The clink of coins in a beggar's cup told him another group was ascending the stairs. He peeped around the column, ducked back to avoid a pair of elderly matrons, waited, and risked another look. Good. The worshippers had gone inside. No one to see him but a crippled beggar. He winked at the beggar and darted through the temple entrance.

Inside the thick wooden doors he skirted the foyer and slipped into a side passage used by priests and temple servants. I read his memories, as down this narrow corridor he sped to the entrance to the apartments where he'd spent his boyhood. Irrin would be ministering to the worshippers in the temple at this hour. With luck old Femory would assist him. the servants would be working in the kitchen area or relaxing in the private patio behind the main temple. If his luck held …

He eased the door open and slipped inside. The small sitting room was empty. He tiptoed across the threadbare carpet, remembering the happy hours he'd spent here on long winter evenings, listening to the marvelous tales told by the priests. Zera! How he'd thrilled to hear old Femory describe the battle scenes in that dreadful contest between Makor and Molor—the mighty clash of their steeds of fire and night, the swordfight which lasted for weeks, shook the world, and washed the land in blood, the uneasy truce which set the River Rethe as the division between the realms of the warring deities. He relived his excitement at the account of how Molor broke the truce and Makor, with the help of Zera, trapped his twin in the land of volcanoes, only to be slain by a spear hurled from ambush.

That's where he'd like to go first! To the Mountains of Dawn where Zera hid Makor's body. He'd hunt for that secret place. What a triumph if he could find the burial place of the god!

Divian, and I with him, hurried through the sleeping quarters to the private chapel where the priests held their own devotions to Zera. It was deserted while the temple was open for public worship. Divian crossed its marble floor, stepped behind the painted statue of Zera with only a quick bow to the raven-haired goddess, and slid open a panel concealed behind a tapestry on the rear wall.

He slid the panel back into place behind him and hurried up the narrow circular stairway. Breathing hard, he burst into the domed chamber. An old woman hunched over a spinning wheel, withered hands guiding the thread, feet working the treadle.

"I've come," Divian announced. "You must keep your promise."

The old woman looked up from her wheel, though she did not slow its spinning. Around her on the dusty floor tangled masses of thread spilled everywhere. Divian waded through the multihued coils. He'd never learned what she wove and why. From within the deep wrinkles seaming her dark face, her black eyes probed his.

"You've gained some small measure of power. Not enough to win our wager." The voice was brittle and ancient as the mountains.

"The power will grow," Divian insisted. "I felt his spirit pass into me, just as that other old woman said it would."

She snorted. "You're a fool to trust that one," she said. "She claims to serve Molor, but she serves no one but herself."

Divian kicked aside a pile of thread. "Maybe, but she said I'd have power, and I do, I feel it."

"Be careful where you step." Her shuttle flew. "Feelings often deceive."

"I've won, I tell you. You were wrong when you said the dark woman was only a dream." He leaned toward her, hands doubled into fists. "Keep your promise, old woman."

She did not break the rhythm of her spinning. "Go, then, foolish lad. Test this power you think you've won."

Thread whirled around him, cradling him within a cocoon of spun silk. I felt him lifted up and flung out across measureless space, and like the snap of a thread the connection between us was broken.

My backside thudded onto cold stone. Jolted into awareness, my contact with Divian broken, I found myself sitting on the top step of the temple. Meeda, panting and wheezing, sat three steps below me.

I easily guessed who "the other old woman" was. Dama Koralie. She wanted to rule the Manor Lands on her own. The dama had somehow reached Divian, taught him the rite of Lord's-Kill, and set him on me. Her attempt with Overseer Vicca had failed, but this one had almost succeeded. I had to get back to the Manor Lands, back to Brid's time to free him and defeat Koralie.

I'd wanted to reach Zera's temple. Now here I was, but I needed to return to the Manor House. However, in my present condition I had no way of getting back there. It could be that in the temple I would find help, perhaps learn how to return safely to the Manor Lands.

But I was not inside the temple, and how I was to get inside without Meeda's help I didn't know. Could I persuade Meeda to enter a Zeran temple? If only Lisha were here to greet me as she'd promised.

But this temple bore only a faint resemblance to the temples I'd seen painted on the screen in Savnar's and Lisha's tent, the one on the mountain, the other in the jungle. Nor did it seem to be the temple of my dreams. Temples to Zera like this one here in Diakos could probably be found in most cities on this side of the River Rethe.

The tap of wood on stone preceded a sharp jab in my back. The crippled beggar stood above me. "He-he-he. Just in time." He poked my shoulder. "You'll catch the worshippers coming from morning prayers. You should do well. Better take off that poncho. It's too rich for a beggar. He-he-he."

Not to do his bidding, but because I was hot and feverish and the stone steps were hard, I pulled off the poncho and twisted out of the empty pack I'd worn since leaving the inn. I stuffed the poncho into the pack and sat on it, stretching my legs in front of me so that my injured feet rested on the edge of the steps.

A loud gong sounded. From the temple a stream of people flowed toward me. Men and women, young and old, they swept around me, a helpless island in their midst. As they passed, coins fell into my lap. A shower of centims, a scattering of decims, and here and there a silver quinto. A single gold valor shone among the other coins. I couldn't tell who'd dropped it.

The worshippers surged into the street. A few lingering children played tag on the temple steps, dodging around Meeda until their mothers shouted for them. The clatter of footsteps on cobblestones receded.

A familiar tap-tap drew my eyes from the emptying street to the beggar who stood on the step below me. "He-he. Did well for a novice." A hand like an eagle's talon swooped down and captured the gold valor. "I'll take my cut. He-he-he. The rest is yours."

His crutch kept my hands at bay. I grabbed at him, but he hopped out of my reach.

Meeda turned toward me. Her face sagged into her chins. "Zerans!" She spat.

"They've been generous." I gathered up my lapful of coins and held it out to her. "Take these—for all you've done."

Her eyes widened. She sat up straight and cupped her hands under mine. I dropped the wealth into them.

I turned toward the temple doors. They were shut.

I crawled over to them and pushed on the carved wood. Nothing happened. I raised my fist and rapped. As in my dream, I bruised my hands pounding the unyielding panels.

"It's locked up tight. He-he-he." The ragged beggar leaned on his crutches and watched my futile efforts. "Priests have gone to eat their midday feast. He-he. Doors won't open again till time for evening prayers." He swung himself back and forth on his crutches, giggling. "Even then you won't get in. He-he-he. They don't allow beggars in the temple." His laughter hung in the air as he hobbled away.

18

COALSACK

The noon sun beat down on the temple steps, deserted now of all save Meeda, who evidently preferred the discomfort of the broiling sun to the contamination of close contact with the Zeran temple. Harboring no such prejudice, I kept to the shade of the portico. The hopelessness of my condition left me stunned. Barred from the temple, I leaned back against the temple doors, unable to walk, thirsty, in pain, wholly dependent on Meeda. If all that were not enough, having lost my contact with Divian, I had no way of knowing where he was or what damage he would do while I lingered here.

Meeda lifted her huge bulk and said, "I'm going to find a better shelter. I'll buy food and drink and come back for you."

Would she really come back? She had no need of me, nor had she any obligation to care for me. The coins I gave her would provide her needs until she could find work. Her hatred of the temple gave her reason not to return. Yet I could not rouse myself to call her back. Instead, I slipped into an uneasy doze.

I watch the flames consume the inn. Somehow it becomes the Manor House. As I rush toward it, its outer wall collapses. Through the flames I see the bedchamber where I'd left Renata and glimpse her lovely face, still as death. I run through the blaze, catch up her limp form, and carry her through the raging fire, charring my feet as I run.

When I lay her on the grassy lawn, I see that her feet and legs are burned far worse than mine. I look into her face and see that it is not Renata but Abbi. I stare at her through tear-dimmed eyes.

The dream-image fades. Clear as spring water, Derli's voice says, "Why are you sitting there wallowing in self-pity, Korth? You have work to do."

"Can't walk," I mumble.

"Ask Meeda to heal you."

My eyes popped open. I looked around. "Derli?"

Too real to have been part of my dream, her voice rang in my mind, but my frantic cries were unanswered.

Wide-awake, my feet and legs throbbing with pain, I watched the shadow of the temple creep down the marble stairs. The shadow reached the fifth step, leaving only the two bottom steps outside its veil. Meeda, arms laden with packages, toiled up those first two steps and hesitated on the line between sunlight and shadow. Seeing her reluctance to cross that barrier, I dragged myself and my pack across the portico and dangled my feet over the edge of the steps. Tossing the pack ahead of me, I cast off my remaining shreds of dignity and thumped down the steps on my buttocks.

Meeda took no notice of my unorthodox descent. "I brought you more cider." She put a large mug of amber liquid into my hands.

With a hasty "Thanks," I tipped the mug and gulped down the cool liquid. I set the mug on the step and wiped my mouth on my sleeve.

"Here." Meeda handed me a slab of cheese on a thick chunk of bread. "Eat this."

I hadn't felt hungry, but now with my thirst assuaged, the tangy smell of the cheese awakened my appetite. I devoured the food almost as fast as I had downed the cider.

"I've rented us a room in the inn," Meeda said when I finished. "Now we have to find a way to get you there."

I frowned at my feet—the oozing sores rimmed with blackened flesh, the mottled yellow and purple skin of the swollen ankles, the red streaks disappearing beneath my trousers. In an inn I could clean my feet in hot water, wrap them in wine-soaked cloths, and rest in bed until they healed. Yet I needed to enter the temple to find where Divian had gone. I couldn't waste time at an inn.

Meeda was watching me, anxious creases furrowing her brow. "Ask Meeda to heal you," Derli had said. But that had been only a dream. If I made such a demand, Meeda would think I'd taken leave of my senses.

I pulled my fascinum from beneath my shirt. It had nearly killed me when I tried to use it before. Dare I try again? It was no longer cold to the touch. I rubbed my fingers along it.

"Ouch!" Pathfinder's thorn pricked my thumb. I grasped the thumb in my other hand and squeezed out a single drop of blood. The crimson globule reminded me of Medara's chatter about pricking her fingers and using her blood to heal me when I lay dying of the nezzi's poisonous bite. I held the thumb toward Meeda. "Heal my feet."

Meeda's gold-flecked brown eyes stared down at mine. Unexpectedly, they filled with tears. She grasped my thumb and touched the tip of her tongue to it. Eyes averted, she sank down on the step beside me and leaned over, placing her hands above my feet. She began to chant, softly at first, then more loudly, in a language I could not understand. Mesmerized, I let myself be drawn into its somnolent rhythm.

A feeling of health and wholeness spread through me into my legs, driving back the pain. My ankles shrank to their normal size. The redness faded. A healthy glow flowed into my feet. The sores dried. The blackened skin fell off, pushed aside by fresh pink skin that spread over the sores. Meeda's chant ended. I stared at my healthy feet.

Meeda leaned back, eyes closed, lips parted, breathing heavily. I stood, relishing the feel of wellness. She muttered without opening her eyes, "It's been a long time, but your blood holds power. I remembered that, but still ... I wasn't sure I'd remember the words of the spell. Sequence has to be just right, you know, and if you get a word out of place, you have to start all over. But I guess once you learn a thing, you never really forget it. That's what Dama Ordell always said."

I stared at her.

The flow of words. The knowledge of healing. The mention of Dama Ordell. The name, Meeda. It couldn't be, but ...

"Medara?"

Her eyes popped open. She sat upright. I recognized the orange-brown hair, the gold-flecked eyes, and the familiar facial contours, hidden in rolls of fat.

Her eyes filled again with tears, and she looked away. "I hoped you wouldn't recognize me. I was so ashamed." Her hands fluttered over her huge girth.

"But how? Only yesterday you—"

"Yesterday for you." She sighed. "Ten long years for me."

"It can't be." I rubbed my forehead. "Before I went back to your time, you were already here."

Meeda-Medara smiled. "When *you* first came to *my* time, I hadn't yet come here."

"First! I was there only once—when we went to the Badlands. How did you get away from Mett's men? What happened to Mett?"

Medara struggled to her feet. "Mett. Well. You came back—or will come—twice more. You—and Derli. And Mett—"

"Derli! Where is she?" Alarmed by the bitterness in her voice when she mentioned Derli, I lost interest in Mett. "What do you know of Derli?"

She bit her lip. Head lowered, she scuffed her feet along the edge of the marble step. "I only know you're better off without her."

"Why do you say that?" I grabbed her face between my hands and tilted it toward me.

The fat chins quivered. "I shouldn't have said it. I'm sorry." She caught my hands and pulled them away from her face.

I clutched her shoulders, digging my fingers into her flesh. "You *did* say it. Why?" I tried to shake her. "What do you know about her?"

"She came with you when my sun song drew you to me, and I knew Molor had sent you, so I figured he'd sent her, too, and that meant not all the falas had fallen prey to Makor's consort. The fala *did* help us, or I thought she did." Medara twisted her head to glance nervously up at the temple. She lowered her voice. "But Zera sent her, not Molor. She's bound to the goddess, I'm sure."

"Derli saved my life. She saved yours." I shook with sudden rage. "I don't care who sent her. What happened to her?"

Medara shrank back as far as her size and the steps behind her permitted. "I don't know, truly. How could I? I've been stuck here—"

A clatter of hooves and the din of wagon wheels over cobblestone drowned out her words. A spavined black horse drawing a bright green wagon with orange wheels stopped in front of us. The horse glared at us with small, mean eyes. Lips curled back exposing long yellow teeth. It tossed its ugly head, whinnied, and reared in its harness with more energy than its sagging form looked capable of. Medara ducked, barely escaping a flashing hoof.

"Hey! Control your horse."

At my shout a figure in mask and motley leaped over the side of the wagon—the juggler, though without his cargo of little heads. "Sorry," he said with a chuckle. "He's an excitable beast. Seems to have taken a dislike to you. Here, Coalsack, calm yourself."

The horse pawed the ground and bared its teeth. Its master jigged beside it.

I confronted the dancing harlequin. "What do you want of me?"

"Of you? Nothing. It's your lady I want." He nodded toward Medara and exploded in laughter.

She clutched at my shirt. "Protect me, Korth."

I stood in front of her, legs and arms spread wide to shield as much of her as I could.

"I want to take her to the fair. She'll sit in my wagon, if she can fit into it, and people will pay three centims to see the fattest wench this side of the River Rethe." He threw back his head and roared.

I crashed my fist into his jaw. He toppled backward and sat down hard on the cobblestones. His back thudded against the orange wagon wheel.

The horse whinnied and stamped. With an abrupt twist, it broke free from the shafts and charged. It reared and came down so close in front of me that its head rammed into my chest. I fell back against Medara, who toppled against the steps. The horse leaned against me. Its hot breath blasted my face; its wicked red eyes glared at me. I tried to push the beast away. It didn't budge.

"Good work, Coalsack. Excellent." The juggler brushed himself off and strutted toward us. He patted the horse's rippling flanks. "Hold them there a bit."

He disappeared into the wagon and emerged with ropes. The horse backed away, and I struggled up. The animal reared and threatened me. As I dodged its flying hooves, the juggler tossed a loop of rope over my shoulders and pulled it tight, pinning my arms to my side. He hauled me aside and bound Medara's wrists. She offered little resistance. Too frightened, I guessed from her pale face and wide-eyed stare.

Coalsack stood guard over me while the juggler led Medara to the wagon. With a shove, he ordered her to back into it. Grunting and straining, she squeezed herself between the bulging wooden sides.

"Coalsack. To the wagon."

At the harlequin's cry, the horse wheeled away from me and eased into its place between the shafts. Its master dashed around and refastened the harness. He jumped up onto a shaft, caught hold of the wagon front, and vaulted over it, landing in the small space left behind Medara. Coalsack trotted into the arcade.

"Jump out, Medara," I shouted.

Medara, face contorted, twisted her shoulders and kicked her legs, trying to pry herself free.

The wagon rumbled into the arcade. Shopkeepers and customers dashed out of the shops along the arcade. They stared at the brightly painted wagon and at Medara's kicking legs. Whooping with laughter, they all trotted after the speeding wagon.

"Grab her! Pull her out!"

No one heeded my frantic pleas. The wagon was moving too fast and they were finding the spectacle too entertaining. I struggled out of the rope, grabbed up my pack, and ran after them, my bare feet scraping over the rough cobblestones. The tender new skin felt every sharp edge; every loose pebble sent a shock wave of pain through my legs. My big toe jammed into a crevice in the stone. I sprawled across the cobblestones.

I picked myself up and brushed the dirt and gravel from the scrapes striping my hands and arms. The crowd followed the wagon out of the arcade, abandoning me in a cloud of dust.

19

SUNBURST

What was I to do? I glanced back longingly at the temple. There lay my hope of following and intercepting Divian. But I could not desert Medara.

Perhaps out of my sight the crowd had succeeded in halting the wagon. I stumbled on bruised feet toward the end of the arcade. My toe throbbed so that I suspected I'd broken it. Already my feet needed healing again. I gripped my fascinum and prayed, "Zera, help me."

I limped past a cobbler's shop and through its open door glimpsed a pair of leather boots on the cobbler's bench. I stepped in. The small, cluttered shop smelled of new leather and the tallow used to polish it. Awls, needles, cutters, and lasts littered the bench. No one was in the shop. The shopkeeper must have joined the crowd following the juggler's wagon. I snatched the boots and held them alongside my feet. Their measure was as perfect as if they were made for me. If only I had the money I'd given Meeda ...

It wouldn't have been enough for boots like these. Expertly crafted of soft leather and so well stitched the seams were almost invisible, the boots were lined with soft silver fur.

I'd lost precious time with this detour into the cobbler's unless ... The deserted street, the empty shop, the perfectly sized boots, and my desperate need hinted that the boots were a gift—whether from Zera or Molor, who could say?

I plopped onto the dusty floor and drew on the boots. The soft fur soothed and shielded the new hurts. I slipped on my backpack and raced from the shop, promising myself I'd return someday and pay for the boots.

I sped from the arcade and turned onto the street that fronted the square. A knot of people blocked the way. Snatches of excited conversation floated toward me. Its import became clear as I drew closer.

"It's real, I say."

"Couldn't be. Too small."

"Who could make a thing like that?"

"Maybe 'twas that small in life. A freak. And that's why, when it died ..."

"It's evil. I say we should burn it."

I guessed what they'd found. I edged around the crowd, hoping to get past while their attention was diverted.

"Here, let us have a look at it back here." In front of me the burly cooper shouted his demand.

Someone called out, "Take the vile thing."

A round object hurtled through the air. The cooper ducked. I put up my hands and caught the missile—a small head, fallen or thrown from the juggler's cart. A shudder seized me. Death had distorted but could not destroy the nobility of the features. I could not name the victim, but a warm rush of affection for him overwhelmed me. I stared transfixed at the face and wept without knowing why.

"He's wearing the boots I just finished!"

The cry startled me out of my trance. A small, bald man in a leather apron pointed a finger at my boots. "He's got on the boots I made for the innkeeper's guest. He must have stolen them from my shop."

I'd foolishly allowed myself to be drawn into the center of the group. With angry mutters they drew their circle tight around me. I looked for a weapon but found none. The cooper planted himself in front of me. I hurled the head at him and dodged around him. Two men tackled me, sending me crashing to the ground. They hauled me to my feet.

The cobbler shook his finger in my face. "A fortnight it took me to make those boots. They're the finest I've ever done, and you've ruined them. What will I tell the innkeeper?"

"He's shamed us all," a woman wailed.

"Whip him," someone called.

"String him up." The ominous suggestion met with shouts of approval from the scowling crowd.

"Let Zera's wrath fall on him." That shout, too, drew hurrahs from the growing mob.

"And would you boast to Zera that in her name you defied her will?" The sharp voice stilled the shouts and jeers.

I looked for the speaker. Above the heads of the mob I glimpsed a red plume. With murmurs of surprise, the crowd parted. The red feather bobbed toward me, attached to a gray velvet hat. The hat sat on the head of a black-haired man dressed in gray tabard over an elegant wine-colored shirt and dark purple breeches.

"The innkeeper!" The cooper's annoyed whisper identified the newcomer. "What's he doing here?"

The cobbler, though, had a quite different reaction. He dropped to one knee. "Sir, the boots you ordered were ready, crafted of the finest material and made to the measure you gave me. This scoundrel created a diversion and stole them from my shop. He's got them on his filthy feet." The little man wrung his hands.

The man, hands on hips, frowned at the cobbler. "Were you not paid the full price in advance?"

"I was, and I'll make restitution. You'll get back every decim."

"You need repay nothing. This man is the honored guest the boots were made for. He's lodging at my inn."

Astonished whispers and disbelieving snickers flowed through the crowd. My own jaw dropped open.

"He? Sir, do you mock me?" The cobbler's indignant gaze ranged over my matted hair and beard, my soiled and ragged clothes.

The man smiled; his blue eyes twinkled. "See how the boots fit him. Surely you can see his are the feet they were made for."

The cobbler, still kneeling, put a trembling hand on one boot and traced the fit of my foot within it. He lifted his pale face, eyes wide with fear, and stammered, "I don't understand."

Nor did I, not fully, but I did recognize the man who called himself an innkeeper. He was Savnar, the fascinator.

Not sure whether I dared call him by that name, I searched his face for a clue to his intention. He turned to one of the men who'd tackled me, a powerfully built, muscular fellow. My arm still throbbed where his fingers had clamped it.

"You, blacksmith. Is the horse I left with you ready?"

"Aye. All shod. A finer, higher-spirited horse I've never seen." He nodded his head in my direction.

A horse! Just what I needed to overtake the juggler. Except that never in my life had I ridden a horse. I had only a vague idea of how to mount one and not the slightest notion of what to do after that.

Savnar clasped my arm and led me along the street.

"Savnar," I whispered, "Again I'm indebted to you."

"Shh," he cautioned. "You owe me nothing. The goddess has seen fit to bless you."

Speaking more loudly, he said, "I regret that you've had an accident, but we'll get you taken care of back at the inn."

I had so many questions that I dared not ask with the crowd trooping along. Savnar led the way to the smithy. Tied to a post in front of it was a huge red horse, its mane rippling like flames.

Savnar's horse.

The questions I'd wanted to ask were driven from my mind by a wave of terror when Savnar unhitched the horse from the post and offered me the reins. "Here, you need a horse. Let me help you mount."

The horse nickered and nuzzled my shoulder.

"Sunburst is eager to be ridden."

I put my right hand on the horse's back. Savnar intended my rescue, but the horse was sure to throw me as soon as I mounted. If I could even manage to do that.

"Why does he look so scared of the horse if it's his?" the chandler's wife wanted to know.

"Get on, if you're really blessed by Zera," urged the cooper with a malicious grin.

The blacksmith, arms folded across his broad chest, stood glowering at me.

Savnar stooped and cupped his hands, leaving me little choice but to trust him. With my heart thudding in my throat, I placed one booted foot into that makeshift stirrup, hoisted myself up, and swung my right leg over Sunburst's bare back. The powerful muscles twitched beneath me. Savnar thrust the reins into my hands. He leaned forward and whispered into my ear. "Trust the horse. Let him guide you. Hold the reins tight, clasp him with your knees, and whatever he does, hang on!" He slapped the horse's flank. Sunburst snorted. I took a deep breath.

The horse bolted. Still holding the reins, I fell forward, clinging to the animal's neck. My knees dug into its sides. I expected it to run to the inn Savnar had spoken of. Instead, the town disappeared in a blur. I shut my eyes and ground my teeth together. My body jounced up and down until I was sure every bone must be broken. I gave up all hope of following the juggler and poured my soul into the effort of hanging on.

The jarring thud of the hooves gave way to a steady, soothing rise and fall like the motion of a boat on a gentle sea. I eased one eye open. Velvety darkness surrounded us.

A spark flew past my face. "Hurry, Korth." Renata's pleading voice startled me. I nearly lost my grip.

Another spark darted near. "Help me." I recognized Brid's plaintive moan.

A swarm of sparks swept by. Each had a voice—the voices of the old lords, who had been silent for so long.

"Fail not."

"Courage."

"Make haste. Time turns."

And a voice I did not recognize. "Soon. Soon I'll be whole again."

The medley of voices died away. I felt the drum of Sunburst's hooves, though what surface they struck I couldn't tell.

I relaxed as we moved onward and began to enjoy the ride. Some instinct took hold and let me ride and handle a horse. *This* horse. Sunburst and I seemed meant for each other.

Sunburst slowed, stopped. Unexpectedly he reared. I locked my fingers in his thick mane to keep from falling off. He settled down a bit but shook his head and pawed the ground restlessly.

The darkness faded. We seemed to be in a cave or tunnel. Its earthen walls narrowed to an oval of light. I judged the opening large enough for Sunburst to squeeze through if I dismounted. I slid off his back and took his reins.

He stamped and snorted. I edged past him. A mummified corpse lay across the path. I stared in shock at the sunken cheeks, the parchmentlike skin, the carefully arranged limbs. The decaying features on that desiccated corpse resembled my own.

I caught hold of Sunburst's reins, as much to support myself as to calm the horse, who seemed as disturbed by the sight as I was. Of all the strange things that had happened to me since performing the rite of Lord's-Kill, this was the strangest. If my eyes were not deceiving me.

I paused and stared at the dead face. What did it mean? Could I be dreaming again? The musty odor and Sunburst's skittishness convinced me this was no dream.

The body lay across the passage, its arms crossed over its chest, its cloak arranged to reveal a green shirt with embroidered work of gold thread, a belt of embossed leather inset with gems, trousers of finest doeskin. The clothes were finer by far than any clothes I'd ever worn, with the exception of the elaborate robes of state I'd donned to assume the lordship in place of Brid.

That occasion seemed so long ago. Was it in my past now, or my future? Brid still lay suspended in some painful half-life. I had not rescued him, had not saved Renata, had not snatched Medara from the juggler. And now here I was, gazing upon a corpse that might be my own. Had Sunburst carried me into the future? But if in this time I had been killed, how could I be here, and what could I do to change whatever had brought about my death? Probably I would only create more of a muddle and disrupt the time line beyond all repair. I would never return to my own time, claim the deathright, and become Manor Lord, the title that I should have been accorded.

I could think of nothing to do but to go forward and confront whatever fate awaited me on the other side of this strange death.

20

THE BEGINNING OF THE CIRCLE

S unburst's nudges and neighs penetrated my stupor. He pushed me back the way we had come, away from the corpse that lay between us and the tunnel or cave entrance. I patted his neck.

"Easy, fellow," I said. "I don't want to go back into that darkness. Come on. We've got to get out of here, even though it means getting past *that*."

Sunburst retreated farther into the black tunnel.

"I'll have to blindfold him," I muttered to myself. Slipping my arms out of my backpack, I let it slide off onto the tunnel floor. I picked it up and took my poncho out of it, then folded the empty pack around Sunburst's head, covering his eyes, and drew the strap through his bridle to fasten it in place. The poncho I threw over my shoulders until I could return it to the pack. I welcomed its warmth in the cool of the cave.

"Now, let's try it." I took the reins and led Sunburst back to the corpse, intending to urge him over it and out of the tunnel.

Poking out from beneath the cloak, a finely worked scabbard caught my attention. With the toe of my boot I kicked aside the edge of the cloak to reveal the sword hilt. On it in gold inlay was a familiar pattern. I pulled out my fascinum and looked at the design on the half that depicted a burial pillar—the trumpet flower drooping from a broken stem with a bee, ready for flight, poised on its edge. In every detail the design on the fascinum matched that on the hilt of the sword. This seemed further confirmation that the corpse was my own, though I didn't understand how such a thing could be.

One thing I did know: I had to have that sword. Steeling myself, I stooped and fumbled with the clasp of the sword belt, got it open, and pulled it gingerly from around the corpse. The scent of decay clung to it. Nevertheless, I buckled the belt around my waist and felt the weight of the scabbard and sword fall into place against my thigh.

Shudders crawled up my spine as I stepped over the body and tugged on Sunburst's reins. He lifted his feet high and stepped across. Together we walked out of that channel of death into a breezy, sunlit afternoon. At Sunburst's vigorous toss of his head, I hurried to take the backpack from over his eyes. I kept the poncho on because the air was chill, and the feel of the soft wool was comforting.

Sunburst whickered and stamped. I kept tight hold of his reins and looked around. We had come out of the cave onto a wide ledge high above a verdant valley. Groves and forests alternated with lush, green cropland. Though the land was changed, I recognized its contours—the Manor Lands. Each time I tried to reach the temple, I was sent back to the Manor Lands. But where the Manor House should be I saw only fields. Gone were the slave quarters, the gardens, the villages of freedmen. The land was wilder, more woodsy. Small frame houses stood here and there among the cultivated fields. It would have been an idyllic scene except that a brown-clad horde fanned out across it, torching fields and axing trees as in the dream-vision I'd had when Divian choked the life from me.

Sunburst nipped at my poncho.

"You're right. We have to hurry." No time to puzzle over the mystery of the corpse. The marauders had to be stopped. If the land below was—or would be—the Manor Land, I could not let it fall to Labonite invaders. I settled my poncho around me and tucked its fringe beneath the sword belt so it would not hinder my grasp of the hilt.

Sunburst trotted forward and stood beside a large rock. Using the rock as a stepping-stone, I mounted. On Sunburst's back I felt a new surge of confidence. Had I not seen my death, yet I lived? What had I to fear? Still marveling at my ability to ride this miraculous horse, I flicked the reins. "Go, Sunburst. Take us down."

Sunburst leaped from the cliff and galloped through the air, mane flowing, tail outstretched. Obeying some instinct, I unsheathed my sword and brandished it over my head. It caught the sunlight and returned it in a flash of golden fire. Rays of light burst from my fascinum. I glanced down. It gleamed like a star on my breast.

Below us heads jerked upward. Eyes widened. I must have appeared a god descending to earth. Axes dropped from hands. Torches were flung down. Men burst into frantic flight. Of the desert horde only the bravest stood their ground.

Sunburst needed no direction from me. He charged one group of Labonites after another. At the sight of us, their faces contorted with terror and they fled in every direction, dropping weapons as they ran. We pressed deeper into the valley, and everywhere we went, the resistance melted away—until we reached a V-shaped point of land formed by the junction of two rushing streams and backed by a thick grove of cypress trees.

Sunburst bounded across the stream toward a knot of struggling men. I'd wondered that the land seemed to have no defenders. Here at last a handful of men mounted a spirited defense. Men in peasant dress warded off axe blows with clubs and the spiked maces called morning stars. In the center of the battle a black head bobbed above the rest and the iron spikes of a morning star glinted in the sun.

A peasant soldier crumpled to the ground. Another backed toward us, one arm hanging uselessly by his side. With his other he flung his club at his pursuer. The man deflected it with his shield and leaped toward his defenseless prey.

Sunburst shot forward, reared, and stomped. The attacker toppled under Sunburst's hooves, his skull crushed. I leaned forward and thrust my sword through the neck of another desert man. Pulling back the heavy sword unbalanced me. Sunburst bucked and I pitched from his back. A brown-clad fighter ran at me, axe raised. I held my sword up like a spear. The Labonite twirled his axe. Before he could hurl it, a morning star crashed against his head. He crumpled to the ground.

I got to my feet and fought alongside my rescuer until the last of the Labonites had fallen, most trampled by Sunburst or felled by the powerful morning star, one or two killed by my sword.

"If not for you and your mace, I'd be dead," I said. "Thank you."

With a bloody hand my lanky comrade pushed his long black hair from his eyes. "No thanks needed. Without you and your horse and your sword, this—" He shook the mace. "—wouldn't've saved me. My friends and I would all be dead." He wiped his hand on his peasant tunic and thrust it toward me. "I'm Peren."

Something—the place, the sword in my hand, the horse beside me, the battle we'd won—prompted me to use my lord name. "Terral here," I said and clasped his hand.

He slapped Sunburst's shoulder. "Some horse you got here."

"He'll do," I said, smiling.

A shock of recognition erased the smile. I stared at Peren's face. Its jet hair had been short and neatly trimmed, but the head tossed from the juggler's wagon had been Peren's.

Sunburst's nudge aroused me. Peren seemed not to have noticed my lapse. His attention had turned to the man Sunburst had rescued.

"Jed, how many of the rest are alive?"

With his good hand Jed pointed to a man who lay in a widening pool of blood. "Only Gil. But look. His life's draining away too fast to stanch."

"Gil. Faithful friend." Peren's eyes filled with sudden tears. He shook his head. "How will I tell his sisters? Jena and Hanna widowed, their brother taken, all in one day. Who'll provide for them with their men dead?"

His grief filled me with compassion. "Let me look at him." I wrapped my fingers around my fascinum and strode to the dying man.

An axe had sliced deep into his side. He was scarcely breathing.

Death could be only moments away. Again I acted according to some buried instinct—I stooped and put one hand across the gaping wound while clutching my fascinum in the other. I concentrated on my heartbeat and on the life that coursed through me with each beat. I willed the fascinum to gather that life force into itself, intensify it, and channel it through my hand into the wounded man.

The bleeding stopped. Strength and health flowed through the wound and spread through the body. As though they were my own, I felt his limbs warm with renewed circulation and his sluggish organs regain their functions.

I grew weak; my head swam. I forced myself to keep my hand on his wound until it closed, the flesh knitted, and my fingers rubbed across smooth skin.

I slumped, my head sagged, my chin fell against my chest. But I could not rest until my work was complete. "Jed," I called, battling waves of dizziness.

Jed knelt beside me in the mud, his broad peasant face filled with awe.

"Jed, what happened to your arm?"

"One o' them desert lice swung the side of his axe against it. It's just broken. If he'd used the blade ..."

"Let me see it."

He twisted around until the arm dangled in front of me. I grasped it. He caught his breath. A spasm of pain contorted his features.

"Hang on," I muttered.

Again I channeled power through the fascinum, this time

concentrating on the strength and firmness of my bones, sending that strength and wholeness into Jed's arm. Weak from the healing of Gil, I couldn't maintain the steady flow. I grew dizzy and spots danced before my eyes. My joints seemed to turn to slush.

Strong hands grasped my shoulders. "Draw my strength, Lord," Peren's voice whispered in my ear. His legs supported my back.

A surge of power coursed through me. The fascinum glowed in my grasp. As I tugged on his arm, the jagged pieces of Jed's broken bone snapped together and the two parts melded, erasing the unnatural division. Torn muscle fiber mended and sheathed the bone. I drew my hand away.

Jed rubbed his arm. "It tingles." He lifted it out straight, slowly bent the elbow. His mouth opened into a gap-toothed grin. "It's strong. Ready to bash more desert lice."

Peren's mace fell at my feet. He dropped down beside it, bent his head, and touched his forehead to my feet. "Your servant, Lord."

Jed knelt beside him. "We are honored, Lord, that a god should come among us," he said.

Taken aback, I shook my head. "I'm no god, just a man like yourselves."

"I can scarcely believe that," Peren said, "but if you are a man, you are no ordinary man, and we owe you our lives and our service."

"Do you not already owe fealty to the Lord of the Manor?" I asked, unsure how to respond.

"Who is that? What manor?" He remained prostrate before me. "We are humble farmers set by Molor to till this valley. We have no leader, Lord, unless you claim that place. You've proved your right to it. Will you take me into your service?"

I grasped him and raised him. His words confirmed that this was the past, not the future. I said, "Not as a servant, Peren, but as my liegeman and friend."

It seemed I had been sent to establish the very lord line into which I had cast so much confusion. Before that could happen, the Labonites had to be completely driven out.

"We waste time. As Jed reminded us, we're not done bashing Dunesmen." I stood, but my trembling legs forced me to lean on Peren.

"My Lord, you're hurt!"

"No, I've merely used up too much strength in the healing. But it'll return. We can't wait. Sunburst does most of the fighting, anyway." I looked for the big red horse, spotted him drinking from the stream, and whistled. He trotted to me, ears back, tail swishing. Peren helped me mount. On his back I felt my strength come back, as though the horse infused me with power. I might be a mere man, but Sunburst was no ordinary horse. He might have been bred for a god.

No time to ponder how such a horse had come to be mine. Shouts and the dull thud of axe blows grew louder. Peren grabbed his morning star. Jed picked up a heavy club and cast a nervous look back across the merging streams toward the westering sun. "Sun'll set in under an hour. Maybe we should just let 'em be—let 'em get caught in there after dark. That'd learn 'em."

"We can't wait," Peren said. A thunderous crash emphasized his words. "Wake Gil. We'll need every hand to save the grove."

Jed knelt by Gil and shook him awake. He would have helped him stand, but the healed man brushed off Jed's hand and jumped up. He looked around, black brows furrowed in puzzlement.

"What's happened? Where're the desert lice?" He stared at the lifeless bodies around him. "Did we win?"

"We won the battle, but not the war." Peren placed a hand on Gil's shoulder. "Listen."

The shouts and axe blows sounded nearer. One crash after another marked the fall of more trees.

With a snarl, Gil snatched up an axe from a fallen Labonite. "We've got to stop 'em." He sprinted toward the grove. A grove that would not be there in my time.

We headed after him, Sunburst trotting to allow Jed and Peren to keep pace with us. The great red horse infused me with boldness. I grasped his mane, and a current of strength flowed through me. I brandished my sword. "For Molor," I shouted.

We plunged into a gray-green world of tall, spearlike trees marching in ordered columns. Between the columns long corridors stretched into the gloom of gathering dusk. A carpet of fan-shaped twigs absorbed the sound of Sunburst's hooves.

I lowered my sword, feeling that the bared blade profaned this quiet sanctuary. Sunburst trod lightly; the men tiptoed, faces filled with awe. I was haunted by a sense of the presence not of trees, but of living beings. I glanced up at the slender, tapering crowns. A sudden impulse prompted me to whisper, "Derli?"

A sigh swept through the pressed leaves. Was it only the wind? A profound sadness fell over me.

The thud of axes sounded nearby and a loud laugh rang out. My sadness changed to rage. I gripped my sword and pressed my knees into Sunburst's side. I motioned Jed to follow me and signaled to Peren and Gil to separate from us and circle around to come on the Labonites from the opposite direction. They dashed off into the gloom.

Jed and I skirted the area where the chopping sounds were concentrated. We found a break in the rows of trees, a freshly formed clearing strewn with logs. About twenty desert men wielded axes, some chopping at the already fallen giants, others attacking standing trees.

Sunburst arched his neck and bucked. I hung on until he settled to earth. He looked back at me and his mane bristled. I slid off his back, hoping I read his meaning correctly.

The great horse charged into the clearing, leaping logs and piles of branches. With loud cries several of the despoilers hurled their axes at him. His form rippled, changed to a sheet of fire. A streak of flame flashed through the clearing. With shrieks of terror the Labonites trampled one another in their rush to escape the deadly lightning.

Jed and I on one side, Gil and Peren on the other blocked their retreat. With an anguished cry a fleeing man spitted himself on my sword. I wrenched the steel from his gut. He collapsed, blood gurgling from his mouth. Jed crashed his club against the head of another desert man, cracking his skull like the shell of an egg. The few Labonites who got past us did not turn back to join battle but sped toward the waning light. We let them go.

Sunburst stood placidly in the center of the clearing. Only the charred axe handles and bits of hardening slag that had once been iron blades showed me I had not imagined the horse's transformation.

I hurried to him. Peren approached more cautiously, with Gil and Jed trailing behind. "What *is* he?" Gil asked in an awed voice, giving a nod toward Sunburst.

"My horse."

"And you say you are not a god?"

"I am not, but the horse may be a god's gift to me, given to allow me to help you defeat the Labonites." It was a theory I'd developed while watching the desert men flee. The explanation may not have fully satisfied them, but it did silence their inquiries.

With sand and leaves I cleaned the blood off my sword and returned it to its scabbard. We dragged the corpses of the slain into the middle of the clearing. By then the day's light had faded to gray, so we agreed to wait until morning to carry the bodies from the grove and build a pyre. My companions' hurried movements and nervous glances revealed their eagerness to leave the grove. I did not mount Sunburst but held his reins and walked beside him. We hurried through the colonnade of trees. I dared not look around but fixed my gaze on the path straight ahead of me. A rustling passed through the trees, so like the whispers of village gossips that I strained to hear the words. But the harder I concentrated, the less distinct the syllables became.

Gil and Jed crowded near me. The club trembled in Jed's hands. In front of us Peren clutched his morning star in a tight grip and broke into a rapid trot. I kept one hand on Sunburst's neck and the other on the hilt of my sword. A chill mist crept over the ground and lifted wraithlike tendrils toward the trees. I shivered despite my poncho.

Off the path to our left a sweet voice burst into song. A bird singing farewell to the day, I thought, but the song continued and I knew it was no bird. I could not distinguish words, if words there were, but the silvery-sweet song spiraled to the treetops, hovered there in winged tremolo, and fell in a shower of crystal needles that pierced my heart with unutterable sorrow. I hid my face in Sunburst's mane and wept, overcome by a deep sense of loneliness and nameless longing.

A chorus of other voices joined the first in harmony so achingly exquisite, its loveliness captured my soul and severed it from my body. I felt myself drawn upward into the cypress crowns, into balsamy clusters of tight-pressed leaves imbued with vibrant presence. A giddy intoxication seized me. I seemed to soar from tree to tree on a euphonic paean—

Strident neighs cut across the melody. I plunged earthward, snapped back into my body with an abruptness that sent me reeling against Sunburst. I clung to the horse until my heartbeats slowed and my head stopped spinning. I opened my eyes and searched for my companions.

Peren crouched on the ground, head bowed, hands clapped over his ears. Jed embraced a tree trunk that I suspected he had tried to climb. Where was Gil? His axe lay abandoned on the ground.

I shook Peren. "Peren. Jed. Gather your wits. We have to find Gil."

Peren stumbled to his feet and together we pried Jed from the tree. Sunburst stamped his feet and swished his tail.

I led Peren and Jed to stand one on either side of the horse's neck. "Keep your hands on Sunburst and let him guide us." I caught hold of the reins, held them loosely, and stood in front of Jed. "Sunburst, take us to Gil."

The horse trotted off through fog and darkness, leading us beneath the dripping trees. A shadowy form materialized out of the mist.

"Gil!" I hurried to the weaving figure and clutched his arm. Offering no resistance, he allowed me to guide him back to Sunburst. He seemed dazed. "Too late," he muttered. "Too late. They're leaving."

"Who's leaving, Gil?"

"The sweet singers. The falas."

Moans and wails broke out around us, and the trees shook. Their shudders spattered us with drops of water, like tears. Sunburst lowered his head; his tail drooped. A wrenching sorrow made me cry out. There followed a terrible emptiness.

Clinging to Sunburst, we plodded past untenanted trees and out of the haunted grove. Away from the grove, the fog lifted. We marched in heavyhearted silence through a starlit meadow. In the distance dark hills pushed their humped backs against a fringe of cloud. Sunburst allowed me to mount, and he and I checked the area for Labonites while Peren, Gil, and Jed made camp in a small stand of poplar trees. Peren wanted to set a guard, and Gil volunteered to stand first watch. But weariness etched deep lines and brushed shadows across every face.

"Sunburst will guard us." I patted the horse's flank. "No one will get past him. We all need sleep."

I set the example by taking off my sword belt, wrapping myself in my poncho, and curling up on the hard ground. Jed and Gil found resting-places near me, and sleep quickly claimed them. Last, Peren stretched out at my feet.

Hot breath blasted my face. I grunted and turned over. Something nudged my shoulder. I groaned and pushed at my tormentor. A hoof pressed into my back, kicked lightly at my side until I came fully awake.

I turned onto my back and peered, bleary-eyed, at the great red horse looming over me. "Sunburst—"

The horse thrust his muzzle against my mouth, smothering my startled exclamation. I patted his nose to indicate I understood he wanted none roused but me. He moved aside so I could rise and nudged my sword belt with his hoof. I picked it up and buckled it on.

With incredible quiet Sunburst picked his way past the sleeping men and I followed. Long wisps of cloud trailed across the sky. A cold east wind made me glad for the protection of my poncho. The plaintive cry of a bird rent the silence. A shiver crawled up my spine.

"Sunburst, wait." I reached for the horse's swishing tail. "Let me mount."

His tail lashed my face. Hooves maintained a steady tattoo on the stony ground. I sprinted for his reins. He broke into a trot that left me loping through his dust. My steps lagged. He slowed to a sedate walk.

"All right. You don't want me to ride. I'll follow you, but go slow." I grasped the hilt of my sword, alarmed at the prospect of being separated from my companions and lost at night so near the desert.

What did I hear behind me? The snap of a dry stick? The chink of rock hitting rock? I peered into a darkness filled with indistinct shapes that could be bushes or boulders—or men. I drew my sword from its sheath and stood, feet apart, muscles tense.

A small animal scurried in front of me. Sunburst gave a muted snort. Feeling foolish, I sheathed my sword and turned back to follow the horse. He headed up a steep hillside. I clambered after him, slipping and sliding on loose stones, groping in the darkness for rocks and branches to cling to.

"Slow down, Sunburst," I called out. "I can't see."

He stopped. I scrambled up to the outcrop where he waited. Surefooted as a mountain goat, he resumed his climb. I followed, setting my feet where his hooves found firm footing. On the crest of the hill, silhouetted against the cloud-veiled sky, he reared and neighed. With a flick of his tail he galloped off into the enshrouding dark. In panic I pulled myself up onto the hilltop. I was alone. The thud of Sunburst's hooves echoed in the distance.

"Sunburst!" I rushed across the rough summit and scanned the dark hillside. A path curved down the far side, but a large boulder blocked my view. I decided to climb it to look for Sunburst.

I took a step toward it. An odor as of scorched rope filled my nostrils. I halted. The boulder shifted shape. With a crackling rustle, batlike wings unfolded and spread wide. From beneath the wings, outstretched arms flexed taloned claws. A head uncoiled from between hunched shoulders. Glowing like coals, two baleful eyes stared into mine. Fangs slavering beneath a curved beak, the living version of the fiend on Dama Koralie's staff sprang toward me.

21

FLUX FIEND

The bat-winged shadow engulfed me, plunging me into a blackness that made the dark night bright by comparison. With the black came an intense cold against which my poncho was useless. I could not move. Terror knotted my guts.

"Grovel, slave," rasped a voice like a rusty saw.

A smothering weight pressed me down. My legs buckled. My knees crashed against icy rock. Hunched over, hands pressed against my thighs, I listened helplessly to the grating laughter. This was no dream. I was confronting a creature out of myth: a Flux fiend.

"Those fools Makor and Molor weakened the Flux of Time with their fighting. I and my kin have waited for a chance to burst our bonds." Each word dripped poison onto my head.

My frozen jaws could not let out the scream of agony that welled up inside me. My mouth filled with acid.

The venomous voice rasped on. "You are my prize. Your floundering about from one shore of time to another opened a passage for me. And you shall open others. Through you I shall funnel time into the maw of chaos. You are my creature. You are the Disrupter."

Talons dug into my head and pushed it against my knees. My body pressed against my legs. My fascinum fell into my hands, and my fingers wrapped around it. Warmth flowed through my hands into my chest and legs. My numbed soul began to thaw.

The fiend let out a shrill screech and jerked upward, yanking me with it. It wrenched its claws from my head, bringing forth freshets of blood that warmed my face. With a dry crackle the creature's wings clapped together behind its back. The terrible blackness retreated.

"Fly, Lord!"

Peren's voice. The fiend swooped on something behind it. A morning star fell at my feet.

I snatched my sword and sprang at the fiend. Time turned fluid. The Flux fiend's movements slowed, as did mine, so that my attacks seemed to take hours or days. Then everything sped. We seemed to pass through many times. Stars streaked across the sky; daylight winked on and was gone. I fastened my gaze on my foe to keep him from dissolving into a vague blur. The speed of my own motions disoriented me. Yet I fought.

The fiend's clattering wings kept me at bay. I hacked at them, tore one, and plunged my sword through the rent. Its tip grazed the malformed body. With a deafening screech and a flap of its torn wing, the demon ripped my sword from my grasp. I stumbled back. It hurled itself at me, slamming me to the ground. Clawed feet gripped me. Numbing cold poured over me. The curved beak descended toward my face, and I writhed in a futile effort to escape. My flailing hand touched the smooth shaft of Peren's morning star. I gripped the shaft, summoned my waning strength, and slammed the spiked orb against the fiend's head.

Time stabilized. The creature yowled and its talons grabbed for my chest, but the claws snared in my poncho. Its frantic efforts to free itself gave me time to beat it again with the morning star. It let out a searing howl, tore its talons free, and grappled for my weapon.

I hung on. We thrashed about, its wings rattling over the ground like dry husks. The creature reeked of scorched hair. Its stench choked me so I could scarcely breathe. Drops of icy venom fell on me from its slavering mouth. Needles of pain stabbed my flesh. It grappled for my weapon but could not wrest it from my hands.

I poured my strength into gripping the morning star and jabbed its spikes into the leathery hide. By the glow from my fascinum I saw the fiend's body shrink. I tore free of the creature's hold and rammed the mace upward. The iron spikes wedged into its throat. With a strangled cry the fiend clawed at the shaft. Willing myself to push harder, I forced the barbs deeper into its neck. It wrapped its wings around itself; its beak stabbed downward. The head of the morning star disappeared, swallowed up into the head of the fiend. The black, misshapen body contracted and melded with the shaft.

I sat up and stared with horror at the thing I held—an ebony walking stick, its head a carved fiend, lifeless except for glittering yellow eyes. I cast it down, but when I tried to rise, I found I was too weak to stand without aid. I was forced to reclaim the fiendish staff and make use of it, much as I hated it.

I pressed the base of the stick against the ground, leaned on the shaft, and hauled myself to my feet. The malevolent eyes glared. I turned the staff so that the eyes no longer faced me and looked around for Peren.

He lay where the fiend had thrown him. Near him lay my sword. I picked it up, sheathed it, and knelt by Peren. His body was cold. I recalled the head tossed away by the juggler. "No!" I raged. "You saved my life. You weren't afraid to attack the fiend. Your courage deserves a better fate."

Dismissing my own hurts, I put aside the staff and lifted Peren. Cradling his head in my arms, I laid my fascinum across his mouth. "Peren," I murmured, "return."

His body warmed. He shuddered and coughed. A wave of relief washed over me as his eyelids fluttered open. Recognition lit his eyes; his lips curved into a smile. "Lord, you're safe."

"And so are you." My smile answered his. "I'm afraid, though, I've spoilt your morning star." I pointed to the staff.

Peren gaped at the shrunken, petrified fiend. He struggled to his feet and lurched forward to peer at the staff. I moved to his side. He tore his gaze from the fiend's wizened face and stared at me, eyes wide with awe. "You transformed that evil thing into a walking stick?" His voice dropped to a reverential whisper. "Who are you, Lord?"

I placed my hand on his shoulder. "Peren, that thing had me helpless. Your brave act of throwing your mace at it freed me to battle it. For that matter, it was when I jabbed your morning star into its throat that it decided to reduce itself. I did nothing to make that happen. You can claim more credit than I."

But Peren dropped to his knees, touched the staff, pulled his fingers back, reached out again, grasped it, balanced it across both palms, and offered it to me. "Lord Terral, when I threw this at the evil one, it only angered him. He struck me a deathblow. I felt my heart burst. You defeated him and called me back from the land of shadows. I'm honored that you used my weapon, but the weapon would have been useless in any hands but yours. Take what it has become as the emblem of your victory."

Reluctantly I accepted the staff from his hands. "I receive it as your gift, Peren, and as a symbol of *our* victory." I grasped the staff below the Flux fiend's taloned feet. A chill invaded my fingers. Stifling the urge to cast the thing from me, I leaned on it and took a step forward. "It will help me down the hill. We need to get back to Gil and Jed. We've left them unprotected. I hope you know the way. I don't know where Sunburst has gone."

"I can find the way down." Peren picked his way around the rocks and waved when he located the path. "Sunburst will come back." The confident assertion drifted to me from the edge of the hill.

I hurried to catch up with him, grateful for the staff to lean on, though the fiend's glittering eyes made me nervous. I was tired and sore, and the descent was harrowing. Even with the staff, Peren had to help me down the steeper parts. When at last we gained level ground, my legs were trembling from exhaustion.

"I have to rest awhile," I said, sinking down onto the grass and wrapping my tattered poncho close about me.

Peren remained standing, shifting from foot to foot. I knew he would have preferred to keep going, but I hadn't the strength. I rubbed my aching calves. "I won't sit here long," I promised. "Don't let me fall asleep. Tell me about the cypress grove—how it came to be home to the falas. Why did the Labonites attack the grove? And why did the falas leave?"

Peren was silent for so long, it seemed he would not answer. He stared off to the east, where the lightening sky gave promise of the coming day. Had I offended him?

At last he said, "Lord, it is said that the falas are the first-born of the gods, the creators of music. I can but tell you the story that is told about them."

He squatted beside me and spoke in the manner of the villagers when they spin tales.

"The falas dwelt in the desert

Before Makor and Molor fought.

Beyond the shifting dunes they lived,

Where time's vast sea flows not.

Falas were ever mischievous

And loved to dance and sport,

But singing was their greatest joy.

Songsters whose music soared

To melodies more beautiful

Than mortals can abide,

They spun fair tales of gods and men,

Of stars and sand and time.

The boldest falas sometimes dared

To wander the lands of men

Gath'ring the stuff of epic song,

Far from their distant den.

They'd leave their timeless state

And put on human skin

To gather tales of pain and grief

That lowly mortals hold within.

And some men they stirred to envy,

To lust, to pride, to war,

Their songs gave some great knowledge,

Others were driven mad.

Those madmen sought the falas' home

Lured by a distant song.

They wandered o'er the shifting dunes,

A sad and hopeless throng.

These became the Dunesmen,

Angry at hopes unmet.

So many took that lonely trek

That Makor's consort wept.

With goddess charm, fair Zera pled

With Makor till she won his will

To cage the falas from men's sight,

Their peerless songs to still.

Molor the Winged rebuked his twin

He bade him set them free.

Blinded by red-gowned Zera's wiles

Makor would not agree.

So the fearsome feud was joined

And raged across the land,

Until Makor the Golden died,

Heart pierced by spear from Molor's hand.

Men called him "Molor Twin-Slayer."

The name brought Molor grief.

He wept for Makor, and his tears

Became the River Rethe.

Molor carved out a valley fair

In fond mem'ry of his twin.

He planted there a cypress grove

Where the falas could freely sing.

The Dunesmen, desolate and crazed,

Bereft of fala song,

Vowed vengeance on grove and valley,

Defying men and gods."

Peren stretched to his feet and looked back at the shadowy hills. "That's the story, as the tale weaver tells it here in the valley. I don't know why the falas left. I never heard them sing before." He sighed. "I could not bear to hear them sing again."

I took up the staff, used it to help me rise, and we resumed walking in silence. I mulled over the tale, wondering how much was truth and how much merely legend.

With a joyous whinny Sunburst bounded toward us, leaping and frolicking like a colt. Beyond him rose the stand of poplars where we had left Jed and Gil. The horse had returned to guard them. I let him nudge and nuzzle me while I patted his neck.

He spotted the walking stick. His ears lay back, his nostrils flared, his lips curled. He snuffled and poked at the translated fiend, gave a loud neigh, and pranced around, ears erect, mane flying, looking as pleased as if he had himself subdued the fiend. I laughed at his antics.

Awakened by the noise, Jed and Gil stumbled bleary-eyed out of their beds of grass and demanded to know where we'd been. Peren and I gave them only a brief account before we threw ourselves down to get some sleep in the short time left until sunrise.

I awakened to a blaring sun directly overhead, rubbed my eyes, stretched, and rose. Nearby, Sunburst was grazing on the thick meadow grass. He whinnied and trotted to me.

"Where is everybody?" I threw my torn poncho across his back. "Have they deserted me like you did last night?"

He showed his disdain with a loud neigh and a toss of his head. I buckled on my sword, took up the staff, and climbed onto his back. He cantered across the meadow toward the grove. I found Gil, Jed, and Peren carrying out the bodies of those we had slain. With the logs chopped by our enemies, they were constructing a huge pyre.

I dismounted and clasped Gil's shoulder. "Why didn't you wake me? I should be helping you."

Gil wiped sweat from his brow. "You needed rest. This work is not for you, Lord."

I argued, but they refused to allow me to join their labor.

By the time they completed the burning, the stench of the pyre hung heavy about us, reminding me of the fiend's fetid odor. I was relieved to leave that place and set off toward the farmland in the center of the valley. Peren's house had been burned by the marauders; that was why he'd led the valley's defense. His family had taken refuge in Gil's home, so we headed there.

Women and children raced through the fields to meet us. The children bounced around, hugging us all. Peren's wife, heavy with child, greeted her husband with a warm embrace. His young daughter, a child of perhaps four years, demanded to be lifted into his arms, where she showered his face with kisses. Gil's three sisters surrounded him, and two of them grasped his hands and gazed anxiously into his face.

He caught them each into a close embrace. "Jena, Hanna, I'm sorry." His voice choked with tears. "Your husbands were brave men. They died fighting at my side. We won the war, but at great cost."

The two women wailed. A loose-fitting gown did not hide Hanna's round belly, against which she pressed her hands. "My baby will be here soon, and now he'll never know his father," she cried.

"The child will know that his father was a brave man who gave his life for us all," Gil said, but his sisters' cries only grew louder.

Jed shuffled his feet and stared at the ground, while Peren's wife clutched her husband as though she feared he might prove a phantom and melt away. Gil's youngest sister, a slender girl with long, dark hair and deep-set eyes, hovered shyly in the background.

Peren whispered into his wife's ear and pried himself from her arms. "Listen," he shouted. "You've reason to mourn, it's true. But you also have reason to rejoice. If it weren't for Lord Terral here, we'd all be dead and the whole valley burned. By his might and his courage he led us to victory. We'll mourn the dead, but tonight we must gather all those who survive and hold a victory feast."

Peren's wife rounded up the children and nudged them toward the house. She caught the hand of the dark-haired girl. "Come, Flora," she said. "These men are tired and hungry. We must draw baths, prepare clean clothes, and start the meal. Jena, Hanna, join us. Work will ease your sorrow."

The bereaved sisters withdrew from their brother's embrace. Peren's wife made an awkward curtsy to me and led them away, Hanna still sobbing and clinging to Jena. Flora, a girl of no more than seventeen, favored me with a shy smile and cast several glances back over her shoulder as the women and children returned to the house. Gil led us to the barn, where we groomed Sunburst and provided him with food and water before seeing to our own needs.

We'd barely had time to bathe and dress before guests started arriving. Their tears dried, Hanna and Jena worked with the other women. Already they had the house cleaned and the floor of the common room strewn with fresh rushes. The savory odor of roasting meat poured from the cookhouse. Gil ushered into the common room with no lack of hospitality men who had saved themselves by hiding when the Labonites came. There were, as he pointed out, only a few who had fought and, like us, survived. For these he reserved his warmest greeting, leading them to seats of honor near Peren and me. The many who had died were named and praised, but the evening was devoted to the living, those who had fought and those who had chosen the more prudent course of remaining to protect their families.

People from nearby farms occupied every rough-hewn bench and chair in the large room that filled the ground floor. Latecomers had to be content to stand or sit on the floor. The room grew hot and stuffy despite the triangular windows that opened outward to admit the cool night breeze.

All were eager to hear the story of our victory and to stare at me and go with lanterns to peek into the barn for awed glimpses of Sunburst. When they asked me where I'd come from and how I had happened to arrive at such a crucial moment, I could only say, "Molor sent me," though I doubted that was true. It didn't seem wise to tell these worshippers of Molor that I'd been sent by Zera, and to say that Savnar had sent me would mean nothing to them.

My answer satisfied them and gave rise to much praising of Molor throughout the evening. Peren stood by my side in proud recognition of his role as my liegeman, and he, Jed, and Gil regaled the guests with tales of our exploits that grew with every telling. Peren swore that a golden glow surrounded me as I healed Gil and Jed. My battle with the Flux fiend became a struggle between two superhuman powers. My protests that it was Peren's brave act that defeated the fiend convinced no one.

The staff received much scrutiny. Losing my distaste for the shriveled fiend, I held the staff up for inspection by each man present, and all marveled at it, but none dared touch it.

The women brought in platters of roast kid and steaming bowls of freshly harvested vegetables. Each new dish was presented first to me, so that I, as guest of honor, might have the first and best portion. I had not feasted so since the night now far in the future when I was, or would be, proclaimed lord through Koralie's deceit.

This dinner, too, was my lord-feast, for before it ended, the valley dwellers at Peren's signal arose and swore allegiance to me, acclaiming me the lord and defender promised them by the One who set them to till the valley.

I made an acceptance speech of some sort. I'm not sure what I said, being by that time surfeited with food and more than a little befuddled from all the wine. The speech must have pleased them. They cheered wildly, and each man in turn swore his personal fealty and promised me a portion of his crop or herd.

Late at night the guests took their leave, first kneeling before me to receive my benediction. When only Gil and Peren and their families were left, I announced my intention of going home with Jed, who lived alone in a one-room shanty, since Peren's wife and children were already crowded into Gil's home. But both Peren and Gil expressed horror at the suggestion.

"Lord, we have a room ready for you," Gil said. "This home, humble as it is, is the best the valley can offer. You shall have no less."

I yielded when I saw how eager they were to show me honor. Tired as I was, I hadn't relished another walk through the fields. Taking my staff, I headed for the narrow flight of stairs. The second floor ran the length of the house but was only half as wide as the ground floor, and was divided into small, cramped rooms for sleeping.

"One moment, Lord Terral." Peren placed a hand on my arm.

The women, who had bustled about all evening serving food and wine, were busy clearing away the remnants of the feast and laying out pallets for those who would be sleeping in the common room. Gil led from among them Flora, his youngest sister. She wore her long black hair in a single thick plait wound through with a white ribbon. A simple pale-green gown accentuated her slimness.

Gil brought her to stand before me, eyes lowered, a rosy flush coloring her cheeks. He cleared his throat and spoke as though presenting a carefully memorized speech. "Lord, you honor me and my family by gracing this house with your presence. Had it not been for you, this house, its fields, the valley, and our very lives would be lost to the Dunesmen. Nor can I forget how you healed me when I lay dying. All I have is yours. So you may know I hold nothing back, here is my sister Flora. Let her be yours tonight or for as long as she pleases you."

My jaw dropped open. In my shock I could think of nothing to say. I stared at Gil and at the blushing girl. "I can't ... you must not ... Gil, this sacrifice ... it's too much"

"Lord, it is an honor for me and for Flora. You shower grace on us by accepting her."

"Gil, I accept your willingness." I leaned on the staff and struggled to marshal my words. "I'm overwhelmed by your generosity. But I don't ask or deserve such a sacrifice."

Flora hung her head, and Gil lowered his gaze and flushed, saying, "Lord, I had hoped to please you."

"Your offer does please me. But I can't accept it."

"Lord," Peren nudged my arm, "a word with you, if you will." He drew me away a few paces and whispered in my ear. "Lord Terral, your refusal will bring shame on Gil and his sister."

"Peren, I can't take her," I whispered back. "She's just a young girl—a virgin."

"And a virgin she'll stay all her life if you refuse her. No man will have her, knowing you would not. Take her for this one night, Lord, and she'll be the envy of every valley woman and the desire of every man."

I tried to comprehend what Gil was saying. "You mean I'm really expected to … Gil's offer wasn't just a polite gesture?"

"Not at all," Peren assured me. "Go back and tell him you accept, if you do not want to disgrace him and his sister, too." Peren pushed me toward Gil and Flora.

A whirl of confusion spun in my brain. I looked at Gil's sad face. I could not offend my loyal and generous host. Tired as I was, the girl's fragile beauty aroused my desire. But was she as willing as her brother implied? "Flora," I asked softly, "Do you not mind that your brother has offered you to me in this way?"

Her lovely, soft amber eyes opened wide. "Oh, no, Lord. I wish it."

Left with no escape, I said to Gil "Very well, I accept."

A wide smile lit his face. He caught Flora's hand, enfolded it in mine, and steered us up the stairs to the loft room prepared for us. A candle flickering on a small table revealed a narrow, low-ceilinged room nearly filled by a wide feather bed. Gil ushered us in, bowed low to me, and backed from the room. His booted feet clomped down the stairs.

Flora's cold hand trembled in mine like a trapped bird. I dropped it and stepped away from her to lean the staff against the wall. I felt my face burning. How could I tell Flora I was as inexperienced as she?

The food and wine lay heavy in my stomach, and I wished I had not feasted so well. It occurred to me to feign drunkenness and pretend to fall asleep. I swayed, lurched to the bed, and dropped heavily onto the quilt. I lifted one foot, stared stupidly at my boot, and tugged at it with clumsy, ineffectual motions.

Flora rushed to my side, dropped to her knees, grasped the boot, and pulled it off me, reached for the other foot and removed that boot also. She grasped my tunic and tried to lift it over my head. I shoved her away.

"I c'n do that." I slurred. "Don' need help."

She stood aside and let me battle my way out of the tunic. I took as long as I could, pretending to tangle my arms in it and to have it caught over my head. Finally I extricated myself from it, hurled it to the floor, and fumbled with my breeches.

I stopped. Flora had slipped out of her gown. Her nude body gleamed straight and pale like the stalk of a lily in the candlelight. Her small breasts, their nipples erect, were like tender buds.

She saw me watching her. Her lips curved into a shy smile. I tugged again at my breeches, clumsy not from feigned drunkenness but from eagerness.

From the corner of my eye I caught a glimpse of the staff propped against the wall. I thought the fiend winked.

22

TREDIENNE

I awoke early the next morning. Flora still slept soundly beside me. I rose quietly from the bed, gathered my hastily discarded clothing, and dressed. I needed a walk, needed to think things through in the cool, fresh air of morning. I could not concentrate here with Flora so near and the memory of our lovemaking so fresh that it clouded my mind to everything else.

I reached for my staff, then drew my hand back and left the thing leaning in the corner I'd put it in the night before. I wished Peren hadn't insisted on my keeping it.

"That stick's your symbol of power and authority, Lord," he'd said. "When people see it, they remember they owe their land and lives to you. You're their Protector."

I grimaced at the title—the same one Medara had bestowed on me. I'd been a poor protector for her. I had to do better in this time.

I left Gil's house quietly and walked slowly to the barn where Sunburst was stabled.

I didn't feel I belonged in this time. That was what I had to think through. How could I be the first Lord Terral? My new friends had named me their lord, but what right had I to that title? If I left, the lord to whom it really belonged would surely come along.

Sunburst had brought me here, by what power I didn't know. But having come here, he must know the way back. He must have the power to move forward in time to the point from which he had brought me.

Though that was not the point to which I wanted to return. First I had to travel to Medara's time and be certain that Mett was installed as lord. Then I had to travel to the time in which Brid and Renata lay in stasis, free them, and make certain that Brid received his rightful place as Lord of the Manor. Only then could I return to my own time and claim the title Koralie had denied me, the only one that I believed rightfully mine.

The clear, beautiful morning invigorated me. On the walk to the stable I could not help thinking what a pleasant place to stay this would be. Here I was honored. Here I had everything I could ask for: a home, friends, a sweet and gentle woman who could become my wife. Our defeat of the Labonites presaged a time of peace at least for the near future. This was a refuge from all the problems that perplexed and beset me. If remaining here changed the future, why should that matter to me? This time would have become my present, and the future as unknown to me as it is to most men.

As I entered the stable and Sunburst gave a welcoming whicker, it occurred to me that I was very different from most men. Most men were not bounced from one time to another as I had been. Few if any were gifted with an invisible companion and a miraculous horse, as I had been. Most men were never forced into a battle with a Flux fiend as I had been. No other was called upon to perform the rite of Lord's-Kill and then denied the deathright that should have made him the Lord of the Manor, nor was any then taken to another time where the title of Manor Lord was bestowed on him when it rightfully belonged to another.

"Why am I different?" I asked Sunburst. "Why have all these strange things happened to me?"

I didn't expect an answer, nor did I get one. But my mind flashed back to my arrival in this time, when Sunburst brought me through some sort of cave and I discovered the mummified body whose features bore such a resemblance to my own and whose sword I had claimed and used to battle the Dunesmen. I felt that the answer to all my questions lay in that cave, bound with that mysterious corpse. Perhaps if I could return there …

I led Sunburst from his stall, and when we were outside, I mounted and urged him into motion, heading in the direction in which I thought the cave lay. With a whinny and a toss of his head he set off at a brisk trot. I guessed that he enjoyed the fresh morning air as much as I. In what seemed only a short time we reached the base of the cliff from which we'd descended as if on wings. On the cliff face high above me I spotted the dark opening that was the cave's mouth. I could see no way to reach it.

"Up there," I urged Sunburst. "Go. You can fly. I don't know how, but I know you did. Do it again. Take me back where we came from. Come on."

The horse stood motionless. My continued urging was futile. He stomped, whinnied, shook his head, pretending—I was certain—to be no more than an ordinary horse, one whose master was stupidly demanding the impossible.

I turned him to ride along the cliff base so that I could search for a normal way of ascent, and after a long ride I found one. A winding path took me to the top of the cliff, but from there I could no longer even see the cave entrance, much less descend to it. And again Sunburst gave no heed to my urging him to take me to the cave.

The sun had already passed the zenith and begun its downward climb when we, too, wound our way down from the cliff and headed back toward Gil's house. We had wandered so far that I was uncertain of the way, but Sunburst found the route with no hesitation.

We reached the stable as the men were returning from the fields. I groomed Sunburst and fed him, reflecting on how strange it was that I knew what to do, though I had no experience with horses prior to acquiring him. It was as though some hidden memory surfaced. Perhaps it was a memory I inherited from Brid when I received the deathright on performing the rite of Lord's-Kill. Though here in this time the old lords were silent. How could it be otherwise? They hadn't even been born yet.

When I finished caring for Sunburst, I went to the house and was startled when on my entrance Flora threw herself into my arms. Hugging me, she said, sobbing, "Oh, My Lord, I was so afraid you had left us."

"We were all worried," Gil put in, coming up beside us and resting a hand on my shoulder. "No one heard you leave, and no one knew where you'd gone. We searched the area and could only conclude that you'd left as mysteriously as you arrived."

Gently I extricated myself from Flora's embrace and placed a chaste kiss on her forehead. I apologized to Gil and his sisters for causing so much concern and told them I had only been riding around, exercising Sunburst and enjoying the beautiful day, and I'd lost track of the time. My excuse seemed to satisfy them.

"Please, Lord," Gil's sister Jena begged, "promise us that you won't go off again without letting someone know."

His sister Hanna reinforced the plea, while Flora simply gazed at me beseechingly.

What could I do? "I so promise," I said.

"May this always be your home," Flora said, grasping my hand.

The high, thin wail of the dying child sent dagger thrusts of pain through my temples. I leaped to my feet, knocking over the inkstand. A black river flooded the sheet of figures spread out on the table.

"My Lord!" The old scribe threw down his quill. My glare stifled his dismayed exclamation. He grabbed his shaker of sand and emptied it onto the dark stream.

I strode to the door of the study I'd had partitioned off a few weeks into my stay and peered into the truncated common room. Hanna, Gil's oldest sister, sat cross-legged on the rush-strewn floor and cradled against her breast the shrieking babe, born two weeks after my arrival and now five months old. Her long hair hung lusterless about her hunched shoulders. The infant's cry drowned out her weary crooning. He'd been a healthy baby until this past week, when what started as a mild fever had grown worse each day. Now he could no longer suckle, and it was clear that the fever was consuming him. We were all sure he would not live through another night.

Near Hanna, two older children sprawled, listlessly braiding rushes. The girl's face was pale and thin, but the boy's was flushed with fever. They had been ill longer than their baby brother, but only now was the illness growing worse.

I touched my cold and useless fascinum. "When is the healer going to get here?"

"When she gets here." Jena, the second sister, emerged from the cookshed with a bowl of thin liquid. She knelt beside Hanna. "See if you can get some of this down him." Without turning from her sister, she added, "Gil only left at daybreak. The healer lives at the edge of the sea marsh."

"I should have taken Sunburst. I could have made the journey in half the time it'll take Gil."

Hanna lifted her head. Shadows ringed her deep-set eyes. "Flora needs you here."

"What use am I to her?" I jerked my lifeless fascinum, wrenched it free of its chain, and hurled it across the room. The broken chain slithered off my neck.

The scribe's hand, trembling and dry as an autumn leaf, touched my bare arm. "Lord, I'll have to redo the figures."

"Do so. I can't concentrate on them now, anyway."

The hand fluttered from my arm. "I'd hoped the records would cheer you, Lord Terral. Never have we had so bountiful a harvest. The tithes will make you wealthy."

"It's no use, Jena." Hanna sent her sister away with a gentle push. "He can't swallow. His throat's too swollen."

"What good is all that food, Master Nicor, to women and children too ill to eat?"

The old man hung his head and shuffled toward the door. His stooped shoulders awakened my sense of guilt. "I ruined your hard work," I said. "I'm sorry."

Shrill screams cut my apology short. I leaped to the stairs and bounded up them two at a time, dashed into the small room I shared with Flora, and fell to my knees beside the bed.

Eyes rolling wildly, head tossing, Flora sucked in a deep breath and let it out in a scream louder than I would have believed her wasted body capable of.

I tried not to look at the mounded stomach that rose above her stick-like arms and legs. "Flora, I'm here. What is it?" I smoothed the damp hair off her forehead. "Flora, what's wrong?"

Her eyes flew open. They stared wildly at the eaved ceiling. "Get it off me. Get that thing off me."

"You're all right, Flora." I stroked her face. "There's no one here but me."

"No. It's here. The fiend. Its claws ... they're tearing me apart." She twisted and writhed, her face contorted with pain. "Its wings ..." She moaned and a spasm racked her body.

I glanced at the corner where my staff leaned, inert, the fiend's eyes hidden against the wall.

"It's only a dream." I held her shaking shoulders. "Nothing's attacking you."

But she struggled against my grasp. Arching her back, she screamed again. Her hands pressed her stomach. "It's here. It's devouring the baby!"

I placed a hand on her taut belly; the child within shifted and kicked.

"Get it away from me. Get it away," she sobbed.

Guilt-stung, I remembered how, after our first night together, Flora had confessed her fear of the staff and begged me to get rid of it. I'd kissed her tears away and promised to destroy the thing. We'd made love again, and that had ended the discussion.

Later, when I mentioned to Peren that Flora wanted the staff destroyed, he'd been horrified. Again he insisted that the staff was a symbol of my victory over the fiend and over the Labonite invaders as well. He ascribed Flora's aversion to it as nothing more than a foolish notion that should be disregarded.

So I broke my promise to Flora and kept the staff. She said no more about it, but I knew by her worried glances that she never got over her distrust of the thing. When I wasn't carrying it, I was always careful to stand it in the farthest corner with its face to the wall.

It had stood there untouched for several days. I carried it only when I left the house on official business, and I had not gone out since Flora became ill.

I stroked her hair and patted her hands. Her screams died away. She drifted into a restless sleep.

Could the fiend be to blame for the illness that afflicted so many members of Gil's household? How else could I explain why, out of this entire valley, only those who had extended their hospitality to me had fallen ill?

First, the son Peren's wife had borne him shortly after our return had sickened and died. Next his wife had grown ill but recovered after Peren moved her and his little daughter, Lonna, to their new-built home. He'd urged me to come with them, but I'd refused. Unless I wed Flora, by valley custom she would have to remain in her brother's home. I was not ready to wed, but neither was I willing to leave her, especially when I learned that she was pregnant with our child.

When the illness struck Flora, I berated myself for not making her my bride. I tried to heal her by the power of my fascinum, as I had tried to heal Peren's child, but the amulet had no effect.

Hanna's children developed the sickness, and the fascinum again proved useless. I sent Gil off to fetch a healing woman he told me of.

Now I doubted that the woman would arrive in time or that, when she came, she would be able to dispel the curse resting on this house.

I snatched the staff and glared at the fiend. "Is this your doing, thing of evil?"

The wicked eyes stared back at me. I carried the stick from the room. The shaft was slick and smooth; the feel of it soothed me. I rotated it in my hands. In Flora's presence the power of the fiend had seemed credible. Away from her, I laughed at her fear. If the fiend were the cause of the plague, would the plague not first have struck me and Peren, Gil, Jed, and the other men who had handled it? The women and children always kept a wary distance. How could it afflict them?

But for Flora's peace of mind, I'd take the staff from the house.

In the common room Hanna's baby maintained its wailing. Jena fretted over the other children, coaxing them to drink the broth the infant had rejected.

Hanna looked up at me. "Flora …?"

"A bad dream," I shouted over the keening child. "The fever …"

"I'll go to her." Jena wiped the children's faces and got to her feet. "Maybe I can get her to take a little broth."

I nodded and crossed to the door. Something crunched under my boot. I looked down. Half-hidden by rushes, my fascinum lay crushed. With a muttered oath I bent and picked it up. One of Pathfinder's fragments had been forced from its setting. I gathered it and the charm into my palm and stared in dismay at the flattened piece of metal. Like a reproachful eye, the empty socket stared back.

I transferred the ruined fascinum and the bit of wood to the hand that held my walking stick. My free hand moved to open the pocket of my belt. The fascinum rubbed against the staff. A pain like the sting of a hundred scorpions shot into my arm. My fingers jerked open. I flung down staff and fascinum.

A tremor shook the house. Blackness engulfed me. I felt as though I was falling through a vast empty space. A vision flashed before my eyes. *A mountain. A temple. The mountain splits. The temple crumbles and slides into the new-formed chasm. The darkness returns.*

A face looms out of the darkness. Renata, laughing, eyes sparkling, hair blowing around her face. The hair bursts into flames, the flesh melts, a grinning skull leers at me, fades away.

Another face, white as frost, floats in the darkness, snowy hair billowing around it. Icy eyes chill me.

"Brinabeth," I moan. "I've failed."

The face recedes. Another takes its place. Purple face, eyes bulging, tongue protruding. Pik, as he'd looked when I'd strangled him.

"Forgive me," *I mutter.*

The face vanishes.

A fourth head bobs before me. Blood from a jagged wound on its crown pours down it, obscuring the features. The head recedes. As the darkness swallows it I recognize the bloody vision.

"Peren! No!"

As if defying my shout of denial, the face bobs in front of me. I cannot shut out the grisly sight.

"Lord Terral! What happened?"

Had the head spoken? I blinked. The bloody vision wavered. A face still peered into mine, but it was Jed's, not Peren's, a living face, unmarred by blood.

I was in the doorway to the common room! I had fallen to my hands and knees. Beyond my reach the staff lay where I'd flung it. Not far from it my fascinum gleamed among the rushes. Whatever had happened, only I had experienced the phenomenon. Hanna still crooned to her wailing infant, and the children still sprawled in the rushes. Jena apparently was in the loft with Flora.

Jed helped me stand. "I opened the door and your staff came flying toward me and you were on all fours groaning like something had attacked you. I thought you'd took sick like poor Flora."

I shook my head. Still dazed, I could only mumble, "The staff ..."

"I'll fetch it for you." Jed moved toward it.

I clutched his arm. "No. Let it be."

He frowned. "Better get you to a chair." He steered me toward the study. "Gil's on his way with the healer. I saw them coming down the rise and ran to tell you."

I stopped. "How soon?"

"Any moment now they should come in the door."

I pushed his arm away and returned to the common room. "I want to be here when they come."

"They're coming?" A note of hope in her tired voice, Hanna swayed to her feet and hugged her baby to her breast. Her daughter sat up, rubbed her eyes, and shook her sleeping brother. He stirred and moaned, but did not wake.

The door burst open. Gil stepped inside and held the door wide for his blue-cloaked companion. The woman entered and swept the hood back from her raven hair.

My mouth fell open. Forgetting my manners, I stared. "Lisha!"

Beneath quizzical brows deep blue eyes met my gaze.

Not Lisha. The woman looked older by perhaps ten years. Her skin was darker, her chin sharper, her face narrower. But the resemblance was startling.

"My name is Tredienne." High booted feet took a single step

forward and stopped. The woman scowled; her nose wrinkled. She extended her arms, spread her hands wide, and leaned forward as though pressing against an invisible barrier.

"Fool!" The epithet exploded from her pursed lips. Her fingers traced a warding sign in the air. She eased forward until she stood between the accursed staff and what was left of my fascinum. Her night-black hair stirred and twisted as though blown by a strong breeze.

Her arms lifted, arced gracefully above her head. Her fingers touched and formed a spire. Face taut with concentration, she issued directions between clenched teeth. "Take up one. Break the polarity."

My vision fluttered from fascinum to staff. "Which one?"

Her arms trembled. Veins bulged on her arched hands. Large beads of sweat appeared on her forehead. "Choose. Hurry!"

I stepped toward the fascinum, wavered, turned, and snatched up the staff. I carried it back toward Hanna. The healer's arms dropped limply to her sides. Gil pushed forward and supported the shaking healer. She leaned against his sturdy arm, but her gaze was directed at me. A blue flame seemed to burn in her eyes.

"That thing can destroy you if you don't know how to control it."

"He knows," Gil soothed, escorting Tredienne to a chair Jed brought from my study. "He is Lord Terral. I told you how he delivered our land, Dama Tredienne."

The healer sniffed. "It must have been chance." She continued to glare. "Maybe there's more to you than meets the eye, but I can't think how anyone clever enough to defeat the Labonites and enchain a Flux fiend could be stupid enough to keep the power staff in the same house with that channeler." She pointed at the crushed fascinum. "And how did you let it get into that condition?"

Embarrassed and ashamed, I mumbled, "An accident," and adding something about underestimating the power of the staff, I backed away.

"Where are you going? Get out of the house with that staff so I can secure the channeler and see to the sick."

Gil cast a worried glance at Hanna and her ailing child. The baby had ceased crying and lay limp in its mother's arms. Afraid it was already beyond treatment, I hurried past it with the fiendish staff and went out through the cookshed. I had hoped to be with Flora when the healer cared for her, but understood now that my presence would obstruct the healing.

I plodded to the barn, holding the staff at arm's length. If I could find an opportunity to talk to Tredienne in private, I'd muster the courage to confess my ignorance of the working of both staff and fascinum.

My fascinum. She'd talked of securing it. What could that mean? Could it be restored? If I could find Savnar ...

No. I'd be too ashamed to let him see how I'd misused his gift, first letting it combine with the fascinum honoring Molor, and then damaging it so carelessly.

I reached the barn and found Sunburst munching the sweet hay in his stall. He nickered and pranced about in evident pleasure to see me. The welcome cheered me. I patted his neck, raised the bar of the stall, and entered, holding the staff. He backed from me and snapped at the fiend.

"I know, you don't like the staff much better than Flora does. I wish I knew a safe way to get rid of the thing. Until I can discover one, it'll have to stay in here, so you'll have to put up with it." I placed the staff in the farthest corner from his stall.

I returned to him and patted his neck.

"Come on, friend. It's been too long since you've been exercised." I hoisted myself onto his back.

He snorted but bent to my will. We cantered off through the fields, a brisk autumn breeze at our backs. I took deep breaths of the hay-scented air, cleansing my lungs of the house's smell of impending death.

But the afternoon ride brought me no peace of mind and answered none of my questions. I'd hoped to find Peren working his fields, but he was not there. I inquired at his house, and his wife said he'd gone off without telling her where he was going or when he would return. Her discovery that he hadn't confided in me only added to her worry and increased my already hefty burden of guilt.

Men at work in their fields and gardens saluted me with deep respect as I rode by, and the thought of how little I merited that respect further darkened my mood. Day waned. Reluctantly I turned Sunburst back toward Gil's house.

A strong scent of fresh herbs greeted me. I entered the common room and found Hanna's older children playing a raucous game on a floor swept clean and bare of rushes. The babe slept quietly in a cradle. Steaming bowls of water strewn with aromatic herbs were set out on the floor in a hexagonal pattern.

Jena emerged from the cookshed carrying a kettle of hot water and an empty bucket. She beamed at me. "They're better."

Her words confirmed the testimony of my eyes. "Flora?"

"Also much better. Eating her dinner. And eager to see you."

"Where's the healer?"

"In there." She nodded toward the cookshed. "Grinding more herbs. All afternoon she's had Gil and Jed hauling water for cleaning and purifying and for boiling the herbs." She set the kettle on the floor, picked up a bowl, poured water from it into the bucket, and refilled it with the steaming water in her kettle. "Watch out, you two." She shooed the bouncing children away from the bowls. "Tomorrow, praise Molor, you'll be able to play outside."

"Peren's gone off somewhere," I said.

"He's restless, that one." Jena filled another bowl. "Always has been, but he's grown worse lately." She straightened from her task and faced me, hands on her hips. "Aren't you going up to Flora? Didn't you hear me tell you she was waiting to see you?"

I started toward the stairs.

"Try not to wake Hanna. She's asleep in the other room—exhausted, poor thing, after being up with the baby so many days. I told her I'd watch him for her, now he's quiet and his fever's gone. She's renamed him Treden in Tredienne's honor."

Treden—my successor and one of my distant predecessors. The lord line was established. Now if I only knew how to reach the other times where as Korth I had disrupted time's ordained flow.

Would I have to live out my life as Terral in this time and wait to be reborn as Korth? And would that birth still occur, after the chaos I'd brought to Medara's time and to Brid's? I entered the loft room so distracted by these questions that I returned Flora's joyous greeting with a light kiss on the cheek and a perfunctory embrace.

Her face fell. Her thin fingers plucked at the yellow quilt. "I've gotten ugly, haven't I?"

"No, Flora, no. The color is back in your face. I'm happy to see you better."

I kissed her again and chatted a bit about inconsequential things. But my paltry efforts only solidified the wall of distance between us, and after a bit of meaningless conversation I left her and wandered back downstairs where Jena was setting out the evening meal.

Though Flora's fever had dissipated, her recovery was slow. I explained her lingering weakness as being due to her advancing pregnancy, but in my heart I suspected the real cause was my neglect.

I persuaded Tredienne to stay with us to care for Flora. The healer's manner toward me had grown more deferential since our first encounter, and I gathered the courage to ask her what she had done with my fascinum.

"It's in a secure place. So long as you have the staff, that's all you need to know." She delivered the answer with such an air of finality that I dropped the subject.

I sat in the study reviewing with Master Nicor his regathered figures. The morning sun streamed through the triangular window and cast a wedge of light around us. I pushed aside the new ledger with its neat lists and rows of figures. "You've done excellent work, Master Nicor. I'm pleased with the prompt way all the farmers have paid their pledges."

"We've needed a leader and protector, Lord." The old man closed the ledger and gathered his ink jar and quills. "When you ride through the valley on your big red horse, there's not one among us whose heart doesn't swell with pride at such a lord."

Master Nicor's flattering words embarrassed me, and I was relieved when a knock on the door spared me from having to reply.

Jena stepped into the room. "Lord Terral, Peren's here and anxious to see you."

The scribe tucked his satchel under his arm. "I'd best be leaving."

I escorted him to the door of the study. In the common room Peren paced back and forth with long strides, like a caged mountain cat. His tunic was travel-stained, his boots caked with mud. He leaped forward when I appeared.

"Important news, Lord."

I drew him into the study and let Jena usher Master Nicor from the house. Peren leaned against the table. "I got word that a Labonite raiding party had entered the valley to the north. I knew how busy you were and how worried about Flora, so I went to check it out, figuring it was most likely just a rumor."

I opened my mouth to scold him for his foolhardiness, but he raised his hand. "Lord Terral, there *were* Labonites, but only a small group. They didn't see me. I sneaked right into their camp at night and listened to them talking. Lord, they're after the falas!"

"The falas!" He had my full attention. "The falas are gone."

"They talked about a system of caves high in the eastern mountains. They said they'd heard falas there in the past few days, and they were sure they could trap them."

I opened the study door. "I'll put on traveling clothes and get my sword. Have Gil bring Sunburst around. We'll leave within the hour."

"Be sure to carry your staff, Lord. It will show the Labonites your power."

23

FALAS

The eastern mountains loomed stark and forbidding above us. We scanned their sheer walls for a path. The jagged slopes reminded me of the temple mountain, but no golden temple graced the icy peaks.

I reined Sunburst to a halt and turned to Peren. "You're certain you can find this system of caves?"

Peren, seated awkwardly on a plodding dun plow-horse he'd borrowed from a neighbor, shaded his eyes and peered upward. Lines of weariness creased his face. I was sorry I hadn't made him rest before undertaking this journey. We got little sleep on the way. When we camped at night, one of us kept watch while the other slept, and at daybreak we set off again. I could have made the trip alone on Sunburst in a third of the time, but Clover, Peren's horse, was old and slow.

"The desert lice cover their tracks well." Peren twisted around to look back the way we'd come. "I'm sure the spot I showed you back there was the campsite where I heard them talking. They said they'd start their climb in the morning and reach the caves by early afternoon. So the path can't be far. It might be easier to find on foot." He shifted and winced. I guessed what toll the unaccustomed ride must be taking.

"You search on foot," I suggested. "I'll scout around on Sunburst."

He nodded and slid off his horse. Walking stiff-legged, one hand on his lower back, he led Clover to a clump of trees, tied him, shouldered his new morning star, and limped toward me with a rueful grin. "No part of me likes that horse. I'll feel better when I've moved around a bit on solid ground."

"I'll leave you to work the kinks out." I pressed my knees into Sunburst's side.

Sunburst broke into a gallop. He leaped easily over tumbled boulders and up a rocky escarpment, hooves scattering loose stones. I can't say how I kept my seat through these leaps except that I somehow anticipated those erratic moves and knew instinctively how to clasp the horse, how to lean, and how to balance myself to prevent being thrown. It was as though I had been riding this horse all my life.

I leaned forward over my staff. "We need to find another cave, Sunburst," I said, sure the horse could understand. "Not the cave through which we entered this time, but a cave where falas may have taken shelter."

He neither slackened nor quickened his pace, but ran off the escarpment, down a gully, up the other side, and on along the base of the mountain.

"Up, Sunburst. Go up!"

He ran on, following his own course. Was he using this means to remind me he was his own creature and did my bidding only when my will coincided with his?

I had grown overconfident in my horsemanship. I clung to

Sunburst's mane and cried out for him to stop, but the wind shredded my pleas and whipped them into the frigid stream of air that rushed past my quaking body. At this speed, we'd be past the mountains and on the banks of the River Rethe in moments. I pulled on the reins. "Whoa!" He flew on.

Desperate, I grabbed my staff, brought it around, and struck Sunburst in the flank.

His mane flared into fire. He reared and I crashed to the ground. My shoulder struck rock with bone-shattering force. If my head had taken that blow, I would have been killed. As it was, I lay stunned and gasping with pain. Through a gathering haze I saw two gigantic winged creatures, a flaming red horse and a black-winged fiend, locked in battle above me. Sparks cascaded from wings that were vast sheets of flame. Leathery wings like thin slices of night beat against the flames. An odor of burning flesh smothered me. The shadows of the end of the world fell over me.

I awoke to a flare of agony in my left shoulder and wondered that I was still alive. Groaning, I tried to move.

"Easy, Korth," a soft voice spoke in my ear.

"Derli?" I mumbled. I tried to sit.

Hands pushed me back. I squinted at the black-edged blur that filled my field of vision. Features swam into focus. A pair of sapphire eyes. Ivory skin. A pert chin. A nimbus of black hair that gleamed blue in the sunlight.

"Lisha!"

"Lie still, Korth." Her sharp voice was tinged with anger. "You took a nasty fall. Your collarbone's badly broken."

"How …? Where …?"

"Shhh. I've pressed the bone back into place and put a healing compress on your shoulder. I'm going to bind your arm to your chest so you can't move it. I'll have to turn you, and that's going to hurt."

She leaned close. I lifted my good arm and touched her hair, stroked her cheek. "You're real."

She gentled. "Of course." Her smile warmed me.

Her lily scent aroused me. My fingers slid to the back of her head and drew her face to mine. Our lips clung together.

Gently she disengaged herself. "Do behave, Korth. You're in grave danger." She slid her arms behind my back and shifted me onto my good side.

I yelped.

"Easy." She wound a strip of cloth around me. "You should have understood that Sunburst was keeping you away from the falas. They're a danger to you."

"Why?" I pulled myself up and twisted my neck to watch her. An explosion of pain knocked me flat. A wave of darkness washed over me.

The sound of tearing grass awoke me. I opened my eyes. Sunburst stood beside me, yanking up mouthfuls of grass and munching with lazy serenity.

"Zera?" I called. I caught myself. I'd meant to call out Lisha's name.

"Lisha," I yelled.

No answer.

It had been a dream, then. I struggled to sit up. Pain stabbed my left shoulder.

Beneath my awkwardly adjusted tunic, my left arm was bound tightly to my chest.

She *had* been here. "Lisha!"

Sunburst swished his tail and continued grazing.

I lay on a stony tongue that stretched from the mountain to lick a sloping meadow. On the edge of the stone slip, half-hidden by the encroaching grass, lay the staff. Astounded, I hitched myself nearer, reached for it, stopped, and glanced at Sunburst. The horse tended to his eating and paid no heed to what I was doing.

I picked up the staff. It felt no different. Except for its wicked, glittery eyes, the fiend was an inanimate carving, its claws sunk into the wooden shaft. Below the claws the smooth wood was cold to the touch. The vision of Sunburst and the fiend locked in battle had been a hallucination.

I set the staff against the stone and with its help hoisted myself to my feet. Unsteady and hurting, I needed the support. I hobbled toward Sunburst. He let me approach and demonstrated not the slightest concern for the staff.

Perhaps I'd only startled him into rearing and pitching me off when I'd struck him with it. But if my injury and pain had conjured up the vision of the battling figures, what about my bound arm and the memory of Lisha's lips pressed to mine?

"I wish you could talk, fellow," I said. "You could tell me whether it was Lisha here or someone else."

He raised his ears and gave a soft whinny that sounded almost like a laugh.

"I've got to get back to Peren, but I don't know how I'm going to mount."

Sunburst nuzzled my side and trotted into the field. Hidden by the high grasses was a rectangular mound nearly as high as Sunburst. Low steps were carved into one side, making it easy to climb with the aid of my staff. From its height I scanned the area again, searching for Lisha or any other person who might have tended my injury. I saw no one.

If I hadn't been dreaming, Lisha had said the falas were a danger to me. But the thought of Derli and all she'd done for me made me disregard that warning.

Leaning on the staff, I threw one leg over Sunburst's back and pushed myself upright on the horse. I placed the staff in front of me in the same crosswise position in which I had carried it before. Sunburst headed docilely off in the direction from which we'd come. All afternoon he kept to a slow, gentle pace, so that the return ride took many times longer but was easy on my aching body.

At dusk we reached the spot where I'd left Peren. Clover was still tied there, but I found no sign of my liegeman. I didn't want to shout and advertise my presence to any Labonites who might be hiding in the area, so I caught Sunburst's reins and guided him around fallen rocks and gullies.

We rounded a high outcropping of rock and Peren stepped out of a crevice. Startled, I nearly lost my balance, but Sunburst righted me with a twist of his body.

"Lord Terral, you're hurt!" Peren loped toward us. With his help I slid off with only twinges of pain.

"It's a long story," I told him when I'd got my footing. "I didn't find the cave entrance. Did you have better luck?"

"Yes." He pointed upward to what I took at first to be merely a dark shadow high on the graying slope. "We're not too late. The Labonites are still there. I haven't seen them, but as I scouted around I heard shouts and curses coming from above me, and when I looked up, I spotted that opening. I couldn't find a way to get up to it, so I settled into a niche to wait for you. I've been getting more and more worried about you." He eyed my bound shoulder and arm. "Who—?"

"I don't know." I led Sunburst into the crevice where Peren had been hiding and, knowing we could not attempt to reach the cave before morning, Peren and I squeezed in beside the horse. As night gathered about us, I told Peren about my wild ride and my fall. I omitted the part about the battling figures, convinced that the vision had been a dream, and I also omitted mention of Lisha, saying only that I had awakened from being knocked senseless to find my wounds cared for and my arm bound, but no trace of my mysterious benefactor.

"It's your staff, Lord. It's protecting you." I couldn't see Peren's face in the darkness, but his awestruck tone told me my tale had increased rather than diminished my stature in his eyes.

The cramped space within the crevice was warm with our body heat and thick with the smell of sweaty horse. Leaning against Sunburst, I grew drowsy and dozed off in that awkward position. A sweet, clear melody awakened me. Pure notes drifted into the niche, making it shimmer with crystalline sound.

Peren gripped my arm. "Do you hear it, Lord?" he asked in a breathless whisper. "It's not coming from outside. I went out to see. It's louder in here—like it's coming from farther back." He pushed against me, forcing me deeper into the niche. I grabbed my staff and edged toward the narrowing rear of the crevice. Sunburst trembled and gave a loud huff. A warning?

With Peren pressing close behind me, I squeezed between the walls of rock, terrified of becoming so tightly wedged that I'd be unable to free myself. The haunting music drew me like a lodestone; I could not go back.

My sword in its scabbard banged against the uneven stone walls. The sound echoed around us. When I tried to adjust the scabbard, it jammed in a crack. I worked to pry it loose. The effort drove waves of pain through my shoulder. I groaned; perspiration poured down me. The sword sprang loose, and my sweat-slick body popped through the tight place like a cork. I tumbled forward and sprawled full-length on the floor of a wide, upward-sloping cavern. Peren toppled in after me. I howled when his weight landed on my injured side. He rolled aside, stood, and with repeated apologies helped me to rise.

Groggy with pain, I slumped against him. But the music would not let either of us rest. Supported on one side by Peren and aided by my staff on the other, I tottered forward. We were no longer in total darkness. Veins of luminescence mapped the cave wall and provided a faint, eerie light. The tunnel or cavern spiraled upward like a circular ramp.

The music welled around us as other voices joined the first. Not even the agony in my shoulder could quench my eagerness to reach those bewitching singers.

I wound round the spiral, oblivious to everything but the music until I stumbled over something large. Jolted into a measure of awareness, I clutched at Peren, regained my balance, and strained in the dim light to see what lay in my path.

"It's one of the lice." Peren probed with the spikes of his morning star. "He's dead. Can't tell what killed him."

A memory stirred. "Danger," I mumbled. "Lisha warned me ..."

But Peren had already stepped around the corpse and headed on up the ramp. "That leaves only four," he called back. "They'll be no match for us."

He disappeared around the curve of the ramp. Thrusting my staff forward and pulling myself after it, I rounded the curve and slammed into his back. He caught me and kept me from falling.

"Look, Lord, another!" He pointed.

A second Labonite lay spread-eagled across our path. Peren bent toward the limp figure.

"This one's still alive." He raised his morning star. "I'll fix that in a hurry."

"No!" I stepped forward and extended my staff to block his blow.

He turned toward me, eyes wide.

"You can't kill a man while he's unconscious," I said.

"A Labonite?" Peren gasped. "It's like smashing a rat."

I poked him with the staff and prodded him away from the fallen man. He went, grumbling, "He'll kill us fast enough, if he gets the chance."

"I hope our standards are higher than his." As I spoke, I turned and nudged the Labonite with the fiend end of my staff.

The man shuddered, sat up, and stared wildly at us. Peren hefted his weapon, and I dropped my staff and grabbed for my sword. But the man let out a tortured shriek, his eyes rolled back in his head, and he crashed back to the cave floor.

Peren leaned over him. "He's dead."

I sheathed my sword and groped for my staff. It felt awkward, top-heavy. It fought my efforts to hold it upright. After each step I had to tug it back into vertical position.

The music summoned us on. I took the lead. We rounded the next bend. A third Labonite sprawled across our path, writhing and moaning. With only one hand, I could no longer control my staff. It tipped toward the Labonite. The fiend grinned down at him. Spasms contorted the desert man's body. His face twisted in agony, and his mouth foamed. I tried to pull the staff away. It was all I could do to hold it.

The Labonite went limp, and I didn't need Peren to tell me that this one, too, was dead.

"At this rate, we won't have to lift a finger against our enemies, Lord," Peren exulted. "No wonder you didn't want me to use my morning star." He chuckled. "Better to let *him* do the dirty work, eh?"

I stared aghast at Peren. He knew the source of the staff; he had experienced the fiend's power. How could he speak of it so casually? And however much he hated the Labonites, how could he so lightly dismiss their excruciating deaths?

But the music blotted out my concern. I grappled with the staff, wrestled it into an upright position, hefted it forward, moved abreast of it, thrust it forward again. My progress was slowed, not helped by the staff. I would have done better to let go of it, but my fingers locked around the shaft and resisted my half-hearted efforts to release my grip.

Peren had not waited for me, so I plucked my weary way onward and upward alone. My shoulder was a fiery lump of agony, my bound arm ached, my bruised body cried for rest. More than the music, which had grown fainter, my concern for Peren forced me to stagger on.

In a haze of pain and exhaustion I passed the fourth Labonite. He sat propped against the wall, a bloody corpse. His bashed head bore the unmistakable imprint of spikes. I shouted Peren's name. My own voice echoed around me, my only reply.

The music ceased. I tugged at the staff. It wouldn't budge. I tried to let go of it. My fingers wouldn't move. I was stuck!

And the fiend unfurled its wings. It flew, dragging me helplessly behind it. I kept trying to take my hands from the staff, but I could not. The fiend's wings clattered upward around the spiraling tunnel. My arms felt yanked from their sockets. My heels scraped against the rock ramp. I let out a scream each time my body slammed against the rocks, first on one side and then the other.

We came out into a wider place. The creature soared upward

toward a high, rocky ceiling. It swooped downward. My fingers unlocked and released the shaft. I fell onto level ground. Dizzy, bruised, aching, I lay still, afraid to try to rise.

"Help me, Lord Terral!" Peren's voice.

I shook my dazed head to clear it.

"Yes, help him, Lord." Another voice. Cold, sarcastic. Koralie's?

"Help me, Korth." The soft plea in Renata's sweet voice tore my heart.

Painfully I managed to sit up, gritting my teeth to keep from crying out. I was in the middle of a large, circular chamber illuminated by the eerie green glow of the luminescent rock walls. Near me, Peren battled to free himself from the talons of the fiend. I staggered to my feet and drew my sword. The familiar feel of its carved hilt gave me courage.

I charged. My awkward sword thrust stabbed the air. The fiend whirled and slammed me onto my back. There I lay, helpless and clumsy as an overturned beetle, legs flailing the air, sword waving in a feeble attempt to defend myself.

"Korth, I can help you. Just swear to serve me." Chilled, I jerked my head toward the sound of that voice. In her purple gown the young Koralie stood against the cave wall, her hands stretched toward me.

"You don't need her help," a voice said. Certain it was Lisha's, I turned my head and gazed around the cavern but saw only Koralie.

"Come to me!" The impatient toss of her head sent her black curls flying. "Don't be a fool, Korth. I have the power you need."

"She's lying," came Lisha's voice again. "You don't need her kind of power. Discover who you are."

I stopped, torn between Lisha and Koralie.

"Beware!" Koralie shouted

The warning drove my attention back to the Flux fiend. The creature loomed larger than ever. With Peren tucked under its arm, it hopped toward me. Its shadow fell over me, blotting out the light. I stabbed upward. My sword raked across tough hide. Drops of stinking slime spattered my hand. The fiend shrieked and leaped back.

My hand burned where the creature's noxious ichor had spotted it. I staggered to my feet, backed toward the wall, and circled, watching for an opportunity to attack. The fiend turned too, keeping its wicked eyes fixed on my sword. The scratch I'd given it must have made it wary.

"Korth, accept my help," came Koralie's urgent whisper.

But the fiend had my full attention. It set Peren on his feet. Peren's head lolled; his morning star dangled limply from his hands.

The demon's beaked mouth opened wide. With a harsh hiss he blew on Peren. I smelled his fetid breath.

Peren lifted his head. His shoulders straightened; he raised his morning star. Eyes vacant, he tottered straight toward me.

"Peren," I called. "What …?"

He swung the spiked club at my head. I parried the blow with my sword. "Wake up, Peren. Don't do this!"

"Take care, Korth!"

Lisha's shout alerted me to the fiend circling nearer my injured side. I swung toward him. Peren lifted the morning star over his head. I spun away from the fiend and raised my sword to ward off Peren's blow.

The fiend pounced. Its talons raked my injured shoulder. I let out a howl and slashed blindly with my sword. The blade wedged into something hard. I jerked it free and hacked at the fiend. It jumped back.

I sagged against the wall and looked to see what had become of Peren.

He lay in a bloody heap, his skull split open.

"Peren!" I dropped my sword and from his lifeless hands I took the mace. With a scream of rage I swung toward the fiend. It froze. For the second time I buried a morning star in its throat.

With a loud hiss the fiend folded its wings about itself. I blinked. Again I held a carved fiend on a staff.

"Give it to me, Korth."

Koralie leaned against the invisible front of her cubicle. "Give it to me," she repeated, her eyes boring into mine. "In exchange I'll free your friend Derli."

Staff in hand, I walked slowly toward Koralie.

"Only Makor's sword can set Derli free," Lisha's voice called.

Koralie frowned. "The staff, Korth."

It tipped toward her. She grasped it and wrenched it from my hand.

A thunderclap shook the mountain. Koralie vanished. My empty hand rubbed the rough and clammy rock she'd stood against. My fingers traced the veins of luminescence. Finally, I wandered disconsolately into the center of the chamber.

What I had seen could not have been real. Yet I *had* lost my staff.

My sword lay beside Peren's corpse. I ran and snatched it up. The sudden movement thrust a stab of pain through my injured shoulder. I stood still, waiting for it to subside. "How I need you with me now, dear friend," I murmured, choking back tears. I stared down at Peren's ravaged face. "If that accursed fiend had not bewitched you ..."

A voice began an angry and mournful song. Other voices joined the first. The words were in a language I could not understand, yet they evoked images of familiar scenes: Peren leading a handful of men against a Labonite force five times as great. Peren fighting desperately to save the falas' grove. Peren attacking the Flux fiend while I groveled in frozen helplessness. Peren leading the valley in declaring me lord.

I knelt beside him. "I was no less bewitched than you, and you paid the price for my folly." I dragged his body to the center of the chamber, laid it straight, arms at the sides, and smoothed his clothes. As best I could, I cleaned the blood from his face with the sleeve of my shirt. Finally, for no reason I understood, I touched the hilt of my sword to his lips.

Again the invisible singers broke into mournful song. I bowed my head and wept.

The dirge ended. I stood, wiped my eyes, and sheathed the sword in its scabbard. Then I spoke to the invisible singers. "You know Peren was your friend and defender. Accept me, too. And if you know where Derli is, please take me to her."

With no transition I stood amid dense foliage. The air, hot and heavy, pressed in on me; I gasped for breath.

Near me a striped lizard basked on a wide silver-green leaf. Large flying insects buzzed around a plant with spiky white flowers smelling of carrion. An insect landed on the pale petals; the spikes snapped shut, trapping it. A small snake slithered across my boot top and disappeared into a thicket. I shuddered. Where was this place, and how did I come here?

Something brushed my head. I jumped, heart pounding. But it was only a vine that, hanging from the thick canopy above and swaying in the moist breeze, had tangled in my hair.

A large scarlet bird darted from the canopy and stabbed my head with its beak. I yelled and drew my sword.

Another bird, a brilliant blue, swooped down. I ran, crashing through brush and dodging vines and tree roots. Shielding my head with my arm, I stumbled forward and skidded in a mud slick. My feet flew out from under me, and I landed on my back in the mud, my dropped sword lying out of reach.

Just as they had in the dream I'd had after being poisoned by the nezzi bite in the time of Mett and Medara, a feathered swarm descended, shrieking.

24

GODDESS

Beaks and talons tore my flesh. I threw my good arm across my eyes to protect them and kicked my legs to ward off the birds. They flew screeching into the air, giving me seconds to sit up before they attacked again.

And attack they did! I let out a yell when a beak stabbed my shoulder. That yell and my flailing arm chased them away. They regrouped for a fresh assault. I used the brief respite to scoot on my rear through the mud to reclaim my sword. The birds renewed their attack. I waved the sword at them, but there was no space to swing it freely. Securing its hilt under my bandaged arm, I managed with my other hand to grab a stout limb and haul myself to my feet.

Now I could use the sword a little more easily, aiming to strike the birds when they darted in close. I hit a couple but managed only to slice feathers off their long tails. My few successful strikes roused the others to greater fury. If only I had Peren beside me with his morning star.

Peren! A pang of grief made me hesitate. A bird darted in and jabbed my cheek. A finger-width higher and my hesitation would have cost me an eye.

It occurred to me to turn the sword broadside to swat the birds rather than trying to skewer them. It worked! I got in more strikes and drove off more birds. But there were so many, and they kept coming despite all I did.

I had to find shelter. I spotted a place where the foliage was thicker and headed for it. I fought my way into it, fending off the birds as I did so. Their attack was hindered by the clusters of small branches, but my progress was equally hindered, and my sword got in my way more than it helped. I cut away some of the thorny branches, but chopping larger limbs might dull the blade to the point of uselessness, and anyway I would have needed both arms for that labor. Already bleeding from the stabs of beaks and talons, I became bloodier still, scratched by twigs and raked by thorns. And all the while the birds shrieked their rage and battered at the thicket in their attempts to reach me.

Shielding my face with my arm, I could scarcely see where I was going. Unexpectedly I burst out into a clearing where I offered easy prey for my feathered attackers. By the short time it took to retreat back to the thicket, I was bleeding from several fresh wounds and cursing the birds in yells bordering on hysteria.

Protected from the birds but not from the thorns, I calmed enough to gaze out into the clearing, looking for some avenue of escape.

There! On the opposite side of the clearing—a building!

A building in this jungle? I stared, unbelieving. Was I hallucinating? I wiped from my eyes the blood or sweat that had obscured my vision. What I saw was indeed a building, but in ruins.

And not just any building.

Its façade, almost obscured by vines, matched that of the temple painted on one side of Lisha's screen, the temple I'd seen in my delirium-inspired dream. I remembered its scarred wooden doors. I rejoiced to see those doors still standing. *But in my dream they'd been locked!* I'd battered them down. I'd do that now if I had to. I couldn't stay where I was. I had to have shelter, and that meant that I had to get across the clearing. Should I wait until dark? I had no idea whether time ran the same here as it had in the Manor Lands. I had no idea, in fact, where "here" was. This whole thing could be a hallucination if it were not for the blood and the burning and stinging of all the jabs and stabs and scratches I'd suffered.

I felt I'd not only find shelter in the temple but perhaps answers as well. Perhaps I would find Lisha here—or Zera. Lisha—or the goddess—could explain why I was being sent back and forth through time and could keep me from causing more deaths as I had caused Peren's.

I extricated myself from the thicket and raced across the clearing, waving my sword to beat off the birds.

Suffering only a few more stabs from sharp beaks, I reached the door. Locked! But the hinges were rusted, the wood that held them rotted. With my sword I easily pried the door free of its hinges and swung it inward. I stepped inside and propped the door closed so the birds couldn't follow.

I was safe! I stood still, catching my breath and giving my eyes time to adjust. Although the sun was shining brightly outside, only a little light penetrated the temple's murky interior.

I was in an antechamber. A plain wooden bench along one side held a couple of stubby candles, but I had no way to light them. I went through the open doorway into the next room and found it less dim.

Apparently the central room of the temple, it was littered with broken statuary. Light came through chinks in the walls and a gaping hole in the roof. I picked my way through the debris and rushed to the one statue still standing.

"Lisha!" I shouted and embraced the stone feet.

In my fever dream the statue had warmed, become alive. But now the feet remained hard and cold. And when I looked up into the carved face, the features remained impassive, the painted eyes stared, unseeing.

I straightened and looked more closely. It did resemble Lisha, but there would be no reason for this ancient temple to hold a statue of the fascinator's daughter. This was a statue of the goddess Zera.

Regretfully I turned away to explore the temple. I hoped to find a time channel through which I could return to—*where?* My own time? Terral's? Brid's? Medara's? The discovery that the temple was real and its ruinous state no figment of my dreams fed my desire to find a way of undoing the damage I'd done in each of those times.

Small side chambers opened off the central one. The light in these was far dimmer, but enough to see that these rooms were bare, walls stripped of hangings, furnishings long since removed. A narrow spiral staircase rose on one side of the temple, its steps warped. Otherwise the stairway seemed sound. With dwindling hope I went up it to a round room in what must be the temple's dome.

The chamber was bare except for dirt and debris blown in by the wind through a gaping hole where the wall had been breached and a panel of the dome's golden overlay had been ripped away. Bright sunlight spilled through the opening. Tangles of cut threads lay trampled among the leaves, dirt, and twigs littering the floor. The sight jogged my memory of seeing through Divian's eyes the old woman spinning in the tower room of that temple. She must have been Uta, mother of the goddess Zera! But if she had been here too, she had departed long ago.

I peered through the gap and found easy access to the temple roof. I stepped partway out, but a flash of vermilion warned me to jump back inside, away from the waiting birds.

I crossed back through the desolate chamber and groped my way down the stairs and back to the central sanctuary. I walked around the statue, meaning to examine it more closely, but behind it I discovered a door so hidden in shadow that I had not noticed it before.

Through it I entered a small room that at first glance looked empty, like all the others. Then in a dim corner I spotted a metal tripod supporting a vertical rod topped with a hook from which some sort of cage dangled. Using one hand, I dragged the contraption to the doorway, where I saw that the hook held a birdcage, tarnished and dirty. On the bottom lay a bird like those that had attacked me. Its eyes were shut and its feathers matted. Dead, surely.

Its beak opened and it gasped. Somehow it still lived.

Its gasps and the fact that its cage and the statue of Zera were the only objects in the temple that seemed to have escaped the worst ravages of time aroused my curiosity. Wanting a closer look, with some effort I carried the cage and the stand it hung from into the central chamber near an opening that provided light.

The cage had no door that I could find and held no food or water. Its bars were too close together to allow the bird to escape. It was clearly near death. I drew my sword, intending to put it through the bars and end the creature's misery. It opened one eye and peered up at me as if in silent appeal. I lowered the sword.

I had no reason to feel sorry for it. Its green feathers and long tail told me it was the same kind as those that had so viciously attacked me. Yet its plight reminded me of my own—trapped here with no apparent means of escape. Like the bird, I had no food or water. The jungle outside might provide both, but the wild relatives of this poor creature were probably waiting to attack me when I left the temple.

With a feeling of hopelessness I left the cage and its pitiful occupant and wandered again around the central chamber. Next to a chink in the outer wall I spied something red. A closer examination revealed a vine that had inserted itself through the crack. From the vine a hung cluster of red berries. They weren't of any variety I recognized and might, for all I knew, be poisonous, but they looked so good and juicy that my mouth watered.

I plucked the cluster and picked one berry. I was about to pop it into my mouth when it occurred to me to test it on the dying bird. If it was poisonous, it would end the bird's suffering, but if the bird revived a bit, I would know the berries were safe.

I carried my prize to the cage, held the berry between my index and middle fingers, and poked them between the bars, which were far enough apart to let me reach the bird but close enough that the bird could not escape. I squeezed the berry so the juice ran into the bird's beak. I stroked its throat until it swallowed. It opened its eyes.

I took another berry and repeated the process, watching for any sign of poisoning. Instead I saw the bird raise its head, and when I put before it the berries I had squeezed, it pecked at the pulp. Moments later it wobbled onto its feet.

"You're a fighter, you are. Maybe you'll make it after all." I gave it a third berry, and after regarding it solemnly, the bird ate it without my help.

I still had over half the berries on the cluster. I ate them—a poor supper, but better than nothing. Soon I would have to find something more substantial.

For now, though, I had to stay here. Light was growing dimmer; the sun had sunk low. It would soon be night and completely dark. I wanted desperately to clean my wounds, but I had no way of doing so. I might as well find a place to settle down and get as much sleep as I could. I was weary and in as much need of rest as I was of food and water. The temple offered shelter but no comforts. I could only find a spot in a side room clear of debris, brush off the floor a bit, and curl up to sleep as best I could on cold stone.

I slept soundly despite the pain in my shoulder, a measure of how exhausted I had been. A loud squawking awakened me, and I sat up in alarm, sure the birds were attacking again.

It was only the caged bird, loudly demanding attention. Hungry again, I supposed.

"You'll have to wait," I told it. "I'm hungry, too, but there's nothing to eat in here. I've got to venture outside, with no guarantee that I'll find anything."

The bird cocked its head as though listening but then resumed its squawking. As much to get away from the noise as to take care of my own needs, I arose, girded on my sword, and ventured outside.

I stopped just clear of the door, looked around, and listened. The jungle was relatively quiet. Soft rustles in the undergrowth probably marked the passage of lizards, snakes, or other small animals. Birds sang in the trees, but I heard no screeches or squawks and caught no sight of my tormentors.

Cautiously I skirted the building and hunted for more of the vine that had provided the berries the bird and I had eaten last night. It proved easy to find, for it covered a large portion of the temple's outer wall. I plucked several clusters of berries and returned inside with my prize.

The bird seemed as pleased as I was. I dropped several berries through the bars into the cage, and it ate greedily, crushing them in its beak, which was soon stained red from the juice. I was reminded of the birds yesterday, their beaks stained with my blood.

To banish that memory I said, "I wonder how you got here, bird. There would be so much you could tell me if only you could talk."

I studied the cage more closely than I had yesterday and confirmed the absence of a door. I couldn't imagine how the bird had been placed in the cage, much less how to get it out. The temple had clearly been abandoned long ago—perhaps hundreds of years ago. The cage looked quite old, but the bird within could not have been captive more than a few days. How had it come here? Who had put it here and why? Another puzzle to add to the many that vexed me.

I sat on the floor to eat my portion of berries and review the dreamlike events that had led to Peren's tragic death by my own sword. I considered all that had happened since I accompanied him on that fatal expedition. I'd been buffeted about by every wind of chance—or of someone's design. The chain of events that began when I performed the rite of Lord's-Kill had to have some meaning, to follow someone's plan. Someone was manipulating me, some force whose identity I needed to discover. Until I knew who was behind it, none of what had happened could make sense.

Now I had the opportunity to reflect and try to solve the puzzle. I considered the possibility that I'd been sent here for that very purpose. I'd been transported here immediately after begging the falas to take me to Derli. Could Derli be here?

"Derli!" I shouted. "Derli, if you can hear me, please speak."

A loud squawk answered. The bird had finished its berries and was demanding more.

I got to my feet. "I'll explore a bit if your friends will let me," I told it. "I'll try to find us something more than berries."

I went back outside and looked around for the birds. Seeing none, I crossed the clearing and reentered the jungle. Here I heard occasional birdcalls and saw flashes of color high in the trees, but nothing attacked me. I found a brook where at last I could drink my fill and wash. The water was not deep and ran so clear that the bottom was fully visible.

Seeing nothing but small fish that posed no threat, I stripped off my clothes and stepped into the water, splashed it over me, and cleaned off the dried blood and grime.

Greatly refreshed, I left the stream and dressed. Next I turned to a task I had neglected far too long. I knelt on the stream bank, scooped up sand, and scoured and polished my sword, a slow job with only one hand. Though I paused often to scan the sky and trees for birds, I glimpsed none and heard only an occasional squawk from the branches overhanging the clearing.

With my gleaming sword replaced in its scabbard, I resumed my search for food. Small animals I couldn't identify scurried away at my approach. If I had to stay in this jungle much longer, I'd devise some sort of snare to catch them for food. For now I was satisfied to find nuts, wild grapes, and tender greens. I wrapped my findings in large leaves I cut from a vine. I was ready to return to the temple, but in which direction should I go? I'd wandered around too much to be able to retrace my steps.

I found my way back to the stream, more by accident than design, and followed it in hope of recovering my trail. Otherwise I might wander around for days.

I stopped to rest and settle on a bearing. With their loud cries and sharp beaks, the birds swooped on me. I leaped up and ran, dodging them as best I could.

The attack was not as vicious as before. After some moments I realized they were herding me in a particular direction, not trying to kill me. Perhaps that had been their intention yesterday as well, and it was my lack of understanding that earned me the stabs of beaks and jabs of talons. After all, they had led me to the clearing that brought me to the temple.

And so they did once again. I kept moving on the course that brought the fewest attacks, and I came out in the clearing before the temple. Carrying the food I'd gathered, I hurried to the door, pushed it open with my foot, and went inside.

The bird squawked a greeting, whether to me or to its friends outside I didn't know. I rewarded it with wild grapes.

"I need a name for you," I told it. I considered while the bird gobbled the grapes. I didn't know its sex, but for some reason I felt it was female. "I'll call you Minna," I decided, using the first name that popped into my mind.

She fluffed her feathers and cocked her head, and I imagined the naming pleased her.

I rested from my tramp through the jungle, enjoyed the food I'd found, and explored the temple a bit more but found nothing new. Remembering my dream, I decided to repair the door. I had no tools, so it was impossible to do the job properly, but using a stone from the debris as a hammer, I pounded the metal hinges back into shape and used long thorns as nails to fasten them onto the wooden jamb, hammering the hard thorns into the soft wood. The work was difficult, given the condition of the wood and the lack of better tools. And of course, the pain of my broken collarbone, which was healing but still protested any excess movement. I hoped the result of my efforts would please the goddess and induce her to end my exile here.

I crossed back through the desolate chamber, where I sat on the pedestal and leaned my head against the statue's legs.

"Lisha, or Zera, or whoever you are, I need your help." I spoke aloud not to the statue, but to the empty room. "Some power, maybe yours, brought me here, and I find only ruins. Reveal yourself as you promised, and as you did in my dreams."

The chirp of a cricket and the soft rustle of a dry leaf stirred by a vagrant breath of air were my only answers.

I looked up at the delicate features, obscured by dirt and veiled by spiderwebs. "Maybe if I clean you off, you'll hear my pleas." With my hand I rubbed the sticky webs off her legs and skirt, as far as I could reach.

I hunted around the temple walls for bits of stone and logs with which to construct a rough platform. What I found I dragged inside with my one good arm. It took some time, but I succeeded in piling my finds into a rickety stepped platform.

I climbed onto the flimsy perch and with the help of large, sturdy leaves, I finished wiping and polishing the statue. I stepped down and surveyed the results.

"You still need a good scrubbing," I said to the empty gray eyes. "But you look a little less neglected."

The stone statue remained cold and senseless.

I glanced around the room. "Maybe if I clean your surroundings, too."

In the days and weeks that followed I chopped and pried out the vines that tore at the outer walls. After my shoulder healed enough to allow me to set both hands to the work, I enjoyed the labor. I fell easily into the daily routine of hard toil. Each night I tumbled onto my bed of leaves exhausted and fell into dreamless sleep.

On my food-hunting expeditions I found a plant with a stiff, bristly stem excellent for scouring; a tree whose bark could be peeled off in long strips and used as polishing cloths; and berries that, crushed and put in water, formed an excellent cleaning agent.

One morning as I slipped the tray out from Minna's cage to clean it I decided to polish the stand from which the cage hung. It suffered from years of neglect, and must have been here long before the cage was hung from it and its occupant left to die. It took me all the morning hours to clean and polish it until it gleamed, and the intricate carving that graced it was at last fully revealed.

With the tip of my fingers I traced the raised engraving. I drew my sword and compared the design on its hilt with that of the stand. The delicately carved lilies on both were identical and had to have been the work of the same artist. I remembered the mummified body in the cave that led to the time of the first Lord Terral. I'd taken the sword from that corpse with a face so like my own.

That recollection coupled with the discovery I'd just made sent shivers down my spine as possible yet improbable explanations occurred to me.

I continued to ponder these possibilities as I renewed my efforts to clean and repair the temple. I shoveled and scraped the temple floors free of their carpet of leaves and broken stones, swept and scrubbed the side chambers. The goddess, freshly washed, presided over the renewed sanctuary with serene air. The cleaning had revived the faded color painted on the stone. The eyes I'd thought gray gleamed a bright blue, so lifelike that each time I happened to glance at them, I quickly dropped my gaze.

I discovered, concealed under the lichens, moss, and layers of grime on the sanctuary walls, life-sized murals painted originally in bright colors. With care I washed off the dirt, scraped away the moss, and exposed the paintings. The years and the jungle mold had destroyed large sections and left only tantalizing fragments.

I stared at the scene on the west wall. In a flaming meadow a black-clad figure, its face obliterated, stood on a rectangular mound and juggled globes of fire. It reminded me of the juggler who'd tormented me so. Could he possibly be the subject of this ancient painting?

The next section of the mural was badly damaged. A red horse leaped from the flames around the meadow, but mold covered most of the horse's body and the entire rider except one arm, which extended forward and brandished a sword. I drew my sword and held it against the painting. Painted sword and real one were identical. And I was certain that the horse was Sunburst.

More than ever I wanted to see the figure on the horse, but the fungi had eaten away the painted surface so that no amount of washing and scraping could restore it. Gone, too, was whatever enemy the horsed figure charged. I guessed it might have been the winged fiend.

Past the blighted section a familiar face looked eagerly toward the charging horseman. In a full red skirt Lisha or Zera smiled and offered a stalk of lilies either to the horseman or to some other figure now lost.

The back wall, behind the statue, was decorated with a repeating pattern of birds and crisscrossing vines. Some of the birds flew free and others were in cages, but all were like the jungle birds. The cages in the painting hung from branches, but they were identical to Minna's cage.

The scene on the east wall, though pocked with gaps, was more complete than that on the west. An old woman sat spinning. The threads she spun gathered into a net, which was flung out in a vast circle against a starry sky of dark blue. Beneath the net, about to be caught in its descending folds, a figure bathed in golden light stood with arms outstretched toward a smiling, red-gowned woman—Lisha— or the goddess Zera. I couldn't see the golden one's face, but I didn't need to.

The scenes roused within me peculiar emotions I didn't fully understand. That last scene moved me most of all. I sat on the floor in the sanctuary and stared at the paintings until the light faded. Night had fallen.

I closed and barred the front doors and retired to my makeshift bed. Through the night while I listened to the muttering of the old building and the angry clamor of the jungle outside its walls, I considered the additional mysteries I had uncovered. I slept little, but by morning I'd pieced my discoveries together into a terrifying theory.

Though the murals were badly damaged, I recognized fragments of the story they told. It was the familiar tale of Makor and Molor. It had to be Makor who rode the flame-red horse. And that horse could be none other than Sunburst! He had been Makor's horse, as immortal as Makor should have been. And now that horse was mine.

The sword held by the rider of that horse was identical to the one I'd taken from the corpse in the cavern. The corpse to which Sunburst had led me.

I recalled now what I had gleaned from the lad Divian's mind—his desire to find the place where Zera had hidden Makor's body. What was his wish? To go to the … the Mountains of Dawn! That was it! That was where he'd been told the goddess had hidden her consort's corpse.

And I had found that corpse in a high mountain cave. I hadn't heard those mountains called the Mountains of Dawn. I only knew them as the eastern mountains. Dawn came in the east. It fit! The corpse had to have been Makor's!

And his face was like mine. The device on his sword was the same as the device on my fascinum. Why had Savnar, the fascinator, carved that device into the fascinum he made for me?

It had to be at Lisha's prompting. Lisha's face was Zera's. She'd been an avatar of the goddess. And—if it had not been a dream—I'd dared to kiss her when she came to care for my broken collarbone. She had allowed that kiss!

I'd sensed a presence in my mind, a presence that was *not* one of the old lords. I was being bounced from time to time, and the presence in my mind was growing stronger with each visit to another time. That presence could be Makor if the goddess was using me to recreate her lost mate.

But no, it couldn't be. Why would she use a slave?

Yet … I'd come a long way since fleeing the longhouse. A slave no longer, I had knowledge and abilities no slave possessed. That did not make me a god.

But so much fit: My horse. My sword. My fascinum. The corpse in that cave. These murals. What could they mean but that Zera intended me to become Makor?

From the tales told by the fire in the longhouse I recalled the legend that Molor had divided Makor's essence into seven parts and had strewn them through time to prevent his resurrection. I had been thrown from my own time to several others. Could I have been sent to gather those parts?

Still, not all that had happened to me was explained by this theory. The juggler. The Flux fiend on the staff that was now Koralie's. And Koralie herself. She'd denied me the deathright. I should have been made Manor Lord after killing the aged Lord Brid. If I had, I would not have gone back in time, would not have begun the lord line.

There was a paradox! Was Koralie allied with Zera? I could not believe it. Koralie acted only in her own self-interest.

Koralie had to be defeated! That was my goal, not to be a god. Especially not a god who caged the falas.

I wanted to find Derli, return to my own time, and confront Koralie. I resolved to defeat her and claim the deathright. To claim my rightful place as Lord of the Manor, as Korth Lord Terral.

I would *not* lose myself to Makor.

With this new resolve fixed in my mind, just before dawn I fell at last into a troubled sleep.

Minna's scolding chatter woke me. I opened my eyes to bright sunlight pouring through the cracks in the walls and streaking the sanctuary. In her cage Minna hopped up and down, squawking. She must be hungry, but after my night's deliberations I had other matters on my mind.

I ignored the noisy bird and went to stand before the goddess's statue, one hand on the hilt of my sword. "Zera, I want answers," I shouted. "Only you could be responsible for all that's happened to me. I demand to know your intention."

The aura of light around the statue's face grew brighter. I hoped that meant I was about to receive the answers I required. But Minna's screeches grew louder and more frantic. She flopped around, shrieking and jabbing the air with her beak. And the light around the statue's head faded.

Frustrated and furious, I dashed toward the birdcage and slashed it with my sword. The blade passed through the bars as though they were wax. Minna leaped up over the swinging blade and darted out of the opening it carved. Talons extended, she flew straight for my face.

I jumped back and my sword arced upward. The sharp edge cleaved Minna's body in half. The grisly pieces splattered against my chest. My blade halted just short of slicing into my forehead.

I swung the sword downward, buried its point in the wooden floor, and leaned, panting and gasping, on the hilt. I hadn't meant to kill her, only deflect her attack.

"No time left, Korth. Hurry! We've got to get out of here."

I snapped up at the familiar voice. "Derli! Where—?"

"Hurry, I tell you."

The temple quaked. Its walls trembled. I yanked my sword from the floor. Derli shouted, "Up the stairs, Korth! Hurry!"

A red haze filled the temple. The ground shook. I glanced around. With a clap of thunder the stone statue of the goddess stepped off its pedestal.

Zera's eyes were blue flames, her raven hair spread out like black smoke.

"Move!" Derli's urgent command pushed me forward a few steps.

"Halt, Korth!"

At the goddess' command I stopped and turned.

Zera took a step forward. The temple rocked.

"Come on, Korth," Derli urged. "Now!"

But I had business with the goddess. "Tell me why you brought me here, Zera," I said, standing my ground. "Tell me who I am."

"I'll tell you nothing until you deliver the fala to me." Zera's voice filled the temple.

"Please, Korth. She'll kill me." Derli's frightened whisper in my ear moved me more than her shouts. I backed away from the goddess.

"Do you flaunt my wishes?"

The temple shook. Stones fell from the walls.

I sped for the circular stair to the tower room, but halted at its base. "We'll be trapped," I panted.

"Maybe not, if we make it to the top." Derli's voice came from the stairway above me. "Run!"

I glanced behind me. Bathed in a red glow, face full of fury, the goddess advanced.

"Do you desert me for a fala?" The angry words set the air ablaze.

Sizzling air scorched my back. I leaped up the stairs.

"You have failed me," Zera shouted after me. "Now you can only be Korth. A slave."

Her words stung, but I kept going. The steps crumbled behind me. At dizzying speed I tore around the spiral. The disintegrating steps threatened to topple me.

"Jump, Korth!" Derli called.

I vaulted into the tower room. In the pale light a misty figure sat spinning. A phantom hand tossed me a single thread. I clutched the gossamer strand and felt the building shudder.

A green luminescence replaced the red glow. Damp chill replaced the heat. An odor of decay made me wrinkle my nose and look down. At my feet lay Peren's corpse, shrunken and desiccated. I'd returned to the cave where I'd fought the fiend. A wave of nausea swept over me.

"Don't look at him," Derli urged. "He lies in an honorable place. Come, I'll lead you out." She began to hum a soft, comforting melody.

Numbly I followed her voice. I had defied Zera, though I now understood that she'd been molding me, gathering Makor's essence within me. Now I'd earned her wrath. I could have stayed and tried to appease her, but I'd made my decision.

I'd resolved to remain Korth, and now I certainly would. The act that had set Derli free had sealed my fate. I didn't regret it. Zera would be a powerful enemy, but in Derli I had a protector. I had to trust her: nothing else was left to me.

Gradually her song eased my mind, drove out my misgivings.

We wound through the descending chambers, past the skeletons of the dead Labonites, through the spiraling passage. I adjusted my sword and squeezed through the narrow channel into the crevice where I'd left Sunburst.

He was standing motionless as a statue. With an anguished cry I rushed to his side.

He swished his tail, raised his head, and gave a whinny of greeting.

"You're alive! You're all right! You waited for me!" My words tumbled out in a glad cascade. I might no longer be on the course to become Makor, but I still had Makor's horse.

Sunburst pranced in place as if in answer. I grasped his reins and backed him from the niche. I led him to the place we had tethered Peren's horse. The rope was broken and Clover was gone. I hoped he'd freed himself and found his way home.

I mounted Sunburst. "Can you ride with me?" I asked Derli.

"No need," she said. "Don't worry. I know where you're going. I'll meet you there."

25

DERLI EXPLAINS

I reined Sunburst to a halt before Gil's farmhouse and combed my fingers through my hair, grown long during my stay in the jungle and now tangled and blown from the thought-swift ride. Sunburst gave a loud neigh.

Hanna's children burst from the door. "You're back!" They danced around me, shouting, "Lord Terral's back. He's home."

So despite Zera's final warning I was still "Lord Terral."

Hanna bustled out. "Lord Terral, we've been frantic with worry these three months." She dropped to her knees and clasped my hand. "We'd given up ever seeing you again—or Peren." She looked around, clearly expecting to see my liegeman following me, and added more hesitantly, "We decided the Labonites must have slain you."

"Peren is dead," I told her gently.

Her eyes filled with tears. "You should never have gone off alone like that, just the two of you. Those desert lice will be the death of all of us yet."

"He wasn't killed by Labonites." I stopped. How could I tell her the truth? "We battled a Flux fiend," I said. "I'll tell you about it later. I'll see Peren's wife as soon as I've bathed and changed clothes. Where's Gil?"

"Working in the fields." She caught each of the children by an arm. "Run, fetch your uncle."

The children scampered off. Hanna drew me inside the house. Jena ran out of the kitchen. "Lord Terral, you've come. I never doubted you'd come back." She rushed to clasp my hand. "We must get Flora!"

"Flora—how is she?"

"She's fine," Jena answered my tardy question. "Tredienne's with her. The birth was rough, as thin as she was after her illness. But the healer took good care of her, and she's getting stronger every day."

"The birth? Flora's had her baby?"

Hanna's eyes sparkled. "You have a son, Lord. A strong, healthy boy."

I didn't wait to wash. I hurried up the steps and into the familiar loft room. Flora sat on the bed cradling an infant in her arms. In a straight-backed chair Tredienne embroidered a tiny white dress.

"Terral." Flora rose with a glad cry, handed the child to Tredienne, and threw her arms around me.

I pressed her to me in a long embrace. My mouth clung to hers.

When at last we drew apart, Flora touched her fingers to my face. "Terral, you've been gone so long. I thought ... I feared you'd never return."

"But I have returned." I pulled her hands down and held them tightly. "Show me my son."

Flora beamed and turned to Tredienne. I released her hands and she took the child back, drew the coverlet away from his face, and lifted him for my inspection.

"He looks like you." She patted the plump cheeks with one finger.

The baby gurgled, and his blue eyes opened wide.

"You weren't here for the naming, so I had to do it." Eyes on the baby's face, Flora spoke shyly. "I named him Divian."

I stared numbly at the bundle of soft pink flesh. My son. But ... Divian?

I remembered the youth Divian, felt again the tightening of his fingers around my throat, the flow of my life into his. It couldn't be this infant, grown. That was impossible.

Yet I traveled through time. Perhaps he could, too. If it was my son, had he—could he have—known I was his father? Did our relationship explain how I could share his consciousness? Where was that youth now? How could he have come to that much later time neither as the infant he was now nor as the very old man he would have been if he had simply lived all those years?

"Terral, what is it? What's wrong?" Flora's thin face paled to a waxy hue, its glow snuffed out like a candle's flame.

"Nothing, Flora. The name surprised me, that's all." I tried to sound reassuring, but my agitation leaked into my voice. Instinctively my hand sought my missing fascinum.

She bit her lip. Tears brimmed in her eyes. "I hoped you'd be proud. I know you never really loved me, but I thought if I gave you an heir ..."

"Heir! No!" I pushed the baby away and stepped back.

Like a crushed lily Flora sank back onto the bed. In her lap the baby squeezed his face into a tight red ball and let out loud wails. Flora made no attempt to comfort him.

"I'm sorry, Flora. It's not you or anything you've done. He's a beautiful baby. I *am* proud." My awkward apology sounded hollow. Flora's head drooped.

Tredienne clamped a hand on my arm. "Leave. I'll give her something to calm her. She's having a hard time making milk as it is."

The healer fairly shoved me from the door. I stumbled down the steps, past Hanna's open-mouthed stare and Jena's worried clucks, and into my study.

I yanked the door shut behind me. I collapsed onto a chair, leaned my elbows on the table, and buried my face in my hands.

"You lost no time getting yourself into a thorough mess here while I was caged."

"Derli!" I lifted my head and peered at the single triangular window through which streamed a mote-filled sunbeam. She must have come in through that window. "When did you get here?"

"Just in time to find out what you've been up to and see you make an ass of yourself. I'd have expected you to have mastered a little diplomacy by now. That poor girl!"

I groaned. "Derli, it's bad enough—"

A sharp knock on the door stifled my protest. I stared at the unpainted wood and willed the intruder to go away.

The door opened. Tredienne swept in, pulling the door shut as she marched toward me, eyes like cold blue diamonds. With a thrill of fear,

I saw again the goddess, angry and vengeful, pursuing me through the temple. I leaped to my feet.

Nearly as tall as I, she confronted me face-to-face. "We must talk. I must know the reason for that scene upstairs." Her imperious tone, the face and form so like the goddess, impelled me to lower my gaze and take a step backward.

Again I pressed my hand on my chest where my fascinum should have hung. The table edge jabbed into my back. I was struck harder by a nettling sensation of Derli's presence. Infused with sudden confidence, I straightened. Hadn't I escaped Zera's wrath unscathed? Why should I fear this woman who was a healer but no goddess? I walked to a chair and held it for her. "Be seated. We do have to talk."

She hesitated, eased onto the chair's edge, still glaring.

I remained standing, arms folded across my chest. "Tredienne, I no longer have the staff of power. I require my fascinum—the channeler as you call it."

"It's safe. When I hear your explanation, I shall determine whether you merit it."

I thrust out my chest and threw back my shoulders. My hand strayed to the hilt of my sword. "I must have it before we talk."

Tredienne's brows arched. Her black hair absorbed the light, throwing her face in shadow. Had I gone too far? I steeled myself to keep my gaze fixed on her eyes. Her glacial stare did not waver.

"I require to know where the staff is. I do not feel it here, but—" She sniffed. Her eyebrows climbed higher. "I sense *something*. A presence—"

"You sense a fala."

My announcement brought her to her feet. "A fala! Impossible!" She inhaled sharply. "Who are you that you could capture a fala?"

"I haven't captured her. She's a friend."

Tredienne reacted to my indignant declaration with a scornful curl of her lip.

"In fact, he set me free." Derli's voice rang with controlled laughter.

Tredienne sank back onto the chair. Her mouth opened and closed several times before her words escaped. "You freed a fala? The legends say Molor attempted to do that and failed."

"Legends don't tell the full story." Derli's voice turned acid-sharp. "If the Winged One had not slain his brother—"

"No explanation is needed, Derli. The dama was going to fetch my fascinum." Deliberately I conferred on the healer the title that would henceforth belong to her and her successors.

Tredienne gave me a measured stare and rose. "I put a warding spell on it. I'll need a little time."

"Do it quickly," I snapped.

She swished from the room. When the door opened I caught a glimpse of Gil pacing in the common room, crushing the rushes beneath his booted feet. My success with the dama gave me the courage to call him in.

He came toward me with arms extended, but his face wore a worried frown. I embraced him, steered him to a chair, and took a seat at the adjoining side of the table.

"Lord Terral, when the children came galloping out to tell me you were back, I let out a whoop and came running. Jena and Hanna said you were with Flora, so I went to the cookshed to wash up. Next thing I knew, you were in here with Tredienne, and Flora was howling upstairs. Lord, if Flora has displeased you in any way—"

"No, Gil, no. Flora misunderstood. I reacted to the name she chose for the child. The name Divian holds evil meaning for me."

Gil's frown relaxed into a wide smile. "Ah, Lord, if that's the problem, it's easily solved. Change your son's name."

So simple a solution had not occurred to me. "I have that right?" I asked.

"Of course. Just as Hanna changed the name of her little one to honor Tredienne."

"Yes, I recall. How is little Treden?"

Gil beamed. "Grown strong and fat. He crawls all around. He'll be walking any day now. I'm as proud of him as if he were my son instead of my nephew." He cleared his throat. "'Course, I'm even prouder to be the uncle of the lord's heir."

I chewed my lip. "Renaming my son will not change one thing: my son cannot be my heir."

Deep furrows creased Gil's brow. He stared at his callused hands. "Lord, I know I'm only a poor farmer, and Flora's nothing but a peasant girl, but ..." He rubbed his stubby fingers across the dusty table.

I jumped up and clapped him on the shoulder. "Gil, you're my loyal and trusted friend. A farmer you may be, but you are not to think of yourself—or Flora—as a peasant. In fact, I intend to select lord councilors, and you shall be the first."

Gil brightened at my declaration, but puckers of worry tugged at his eyes and mouth.

"And, Gil," I went on, "Treden is to inherit the lordship. So you *are* the uncle of the lord's heir."

Gil's mouth dropped open. "Treden? Not your own son, but Treden?"

I nodded.

"Then Flora *has* displeased you."

"No, no. It has nothing to do with Flora." I sighed. "How can I make you understand?"

"Let *me* try."

Derli's voice brought Gil to his feet, staring wildly about the room.

"I'm sorry, Gil." I placed my hand on his arm. "I should have warned you we weren't alone." I paused, unsure how to introduce an invisible companion.

"I'm Derli," she said, solving the problem for me. "I'm witness that he's appointed you first lord councilor and your nephew Treden his heir. A vow made before a fala is broken at the vow-maker's peril."

"A f-fala?" Gil clutched my arm. "Here?"

"As for why Lord Terral cannot claim his son as his heir, you know he came to you from outside this valley. He has neglected to tell you he's promised to a powerful and jealous woman. It is to protect this valley from her wrath that he refuses to name his son as heir."

Ashen-faced, Gil stared at me. "Is this true?"

Derli answered before I could speak. "Of course it's true. Don't you know, man, that a fala cannot lie?"

"Forgive me, I didn't—"

"Now you understand why I could not wed Flora," I put in, taking quick advantage of Derli's strange tale.

"And the child—he's in danger?"

"He may be. I'll try to protect him." I rubbed the hilt of my sword.

Gil stood. "I'll explain to Flora." He bowed and left the room.

"Thanks, Derli," I said. "Your story was a marvel."

"It has a strong basis in truth. Lisha expects you to find your way back to her."

"Lisha! You mean Zera, don't you? Lisha was just her avatar."

Derli's tinkling laughter came from directly above my head. "Korth, if you've figured that out, you don't need to ask me anything more."

I raised my eyes toward the ceiling. "You never answer my questions anyway. And what was that nonsense about falas being unable to lie?"

She laughed again. "Easiest lie I ever told," she said.

26

VISITORS

With one finger I rolled the mutilated fascinum back and forth in the palm of my right hand. Like the eye of a blind man, the empty socket that had held the missing fragment of Pathfinder stared back at me. Tredienne sat watching me, saying little but observing me with sharp eyes and a worried frown.

On Derli's advice I told the healer most of what had befallen me from the time of my summoning to perform the rite of Lord's-kill. It was a tremendous relief to me just to be able to share the story with another person. I did not tell her of my conviction that I'd been chosen by Zera to become Makor. Nor had I confided that to Derli. I couldn't bring myself to put in words what to others would seem boastful but to me was my greatest fear.

At the conclusion of my tale, Tredienne eased her chair against the wall, out of reach of the fan of light that spread from the window. At last she spoke, slowly and thoughtfully: "In one sense, Lord Terral, we are all pawns of the gods. They play with us, but they do allow us some freedom, some possibility of self-expression. They sometimes seem to favor those who most defy them. Your blunders have been caused not so much by your own blindness as because you are being pulled between opposing powers. It is not clear to me what those powers are—or how many. But I suspect that you are of interest to them—of *value* to them—because they cannot predict the outcome of their contest." She allowed herself a tight smile. "Whatever that contest is, it is being played for high stakes. And you, Lord Terral, have the power to decide the outcome."

I considered her words. "The players in this game aren't gods," I said. "Not all of them. Lisha may be a manifestation of the goddess Zera, but—the juggler? And Koralie is certainly no goddess."

"But Koralie has summoned immortal forces," Derli put in. "Forces far beyond her ability to control, though she may not yet realize that. And you don't know who—or what—the juggler is."

Tredienne nodded agreement.

I suspected that Derli knew more about the juggler than she'd told me. As I thought, I continued to roll my fascinum, watching how the light played on it, toyed with the charm's rough edges, creating a pattern of spikes and shadows that shifted as I turned the cylinder. It gathered the sunlight and grew warm in my hand.

The shifting pattern had a hypnotic effect. Tredienne again lapsed into silence, her eyes closed, her fingers tracing tight circles on her homespun skirt. Derli hummed a low, sweet melody, which she may have intended as an aid to concentration, but which was instead lulling me into a dreamlike state. I scarcely noticed that the fascinum was growing hot.

Blue flame erupted from the cylinder on my palm. Derli's melody ended in a discordant shriek. I hurled the blazing object to the ground.

A dark funnel cloud formed in front of me. From its center, a taloned claw reached toward me.

I shrank back and the thing withdrew into the black whirlwind.

"Your channeler, Lord," Tredienne shouted. "Take it up. Don't let that fiend pass."

The fascinum lay at my feet, its flames extinguished. I snatched it up. It froze to my hand.

The swirling murk slowed, took form. Like a pale moon in a stormy sky, Koralie's face breached the darkness.

Tredienne was on her feet, swaying, arms flailing. "The channeler," she shouted again. "Use it. Before she gets through."

My hand burned with cold. Frost whitened the skin on which the fascinum rested. I thrust my palm to my mouth and pried the cylinder from it with my teeth. On my tongue the metal warmed.

Koralie's face faded into the black cloud. The phenomenon folded in on itself. Derli let out a low whistle. The blackness thinned, vanished. Again sunlight streamed across me from the high window behind me.

Tredienne sank to her knees beside my chair. "That was close. She's strong. And clever. I was ill-prepared, despite what you told me." She rose and paced the room with rapid, even steps. "I must discover how she was able to act so quickly. I was in the midst of refocusing the channeler. She must have sensed its flow of power."

I popped the fascinum from my mouth and stared at it, glistening in my palm. "Why do you call this a channeler? And what do you mean by 'refocusing' it?"

Tredienne halted in midstep and swung toward me. "The fala did not instruct you?"

My blank look must have been sufficient answer. Hands on her hips, Tredienne stared at the stream of sunlight. "Fala, were you not sent for that purpose?"

"He did not welcome my instruction." Derli sounded defensive. "He seemed to do well enough without it."

"So you disobeyed your mistress," the healer snapped.

"I am a free fala." Derli's haughty voice bounced off the wall.

Tredienne shook her head. "The Lord Terral's account shows clearly that you were sent to him by the girl Lisha, who, as he said, was surely a manifestation of the goddess Zera. Can you deny you are in bondage to Makor's consort?"

Derli sniffed. "I was. I am no longer. He set me free."

Tredienne's brow furrowed so that a deep crease divided her forehead. "I question that. But if it's true, it proves what I said about him. If he could wrest you from Zera's power ..."

I crashed to my feet. I had to stop that line of reasoning. "Enough of this." I grabbed Tredienne's arm and shook it. "Have you forgotten that Koralie is trying to enter this time?"

Tredienne dashed the heel of her hand against her forehead. "Molor! Yes!" She spun toward the door. "I'll have to find stronger spellbinders." She paused, hand on the latch, and looked back. "Put that channeler back on its chain and keep it around your neck. We must find someone who can repair it. Its lost eye must be replaced so its paths will flow true."

She opened the door. I hurled questions at her retreating back. "Who can repair it? How can I guard against Koralie's return? How am I supposed to use the channeler?"

Tredienne marched to the outside door. "Ask the fala," she called without breaking stride.

I pulled the study door shut. "Derli?"

"Korth, there are questions only the asker can answer."

"You're talking in riddles."

"I'm speaking truth. There are questions to which you must forge the answers." Derli's voice was soft and earnest, but her gentle tone did not appease me.

"Tredienne said Lisha—Zera—sent you to instruct me. You didn't deny it."

"Nor do I now."

"Then, why," I thundered, "do you stubbornly refuse to tell me what I must know."

"What you must know and what you wish to know are not the same." The sharp edge was back on her voice. "I've never refused to tell you what you *must* know."

"The operation of the fascinum is something I *must* know." Mimicking her tone, I shook at the empty air the fist that clasped the fascinum. "It was a gift from Zera. Is she using it against me now?"

"Korth, beware."

My hand shimmered with golden light. I stared, forgetting my anger. A sharp rap followed Derli's warning. I thrust my hand behind my back. The door burst open.

Pale and trembling, Gil stood in the doorway. "I'm sorry, Lord Terral," he stammered. "She won't listen to me."

Flora pushed past him. Eyes smoldered in her livid face, her hair flew in wild disarray. She clutched the baby to her breast.

She thrust her face near mine and screamed, "You will not accept this child as your heir, and you claim the right to rename him?"

I stepped back. "Flora—"

"I won't hear you!" She stamped her foot. "You've rejected your son. When you would not wed me, I should have known I had no hope. But I thought a son—an heir—would bind you to me." Tears spilled down her cheeks. She made no attempt to wipe them away. "Instead you reject the child and offer the final insult—you choose in his place my sister's son. What claim can Treden have on you, that you prefer him to your own son?"

"Flora, try to understand. I—"

"You're to wed someone else—that's your explanation? And you've kept that a secret all these months?"

Gil touched her shoulder. "Flora, a lord has the right—"

She swung away from her brother. "Not even a lord has the right to rename a child he disowns."

The baby squirmed and whined. She shifted him against her shoulder and held him in place with one arm. "I've named my son Divian, and Divian his name will remain."

I stepped nearer and closed my fingers over hers on the child's back. "Flora, listen, please. I—"

Her free hand shot into my face; her nails marked my cheeks.

Gil grabbed her and dragged her back. Unthinking, I rubbed my face with the hand that held the fascinum. Its dazzling light struck Flora's eyes.

She screamed, screwed her eyes shut, and dropped the baby. I grabbed for him, caught him, but dropped the fascinum.

The baby shrieked, Gil moaned, and Flora screamed, "I can't see! I can't see!"

I rocked my wailing son in my arms. Flora collapsed against Gil. He hugged her to him and eased her from the room.

On the floor the fascinum blazed white. I backed away from it, covering the baby's eyes. The light became a sun, eclipsing my momentary glimpse of Gil and his sisters cowering beyond it.

What could I do? Where was Tredienne? My fear for my child paralyzed me. I dared not pick up the fascinum while I held him, and I could not get past it to give the baby to his mother or his aunts.

"Korth!"

Derli's cry alerted me to a black column rising from the middle of the effulgence. I shoved the table aside with my body and leaped toward the window.

"Korth, I'll do what I can," Derli shouted.

The black column was acquiring a familiar form. The light shrank as though absorbed into the darkness.

Koralie threw back her hood. "I've come for you, Korth." She extended the staff.

I clutched the babe in one hand and reached for my sword with the other. My fingers closed around the hilt.

"Oh, no, Korth. You can't fight me with the sword." Koralie laughed softly. "If you were to kill me here, the flow of time would be forever changed."

Knowing she spoke truth, I took my hand from the sword. She stepped toward me.

I shrank from the staff. Its fiend's head grazed the baby's arm. He howled.

A fresh burst of white light flared from the fascinum. Koralie whirled and pointed the staff at the light. The brightness expanded. Out of its midst stepped Medara, young and slender as when first I met her. The black mist again swirled around Koralie, who seemed to shrink into it.

Medara stretched her hands toward me. "At last I've found you. Come quickly. I've opened a way."

I grasped her hand and let her pull me into the light.

"You have to pick up the fascinum," she ordered.

I transferred my son to her arms and reached into the heart of the sunburst. Unburned, my fingers found the hard cylinder and closed around it. But when I tried to lift it, I couldn't. The charm had acquired a weight that dropped me to my knees. My back arched. My muscles were tight cables. Sweat streamed down my face and neck.

Pain shot through my arm and into my body. I collapsed on top of the fascinum, overcome by a sensation of being turned inside out.

The feeling waned, leaving me weak and trembling, and the fascinum in my hand reduced to its usual lightness. Blinded from the departed radiance, I stumbled to my feet. I squinted toward the baby's loud cries and resolved a large blur into the outline of Medara holding the screaming, kicking infant.

"There, there, poor thing," she crooned. "You've had a fright, but you're safe, though why you're here and when and how we'll get you back to your mother, I don't know. But, shhh, it's all right. We'll find you a nursemaid and keep you safe and well cared for, never fear."

My brain stopped its spinning, my vision cleared. I rubbed my eyes. I was standing on a rush-strewn floor in a large bare room illuminated by sunlight streaming through a high, round window.

I'd returned to the room of the old Manor House to which Medara had summoned me, preventing Koralie's attempt to hurl me into the void. How long I'd been gone from here I had no way of knowing, but clearly Medara's power had grown since I'd been snatched away.

The baby quieted, clutched a fold of Medara's loose gown, and sucked on it. I glanced around the room.

"What happened to Koralie?"

A smug smile preceded a torrent of words. I'd forgotten her capacity for verbiage.

"That was a neat piece of work I did: turned her own spell against her and locked her out of the very channel she'd opened. She's stranded, won't be able to get back to her own shore without the beacon." She pointed to my hand, clamped around the fascinum, and took a quick breath. "If she tries to use that power staff she's got, it'll carry her where she'll least want to go."

"Where is that?"

"Why, the Time Flux, of course. That thing stinks of Flux."

A sharp voice said, "You're a fool if you think she's a stranger to that realm."

Medara jumped and cast a furious glance in the direction from which the voice had come.

"Derli!" I cried out with relief. "You came with us!"

"Had to. I couldn't let you flounder around on your own."

Derli's presence calmed me and eased my fears. I laughed.

"You have nothing to laugh about, Korth. If Koralie stays in the first lord's time, can you imagine the damage she can do without you and me to stop her?"

"Tredienne—"

Derli interrupted. "The first dama's a clever woman, but she's not in Koralie's class. Unless we get back fast, you'd better hope this foolish girl is wrong about having stranded that witch."

"Foolish, am I?" Medara huffed. "Didn't I cast a binding spell strong enough to find Korth and take me to him? And didn't I pluck him from the talons of the witch-woman? And bring him here to bring Mett to his senses and defeat the Flux fiend? Did I do that with no power? With no command of spells? Did I not—"

"No, you didn't," Derli shouted, so close to Medara's ear that the girl jumped and clapped a hand over that ear, nearly dropping the baby. "You did *not* bother to calculate the consequences of your spells."

The child let out another loud wail.

Derli's voice swelled to drown Divian's cries. "You're a danger to everybody. Think what your spells did to Abbi and Pik. Now you've put Korth and his child in danger and you've—"

"I rescued them from danger," Medara shrieked, scowling at the air. "Korth is needed here. Has your brain no more substance than your body, that you can't understand that?"

"I understand that you gave no consideration, as usual, to the consequences of your action, and you put your need above needs of others that might be more urgent. Did you hear me say that the baby you're holding is Korth's son? You've separated him from his mother and his rightful time and—"

"Korth's son?" Medara yelled over Derli's accusations and the baby's frightened wails. "Well, then, he belongs with Korth, doesn't he? And I've done no more than save him from that witch-woman as I did before. She's the one twisting time, and I'm trying to set things right, and you should be helping me and not—"

The baby howled louder.

I sucked air into my lungs. "HALT!" The command exploded from me. My breath took form and hovered before my face, a shimmering mist. Within it, my shouted syllable acquired a life of its own, rumbling and rolling in a prolonged echo that filled the room with its repetitions.

Makor was still within me. Without meaning to, I'd let him take control.

Awe and terror etched on her face, Medara dropped to her knees, and only the baby's grasp on her robe kept him from falling from her shaking arms.

Beyond the hovering exhalation I sensed—though with what sense I could not say: not vision, but some inner sight—a vibrant and complex pattern of force.

"Derli?" My whisper wafted against the wall of solidified sound and shattered it. The mist dissipated, the echoes died away. And still I perceived—felt? intuited? imagined?—that complex presence. I reached toward it. "Derli? I *see* you!"

"Your senses are waking, Korth. The goddess hasn't turned against you." The pattern shifted with her words. "It would have been better, though, not to have started with the Potent Command. You've apprised the whole household of your presence."

"And of his power," Medara offered in a subdued voice.

"A power he'd better not advertise until he knows how to control it," Derli snapped, her pattern expanding and contracting in dizzying whorls. "Korth, you could destroy us all."

"I only meant to make you hear me," I countered. "You two were yammering like fishwives."

If Derli was right, I hadn't foiled Zera's plan. Makor was growing stronger in me. I had to exercise more care.

I helped Medara to her feet. "What's happened here?" I asked her. "Has Mett been installed as lord?"

She nodded. "He kept his word about that. And he kept his wild men from hurting me. But he brought the men with him. And that evil Scrug never lets him out of his sight. We reached the Manor House, and no sooner did we set foot over the threshold but Dama Ordell began to shriek and moan and whimper, and when I got to her, her mouth was foaming and she was in convulsions, her eyes rolled back, her fingers clawing at herself. 'Get it away,' she said over and over, though nothing was there that I could see. 'The Flux fiend. Get it away.' No spell I tried brought her any comfort. Blood gushed from her mouth and she choked and died, and we found she'd bit clear through her tongue."

Tears streamed from Medara's eyes. Sobs fragmented her words. "I knew I'd caused her death. When I heard Dama Ordell's ravings about the Flux fiend, I knew it was Scrug. I'd brought a Flux fiend into the Manor House along with Mett. They're clever at disguises, fiends are, and he'd fooled me and, worse, he'd fooled Mett until he had him in his power. He knew I'd recognized him, so he had Mett lock me up here in the tower. I warded this room with the strongest wards I could fashion and set out trying to find you and bring you here to set things right." She stretched one hand toward me in a pleading gesture.

As if in imitation, my son, cradled in her other arm, reached out to me with both his tiny arms.

I moved to take him from her. A shout stopped me.

"Ho! Who shakes the earth with a Potent Word? Come forth and let me meet you!"

I recognized Scrug's voice, calling from the tower steps.

"He can't get in," Medara sputtered, her face white. "The wards—"

"No wards will hold him when his prey is here." In her agitation, Derli set up such a sparkling disturbance that I wondered how I could have been blind to her till now. "Korth, you must flee. You aren't ready to face him. It's Mett's job to cast out the fiend."

I looked at my fascinum. Could I use it to follow her counsel?

Too late. In a shower of sparks two figures burst through the doorway. Attired in the robes of a lord councilor, Scrug shoved before him a struggling youth. He held a jeweled dagger to the lad's throat.

The youth was Divian.

A thin wail drew my eyes from the glaring lad to his infant self. In Medara's arms, the babe began to fade.

27

BATTLES

Divian twisted and squirmed in Scrug's grasp, but the scrawny scarecrow was stronger than he looked. The youth's face was red, his muscles corded, but Scrug only grinned at Divian's efforts. To my horror, the boy grew weaker, and he, like the baby, began to fade. Before both manifestations of my son faded out of existence I had to do something.

Sword in hand, I stood in front of Medara and the baby. I risked a glance behind me. The infant lay limp and almost transparent. Through his body I could see the beige weave of Medara's dress. I turned back to face Scrug, but he was using Divian as a shield. I circled round him, but he was quick to keep Divian between him and me. No matter how I tried to find a way, I could not attack him without putting Divian at great risk.

Derli's glistening manifestation hovered near me. My blade gleamed in the tower room's wash of golden light. The lily device on its hilt kindled the memory of what I had learned in the jungle temple. "Zera." I breathed the name and followed it with a louder, "Makor!"

Scrug laughed the raucous, jeering laugh I remembered too well.

"You waste your breath calling on a dead god and an exiled goddess." He peered at me over Divian's head. "A fool such as you cannot have uttered a Potent Command."

"My strength is greater than you think," I boasted, infused with sudden confidence.

I opened the hand that held the fascinum. "Medara, use your power and the power of this channeler to open a time gate."

"I'll call on what power I possess, but you'll have to open the channel," she said.

There was still much I didn't know. "How do I—?"

"Breathe on it," Derli instructed.

I raised the fascinum to my mouth, pressed my thumb over the empty socket, and blew on the cylinder. It warmed in my hand. I thrust the hand toward Derli. "Get the baby and Medara out of here," I said to the bristling air. "And return Koralie to her own time."

She whistled. "Is that *all?*"

"Get going!" I opened my hand. The fascinum exploded into light, swallowing Derli's manifestation.

Medara stepped into the radiance, and she and the child vanished. I counted to five and closed my hand. The light faded. I was alone with Scrug and Divian.

Divian's color returned. He renewed his struggles. Scrug jerked Divian back against him and drew his blade across the lad's throat. The blade reddened. The youth gasped and tried to draw back. I felt the boy's tension as if it were my own. In a sense, it was—he retained a portion of my consciousness.

Divian's wrath seared that shared consciousness; like a poisonous river, a current of bitterness flowed between us. Swept by that fierce anger, I jammed the fascinum behind my belt and gripped my sword hilt with both hands. "You're wrong if you think the lad will serve you as a shield."

"Ah, would you kill your own son?" The fiend spoke in honeyed tone.

"His *son*? I'm not his son." Divian screeched the words.

Scrug laughed. "Ah, but you are, though he's been a poor father to you, abandoning you when you were a baby."

Divian stared at me with hate-filled eyes. "It's not true. It can't be."

"It's true," I said. "Though I never meant to abandon you."

"Let me go!" Divian shouted then to Scrug. "He's your enemy, isn't he? I'll kill him for you."

The force of his hatred impelled me to thrust my arms forward until my sword point reached Divian's chest. I checked the strike, drew back the sword; blood seeped from the shallow wound.

Divian's face was scarlet with rage; his eyes smoldered.

I fought against the fury I was sharing. The strength of Divian's bitterness clouded my mind and tugged at my sword arm, begging me to strike. I had to hold back. The Flux fiend wanted me to kill Divian, and so further disrupt the time line. A mighty effort of will tore my consciousness free enough of Divian's to let me focus my attention on Scrug.

His knife hand did not relax its pressure against his prisoner's throat, but his gaze fastened on my face. His lips parted in a toothy grin. "You restrain yourself from killing. I did not, after all, select a worthless shield."

I scowled and lowered the sword until its tip touched the floor. "Why do you hold him captive?"

"Perhaps to serve as a weapon." He slid his knife away from Divian's throat, exposing the red line it had drawn. "Suppose I place this knife into his hand? Will he spare you as you spared him?"

Divian writhed and fought to grasp the knife. I had no doubt where he would plunge it should he seize it. I lifted my sword and assumed a fighting stance. I felt a certain pride at what I read in my son's emotions: defiance, anger, and hatred, but no fear and none of the hesitancy that so often colored my actions.

I glared at the Flux fiend. "You can't force me to slay my son."

"Then I *will* let him kill you. It matters not which of you dies."

"So I'm no more important to you than he is?"

Scrug threw back his head and howled with laughter. The hideous sound held me in thrall and apparently Divian as well. Neither of us could move until the fiend spoke. "The ordered flow of time offends my nature. Your death—or the death of your son—will twist time and send it back into the Flux." He loosed his hold on Divian's arm.

The boy lunged for the knife. The fiend let him take it, backed off, and watched while Divian, eyes on my sword, hunted for a weak point in my defense.

"You won't find it," I said. "I know your thoughts."

He clenched his jaw. His gaze never left my sword, and his intention did not waver.

I felt a sudden burning at my waist. The fascinum! Derli and Medara must be trying to return. I had to open the channel immediately, lest they become trapped with Koralie. But reaching for the fascinum would give Divian the opportunity he waited for. I'd have to kill him before he killed me. Unless I took a gamble.

"Divian. Here!" I lifted my sword and tossed it to the floor in front of him.

Startled, he dropped his knife and grabbed for the sword. Hands gripping the hilt, he straightened and tensed for the spring that would drive the blade into my heart.

But I'd dug out the fascinum. With my thumb over the empty socket, I blew on the channeler and, using Makor's power, shouted across it, "HALT! TURN!"

The words boomed into the air. The house rocked. The window shattered; its glass crashed to the floor.

Divian staggered back. Holding the sword, he spun around. Scrug retreated before him.

I closed my hand. "Divian, Scrug is your true enemy. Attack him, not me."

Despite the power of my shout, my son hesitated. I held my breath.

I won the gamble! With a roar, he plunged toward Scrug. I opened my hand and willed the fascinum to burst into light.

A sun swam before me. In its core my tortured eyes distinguished the tiny silhouettes of two women—one dark, the other light. The dark figure brandished a staff. The light figure stood her ground and flung her arms wide over her head. In the act of striking her opponent, the dark woman vanished. The second, hands at its sides, shrank, lost her human appearance, took on the familiar contour of the fascinum. The radiance faded.

In the air in front of me a faint blur as of beating wings signaled Derli's presence. "Where's the fiend?" Her voice was strained, weak.

"Divian's chasing him with my sword." I wiped sweat from my face. "Where's Medara?"

"She battled Koralie and forced her back into her own time. But Koralie wounded her. She couldn't get back."

That explained the tiny figures I had watched. "The baby?"

"Safe. We took him—"

A loud scream came from the stairs. Divian!

I dashed to the stair landing and peered down in time to see my sword clatter from Divian's hands. He backed against the wall, and I felt his fear. The fascinum dropped from my hand.

The thing that loomed over my son had shucked its human disguise. Three horned heads jutted from a huge, worm-like body. Powerful arms reached out from the first segments of that body. One head, a slavering wolf with fiery eyes, snarled and snapped at the terrified youth. Long, splayed fingers wrapped around my son's throat.

I hurtled onto the stairs and struck at the thing with my bare hands, clawing at its powerful arms, kicking and pounding, dodging those hissing, snapping heads.

My attack restored Divian's courage. He tore at the hands that gripped his neck and kicked at the coils of the long, serpentine body. Father and son, we battled together.

I stretched to retrieve my sword. A barbed tail shot out and whipped the weapon away from my reaching hand. A serpent's head sank fangs into my shoulder. Torrents of paralyzing pain coursed through my body. Time slowed, wavered. I couldn't move. Divian, too, hung helpless in the Flux fiend's deadly grasp.

Mett leaped up the stairs and launched himself at the creature. He drove his long-bladed knife into the thick neck. Foul-smelling gore bubbled from the wound, and one by one the beast's heads sagged.

The wolf's jaws opened, freeing Divian. The serpent's head released my shoulder. I sank to the step. My hand closed on my sword. I drove the blade upward through the creature's coils. My son's limp body toppled beside me. The fiend's heavy corpse crashed down on us.

I wander a barren, horizonless plain. A gray mist hangs in the motionless air. Dull gray rock stretches beneath my feet. I trudge onward with no aim of arriving anywhere. I remember no other existence than this. I am a shadow in a shadowland.

Something finds me in this nowhere place. Some part of me lost long ago. It latches on to me, and though it brings no ordered thought or specific memory, I feel more complete, more aware. That regained spark of consciousness lets me see a will-o'-the-wisp bobbing before me, an interruption to the nothingness. I follow it. It slows and I catch up to it. "Father?" it whispers. "Father, we have to go back."

Go back? The words hold no meaning. Who is this that calls me father? How came he into my death?

"Father, hurry before the way closes." The vague luminosity drifts away, but its plea stirs the ashes of memory. I sigh and stumble down a tortuous path between slick walls of ice.

I skid on loose rock, fling out hands I'd forgotten I had, clutch at the smooth walls on either side. I slide down the incline. The wraith who'd summoned me floats ahead of me. I pick myself up, mutter a curse, and dash after it. A sharp pebble wedges between my toes. The jabbing pain slows me, but I don't stop, imbued with a new sense of urgency.

The rough descent brings me from the timeless realm into that fiend-haunted verge where time's waters lap the timeless shore. I stop. I know this place—or that recovered bit of consciousness knows it. The Flux, where Time fountains forth from Not-Time and the Flux fiends try to lap it up before it finds its proper channels.

"Wait," I call to my guide. "We'll lead fiends back with us through any opening we make."

"They're probably already through. Derli's held open the channel." He points to a small black hole. "Come on. We'll take care of 'em like we did the others."

I understand none of what he said, but the promised change in my condition makes me follow. My insubstantial companion sweeps through the opening like wind. I dart after him. Darkness swallows us. I limp, hands extended, through rustles, snarls, and hisses.

Black fades to indigo. Indistinct shapes swirl around me. Clearly visible in the waxing light, the statue of a young woman bars my way. Long brown hair drapes its shoulders, a rope belt gathers in the waist of the rough beige dress that hangs to midcalf. Bare arms rest on slim hips; slender fingers interlock across the abdomen.

My gaze lifts to the closed eyes, flared nostrils, and parted lips. A jolt of recognition shakes me. This is no statue. A name pops into my mind.

"Medara!" I grasp the cold hands, their texture like fine ivory. "I remember! Koralie wounded you and left you here in the not-life. You must return. I'll provide an exchange."

I peer around, tense, lunge at a shadowy form. It lacks the substance it would gain in the outer world, and so, in fact, do I. I grapple with the thing as smoke with steam. We flow round each other, twisting, intertwining, mingling our essences in the encounter, and withdrawing in mutual abhorrence. Weakened, I thrust my remaining force into the speaking of words that bubble up from some hidden reservoir. The words blast the creature into shreds that fade into the mist.

The words ripple over Medara, tingeing her skin with pink. Her fingers relax; her eyes open. With a startled look she gazes at me for a moment, then turns and steps through some exit invisible to me.

Drained, I collapse on the now empty ground where she had stood.

"**K**orth, Mett's breathed life into you, and I've worked my best healing spell, and Derli's been singing to you, so now you have to do your part. Derli sent Divian to fetch you, and he's come round, so you must too."

With every word needles of pain jabbed through my eyes into the void behind them. Small chunks of remembrance fell into that void like bits of plaster from a cracked wall. I lay still and sorted these jumbled bits of mosaic into a coherent picture. I discovered pieces of two distinct yet overlapping sets of memories, like two murals painted on one wall, one covering part of the other. The implacable voice and the throbbing in my head made me despair of sorting it all out.

"Medara, be quiet, can't you? Let me try to sing him around."

The rush of words ended with a loud sniff. A low, sweet humming soothed my disordered mind; its melody created an intense yearning for some lost, elusive joy.

The sharp longing herded my memories together. I searched them and recalled that I was Korth, though another name nagged at my mind. I was no longer only Korth. I remembered Derli ... and Medara ... and Divian. Fighting with the Flux fiend. Mett killing the thing.

I remembered my dream.

Dream? More than a dream, its vividness told me. I *had* been on that timeless shore. And there I'd absorbed another portion of Makor's essence. I was closer to becoming Makor revivified. But if Makor became stronger, what would happen to Korth?

The tempo of the melody quickened, infused with an urgency that yanked me into wakefulness. I opened my eyes.

Medara clapped her hands. "Praise Molor!"

A cluster of sparkling threads swirled around my face.

I smiled. "Thanks, Derli."

Mett approached and dropped to one knee. "I thought I'd slain you along with the fiend."

I shook my head. "Death doesn't seem able to hold me."

Mett lowered his gaze. "Lord, forgive me for bringing that thing here, for not recognizing—"

"You recognized it when it most counted," I said, grateful for the distraction his words provided. "You saved my life—and my son's. Help me to rise."

"Thank you, Lord." Mett grasped my elbow with one hand and slid his other beneath my shoulders.

Divian, no longer my enemy, stepped to my other side, stooped, and grasped my other arm. He and Mett hoisted me to my feet.

When my swimming head had gained a sense of balance, I

motioned them away and stood alone. Something sharp stabbed the tender flesh between my toes. I grabbed my son's shoulder, balanced on one foot, and tugged at the boot on the other. With Mett's help I pulled it off and plucked out the rough-edged pebble lodged between my toes. Supported by Divian, I stared at the offending stone while Mett replaced my boot. It offered proof that I had been in that timeless realm of shades.

"Korth?" Medara's tentative call roused me.

"I'm all right." I tossed the pebble into the air, caught it, stored it carefully in my belt pocket, and glanced around the tower room. "Where's my sword?"

"Out there." Medara pointed toward the stairs. "You'd impaled the creature on it, and when Mett and I rolled the thing off you—it took all our strength to do that; the thing must have weighed twenty-five stone—we found we'd rolled you over with it, you had such a death-grip on the hilt. We had to pry it from your hands, with you and it all sticky with the creature's gore. Not knowing whether you were dead or alive, we brought you up here and went back after Divian, and we had to rush, with no time to think about the sword, so it's—"

I interrupted. "Are you trying to tell me the sword's in that monster's carcass?"

A hurt expression on her face, Medara nodded. "I was about to say that."

"Fetch it!" My curt command sent both Medara and Mett hurtling toward the stairs.

I hadn't meant to speak so sharply. My peremptory command had come more from Makor than from me. He had gained strength. I had to resist, discover how to fight back.

"I have to find my fascinum," I said, speaking softly. "Might anyone know where it is?"

"It's here, Korth." Derli spoke from the landing. Below her shimmering presence shone the glint of electrum.

"I'll get it, Father." Divian jumped toward the stairs, returned in seconds holding the fascinum aloft like a prize. Derli glistened in after him.

With a smile and a word of thanks I accepted the fascinum and cleaned it on my shirt. My son watched, his face etched with a mixture of awe and pride.

Moved to take advantage of his changed attitude toward me, I said, "Divian, if you've decided not to kill me, you might join me in tracking down any Flux fiends that slipped back in with us. We've got to stop them before they create more problems than we can straighten out."

His chest swelled, and his face flushed with pride. "We'll get 'em. They don't stand a chance."

I grinned until a tardy recollection clamped my teeth together. Divian's presence either in the time into which he'd been born or the time in which he'd grown from infancy to young manhood could create time-shattering anomalies. And the infant Divian—where was he? I had to be very sure that babe and youth never occupied the same time.

"Derli, you started to tell me what you and Medara did with the baby. Where is he?"

The clustered sparkles shifted quickly through several different configurations, betraying her agitation. "He is safe, Korth, truly," she said. "We didn't land in Flora's time, and we had no time or way to find our way back to it."

"So where is he?"

"In the care of the priests of the Temple of Zera in Diakos." She spoke rapidly, while her lights flickered and shifted. "They'll hire a wet nurse for him. They often take in orphans and raise them to serve in the temple. Medara made the arrangements, though as a devotee of Molor she didn't like the idea of leaving him with Zerans. I convinced her we could do nothing else with the little time we had."

"Stop! You sound like Medara. What time was this?"

The flickering slowed; the pattern clustered tightly into a single, even gleam. "About sixteen years before Lisha and Savnar saved a certain runaway slave from being beaten to death," she said.

That answer relieved my mind a bit. Divian *had* grown up in that temple—not the upbringing I would have chosen for him. And I had no idea what I could tell Flora if I got back to her time. She'd never forgive me for carrying her son away, never understand why I couldn't return him to her. But Derli was right; the baby was safe.

At least, I hoped that was true. My son had shown himself as capable as I of disrupting the time line by shifting into times when he didn't belong. I already regretted my rash promise to let him join me in searching for the Flux fiends.

I had to safeguard time's flow without endangering my son's life and without delaying my pursuit of the fiends. Another impossible task to add to the list of those I faced.

Well, the more impossible the task, the sooner I'd need to start on it. The first time I needed to go to was the time of the first Lord Terral, and that was one of the places to which Divian could not accompany me. I had to protect Flora and assure her that our son was safe. How could I do that unless I believed that he was safe?

My son had to stay in this time. Here he'd be protected and wouldn't disrupt the time line by appearing in the same time as his infant self. It was unlikely that he would encounter another Flux fiend here—they'd have dispersed to other times by now, I decided, drawing on Makor's knowledge.

Medara returned, followed by Mett with my sword held at arm's length, its blade corrupted with slime and gore. The noxious fluids had blackened the silver hilt.

I motioned for Mett to drop the sword onto the rushes. Divian's face wrinkled in disgust.

"Son, would you please see if you can get around that monstrosity on the stairs? If you can, summon servants to have the thing removed and burned. Then find me a sandstone to clean and polish this sword."

His face displayed his reluctance to leave, but he did as I asked. When he was out of earshot, I turned to Medara and said, "I'm going to entrust my son into the care of you and Mett. I can't take him where I must go. He'll want to come, and I doubt I can make him understand the danger. He may try to bridge time on his own. You must be certain he doesn't succeed. I expect you to keep him here and keep him safe."

Medara's lower lip thrust out; her forehead puckered. "Protector, if you must leave again, let me accompany you. My spellcasting will help you defeat the Flux fiends, and I can prepare your food and clean and mend your clothes." She cast a critical eye on my ragged shirt and filthy trousers. "I can spin and weave. I know healing herbs and restorative potions, I can—"

I interrupted. "Woman, have you forgotten? As dama your job is to preside over Mett's household and to find and prepare your successor."

"And do no more meddling with the time channels," Derli put in, her sparkling pattern hovering by my shoulder.

"I haven't meddled," Medara protested. "I called the Lord Protector here in time of great need and by Molor's will. You can't deny it. The Flux fiend had to be killed, or who knows what would have happened, and Mett wouldn't have done it—would you, Lord Mett? —if Korth hadn't made the thing reveal its true form and—"

"Quiet," I said. "This arguing is pointless. What's done is done, but from now on your place is here with Mett. Not to mention that I ordered you to see after Divian."

"Why do I need seeing after?" Divian strode into the room, eyes sparking. He carried cloths and a sandstone.

I took the things from his hand. "How'd you find these so soon?"

"The servants were all huddled in a room below the steps, scared out of their wits. I told them what had happened, gave your order, and had them fetch what you needed. Now answer my question. Why is Medara to look after me?"

"Because you're young, and I've given you a dangerous assignment." I knelt on the floor, took a cloth, and commenced scraping the thickened gore from my sword. "The Time-Flux spawns devious and deadly creatures, as you've seen."

"Medara's scarcely older than I am. Where will you be?"

I passed over the matter of Medara's age. "Son, the fiends have by now already dispersed throughout Time's flow. I want you to hunt them here while I search another shore."

"So." His face went sullen. "You don't want me. You're going to abandon me again."

I shook my head and reached for a clean cloth to polish the hilt of the sword. "I didn't abandon you in the first place. I'll explain that, but first I think we both need to get cleaned up. I can't stand having this stinking stuff all over me and my clothes. I'd guess you're as ready as I am to get it off you."

"Can't we talk first?"

"What I have to tell you will take some time, and you'll have a lot of questions. We need to sit down together and take our time if I'm to satisfy all your doubts. I understand your impatience, but if we get cleaned up, we can sit somewhere, have a meal brought to us, and eat as we talk. This isn't something we can rush through."

"How do I know you won't duck out on me?" he said, frowning.

I straightened and looked him in the eye. "I promise I won't. I want you to trust me. I want this conversation as much as you do. Please believe me."

He nodded slowly. "I'll trust you—this time."

"Then let's have the servants prepare a bath for each of us and see if they can round up some clean clothes."

Medara, who'd been listening, in silence for once, said, "I'll give the orders," and hurried off, glad, I suspected, to have a reason to be away from me.

Feeling greatly refreshed after a good scrubbing, I dressed in clean clothes provided by Mett. They weren't a good fit, but my own clothes were ruined, so I couldn't be choosy. I put on my sword belt, but left my sword on the table where I'd laid it while I bathed. It wasn't far, should I need it, but I wanted to be relaxed and comfortable while I talked to Divian. I did make certain my fascinum and the stone I had brought from the Flux were still safe in the belt pocket. At last I sent a servant to tell Divian I was ready for our talk and sank into a chair. Near it shimmered the constellation of sparkling lights that was Derli.

"Are you going to explain everything?" she asked.

"I'm going to tell him all that has happened to the slave Korth since I was summoned to perform Lord's-Kill."

"So ... Not everything, then."

When I didn't answer, she said, "I judge from the things you did, from issuing Potent Commands to unmasking a Flux fiend, that you aren't just Korth any longer." Derli's tone, no longer bantering, had become reverent, fearful even.

"No. I suppose you knew all along what I just figured out in the jungle temple. That Zera means to use me to bring Makor back." I paused, waiting for a response, but none came, so I continued. "I'm more than Korth. More than the Lord of the Manor. But I'm not a god. I have a little of Makor's power, and I've been using it. But I still have all my own weaknesses."

Her only response was a low whistle. Unable to interpret that reaction, I asked a question of my own: "Derli, when we were in the jungle temple, why was Zera so angry with you? I know she was no friend to falas, but she *had* sent you to be my guide."

She sighed. Her voice, when at last she spoke, was low and sorrowful. "Guide? Not exactly. I was to warn of danger and protect you if I could. I did those things well enough to satisfy her, though not to the extent you would have liked. But I broke the oath I'd sworn to her."

"What oath was that, and how did you break it?"

Again I waited as the silence stretched until with another sigh she said, "I broke it first when I sang to you in the inn. After that, well … I was sworn to accompany you without offering you any kindness. I was supposed to make you resent my presence, so that when you learned, as you inevitably would, that I am a fala, you'd turn against all falas."

Ah! "And instead you made me appreciate you and all falas." So many things that had puzzled me became clear.

"We'll speak of none of this to Divian," I said. "But tell me, how did he reach me when I was lost in the Flux?"

"He called on Uta. She seems to favor him."

"Yes. Another mystery. Why? And why did Uta, Zera's mother, help us escape her daughter? How did she even come to be there in the temple when we fled from Zera?"

"None can interpret Uta's weavings, but I sensed her presence in the temple and guessed she would help us. She never agreed with her daughter's plan for the falas."

"I'll ask Divian about Uta when we have our talk." Suddenly aware of how much time had passed, I added, "Shouldn't he be here by now?"

"Should I go find him?"

"Yes ... No, wait." I took my fascinum from my belt pocket and warmed it in my hand. "Let me try to call him with this."

"I don't think that's a good idea ..."

I'd already raised the fascinum to my mouth. Breathing over it, I called, "Divian!"

"Uh-oh!" Derli's voice echoed strangely.

I was caught up into a swirl of fog.

28

CAUGHT

The fog cleared. I stood in the middle of a cobblestone street. The place looked familiar, but I had no chance to look more closely. On the path before me a coal-black horse pranced. Astride it sat the juggler.

"Did you bring me here, fool?" I demanded, glaring at the masked figure.

"Your own folly brought you here," he responded, grinning maliciously. "You still don't know how to use that thing properly." He pointed at the fascinum still in my hand.

"How would you know?" It was all I could do to restrain myself from using Makor's power against him.

"I make it my business to know where and when you are." He laughed and added, "You don't make that easy, you know. Oh, and I think this little gift is long overdue."

He pulled one of the small heads from a bag and tossed it to me. "So many deaths you're bringing about," he said.

I caught it and looked into the face of Flora. I stared at it, too stunned to speak. *She isn't dead.* I amended the thought: She hadn't been dead when I last saw her. I hadn't saved those represented by the first five heads. Could I save Flora?

The juggler flicked the reins, and the horse raced off, leaving me holding the head, with the memory of Flora now fresh in my mind.

"Who *is* he? Derli, do you know?" I looked around, expecting to see her glistening nearby.

I saw nothing, and no one answered.

"Derli?" I called again. And again. And again.

She hadn't come with me. Maybe she'd remained in Medara's time and could explain to Divian that my disappearance was a terrible accident. That I hadn't deserted him. But she'd been so close to me when I'd been swept away. I very much feared that she'd been caught and hurled to a different time than this. Or trapped in a time bubble as she'd been before.

I groaned. Just as things had seemed to be going well, how could everything have gone so wrong? I tried to blame the juggler, but I knew the fault was mine. My carelessness with the damaged fascinum had sent me here.

Not able to bear looking longer at the head that wore Flora's face, I set it down under a tree and left it, though I could not so easily escape the burden of guilt it had placed on me.

Where was I? I looked around, hunting some familiar landmark.

It didn't take me long to find one. I hadn't walked far along the cobblestone street before I spotted the cobbler's shop from which I'd stolen the boots. I was back in Diakos.

Had I transferred back to that same time? If so, I could perhaps find Savnar and get my fascinum repaired. On my previous visit here, he'd claimed to be an innkeeper. I didn't know where the inn was, but on this visit my clothes were clean and neat, so I wouldn't attract attention if I asked a passerby where to find an inn.

I missed Derli terribly, felt vulnerable without her beside me. And I felt defenseless without the sword I'd left behind, though I sensed no danger. The town was quiet, its people going about their usual business. I approached a greengrocer. "Good sir, I'm a stranger here. Can you direct me to an inn?"

"There's a fine one not far from here," he answered, and supplied me with the directions.

I reached it after only a short walk, went inside, and was greatly relieved when Savnar came forward and bowed in greeting. Before I could greet him by name he gave an almost imperceptible shake of his head, grasped my arm, and drew me past the tables where diners were being served and into a small room, an office of sorts.

"I wouldn't have expected to see you here, Savnar," I said. "You said you traveled around."

He smiled. "Oh, I do. I do. And here I'm known as Ander the Innkeeper, not Savnar. And not as a fascinator, though I ply that trade most often when I travel."

"That's what I wanted to see you about," I said, drawing out the damaged fascinum. "I need this repaired."

Savnar plucked the fascinum from my hand and examined it. His eyebrows lifted to his hairline and a shudder coursed over his body. "It's been joined to another," he said, frowning.

I nodded. "The joining increased its power. Can you restore it?"

"Perhaps." He turned it round and round in his fingers. "A piece is missing."

From the pocket of my belt I took the pebble I'd brought from the timeless realm and handed it to him. "This may fit."

He peered at the faceted bit of gravel and set it gently into the hollow from which I'd lost Pathfinder's thorn. "Yes," he murmured as though he'd forgotten my presence. "Yes, the fit is right. And the power!"

"So you can repair it?"

He smiled and his eyes sparkled. "It presents a challenge, but I've always liked challenges."

"I need it as soon as possible."

"I understand," he said. "I can have it ready tomorrow. In the meantime, you're welcome to stay here as my guest. I'll have a room made ready. Please enjoy a meal in the dining hall while that's being done."

I was only too glad to accept his hospitality.

Cautioning me to remember to call him Ander, he led me back to the dining hall, where I took a seat at a long table with other diners. Seated near me were three red-robed Zeran priests. I served myself from the communal bowls of vegetables and platters of meat and busied myself eating, not wanting to be drawn into conversation with my fellow diners. Especially I didn't want questions from the priests.

I paid little attention to the chatter around me until Someone asked one of the priests, "Have you found the missing boy?"

The one to whom he addressed the question replied briefly, "Not yet," and served himself a generous helping of a vegetable soufflé.

"What boy is that?" I couldn't resist asking, though I was sure I knew the answer.

"A youth we raised in the temple from his infancy," the priest responded curtly.

As his portly companion carved the generous portion of roast he'd placed on his plate, he offered with similar generosity, "The baby was brought to us by a woman who refused to give her name but swore she was not the child's mother. She also swore that the babe was in danger and needed our protection. 'His name is Divian,' she said and thrust him into the arms of the attending priest, and then, according to that priest, she simply disappeared."

The third priest chuckled. "That was old Samri, as I recall. He was prone to wild imaginings. I doubt there was anything mysterious or unnatural about the woman's departure. And now that the boy is nearly grown to adulthood, he's probably run away because the cooper we apprenticed him to was too hard a taskmaster. "

"Perhaps, perhaps not," the second priest said, pausing in his attack on the roast. "He could have been stolen away, possibly by the strange woman who came to the temple and asked questions about him shortly before his previous disappearance."

"I suppose it's possible he was lured away," the third priest offered. "He was ever curious to learn who he was and where he'd come from, and he'd go with anyone who promised, however falsely, to satisfy that curiosity."

I was sure the boy they spoke of was Divian and the "strange woman" could have been Koralie, possibly disguised, or a servant sent by her. It had to have been Koralie who taught him the rite of Lord's-Kill and sent him to kill me when I was here in Diakos previously. Satisfied that I'd solved that mystery, I didn't engage in further conversation but finished my meal and left to see whether my room was ready. It was and I went there, locked myself in, and stayed there until morning, glad of the opportunity for a good night's sleep.

In the morning I sought out Savnar and found him overseeing the serving of breakfast. We repaired to the same small office he'd taken me to the night before. True to his word, he had my fascinum waiting. He presented it to me wrapped in a silk cloth, which I unfolded to reveal the amulet, its scratches and dents gone, the formerly nondescript stone polished to a rich mauve and set between the two fragments of Pathfinder where it sparkled like a gemstone.

I turned it about in my hands. "It's beautiful! And I feel the power it holds."

He shook his head. "The fascinum is only a channeler of power. The power comes from within you."

"Within *me*?" I almost dropped the amulet. "What power do I have?"

"I think you know the answer," he said with an enigmatic smile.

He knew!

And why should he not? He'd claimed as his daughter Lisha, the avatar of Zera. She couldn't be his daughter, of course, but I knew whom he served and how much in her confidence he must be.

"It's not a power I want to draw on," I said, reckoning it useless to deny that I knew whose power he meant.

"Where is the fala?" he asked abruptly.

"I don't know. She was with me when I tried to use the broken fascinum, and instead of accomplishing what I intended, it brought me here. She didn't come with me. She may be trapped."

Savnar nodded and sank into a chair. "It's likely."

"I mean to find her," I said.

That won me a sharp look from those piercing blue eyes. "She's no stranger to being trapped and held captive."

"All the more reason to find her. She's suffered enough."

"I think her capacity for enduring suffering is greater than you can imagine," Savnar said. "You should forget her and go to the temple."

The temple here in Diakos was one place I did not intend to go. "I've left things undone in several times," I said. "I have responsibilities I can't ignore. I have no time to visit the temple."

"A visit to the temple might resolve your problems."

"I doubt it." I stood in front of his chair and looked down at him. "I know what Zera wants of me. It's not what I want for myself."

"Then you're a fool after all," he snapped, standing abruptly, so that I was forced to step back.

I was afraid, but I refused to back down. "A fool for wanting to remain myself?" I asked. "A fool for thinking I'm more than an empty vessel she can fill as she chooses?"

He backed from me and resumed his seat, regarding me for a long while. I waited, not willing to speak until he did.

At last he said, "I think, Korth, that you have grown too strong to be merely an empty vessel."

Not knowing how to respond to that, I kept silent and waited for him to say more.

It was a long wait. But at last he looked around furtively as though afraid someone might overhear, though there was no one else around. He stood, went to a locked cabinet, and opened it with a key dangling from a chain around his neck. From a shelf within it he took a princely saber with a jeweled hilt.

"I see you've lost his sword. This was also his. Bear it with pride and don't lose it." He placed it in my hands, resumed his seat, and continued. "The fascinum can take you where you want to go, but like it or not, it does so by Makor's power. I can show you how to use it to go where you want and stay as long as you like, but if you accept my help and use the fascinum, the time will come when you must return here—to this place at the exact moment you leave. We can delay the goddess's plan. We cannot disrupt it."

"You mean *you* can't."

"I mean precisely what I said. If you refuse her gift, you will not have the power to oppose her. If you accept it, you won't want to."

I pondered that statement for longer than he liked. He drummed on the arm of his chair, and finally said, "I've made you a generous offer. I advise you to take it before it's withdrawn." When I still hesitated, he added, "I'm not your enemy, you know. I'm trying to help you."

He seemed sincere. And also frightened. It was his fright that convinced me. I took a deep breath. "All right, then," I said, "Show me how to use the channeler correctly. I want to find Derli."

"That may not be possible. You can use the channeler to reach a specific place, but not to find someone whose whereabouts you don't know."

"Can I use the fascinum to call her to me?"

He shook his head. "Choose a place. Now. Quickly."

His sense of urgency bordered on panic. I had to leave now or lose the chance.

I'd intended to go back to Medara's time, aiming for the exact moment I'd left. But a picture flashed into my mind and would not go away. The picture of Flora's face as I'd last seen it, both angry and fearful. And her face on the head the juggler had tossed to me, its expression sad, desolate.

"I've chosen," I said.

"Picture the place and time as clearly as possible," he instructed. "Hold the fascinum like this." He demonstrated how to place my fingers on it in a specific configuration as I raised it to my mouth. "Breathe on the fascinum while you keep the image of your destination clear in your mind. The channeler will take you there."

I placed my fingers exactly as he'd instructed and concentrated on a mental image of Gil's house, asking for a time shortly after I'd let Medara draw me away from there. Derli, too, came into my mind as my breath warmed the fascinum. Relief flooded Savnar's face. I felt a momentary disorientation as that face faded from view.

My abrupt appearance in Gil's common room caused screams and shouts from Hanna, Jena, and the children. The light streaming though the high windows indicated a midmorning hour. I scanned the room. No Flora. No Tredienne.

"Calm yourselves," I cried above the clamor.

The noise subsided. The children hid behind their mothers. Jena was the first to find the courage to speak.

"Lord Terral, is it really you?" she stammered in an awed voice.

"It is, Jena." I stretched my hands toward her.

Hanna gave a cry and threw herself at my feet. "Oh, Lord, if you'd only come back sooner!" She burst into sobs.

"How long have I been gone?" More time must have passed than I'd hoped.

"Two weeks," Jena said. "And Flora's been wild since you took her baby from her. She ran off this morning, with the madness on her. I think she meant to kill herself. Dama Tredienne went to find her and hasn't come back."

The fear on the sisters' faces made me recall Flora's volatile and fragile nature and recognize the seriousness of her disappearance. "Where's Gil?"

"He's hunting for her, Lord," Jena answered. "So is Jed. And Dama Tredienne, as I said. But ..."

"I'll join the search. On Sunburst I may have a better chance than the others." I headed out. My poncho, cleaned and mended, hung on a hook by the door. Touched by that evidence of the family's faith in my return, I caught it up and slung it over my shoulders.

I dashed to the barn and led Sunburst from his stall. "No time for a proper greeting," I said. "I'll make it up to you later." He stood still while I mounted him. So still that I wondered whether he would obey me. He'd been Makor's horse, the deathless horse of a dead god. Perhaps Sunburst would sense that I'd rejected Zera's intention to bring about Makor's rebirth in me. I pressed my legs against his sides. "Go, Sunburst. Fly with the wind."

With a glad whinny he sprang into the air, hooves sparking, mane shimmering. We streaked across the valley swift as hungry flames. But the tableau at the edge of the stream beside the cypress grove told me I'd arrived too late. I'd failed again.

Tredienne cradled Flora's head in her lap. Flora's long, dark hair trailed like waterweeds over Tredienne's knees. Rivulets of water streamed from it. Flora's gown, caked with mud, outlined the contours of her thin body. Her eyes stared sightlessly. The dama brushed a fly from the parted lips.

When I dismounted and hurried to them, Tredienne looked up with a blank, dazed face. "I found her wedged among the rocks of the streambed. I tried to breathe life back into her. Her spirit was too far gone, swept by the current out to sea."

I knelt, took Flora's cold, stiff hand in mine, and felt the truth of Tredienne's words. If only I had come sooner. A tear fell and splashed on Flora's hand.

"The loss of her son dealt a deathblow to her spirit," the dama said. "I've watched her constantly, knowing she courted death. This morning, tortured with restlessness, she wandered through the house moaning and wringing her hands. The calming potion I made her drink had no effect.

"Gil had left for his work in the fields; Jena and Hanna were cooking and washing, and the older children had gone to visit Peren's widow and children. I was alone with Flora in the common room. Suddenly she said, 'My son is back. I must find him.' She rushed outside. I ran after her, but before I could catch her, powerful forces swirled around me. I could see Flora running farther and farther from me while I was caught, unable to move."

"What did you see? Or sense?"

"I saw nothing. I sensed diverse powers locked in conflict. I was buffeted by anger, fear, and hate on the one hand and confusion, hopelessness, and loss on the other. I'd blundered into the clash of forces, and they held me helpless as a fly in a bottle until the forces burst apart and vanished. I was free, but by then I'd lost Flora. I ran to the field where Gil and Jed were working and told them. They went south and west in search of her while I went north. And found her too late. Gil will have to be told." She stroked Flora's hair, pressing water from its limp strands.

"I'd better do the telling," she added, avoiding my gaze. "I'm not sure how he'll take the news. He's beginning to feel that the personal disasters—Peren's death, the baby's disappearance, Flora's madness—cancel the obligation he owes you for saving the valley. Your absences have made him feel he was wrong in upholding your lordship. When he learns of this—" She shifted Flora's sodden corpse.

I nodded, bent, and lifted Flora's body from Tredienne's arms. "I can't blame Gil. He has sound reason to turn against me. But a rebellion led by Gil would change the flow of time. I have to prevent that. Don't seek him out yet. I'm going into the grove. Wait here with Sunburst until I return."

I carried Flora in among the cypresses, down the cloistered lanes between the columns of trees, to the heart of the grove. Surrounded by the silent sentinels, I laid her on the crisp, dry fans of cypress that littered the ground. Kneeling beside her, I kissed the icy lips and whispered, "Goodbye, Flora. Forgive me for what I did to you. And what I'm going to try to do now."

Tredienne's account of the forces she'd felt gave me both fear and hope. The urgency that had drawn me here should have eased when Flora died, but it had not. That might be due to Divian's presence here, but there could be another reason as well. Acting again by instinct, I drew out my fascinum, murmured over it, and used it to direct that murmur throughout the grove.

"Derli," I called. "If you've taken refuge here, come. I need you."

My voice rustled through the cypress needles, a dry wind rattling the trees. The echo died away, leaving a sepulchral stillness. Like a supplicant in the temple, I waited in the muted light.

A sigh. A whispered snatch of song, sad and lovely, like a dying flute.

Flora's body shuddered. Her breast rose and fell. Her eyelids fluttered. I took her hand, felt the flesh grow warm. I slipped my arm beneath her shoulders, raised her to a sitting position, and steadied her against my breast. "I'm sorry, Derli."

Her hand gripped mine.

I squeezed her fingers. "Have courage. This will not be forever."

"Will it not, Korth? There is more than one way to trap a fala."

Her sad smile tore at my heart. "You didn't have to come," I said. "But I'm very glad you did. I need you. There's an evil here, and when Flora ran off she told Tredienne she sensed the presence of her son. If Divian is here ..." I had no need to finish. She nodded and gave me her hand.

I helped her to her feet. Together we walked from the grove.

Tredienne jumped up and ran to meet us, face alight with astonishment. "Lord Terral, you restored her!" She touched Flora's hands, her cheeks, looked into her eyes.

Her arms fell to her sides. She stepped back. The light left her eyes.

"No power could bring Flora back from the timeless realm, Tredienne," I said. "This is a necessary deception. You alone will know the truth. Gil and his sisters will believe that Flora has been restored to them."

"But how long will the fala keep this flesh? When she withdraws, they'll know you deceived them, and the harm will be more grievous."

"She will not withdraw." I took Flora's hand.

"I've yielded my freedom," Derli said. "I cannot leave this flesh at will."

The pain in her voice stabbed my conscience. I released her hand. I should not have subjected her to this imprisonment.

Memories haunted me—of Brid, of Renata, of Divian, of Koralie, of the Flux fiends I'd loosed on the land. Everywhere I sowed disruption, suffering, and death. I was doing Molor's work, not Makor's. I did need Derli's help to undo the damage I'd done. I needed her presence with me. And she had come willingly this time, not as Zera's agent but as my friend.

I whistled for Sunburst, and he trotted to me. I patted his neck and kept my hand in his mane as I spoke to Tredienne. "We have to leave, though not for long, I hope. I have to find Divian. You said Flora felt his presence." My broken promise to him haunted me. What anger and hurt he must have felt when he found me gone! "He's no infant now. He's a young man with a bitter heart and the ability to disrupt time. I don't know how he came here, but he's got to be stopped."

I put my hands on Flora's waist to lift her to Sunburst's back.

"Wait." Tredienne's sharp command stopped me. "Search for your son if you must, but if you mean to have the fala carry out this deception, she must return to the house at once. Have you forgotten how frantic everyone is? If I go back alone and tell them you found and restored Flora, then carried her off, will they believe me? And if they do, will they continue to trust you? No, they must see this woman and think it is Flora and believe that you have saved her if you're to retain their trust and loyalty."

"She's right, Korth," Derli said. "I'd rather be with you, but in this flesh I'd be more of a hindrance to you than a help."

I wanted to argue, but I saw the truth of Tredienne's counsel. Much as I wanted Derli with me, I needed her as Flora to heal the hurts I'd caused Gil and his family. So I only said, "I'll come back as quickly as I can."

Flora's hands caught hold of mine. "It may take longer than you think, Korth. Divian *is* here—or was—and he didn't arrive alone."

"What do you mean?"

Derli gazed at me through Flora's troubled eyes. "I fled from Zera and she followed me. She would have caught me, but a time storm slowed her. Divian, caught in it, bounced between times like a ball on a string. Koralie appeared for an instant. I'd guess the storm was of her making, but she couldn't control it, so she withdrew. The storm brought Flux fiends, ravening after prey. At least one prowls this time."

I groaned. "I'll have to find it as well as Divian. No matter how long it takes. And Zera—she's here, too?"

"I don't know. She was, but I don't think she is now. If she were, I wouldn't have been safe in the grove where I hid, even though it's under Molor's protection."

"I doubt she fears Molor," I muttered. Louder I said, "All right, go back to the house. Derli, as Flora you can act for me with Dama Tredienne's help. I can trust you, as I could no other. You'll free me to mend the damage left by my earlier blunders. You and the dama will help me establish the traditions of the Manor Lands.

"Tredienne, you'll groom Treden to be my successor and train Peren's daughter Lonna to be dama after you. You will know when my spirit passes to Treden, and in the same way will each dama know when the inheritance has passed from one lord to the next."

Tredienne placed her hand on my arm. Her low voice was filled with concern. "My Lord Terral, don't speak as though you might not get back. Call on Molor for help. He'll keep you safe."

"Better to call on Zera," Derli said. "She's angry with me, but she still favors you."

"I'll call on them both, if I must," I said, searching for Derli in Flora's amber eyes. "Have courage. I'll come back to you, though I don't know when. I can't say where this search will take me."

Flora's eyes filled with a fala's tears. Unable to bear the pain I was causing, I turned away to mount Sunburst. "Hurry," I said to Tredienne. "Get home before nightfall."

Sunburst and I streaked north toward the Desert of Labon.

29

ICE

In the hills that fix the bounds of the Manor Lands I sensed a wild power sitting on the stony heights calling to the desert men, stirring up the desire for conquest, the hatred of the valley, the need for slaughter. Somehow I knew how to trace that calling. Lord's power—or Makor's? No time to think about it. I traced the power to its source.

The thing looked harmless—a bare-branched tree, twisted and gnarled from warring with the wind. Yet no tree had the charnel stench that rolled from that misshapen sentinel. The battle lust raged in me. I slid off Sunburst. He reared and struck the trunk with his hooves, while I drew my saber and slashed the encircling limbs. Twiggy fingers clutched at me. Thorns jabbed into my flesh. I ignored the pain and hacked at the limbs. Sunburst stomped on the dismembered pieces, grinding them into the hard earth.

With a shout of victory, I lifted my saber over my head and with all my force brought it down on the torso, splitting it lengthwise from top to bottom. The two halves fell away from each other. I chopped at one half and Sunburst trampled the other. Not until only battered chips remained did I stop, wipe sweat from my face, and rest my aching arms.

In the fading light of dusk the splintered fragments wriggled and twitched. The bits and pieces rounded themselves into small, dark, furry bodies. Legs sprouted from them, and long noses, and mouths full of sharp, white needles that glinted in the last rays of the departed sun.

I kicked and stabbed at the things, and Sunburst slammed his hooves into them. But some of the tiny creatures scurried off into the darkness. We flattened and ground into the dirt all that remained and hunted the ones that escaped, but they scattered and hid.

We were searching them out when a sudden sensation of fear and fury halted me. Divian! Through the tenuous link between us I was picking up a sudden strong emotion. He was in trouble.

I called Sunburst from a pile of stones he was kicking apart. "We'll have to let the rest go, Sunburst," I said. "They carry only a trace of the power that was in the whole, and not much of the intelligence. We can't let them delay us any longer."

Sunburst trotted to me and rubbed his nose against my hand. I scratched his head, shifted to his side, and mounted. "Now we know the origin of the nezzi that bit me in Medara's time. No wonder it poisoned me. I hate to let the scabrous pests run free, but we have to find Divian. He needs us."

The great red horse snorted, tossed his mane, and broke into a canter. I headed Sunburst in the direction from which the sense of Divian's presence seemed strongest.

That sense waxed and ebbed. I could not read my son's thoughts, perhaps because he was too far from me, or perhaps the link between us had grown weaker. The impression of danger grew no less, and I ached to reach him, but no matter how fast I rode, I could not seem to breach the distance between us.

Dawn found Sunburst still cantering through the stony hills that bordered the Desert of Labon. If Divian knew I'd been lord in this time, he might have gone to the Labonites to stir up trouble against me in revenge. That would be a dangerous course and might explain the impressions I was still receiving.

But Sunburst turned not toward the desert but in the opposite direction, toward the mountains.

"Sunburst, are you sure this is the way? He's not in the desert?"

Sunburst continued to climb the rugged paths that led to the mountains. I trusted his instincts, and besides, the feelings I was receiving from Divian did not lessen as the horse moved higher into the mountains. Neither, however, did they grow stronger.

To my great relief Sunburst did not take the way to the cave where Peren and I had found the falas and where Peren lay entombed. He selected a different path, one so twisting and tortuous no horse but he could have negotiated it. We had climbed a great distance when abruptly Sunburst halted.

Then I felt it. Or failed to feel it. The connection with Divian was gone. Try as I might, I could raise no sense of his presence.

We might simply have taken a wrong turn, but I didn't think so. Either he had been killed or he had somehow transferred to another time. In that case, had he done so deliberately, or had he been taken somewhere against his will?

I had no answer. "What do we do now?"

The great red horse leaped into the air. As had happened the first time I rode him, he took me through the paths between times. This time, though, I understood what was happening when the earth receded and the heavens rolled around us.

We passed in minutes from starlight to bright sun to cloudy night to blue daylight. Sunburst's hooves clattered over a rough stone lane. Ahead of us stood the Manor House. Its appearance told me we'd returned to Mett's time. I had the wild hope that Divian had sensed my presence as I had sensed his, grown afraid, and returned where I had ordered him to stay. Certainly, Sunburst had brought me here for some reason.

I dismounted, ordered Sunburst to wait, and hurried to the front entrance. No one responded to my pounding on the double doors. Where were all the servants? I tried the doors, found them neither locked nor barred. Muttering at this carelessness, I entered and passed through the foyer and the large reception room before I spotted a young servant woman hurrying along the corridor leading to the lord's quarters. With several long strides, I caught up with her.

"Is the Lord Mett in? And Dama Medara?" I asked, not bothering to explain my presence.

Her eyes widened. "Lord Mett is in, b-but n-not the dama."

I'd guessed right about the time Sunburst had brought me to. But what was this girl so frightened of? And where was Medara? "I must see the Lord Mett at once."

The girl made a hasty curtsy and ran off as though a fiend were behind her. She returned in seconds with Mett.

Seeing me, he paled and dropped to one knee. "Great Lord, I—"

"Where's Divian?" I interrupted.

He prostrated himself on the polished wood floor, and that action dashed my hope of finding Divian here. "Lord, slay me," he said. "I betrayed your trust."

I bent, grasped his shoulder, and yanked him to his feet. "My son is gone. I know. But how? Where's Medara?"

Mett raised his troubled eyes to mine. "Gone with him, Lord. While I was busy disentangling the Manor affairs, they spent their time together. I assumed she was carrying out your command. Too late I discovered he'd persuaded her to spell open a channel through time."

I scowled. "When and how did you discover this?"

Mett gestured to the girl who'd fetched him. "Her maid—Katrina—told me."

I turned to the girl. "Do you know where they were going?"

She curtsied again. "No, Lord. She wouldn't let me watch. And I'm not far enough along in the craft to—"

"She was training you? To take her place?"

Katrina nodded.

"This was no sudden impulse, then. The hussy planned it."

Mett agreed glumly. "Your son has a great deal of charm. He played on her weaknesses. I should have seen it before it was too late."

"Never mind. I have to find them. How long have they been gone?" My fingers tapped the hilt of my saber.

Katrina's nervous smile accompanied another curtsy. "Three days, Lord. But I couldn't report it till today. The dama had put a binding spell on me. I lacked the skill to break it. But this morning it weakened and I ran to tell Mett Lord Terral what I'd seen."

"Didn't Medara give you any hint of what they planned?"

She shook her head.

"Nothing?" I persisted. "What did they take? What did they wear?"

Katrina thought awhile, chewing on her lower lip. At last she said, "Medara carried a warm journey cloak and wore boots. Divian carried a large knapsack into the tower room, and he, too, wore sturdy boots and had a heavy cloak. Oh, and a coil of rope."

I thought immediately of the mountain we'd been climbing when I'd lost contact with Divian. I was sure Divian had intended to see Flora, but the clothes Katrina described suggested the mountains as their ultimate destination, though at first I could not imagine why. Then I recalled how on the day I met him, when my consciousness had linked with his, the youth Divian had gone to find Uta, wanting to go to the Mountains of Dawn where Zera hid Makor's body. I recalled his exact thought: *What a triumph if I could find the burial place of the god!*

Might he have found the body that looked like mine—Makor's body? The murals in the jungle temple had led me to suspect that I bore a physical resemblance to the god Zera had intended to be reborn in me. Her power must have shaped my physical attributes while I was in my mother's womb. But molding my inner self was another matter, one she at which she had not succeeded. Not yet.

I could not allow those memories to distract me from finding my son. If he'd gone to the eastern mountains, the fear and anger I'd felt from him could only have meant that something had gone wrong.

I had to find him quickly. "Katrina, Medara knew a very effective summoning spell. Did she teach it to you?"

"No, Lord. I hadn't progressed nearly that far."

"What did she teach you?"

"How to heal minor hurts. A little divination. She taught me about the deathright and how to find the lord's successor." She cast an apologetic glance at Mett.

Perhaps in sympathy for the girl he said, "Katrina tried using divination to search the time lines for Medara and Divian. But without any success."

"I'm not ready for that sort of thing," Katrina said, her eyes filling with tears.

"But you know something about it?" I asked.

"Not enough." She was sniffling now.

"Dry your eyes and blow your nose," I ordered her. "You're going to try again. I'll use my fascinum to boost your power."

Instead of doing what I asked, she burst into loud sobs.

Mett grabbed her shoulders and shook her. "Stop that!" he said. "Lord Terral is only asking you to try. What you couldn't do alone you may be able to do with his help."

Her sobs subsided. "I'll get the things I need," she said in a choked voice.

She wasn't gone long. Apparently she needed nothing more than a candle and a basin of water.

"Medara always used the tower room for her spells," I suggested. "Maybe it would help to go there?"

"I was never allowed there," Katrina said, still sniffling a bit.

"You have my permission to enter the tower room as much as you need while Medara is gone," Mett said gravely.

His pronouncement seemed to give her confidence. Carrying the water basin carefully so that it would not spill, Katrina led the way up the several flights of stairs to the tower. I followed, carrying the candle she'd brought, while Mett brought up the rear.

The tower room had a stale smell, as though it had remained closed and unused since I took my departure from it after defeating Scrug. Dust motes floated in the stream of light from the high, round window, making me think of Derli. How I wished she were here!

Katrina set the basin of water on the floor in the center of the circle of light. The three of us gathered around it and waited until the water settled and was absolutely still. Katrina took the candle from me and lit it, then held it so the flame was reflected in the water. Her hand was shaking badly. The reflected light juddered and danced in the water.

I put my hand over hers to steady it and grasped my fascinum with my other hand. I tried to channel power from the fascinum to her, but her fear blocked my effort. She chanted in an uncertain voice that faltered all too often. I could not recognize many of the words, but she repeated the name Medara over and over.

I grew impatient. This wasn't working. Hot wax from the candle was dripping onto my hand, and I was trying not to sneeze from the scent of the melting candle. Its light was barely visible in the sunlight pouring through the window. "Enough!" I said, grabbing the candle from Katrina's hand and extinguishing the flame.

The girl cringed. Tears filled her eyes. "It's no use, Lord. I told you I couldn't do it."

"You tried. That's all I asked. Now let me see what I can do on my own." The power I had tried to pass to her had built up inside me. I kicked the basin out of the way. Its water splashed over my feet and spilled across the dried rushes that lay crumbling on the floor.

Mett pulled Katrina back toward the door.

I centered myself in the stream of sunlight, spread my arms wide, and poured all the gathered strength into a single shout: "Medara!"

Why hadn't I shouted Divian's name? In my impatience, I wasn't thinking clearly, and Katrina's many repetitions of Medara's name had made it foremost in my mind.

With the thunderous sound of my shout light flared around me, and I stood bathed in a golden glow. I was dimly aware that Mett and Katrina had fallen prostrate. My attention was focused on a wraith-like form that appeared on the edge of the stream of light.

The form solidified. Medara stood before me in journey cloak and boots. She fell to her knees, her head touching the floor.

"Rise, woman, and explain why you betrayed my trust. Where is Divian?"

She didn't move. In a single stride I reached her, grabbed her arms, and yanked her to her feet. "Answer me!"

Medara for once was speechless. Trembling, she stared at me and her mouth opened, but no sound came out. When I released her, she dropped back to her knees, but kept her upturned face fixed on mine as though powerless to turn away.

I stepped away from the circle of sunlight, into shadow. Somehow I gathered my wits and forced myself to speak in a low, even voice. A human voice. "Medara, I sense danger to my son. You must tell me where he is and what's been happening to you both."

She burst into tears. "Lord, I'm sorry," she wailed amid sobs and hiccups. "I kept watch over him as you commanded. I never let him out of my sight, and that's what led to the trouble."

"What trouble?" My forced calm was slipping away. I heard my voice grow louder. "You were to prevent him from moving through time. Instead you went with him."

She wrung her hands. "He begged me. He made love to me. I couldn't resist—"

Again I lost control. "Never mind that!" My shout drove her face to the floor, hands over her ears. "Where is Divian? What trouble is he in?"

Her muffled answer was lost into the floorboards. I grabbed her hair and yanked her up. "Speak so I can hear you."

She took a deep, sobbing breath and without meeting my eyes launched into a long, rambling story.

"That witch tried to grab him. We were going back to find his mother, you know, because he'd persuaded me to tell him the story of his birth, at least what I knew of it—how he was snatched away as an infant to save him from Koralie. We almost reached that time when she found us. I fended her off the way I did before, but while I was doing that, the time storm caught him and I lost him for a while, and the fala was cursing me, and then I didn't know where or when I was, but I saw

Zera and I was that terrified I couldn't move or speak, just like now when I saw you all golden and terrible, only it wasn't me she was mad at, it was the fala, but she's fearsome, Zera is, and I don't see how anyone can worship her, and maybe she *was* angry at me, too, for bringing Divian into her temple when he was a baby and leaving him there. I'll never go into her temple again, I know that. Even if she wasn't mad at me, I caught the crosswinds of her rage and I expected to die, but then she was gone, and I caught up with Divian—was dumped on the ground in front of him, actually, though I don't know by what power." She drew a quick breath and went on. "Molor's, I suppose, because if the Winged One wasn't looking after me I don't know what saved me. But we had to run, and I kept saying we needed to get back to this time, but he wouldn't listen, he's that stubborn. Even though a Flux fiend was after him, he kept going, into the mountains east of the valley. He *would* explore the caves, though I kept telling him they'd be a good hiding place for fiends, and I was right, too, but he didn't care. He was hunting Makor's tomb, of all things, and wouldn't hear of giving up though I kept telling him what a crazy idea it was. He was climbing up to a ledge where he saw a cave opening, and then something swooped us away like an icy whirlwind, and I heard the voice of the goddess, and I knew it was her, though I couldn't see her, She was cursing Divian, and we were on another mountain, only this one was a mountain of ice too slick to climb and we were stuck on a wide ledge about halfway to the top, with no way of going up or down, and 'You'll stay there,' she says, 'until your father comes for you, and if he never comes, you'll rot or freeze, I don't care which.' And it was so cold we were shivering and hugging each other to keep warm, and Divian kept telling me to do something, but what could I do? I tried a summoning, but it didn't help. And then you called me and here I am."

By the time she finished, my ears were ringing and my brain was busy trying to sort out the strange tale.

Mountains of ice. "Can you find the spot again?"

"I—I'm not sure. Not the spot, no. Not by itself, I mean. But I think I can find Divian. Except I don't know how to reach him."

"Sunburst will carry us there," I said. "If you can just point him in the right direction."

She stood, then, and adjusted her cloak. "I'm ready," she said.

I was ready, too, but Mett cleared his throat. "Lord," he said diffidently, "if you could wait just a bit. I'll have the servants prepare a meal before you go. And while it's being readied, perhaps Medara could give Katrina a bit more instruction. In case the Dama Medara is gone for a long time, you understand."

I understood. It was very possible that the Dama Medara would not return. I felt no need for a meal, but the offer was only an excuse to give Medara a bit of time with Katrina. Reluctantly I consented to wait, not just for the serving of a meal, but for another whole day while Medara gave Katrina an intensive course in the arts of being dama.

It was a day I bitterly resented. It seemed to last forever, especially since I had nothing to do while Medara was closeted with Katrina. Mett was not an easy man to talk to, and I was in no mood for conversation in any case. I paced back and forth and cursed the delays that haunted me at every turn of my life.

I forced myself to be calm and use the time to think things through. When I'd called Medara from another time, I'd used power not mine but Makor's. They'd all seen Makor in me. I'd come very close to letting Makor control me. I couldn't let that happen again. I had to resist; I could not let Zera win. But my resistance was wearing low when the time finally passed and Medara declared her pupil ready to serve as dama in her stead. What Katrina still did not know—and that was a great deal—she'd learn through experience. Medara had passed on all the spells and secret knowledge she'd learned from Dama Ordell.

Wasting no time, I mounted Sunburst, and Mett lifted Medara up behind me. Medara locked her arms around my chest and we set off toward the eastern mountains. The ice mountain was no part of that range, but Medara felt that from there she could sense the direction to take through time and space to reach Divian.

I did not share her confidence, but when we climbed into the eastern mountains, we stopped and Medara dismounted. She sniffed about like a nezzi, whispered into Sunburst's ear, and climbed back onto the horse. She clung to me as off we went, Sunburst flying as he did when we passed through time.

Swift as Sunburst sped through clouds and cold and darkness and mist, the journey was a long one, and I was greatly relieved when finally we passed into light.

Sunburst galloped over a desolate plain edged by the shadows of a jagged range of mountains. Icy spires spindled the clouds. I gazed up at the white peaks. Was that the glimmer of gold on a distant summit? I dug my heels into Sunburst's side as though he could go faster.

I think he tried. But his flying hooves crashed against an invisible barrier. Sparks flew around us. I clung to Sunburst's neck to keep from being tossed into empty space. Medara clutched me so tightly I could hardly breathe.

"Easy, fellow. Easy," I said to Sunburst.

I couldn't see what had stopped us. Unable to find any barrier, I urged Sunburst forward. He limped a few steps and halted.

I dismounted and checked his front legs. The unexpected blow had lamed him. I rubbed Sunburst's legs and patted his neck. "Can you walk without our weight?"

He whinnied and bobbed his head.

I helped Medara down. "Looks like we'll have to walk from here."

No longer carrying us, the fiery horse moved more easily. The three of us marched at a steady pace toward the towering peaks. Medara trudged along in silence, not complaining, though her legs must have grown as tired and her feet as sore as mine.

The mountains remained distant. Nightfall brought us no nearer. I drew my poncho around me and plodded on, ignoring my aching feet, until Medara's stumbling shuffle forced me to stop so she could rest. I rested, too, leaning against Sunburst, but only for an hour or two. Then I urged both Medara and Sunburst back into motion.

A cold wind blew from the mountains, stinging our faces, slowing our steps. Something white, a patch of mountain fog perhaps, hovered above the path ahead of us. Leaning into the wind, I pressed forward ahead of Medara. The patch of white grew, took form. I halted.

The ghostly figure of Dama Brinabeth floated before me.

Medara screamed. The specter ignored her and addressed me. "This way is closed to you while Brid lies torn between life and death." Her words came in icy blasts that froze my soul. "Unless you free him, your son's life is forfeit. The Winged One has sent me from the timeless realm to bring you this warning."

"Dama, I believe my son to be in grave danger, and I have already delayed too long in going to him."

"You know the danger to Brid, and you have delayed even longer in going to him. And to the woman whose fate you bound with his."

I could not deny the truth of her accusation. My rescue of Brid and Renata was long overdue. But Divian ... "What of Medara?" I indicated my companion. "Will you allow her to join Divian?"

She reached down and touched Sunburst's foreleg. "The horse may carry your son's companion to him. You may not go there until you have fulfilled your obligation to Brid and restored the time line. This is Molor's will."

She faded like hoarfrost. Medara trembled with fear. Unable to speak, she appealed to me with her eyes.

I urged her to be brave and lifted her onto Sunburst's back. "Take her to Divian," I said.

The horse galloped forward, rose into the air, and like a dying flame disappeared into the mist.

Shivering, I drew out my fascinum. "Forgive me, Divian," I whispered. "You'll have to wait a little longer, but at least you won't wait alone."

My breath was cool. The fascinum warmed slowly. I stomped my feet and rubbed my hands together, and at last a burst of heat surged through the channeler.

I pictured the Manor of the young Koralie's time.

The fascinum obeyed. In a breath the water sculpture played before me in the Great Room. Beside it Koralie leaned on her staff, her hands cupped around the head of the fiend so that I could see its glittering eyes. The dama smiled. "Welcome, Korth Lord Terral. I've been expecting you."

30

FIRE

The water sculpture's sparkling spray caught the reflection of Koralie's purple velvet gown and played with it, mixing it with mirrored candle glow to create a cascade of sparkling lavender. The candlelight softened the sharpness of Koralie's features and emphasized the long sweep of her lashes, the deep mystery of her dark eyes. Her raven hair flowed over her shoulders and caressed the satiny curve of her breasts above the low-cut gown.

"I've waited long for this meeting, Korth." Her voice was low and seductive. She took one hand from the fiendish staff and thrust it into the spray. "You've grown strong." Her smile showed sharp, even teeth. "You bring great power to the lordship." Her dripping fingers touched my wrist and traced the elemental symbol of fire on my flesh. The scent of myrtle swirled around me. My pulse raced. The mark on my wrist burned like a brand. I could feel the spell she was casting taking effect, making me desire her. Making me willing to obey her.

But I was wiser now. I stepped back and drew out my fascinum, letting it hang outside my shirt. "The time for my lordship is not yet come. This time belongs to Brid."

She laughed like a tinkling bell, though her eyes strayed to the fascinum. "Are you not lord in every time, Lord Terral?"

"A lord may not toy with his trust." I rubbed my wrist. "You must wait your proper time."

"My proper time!" She spat. On the staff the fiend's eyes sparked. "When Brid dies of old age, I too shall be old. Shall I contain my ambition until then? Curse Lord Stamsel for lingering so long before passing the deathright to his successor. Brinabeth grew old and her hair turned white with waiting. The more fool she! I'll not do the same." Again she thrust her fingers into the flowing water, placed them on my cheek. Her voice softened. "Think, Korth, what our combined power can accomplish while we are both young and our strength is at its height."

I caught her hand and drew it from my face. Her fingers entwined with mine. Her other hand, holding the staff, circled my waist. The fiend pressed against my back. Her body, warm against mine, kindled fire within me. Her lips found mine. Drowning in her scent, I clasped her shoulders, held her tight against me.

With a silent call to Makor I channeled my body's fire into the fascinum pressed between her breasts. She screamed and leaped back, clutching the burned skin. "You brand with water, I with fire," I said.

Eyes blazing, she hurled the staff at me. I caught it one-handed and held it by the heel. Letting the fiend's head hang just above the ground, I swung it back and forth.

"I'm footsore and weary and have no more time for games," I declared. "Take me to Brid."

She splashed water on her chest, but the red imprint of a grave pillar remained on the ivory skin. "You have no gratitude, Korth. Who made you lord? Who opened to you the doors of power? Who taught you to traverse the time channels?" Warily she eyed the swinging staff. "I have done you great good, and you repay me with evil."

"You delude yourself if you believe you did any of those things. You can no longer distinguish evil from good. Lead me to Brid."

She lunged for the staff, caught its head, and ripped it from my grasp. "I underestimated your strength. I think you underestimate mine. Very well, we'll go to Brid, and see which of us is stronger."

She removed a candle from the candelabra and, with it in one hand and the staff lifted like a baton in the other, she marched off. I limped after her, thinking how foolish I'd been in calling on Makor's power. I'd had no choice. Koralie was too strong to battle on my own. Yet every time I used his power I came closer to that point when Korth would be subsumed in Makor. Could I already have passed that point?

No, not yet. Even when I let the power flow through me, I knew I was no god.

We wound through the darkened corridors of the oldest section of the Manor House. She led me into the concealed passage. This time no false barrier impeded our entrance. I recognized the low, curtained archway that admitted us to the familiar cell. I hurried to the narrow cot on which Brid lay. His beard had grown so long that it hid his chin and neck. His bones showed through transparent skin; his closed eyes were sunk deep in the skull-like face. I could detect no breath in the emaciated form. Had Koralie cheated me?

"He lives," she answered my unspoken question. "To end his life is a task for your hands, not mine."

She set the candle into a holder on the bedside table and looked down at Brid's face. I edged along the other side of the cot and stood opposite her. We locked gazes across Brid's pitiful visage. Koralie gripped the staff. I lifted my hand to my fascinum.

With the staff Koralie drew a symbol in the air between us. A trail of flame marked the movement of the staff, and loops of smoke formed a glyph of power.

I raised my fascinum to my lips and blew across it. A blast of wind tore the glyph apart and scattered the smoke.

With a grim smile Koralie raised her staff and twirled it around her head. A swirl of flame cascaded down, enclosing her in a cocoon of black smoke and showering the bed with sparks. I swatted the smoldering sparks, making sure I got them all before they transformed the cot into a pyre. Again I blew across the fascinum and sent a wind to whip away the twisting column of smoke.

I stared at empty space.

Tricked! Koralie was gone and the arched entrance had also vanished. Four solid stone walls enclosed the room. Exhaustion weighed on me like a cartload of rocks, putting the spell that sealed me in beyond my power to break. Especially distracted as I was by the burning pain that throbbed through my feet.

I sank down on the floor and pried off my boots. Gingerly I probed the raw and blistered flesh and wished Medara was here to heal the hurt. In my sleepy dream-state, the memory of Medara led my mind to

Divian and my interrupted journey. And to Derli, who waited in her prison of flesh.

I sat up. I recognized this near sleep to be another of Koralie's spells. I grasped my fascinum and pressed it against my forehead, focused my mind strength, and wove a barrier against the spell.

My mind cleared. I addressed the air. "I shall sleep, Koralie, but not at your command."

I made another circuit of the room, tracing warding signs on the walls. Koralie had sealed me in; I sealed her out.

Satisfied that the room was secured against her return, I peered down at the frail figure on the cot. Koralie hadn't bothered to throw a coverlet over him. I shivered at the thought of his lying all this time in the cold and damp in only a peasant tunic, and faded, thread-worn breeches, the clothes gray with dust.

I wrapped my poncho around me, squeezed onto the narrow cot beside him, and spoke over my fascinum a plea to be drawn to Brid's place of torment.

My limbs grew heavy, my heartbeat slowed, numbness crept over me.

I floated in a darkness that drove out everything but pain. Caught on the Flux where life and notlife meet and time and timelessness converge, I was stretched between the opposing forces like a frayed flaxen thread. The moans of unseen sufferers recalled my mission.

I did not wish to do the thing I'd come to do. Better to go back and escape the torture. Already accepted as lord in Brid's stead, I could release him from his suffering in the way Koralie had suggested—it would be a simple mercy to close my fingers around his throat and quench the feeble spark of life.

Fingers. Here I had none, nor any corporeal form. Yet the pain was real. How had Brid endured it for so long? "Brid! It's Korth. Brid?"

"Here," a faint whisper answered my call. "Help me!"

"I've opened a way for you." I whispered in return. "Follow it back."

"And you?" His question smote my conscience. I'd been tempted to return alone. He, whose suffering had endured much longer than mine, thought immediately of me.

"I must remain here," I said with a firmness that brooked no argument, "but I'll be with you in your mind as you have been in mine. Go."

A point of light appeared, grew larger. "Trace the light to its source," I instructed, recalling my previous sojourn in this gray land. "When you wake, you will be weak and in need of help. Summon Brinabeth."

Brid awakened, and I awakened with him, though my body remained still as death. As I had shared consciousness with Divian, so I shared with Brid.

Confused, disoriented, and frightened by his physical weakness, he tried to sit up but sank back onto the mattress with head whirling. Black spots danced before his eyes.

After two more unsuccessful attempts, he managed to drop his legs over the side of the cot and sit hunched over, head between his knees, fighting dizziness.

Summon Brinabeth, I mindspoke.

I do not think he remembered our meeting or knew that the words within his mind came from an alien source. Nevertheless, he lifted his head and in a tremulous voice called, "Dama Brinabeth, help me."

His head fell again to his knees.

The sealed walls were no barriers to Dama Brinabeth. Her ghostly form wafted through the solid stone. Her touch on his brow was no more than the brush of a snowflake, but it cleared his mind and eased the dizziness.

"Courage," she said. "This room is warded. I must discover how to breach the wards to allow Kast to enter and carry you out. Lie back and rest while I read the signs."

He stretched back on the cot and noticed for the first time my body lying beside him. Startled by the belief that he lay next to a corpse, he rolled aside, toppled off the narrow cot, and knocked over the bedside table. The fall extinguished the candle. Groaning, he tried to lift himself from the floor. In the darkness the figure of Brinabeth glowed with its own pale, unearthly light. I'd forgotten that he didn't know she was dead. He fainted, and I lost my window on the outer world.

When I regained it, Brid was no longer in the cell. He lay in a large, soft bed, his head supported by pillows, a warm counterpane thrown over him. Kast stood by the bed. The warmth and comfort reassured Brid; the presence of Kast instead of the spectral Brinabeth provided needed contact with normalcy.

Kast bent over him. "You're safe, Lord Brid. I've brought you to my chambers to guard you and keep your return secret until you regain your strength. Here's water, and I've sent for food."

He held a crystal goblet to Brid's lips, and he drank. I felt his pleasure in the cool, pure liquid.

A knock at the outer door heralded the arrival of the promised food. Brid's eyes followed Kast through the sitting room. I tried with Brid's vision to see whether Renata lay on the lounge in that front room, but only a tantalizing corner of the lounge was visible through the bedroom door.

Kast returned bearing a tray with a soup tureen and a fragrant loaf of fresh-baked bread. To my astonishment the haughty lord ladled broth from the tureen into a bowl and held the bowl to Brid's lips. When Brid had taken several sips, Kast broke the bread, soaked a piece in the broth, and placed it into Brid's mouth.

When he'd gone to get Brid, Kast must have seen me lying on the bed where Brid had lain for so long, but he made no mention of seeing me there. He knew I lived and had somehow fallen into the same state that Brid had endured. He no doubt still considered me an enemy, and probably felt I was receiving my just punishment, perhaps believing that Brinabeth had consigned me to that fate.

After finishing his meal, Brid fell into a natural and healing sleep that left me in limbo, the first of many periods of nullity before he grew strong enough to rise from his bed and walk unaided. During this time I had too much opportunity to wonder and worry about the condition of my own body, which must still lie on the cot in that hidden cell.

Kast kept close watch over his patient, but he'd left the room when Brid decided to test his legs. He stumbled to the window, leaned on the sill, and gazed out at the garden.

Brid, hear me, I mindspoke. *The first Lord Terral speaks to you.*

Only the support of the sill kept him from falling. "Who? ... How?"

Don't be afraid. You are the Inheritor; have you not heard the voices of the past lords?

"They were faint and indistinct. Your voice booms out over my own thoughts."

I share your consciousness in a different way from the other lords. I told him how I'd swum against time's current to bring him back from the void to which Koralie had sent him, how I'd taken his place and left my body in the hidden cell where his had languished for so long. I explained what he must do to release me.

He straightened and tottered toward the door.

Wait, Brid. You don't have the strength to confront Koralie.

"Shall I let you grow weak and helpless as I did? Shall you suffer as I suffered? No! By all the lords who preceded me, I swear to free you and wreak vengeance on Koralie."

Don't be a fool. You're no match for her. You can barely stay on your feet.

"But with the old lords lending me power ..." He paused, his hand on the knob of the door to the outer room.

Not enough. Give yourself two or three days more.

His hand clenched the doorknob. I felt his stubborn resolve. *Go on,* I said. *Enter Kast's sitting room and walk around in it. Test your strength.*

He opened the door and padded into the sitting room. A large oil lamp on a stand provided illumination. Brid glanced at it and headed resolutely toward the outer door.

Look around before you leave the safety of this suite, I cautioned. *You may need a weapon. See what you can find.*

He stopped at the door, turned impatiently, and swept his gaze around the room. I achieved my purpose. His eyes settled on what seemed to him to be a wax figure on a lounge. Drawn by the sight, he moved closer.

Renata lay as she had when I had last seen her, except that the fresh red blood that had soaked the bodice of her gown had become a dried brown stain. Her condition, so like that from which he'd been rescued, aroused a deep sympathy. He bent over her, placed his lips on her mouth. I felt her icy lips warm beneath his kiss. Her eyes flickered open. I remembered all too well that Brinabeth had said Renata would be restored if and when I had restored Brid.

Brinabeth had kept that promise. Renata was saved!

I hadn't forgotten that of all the juggler's shrunken heads, Renata's had been the first one I could name. To one I had yet to give a name. Of the others whom I had later named, all were dead, and directly or indirectly I'd caused those deaths. Brinabeth had died of a spell set by Koralie, but I had made it possible by becoming Koralie's tool. Pik I killed defending myself, but I had been at least in part a cause of the madness that drove him to attack me. I'd killed Peren accidentally, but my carelessness and folly had thrust me into the plight that caused that accidental blow. Those deaths I mourned and regretted. I'd killed

Ordrain in a sword fight, but it hadn't been a fair fight, with Derli helping me by distracting and finally blinding him. Had I learned enough from those deaths to avoid causing the two remaining? That Renata lived encouraged that hope.

Brid knelt beside her, enfolded her hands in his, chafing them to restore the circulation. A weak smile rewarded his efforts.

My delight to know Renata lived and to see her awaken blinded me to the intensity of Brid's attraction. I spoke in his mind, telling him who she was and of the knife wound she'd been dying from when Brinabeth cast a spell on her and entrusted her into Kast's care.

"Renata," Brid murmured. "A lovely name."

Her eyes focused on his. Her smile grew stronger.

Gently he eased her gown from her shoulder, exposing the knife wound above the curve of her breast. The wound was closed, nearly healed. He touched it lightly, let his fingers wander over the velvet skin.

Brid! My mental rebuke jolted him. He drew the gown back in place.

Renata's eyes had not left his. In a voice soft as a caress she whispered, "Who are you?"

"I'm Brid Lord Terral."

The reply should have puzzled her, for was *I* not Lord Terral? She only smiled and laved him with her eyes.

Brid, leave her. She's safe for now, and I still need your help.

He ignored my plea.

You'll have a hard time making him believe that, with her gazing at him the way the moon eyes the sun. Kadry's booming voice startled me. I'd forgotten the old lords' presence with me in Brid's mind.

Pity you didn't let him wake you when he wanted to. You may not get his attention again.

I feared the truth of Maxin's wry comment.

Ungrateful wretch! Mett's voice rasped.

Lucky I'm caught up with my rest. Sleep won't interest him for some time, if I know the signs.

By Molor, Stamsel, do you think of nothing but sleep? Can't you see Brid's distraction can be fatal to Korth?

Of course, since my consciousness was in Brid's mind, these voices were as audible to him as they were to me, but he brushed them aside like annoying flies.

What do you advise, Lonness? Treden asked.

It was Ladin who responded. *If he won't heed our warnings, there's little any of us can do.*

Ladin's sober assessment proved true. At that moment Kast returned and rushed to Brid's side. "My Lord, I'm glad to see you improved and this woman awakened from her long sleep. But you tax your strength and hers as well." He caught Brid's arms and lifted him to his feet.

Renata clutched the sleeve of Brid's dressing gown. "Stay," she pleaded.

Kast plucked Brid from her feeble grasp and propelled him firmly into the bedchamber. "I must speak to you of a matter of great importance. I'll send for serving women to care for Renata." I noticed that Kast did not accord Renata the title of Lady that I'd conferred upon her. He pushed Brid onto the bed and left.

Brid sat up and glared after him, but he had exhausted himself and did not try to rise again. Kast returned, closed the door between the two rooms, and drew a chair up to the bedside.

"My Lord, I've had servants scouring the house and lands in search of Koralie. She is not to be found. Wherever she's hidden herself, she'll be plotting against you. I'm glad to see you able to walk about. I can reveal your return to the other councilors."

"The Lady Renata ..."

"Renata holds no title. Now that she's awakened, it's not seemly for her to remain here. I've ordered her moved to other quarters."

"Where?"

Kast dismissed his question with a wave of his hand. "The other councilors are on their way. They'll have questions. We must discuss your answers."

"No! I want an answer to *my* question!"

"Lord Brid, she is not worthy of your concern. I assure you that she's safe and well cared for—despite the fact that she is most assuredly a worshipper of Zera."

"Zera! But still—I want to know where she is. I'd like to see her." He was stubborn, and I could see in him the strong lord he was destined to become. I was sending him mental warnings throughout this exchange with Kast, and he was ignoring them in his single-minded determination to know more about Renata.

I thought he'd forgotten me until he said with clear impatience, "Very well, I'll leave it for now, but there's something I must do, an obligation to fulfill, once this meeting with the councilors is over."

"My Lord, the councilors are coming here because I assured them that you are too weak to leave your bed. Please don't make me seem a liar. You are weak yet, and while you may walk around this apartment, you are not yet fit to prowl about the Manor House."

It's fine, Brid, I sent. *He's right, and I can wait a little longer. It's important now that you win the councilors over and convince them of Koralie's duplicity.*

He yielded then, and I resigned myself to remaining in this painful state a bit longer.

The wait proved longer than I'd expected. I had plenty of occasions over the next several days to recall the many things that had conspired to keep me from restoring Brid. Now I waited for restoration, and with the waiting my presence in Brid's mind grew weaker. At first I'd been scarcely aware of that part of me that languished beyond the shoals of time. But I felt increasingly drawn, stretched painfully between Time and notTime until the attenuated thread of being that clung to Brid's thoughts had little strength to make itself heard. Brid had to act. I tried to convey the urgency, but the councilors kept him so busy he had neither time nor energy to spare. I suffered through five days of preparations and instructions leading to the investiture ceremony.

That ceremony was less elaborate than the one I'd been put through. Brid still tired easily. At the feast an empty chair on Brid's left symbolized Dama Brinabeth's authority and Koralie's perfidy. When the dama was invoked, her ghostly presence filled the chair, terrifying the guests. The three councilors seemed unsurprised by the apparition.

When Brid retired to his chambers after the dinner, I mustered what little force I retained to remind him of his duty. The old lords chimed in to back my request.

Brid took up a lamp and went into the hall. I could give him little guidance, and the cell was well hidden. Not knowing what else to do, he made for the servant quarters and caught the house servants doing their own celebrating with the leftover food and wine. They quaked at the unexpected appearance of their new lord.

He reassured them with warm smiles. "I'm glad to see you enjoying yourselves after all your hard work," he said. "No, no, don't stop eating. Why should so much food go to waste? I didn't come to spoil your evening."

He had come here with the intention of asking about secret passages and hidden rooms. But he was quick to grasp this opportunity to discover where Renata was being held. He peered at the empty bottles and glasses. "You haven't much wine here for toasting your new lord. Let's have some brought up from Lord Terral's private stores. Wine steward, have you the key?"

At that ruddy-faced gentleman's enthusiastic nod, Brid clapped his hands. "Hurry, then. Bring up enough for a real celebration."

The man scurried off, and Brid strolled around beaming, patting shoulders, squeezing hands, pausing to question each awed man and maid. Was he contented with his work? Did she feel she received sufficient wages? Were unreasonable demands ever made or additional duties imposed without extra compensation?

His final questions he addressed to all. Had those who'd prepared and served his meals while he was an invalid in Kast's chambers been rewarded for that service? No? And what of the other invalid, the Lady Renata? Surely those entrusted with her care deserved generous bonuses. Who were they, that he could see to their payment?

Hesitantly a tall, gaunt woman stepped forward and confessed to preparing and serving the lady's meals. "A service I'm glad to render, Lord, and I never considered it more than my duty and privilege, but it does get a bit tiring, climbing all those steps three times a day."

Brid sounded horrified. "You alone do this? No one helps you? You yourself make all those wearying trips up— let's see, how many flights of stairs is it?"

The woman drew herself up and with the pride of a martyr said, "Five flights to the east tower room, Lord."

I had to admire his cleverness, though I seethed at the delay this would mean for my rescue. With the promise of a purse of gold, he wheedled the tower room key from the woman and left the servant wing. Undeterred by the late hour and with no sign of weakness, he ascended the five sets of stairs to the tower.

When Brid unlocked the door and peered into the room, Renata jumped from her chair clutching about her a dark green robe that emphasized the creamy whiteness of her skin. The fear on her face changed to joy and relief when she recognized her late night visitor. Her cheeks glowed; her sapphire eyes sparkled.

This was the tower room in which Medara had worked her spells, furnished now, its floor carpeted. But of the furniture I caught only the barest glimpse. Brid's gaze fastened on Renata and clung there.

Brid refused to heed my voice. The danger to me and to the time line from his delay, the pain of being suspended between two opposing states, the frustration of my failure to communicate with Brid, built up a tension that begged for release.

When Brid drew Renata into his arms, I abandoned myself to the joy of their kisses, their tender caresses, the shudders of ecstasy as their bodies joined, his urgent thrusting and tornadic release, the two lying entwined in each other's arms murmuring sleepy confidences and listening to the harmony of their mingled heartbeats.

But instead of Renata's rare beauty, I saw only Derli in Flora's body. That image of her—trapped, lonely, awaiting my return—cooled my ardor.

I was relieved when Brid left Renata sleeping and crept downstairs in the deep silence of pre-dawn.

The next day Brid could think of nothing but Renata. He ignored my weak voice, forgot my plight. He'd made up his mind to wed Renata. The councilors had to be persuaded. He visited each one separately to plead his case.

"Don't be a fool!" Kast exploded. He fingered the carved bird on his dagger's golden hilt. "You beg trouble. She was beloved of Korth, who was a tool of Koralie. Your lordship is safe only while by Brinabeth's power Korth lies in death-dream. Renata is dangerous. She'll plot for his release. This infatuation of yours has the smell of a plot of Koralie's." As usual, Kast had everything twisted.

His adamant refusal inflamed Brid, who made no attempt to correct his notions but marched from the room and went straight to Hulsin.

"Renata, eh?" Hulsin twirled his fascinum of braided hair. "The mandolin player. Korth had an eye for her, too. She's a freedwoman, though Korth named her a lady." He dropped the silver chain and let the circlet of hair fall against his chest. "If you confirm the rank, you confirm his lordship. You're playing with fire. Leave her alone."

Hulsin was unbendable as an iron rod. Brid stalked off to Boral's apartment.

Boral's reaction was less intense but no more encouraging. "You've enough to do learning your duties as Manor Lord. This is no time to worry about taking a bride—a Zeran, at that. You'd stir up all sorts of trouble. Furthermore, you'd put her in grave danger. Have you considered that?"

He hadn't. He considered it now and decided that for her sake he must renounce the love he felt for her. At the same time, though, he wondered whether she and I had been lovers. I tried to convince him that we were not, but my voice was weak, and what message got through did not convince him. He had to talk to her again, to ask her if the charges the lords raised against her were true.

That night, near midnight, Brid climbed again to the east tower room. He recounted to Renata the reasons he'd been given for denying his petition to wed her. She assured him that she and I had never been lovers, nor had she encouraged my clumsy advances, which she described in embarrassing detail. She begged him to dismiss his councilors' advice. Their love would defeat Koralie; its strength would overcome all opposition. She convinced him not only with words but followed those words with passionate kisses.

Brid surrendered to that passion. I could not bear to participate again in his lovemaking. I let myself be claimed by the pain of the Flux.

I could scarcely get back into Brid's consciousness, so weak was I, and so full of Renata was he. He muddled through the day's obligations with her face floating before him, and at night he slipped again from his suite and stole through the darkened halls toward the east tower.

He ascended two flights of stairs. The acrid odor of smoke broke through his enraptured thoughts. He raced up a third flight of stairs and rounded the smoke-filled landing. Flames leaped at him from the fourth staircase. The heat drove him back, but his love spurred him on. He dashed toward the red tongues of fire. Powerful arms caught him, pulled him back. He struggled in an iron grip.

"Calm yourself, Lord Terral," Kast's voice ordered. "You can't reach her. It's too late."

With a strength born of grief and rage, he tore free of Kast's hold and hurtled toward the flaming stairs.

A white figure, arms outstretched, barred his path. He skidded to a halt, frozen by Brinabeth's icy gaze.

"Turn back. Run." Her sharp commands sounded above the crackling blaze. "Fetch Korth."

31

PARTINGS

The white wraith of Brinabeth glided before Brid, guiding his running feet to the hidden cell. With a wave of her hand, she dissolved the wards.

"Hurry," she said. "Do as he tells you. I'll provide the exchange. My return to the timeless realm is overdue."

She vanished from Brid's sight, and I felt her cold, scant presence beside me in my prison. She passed to me the arcane spell that Brid must use to free me from my exile.

The past lords put aside their differences and joined themselves to my enfeebled essence. Even the whisper-thin soul of Chevor added its puny force. Thus bolstered, I passed to Brid the words to summon me back to my body.

Brid's voice rang out in a call that thundered in my ears. My eyes flickered open. Brid helped me to rise. "Fire. Renata's trapped. Hurry!"

His plea drove me up onto shaky legs. I took four or five deep breaths. "Hurry!" he urged again.

But I had lain helpless too long. I not only lacked the strength to hurry, I could barely stay on my feet.

He dashed through the passage and into the main corridors, and I tottered after him. He was soon lost to my sight, but the suffocating smell of smoke told me the way he had taken. I soon came upon brigades of servants bearing buckets and tubs of water. They scarcely took time from their task to indicate the stairs Brid had climbed. I paused at that stairway, but the first of several leading to the tower. I was too weak to climb even this one.

Although my own infatuation with her had long since cooled, I understood Brid's grief at the possibility of losing the lovely Renata. I felt his desperation. This was no time to refuse the power I could call on, though I knew the price of that calling. I raised my fascinum to my mouth and breathed over it the name, "Makor!"

Power burst from the fascinum in a flash of light. I felt Makor's power fill me. It told me what I must do.

"Sunburst, to me!" My shout echoed across time's ocean until it blended with an answering neigh and the steely drum of hoofbeats. By then, my strength returned and increased, I'd climbed the stairs before me and headed through the smoke-filled hall to a second stairway.

The great red horse took form beside me—the horse of a god. And with a god's power I matched my pace to his, leaped to his back, bent, and clasped his neck. Through the billows of smoke we flew, into the hungry flames where no horse but Sunburst could have gone, up the crumbling stairway where none could follow, through an inferno of exploding beams and falling timbers, to the flame-engulfed tower room.

Leaning from Sunburst, I snatched up the still form huddled on the floor beneath the window. I straightened, and Sunburst leaped through the window as the tower collapsed around us. Sunburst and I glided on a swirling cloud of smoke to the garden five stories below.

The fire died. It had done its worst. The entire east wing of the Manor House was a smoldering ruin. And in my arms I held the sooty corpse of the lovely Renata.

The flames that killed Renata also burned away most of what was left of Korth. Like a phoenix from its pyre I emerged as Makor from the conflagration, filled with the powers I'd forgotten. I cast a bidding into the reeking air.

Brid ran toward me and dropped to his knees. "Lord?" His voice trembled with awe.

"Up!" I ordered. "Look at what your stubborn delay has wrought." I forced him to gaze at the scorched remains of his beloved.

With an anguished scream he backed away from the tragic sight. "Renata," he sobbed, and repeated, "Renata!"

More gently I said, "Because you have seen this consequence of your folly, you will be a wiser and better lord. Wisdom is never gained without price. Fetch a shovel. We will make a grave and lay her to rest."

Brid stared at me with pain-dulled eyes. Though he must have known he had answered the call of no mortal man, I think he did not yet realize he faced a god. "Go," I said.

He moved off as if in a dream, returned with a shovel, and followed Sunburst and me deep into the woods. In a hidden clearing Brid dug a shallow grave. I dismounted and eased my sad burden into it. Brid stood blinded by tears. I took the shovel from his hands and covered the grave myself.

When I finished, I placed my hands on his shoulders and forced him to look at me while I gave instructions. "Have a grave pillar made, with a design of vines and lilies. Renata was a follower of the goddess. This spot alone of the Manor lands shall henceforth be sacred to Zera."

He nodded, still too dazed to understand who spoke to him. I led him back to the Manor House. At the garden entrance I stopped. Among the shouts of the servants searching out live embers and clearing debris from the ruined east wing I identified Kast's lusty bellow and guessed he and the other councilors were directing the work.

They would have to manage without Kast. I needed his strength. A word spoken over my fascinum drew the haughty lord to me. Soot streaked his face and hands; his brocaded vest was soiled and torn.

He raised his arm to his forehead, wiped away a corona of sweat, and glared at me. As Brid had been blinded by grief, he was blinded by anger. "Why did you call me from my duty? Haven't you troubled us enough?"

"I require your aid. Koralie is the troubler, not I. The fire smelled of witchcraft. It had to be her doing. We must deal with her."

His lip curled. "Who are you to deal with that witch? Disrupter!" He spat the epithet.

I straightened and let my regained power break forth in a dazzling burst of light. Sunburst shimmered with a fiery radiance. "I am the first Lord Terral, sent to this time to heal the lord line, not disrupt it." I withheld the greater truth. The partial explanation would do for these followers of Molor. For now.

Brid covered his eyes.

Kast fell to his knees and bowed his head to the ground. "Forgive me, Lord," he pled in a muffled voice.

I dismounted and raised him to his feet. "You've acted rashly, but always out of concern for the Manor Lands. You need no forgiveness. Join your strength to mine and Brid's."

I grasped one of Sunburst's reins. My other hand caught hold of Brid's. Kast took Brid's other hand in one of his and the second rein in the other. Stretching our arms, we formed a wide circle.

I raised my head toward the smoke-stained sky and chanted:

"By the power of the Twins I call thee.

By the will of the Twins I bind thee.

Now does thy fate befall thee,

For the Twain I send to find thee—

Winged Molor, in restless flight;

Golden Makor, by death-won might.

Bring Koralie to me here.

Koralie, I command thee, appear!"

With a loud thump, like a large bird brought down by a hunter's arrow, Koralie plopped into the center of the circle.

She rolled over onto her knees and thrust her staff before her like a shield. "Who summons by the Twins?"

"I." Dropping Brid's hand and Sunburst's rein, I stepped toward Koralie.

She sneered. "You think to gain power by a spell that invokes a dead god?"

I folded my arms across my chest. "It drew you here."

"To laugh," she said. "And to punish you for your temerity." She lifted the staff toward me; the fiend's evil face leered into mine.

I did not move. She spoke a releasing spell. The fiend blinked and flexed its claws. Its body straightened. Its leathery wings unfurled. Unflinching, I stared into its yellow eyes. As Makor, I had no fear of the thing. "Turn!" I ordered.

It twisted on its shaft and lunged at Koralie. Its talons clawed her shoulder. She screamed, dropped the shaft, and tried to tear herself free.

I unfolded my arms and caught the headless staff. "Retreat!"

At my shout the fiend shrank back onto the shaft and curled into its captive position. I held the restored staff toward Koralie. She backed away, clutching her torn gown. Blood streamed from the deep gouges on her shoulders.

"Take your staff," I said, looking into her eyes.

She could not break her gaze from mine. Her hands stretched slowly toward the staff. Her fingers closed around the shaft.

"You claimed this staff as yours, Koralie," I said. "You will keep it ever with you. If you abuse your power or attempt to unleash the Flux fiend, it will turn on you and complete its kill."

"I don't want the staff." She held it out. "I renounce its power."

"Too late." I continued to hold her gaze. "You will carry the staff until I choose to take it from you. If you try to put it aside, you will release the fiend and it will destroy you."

I beckoned to Brid and Kast. They stepped to either side of Koralie.

"Brid Lord Terral, Koralie must complete her service as dama. To punish her as she deserves would disrupt the time line. You must let her grow old in your service, obedient to your wishes, growing herbs, healing the sick, birthing babes, casting fortunes, overseeing the house servants, spinning and weaving."

Koralie's face grew sourer with each addition to the list.

"Kast, see that she fulfills her responsibilities. If she grows lazy or tries to work counterspells, you have only to touch your dagger to the staff. Demonstrate."

Kast drew his dagger and touched its jeweled hilt to the fiend's arm. The arm shot toward Koralie. She screamed.

"Back!" At my order the arm pulled back and the fiend reverted to its petrified state.

"Kast, persuade Hulsin and Boral to allow her to serve as dama," I commanded. "Brid Lord Terral, yours will be a long lordship and a prosperous one. Your first task will be to oversee the rebuilding of the east wing. May you find solace in that work.

"Dama, long years will pass before you and I meet again. I counsel you to find joy in your duties. If you allow hatred and bitterness to fester in your heart, your rage will consume you."

She glared at me and did not speak.

Kast fastened a shrewd gaze on me. "Surely no Manor Lord, not even the first Lord Terral, has had such power at his command. I think you are more."

"You've gained wisdom," I said. "But for now it is best to see me as the first Lord Terral, who has no more to do in this time."

After a last speculative look at me, Kast took Brid's arm and led him toward the house. Staff in hand, Koralie trailed after them.

Alone in the garden I leaned wearily against Sunburst. That I had failed to save Renata caused me sorrow. At least Brid was restored. Though to do so I had had to let Makor through after working so hard to suppress his growing power.

I was thinking as Korth! Makor's power had flowed through me, but the god had *not* completely taken over. It seemed I need not yet lose myself by becoming Makor. Could he be as reluctant to return as I was to yield to him? Another possibility: of the juggler's seven heads one remained unnamed. I'd failed to save the six I'd named. If I failed with the seventh, perhaps Makor's restoration could not become complete.

Much as I wished to remain Korth, I also wished to cause no more deaths. My deepest desire was to go back to Derli. To do so, I'd have to draw on Makor's power without becoming Makor. I had no choice if I was to find and rescue Divian.

Sighing, I warmed the fascinum with my breath and spoke my son's name over it. Nothing happened.

I pictured the mountain where my quest had led me until Brinabeth had turned me back. I willed the channeler to take me to that place.

Again, nothing happened.

I mounted Sunburst and tugged at his reins. "Take me to the mountains where you left Medara," I said. "Lead me to my son."

The red horse tossed his mane and neighed but did not move.

How could I find my son if neither Sunburst nor my fascinum would cooperate?

A masked figure in belled cap and motley flashed before my eyes. I recalled the juggler's taunts at our last meeting, when he'd stolen my sword. He knew where Divian was. I didn't know where the juggler was, but I knew a place he might be.

I leaned low and spoke into Sunburst's ear a command to take me to the inn where I'd begun my journeys in time, selecting a time several years before my first visit there. He neighed and sprang into motion. In a moment the Manor House was far behind us.

I rode wrapped in my thoughts, only dimly aware when Sunburst streaked across the bridge over the Rethe and entered Zera's domain. We took the bridge over the death-marsh and followed the lane past the trapper's shack to the inn, still intact in this earlier time.

I dismounted. "Ho!" I shouted.

A thin-faced youth came running. "Good sir?"

"I come to break my journey here. I'd like my horse fed and groomed." I took a decim from my belt pouch and placed it in his hand.

The lad's eyes sparkled. "I'll see to it, sir."

"What time is dinner served?"

"Just after dusk, sir, but I warn you not to expect much. The cook quit this morning and my master hasn't found a replacement."

I thanked him for the warning, watched him lead Sunburst away, entered the inn, and looked around. Behind a desk stood the innkeeper I remembered, though several years younger than before.

Not seeing the juggler, I took a room. Always before, he had found me. I hoped this time would be no different.

Washed and rested, I appeared for dinner at the appointed hour. As the servant lad predicted, the food was wretched: stale bread, scorched meat, half-cooked vegetables. I surveyed the table and its reflection in the mirrored wall behind it. Only one other guest had braved the innkeeper's cooking: a man of middle age wearing the red and gold robes of a Zeran priest. He motioned me to the seat beside him.

"Not the best of fare," he said, waving a long-fingered hand at the unappetizing array. "But weary travelers have to eat. A bit of pleasant conversation might improve the taste."

I nodded, accepted the serving bowls he passed me, and speared two or three vegetables that looked edible.

"Your poncho marks you as one who bears the goddess's favor," the priest said. "Are you journeying to the temple?"

I shook my head. "I have sought it and may do so again, but now I travel in search of my son." To discourage further conversation I sipped wine from a tall-stemmed goblet.

My companion carved a blackened chunk of meat and placed a piece on my plate. "Ah, he is lost? It is a hard thing to misplace a son."

Frowning, I dragged an undercooked turnip back and forth across my plate. "My son is rash and impulsive. He's lost himself."

"If you go to the temple, the goddess may find him for you."

"I haven't pleased the goddess of late. I doubt she'd trouble herself."

"You can't be sure until you've tried." Chuckling, the priest reached again for the platter of meat. He picked up his knife and hacked at the burnt slab.

A tinkle of bells interrupted his carving. The knife clattered to his plate. My gaze jerked toward the doorway.

The juggler leaned against the doorframe and tossed a single head from hand to hand. "Why not ask *him* to send you to your son?"

The priest rose from his seat. "You dare—"

With a peal of raucous laughter the juggler waved his hand toward the mirror. "Look! I'll show you where he is."

The reflection of table and room dimmed and faded into a high, jagged mountain of green ice. On a narrow ledge halfway up that slick, forbidding wall two figures struggled, perilously near the brink.

The ledge loomed nearer; the figures grew larger. Wielding my sword, Divian battled a beaked and bat-winged fiend. Its scaled arms fended off Divian's thrusts. Sharp, dagger-length nails swiped at my son. His clothing was tattered and soaked with blood. He swayed, exhaustion lined his face, and his knees trembled. He fought with the mechanical movements of one ready to collapse.

Behind them was Medara, on her knees, hands gripping rocks, tear-streaked face intent on the battle, waiting, I guessed, for a chance to hurl the stones at the Flux fiend.

With a cry of rage I leaped toward them—and crashed against unyielding glass. The scene faded. I spun around, my saber in my hand.

The juggler was gone.

I grasped the priest's robe and hauled him toward me. "Send me to Divian. He said you could."

He pushed against my chest. "Sir, I'm forbidden—"

But I was beyond reason. My rage drew forth Makor's power. And

I recognized the priest. Or Makor within me did. Savnar had warned that he would appear in other guises. He had, and now they were all clear to me: the old nut-gatherer, the beggar at the temple, Ander the Innkeeper, and now this priest. All were manifestations of Vandesar, who had been Makor's liegeman and no doubt Lisha's attendant since Makor's death.

Vandesar. I not only knew him, I recognized something else. His was the seventh head, the last one remaining to be named. He must not die as the others had. But I didn't have time to think about that now.

"I know you, Vandesar," I said. "You are sworn to Makor, not to Zera. You must send me! Now!"

He flinched. "May Zera forgive me." He traced a mystic symbol in the air. "Go, Lord."

Instantly I lighted on the frozen ledge, inches from Medara. She gasped. I lunged forward and stabbed my saber into the creature's scaly armor.

It penetrated the hide and struck bone. The blade snapped. Waves of pain shot up my arms. Snarling, the creature lunged at me. I ducked and feinted toward the wall of ice.

"Divian! My sword!"

He slid the sword across the slick green ice. I caught it and with a shout drove the blade deep into the Flux fiend's breast. It let out a yowl, reeled, and toppled backward. Its shuddering wings caught Divian and swept him from the icy ledge.

Medara screamed. I sprang to the rim. "DIVIAN!" I thundered with Makor's power.

His descent slowed, stopped. He twisted slowly like an insect caught in a spider's strand.

I took a deep breath and called him to me, my words cleaving the frigid air. He rose a bit and stopped. I strained. He floated higher. "Come!" I poured into the command all the power I could summon.

He drifted upward once more but stopped just out of reach. His body brushed against the ice. With a screeching groan and a sharp crack the ice parted, sucked him in, and jammed together, sealing him in a bubble beneath its surface.

I turned and stared at the fallen Flux fiend. It lay still and rigid. It could not have trapped my son. I lifted my gaze upward, where sunlight glinted on crags and spires of ice.

On a pinnacle high above us stood …Lisha? No, Zera, her red robes fluttering in the thin air.

"Release him!" I shouted.

"Come to me!" she called back.

"I can't scale this mountain."

"If you wish, you can. You know the way."

"Release him."

"Join me."

"I cannot."

"Then he must stay sealed."

I shut my eyes, grasped my fascinum, and sent Makor's force through the thick ice to the bubble in which Divian lay trapped. He slept, but his heartbeat was strong and even. "Sleep on," I whispered though he could not hear. I wrapped him in a blanket of warmth.

I looked up. "Zera?" I called. "Goddess?"

"You know me and yet refuse to come? You choose your fala and your bastard son over me? Pfaugh! I should have left you a slave." With a toss of her head and a whirl of her robes, she was gone.

Medara wept hysterically. I pulled her to her feet. "I'd hoped you'd found a way to get Divian to a place of safety," I said.

"I-I cou-couldn't," she said between sobs. "None of my spells would work here. Something blocked them. And he didn't want to come. He wanted to go to her." With an upward lift of her head she indicated the place where Zera had stood. "He has the idea that she's his mother."

"He thinks *Zera*—" I began incredulously, then started to laugh. "That fool boy. Didn't you tell him how mistaken he was?"

"I tried, but he wouldn't listen. And I never heard the story of his birth. I only knew his mother was from the time of the first Lord Terral."

It was true. I'd never taken time to tell Medara of Flora. And Divian had been reared in the Zeran temple with no knowledge of his parentage. Koralie had told him of the rite of Lord's-Kill and showed him how to recognize me, but she couldn't have told him he was my son. He hadn't learned that until our battle with Scrug. To make him more reckless, Koralie might have hinted that he was the son of Zera.

These musings had distracted me from Medara's continuing prattle. Knowing how long it took her to reach a point, I was used to shutting out most of what she said. But I caught a few words and sensed I'd missed something important.

"… of course I shouldn't have, but it was so cold on that ledge, and we couldn't go up or down, as I said, we were stuck there to freeze, or it seemed like we were freezing, though we tried hard to keep each other warm, and I didn't know the spell would even work—none of my others did, as I said, so I doubted that one would, but when you're that cold you get desperate and try anything you can, and—"

"By the Twins, Medara, what are you saying? What did you do?"

She gave me a curious look. "By Molor, you mean," she said. "And don't think I didn't beg the Winged One for help. I cried and called out to him over and over, but he wouldn't answer, so that's why I tried the other thing, though as I say, I didn't think it would work, but—"

"Come to the point, Medara. What did you do?"

She hung her head. "Well, I didn't mean to do it, of course, but I brought the Flux fiend here."

"*You?* How?"

"I told you, I only meant to keep us from freezing to death in the night, it was so cold, and I couldn't conjure up a fire no matter how hard I tried, so I thought of the warmest place I'd ever been, and that was the Badlands, when we were hunting Mett, and his desert men took me across the lava lake and left me on that hump of land, you remember how hot it was. Well, I tried to think of that heat and imagine it around me here, and just, you know, *imagine* it was warm the way it was there. So I pictured the lava lake and all the heat rolling off it and the blasts of steam and all that …"

Her words brought back the memory of Derli in Abbi's body wading across that burning lake, suffering to save me. The anger I'd felt then toward Medara came back and grew as she continued her tale, prolonging it deliberately, I was certain.

"It seemed to be helping a bit—the memory of all that heat—so I kept on adding to the pictures, bringing in all I could remember of that terrible place," she continued seemingly interminably. "The sun's burning heat, the fountains of lava, blasts of steam from vents you didn't see till they opened in front of you and nearly burned you up. I was picturing one of those in my mind, when it seemed I could really see it in front of me, a little piece of the Badlands right here on the ice shelf, though of course I knew it couldn't be, or thought it couldn't, but the burst of heat was real enough, and where there'd been ice there were red-hot stones, and a great gap opening in them, and Divian saw it too, so I wasn't dreaming. We backed off from it, not just because of the heat, but something was climbing out of the gap. It looked like Pik at first, and I started to cry out to him, but then he changed and it was the Flux fiend, and when he was out of the gap and standing, the heat and lava and sharp stones all faded away but the fiend was still there, standing on the ice shelf, grinning at us. We just stood there staring at one another for a few minutes, then the fiend lunged for Divian."

"So you opened the way for that thing to attack my son," I said, my voice taut with fury, not just for this one foolish act but for all the things Medara had done to endanger and destroy others.

"But I used my powers to channel strength to him while he fought it, or he would have been killed long before you got here, so I saved his life, you know, and I—"

"Silence!" I sheathed my sword, lest in my anger I use it against her.

She shrank from me and cowered against the ice.

"Foolish girl!" I grabbed her arm. "I know the punishment for you."

I took my fascinum, warmed it in my hand, and spoke into it. The walls of ice receded. The walls of the dining room closed in around us. The room was empty; the priest had gone. I summoned the innkeeper.

"You need a cook," I said when he appeared. "Take this girl. She'll work for no wages save a room to sleep in and the food she eats." I thrust her toward him. "Let her grow fat in your employ. Keep her here until I return."

I left the innkeeper gaping and strode out to the stable. The boy I'd met when I arrived ran toward me and threw himself at my feet. "Forgive me, sir. I don't know how it happened." He shielded his head with his arms as though he expected me to strike him.

"What are you talking about, lad?"

"Your horse, s-sir," he stuttered. "I—I fed him and groomed him as you told me. I was sure I'd closed the stall door. I was leaving the stable when a red streak flashed by me. I went back in, and your horse was g-gone." He began to sob. "I've looked everywhere. He's run away, and I'll lose my job and—"

"Quiet, boy. It's all right. I won't report you."

"You—you won't?" He lifted a face streaked with tears and dirt. "I'll pay back the decim."

"Keep it. You've done nothing wrong. The horse will come to me when I need him."

As Sunburst was gone, so was Makor's power. Makor had come to rescue Brid, find Divian, and fight the Flux fiend. But now he left me, as Sunburst had. My rejection of Zera must have caused him to withdraw. I wondered whether he would ever return.

Perhaps I should have yielded and gone to Zera to save my son. But I knew what the cost of that yielding would be. Zera could be gentle and loving. Her avatar, Lisha, had reminded me of those aspects of her. But she could also be stubborn and vengeful. I'd had a taste of those aspects already.

I walked through the darkness to the road in front of the inn. Clouds obscured the stars. I stared upward at the river of their dark flow.

"I'm sorry, Divian," I said to the empty air. "I'll try to find a way to rescue you without accepting Zera's terms. It may take a while. May your wait teach you patience." I pulled out my fascinum, raised it to my lips, and pictured Flora with Derli's essence sparkling in her eyes.

32

SORROW

A trifle unsteadily Gil rose and lifted his glass, his face flushed and beaming. His relief when I'd explained that the witch who'd prevented me from wedding Flora had been vanquished was evident again in the pride with which he proclaimed, "A final toast to our lord and his lady before they retire to their bridal chamber. May their union be prosperous and fruitful."

Crystal chimed, and cheers rang out around the tables crowded into the common room. I rose and clasped my bride's hand. My other hand rested on Gil's shoulder. I said, "Wife's brother, wise counselor, dear friend, to your ever gracious hospitality, your unfailing patience with my long absences, your wise leadership during those absences, you have added this greatest boon of granting me your sister's hand in marriage. Already I've named you Head of the Lord's Council. I can do no more than commend you to Molor and ask for you his enduring favor." I squeezed his shoulder.

Wild applause filled the common room. Gil gripped my hand. Hanna and Jena kissed their sister's cheek. Only Tredienne, seated on Gil's left, did not share in the gaiety but stared into the wine in her glass as though reading a tragic tale in its red depths. I refused to allow Tredienne's gloom to dampen my joy. Waving and smiling at the crowd, I led my bride to our room and shut the door against the din below.

I gathered Derli, in Flora's body, into my arms, kissed her, and carried her, laughing, to our bed. Her arms tightened around me, pulled me close against her. "I wonder if I'm dreaming, Korth. I can't believe you came back."

"How could I not come back to you?" I kissed her mouth, her chin, her neck. "Did you think I would leave you to suffer alone, imprisoned in Flora's body for who knows how many years?"

I felt her shudder. She pressed her face into the hollow of my neck and shoulder. "I fear for us," she whispered. "This isn't what Zera intended—our being together like this."

"Hush. This is no time to think of her." Of course she was right, and we both knew that my return here and our wedding would bring eventual retribution. We'd discussed it before taking this step. But by refusing Zera and thus blocking Makor's full return, I'd won more time to live out my life as Korth before yielding to the inevitable. I was willing to pay the price, and Derli was resigned to it. My deepest regret was that my happiness was bought at Divian's expense. There would be an additional price for that, I was certain. But I suppressed that knowledge, refusing to let it spoil this night and as much time thereafter as might be granted us before the goddess acted.

I opened the fasteners on the back of her gown and peeled the dress from her shoulders, pausing to kiss the creamy flesh.

I helped her slip off her lacy gown and whispered in her ear, "Now, my love, I'm going to teach you the advantage of flesh."

My mouth caressed her breasts, and the nipples hardened beneath my kisses as Flora's body responded to a fala's desire. Her fingers plucked urgently at the buttons on my shirt and trousers. Clothes discarded, I snuffed out the candle and lifted her onto the bed.

How rich with love were those early days! As lovesick as Brid had been for Renata, I rejoiced in the ever-changing wild harmonies of our bodies in concert.

I never tired of Derli's ready wit. When the oversight of the Manor lands grew tiresome, when crop failure or illness or threat of Labonite attack made me anxious and foul-tempered, she knew how to cure with a tender touch, an understanding caress, a soothing song. Her easy laughter never failed to brighten my mood and restore my sense of perspective. Our love deepened from month to month and, as time passed, from year to year.

Derli reminded me often of Divian's plight. Not that I had forgotten my son. I grieved for him, but she and I both knew that no matter how long we lingered here, when we—or I—made the jump in time, it could be to a time only moments after Zera had sealed Divian in ice. We also both knew that as Korth I was no match for Zera and would have no hope of freeing Divian. I would have to give way to Makor and let him do it. And in yielding my will to his and letting him come fully forth, I would be lost as Korth and Zera would have won.

So I lingered, letting the years roll by, enjoying being a mere mortal,

Korth to Derli and Lord Terral to everyone else. Makor remained submerged. I was free to love Derli and relish the time I spent with her.

We were rarely separated for more than a day, but once an unusually strong Labonite attack took me from her side for three months. A hard-fought battle on Manor land left many dead on both sides. Seeking revenge, we pursued the enemy deep into the desert. Using nezzis to track down their camps, we fought them on their own ground and drove them to take refuge in the Badlands, where we left them, their numbers greatly diminished, and returned weary and wounded, to our homes.

Flora/Derli raced across the fields, her skirt billowing, her bare feet sending up silver sprays of dust. I dismounted and dashed toward her. Laughing and crying, she hurled herself into my arms, and I whirled her around, drinking in the sweet smell of her, the warm softness of her body. My exhaustion vanished. We ran hand in hand to the house, leaped up the steps, laughing like children, tore off our clothes, and tumbled onto the bed. The whole household must have heard Derli's happy squeals and my rollicking laughter. The bed creaked and groaned and the walls shook with our frenetic love-making.

Much later, calm and content, lying in her arms, I said, "Dear love, I'll never leave you again."

Her fingers traced my lips and stroked my beard. A note of sadness crept into her voice. "You will, though, Korth. One day ..."

"Hush!" I twisted around, clasped her to me, and kissed and consoled her till our passions rose again and we thrust aside the awareness of what our futures held.

I knew too well, though, what she meant. Streaks of gray dusted her dark hair; her ageless spirit looked out through eyes nested in tiny wrinkles.

A few days later we carried a basket to the stream and picnicked on the rocks along its bank. She dangled her feet in the stream and, giggling, dipped a handful of the clear water and flicked it at me. I caught her wrist, gave it a playful smack, and pulled her to me. She snuggled into my arms. "Korth," —she alone called me by my slave name— "Korth, this body's getting old. I feel the changes. My bones ache and creak, and my skin is going flabby. I don't like it, Korth. You don't change. Even though you don't draw on Makor's power, Makor must keep your body young and firm. Soon I'll look like your mother, then your grandmother. And how will you love me then, my dearest? How—"

I stopped her questions with a long kiss. "I'll love you no matter how your body changes, because it's you who wear it. Don't fret. The more worn and aged your body grows, the nearer your release."

She sighed and hid her face against my shoulder. "I'm not in a hurry for release. Separation from Flora's body will mean separation from you. I can't bear that, Korth. I can't."

I hugged her tight against me and rocked her, smoothed her hair, covered her with kisses. "We have long years ahead of us," I lied. "You'll tire of this flesh and of me before they end."

She smiled and returned my kisses, and made love on the stream's edge, and afterward she sang me to sleep.

She must have known then what all too soon became apparent to everyone: Flora's body, lacking its original tenant, aged early. Twenty years had passed. Flora should have been in robust midlife, but her withered body was that of an old woman, far older than her sisters and Gil. Derli never complained, but I saw the suffering in her eyes as her shoulders hunched, her face became lined, her hair grayed and thinned.

In truth I loved her no less, and during her last year I scarcely left her side. On days of warm sun I carried her outside and we sat on a wide wooden swing Gil had made and hung from a sturdy limb of the oak tree by the cookhouse. Hand in hand we swung gently and talked of old times and laughed together, and sometimes we wept a little.

The time came when she could not rise from our bed, and I lay in it with her, holding her, stroking her, giving her warmth.

Early one morning at her whispered request I wrapped her in blankets and carried her from the house while the household slept. I woke only Tredienne and told her where we went. She alone would understand.

I carried Derli in Flora's failing body to the cypress grove. Deep into the solemn lanes I trudged, and in the shadowed stillness I laid her down.

"Love me one last time, Korth," she whispered.

Gently I complied. Like a dying rose she opened her faded petals to me. As in a great concerto, though the trumpets were muted, the melody was there, its intricate harmony intact. The fading notes rose to a final, glorious crescendo. There could be no encore. I withdrew, and with a sigh and a shudder Flora's body yielded to death.

Blinded by tears, I wrapped the blanket around her and rose

clumsily to my feet, clutching the trunk of the nearest cypress for support. From the tall tree's crown an aria, sad and haunting and wild, floated down, its melody tearing at my heart. I stood frozen until the last pure notes swept off with the wind.

In the terrible stillness that followed, I bent, picked up Flora's corpse, light as a dry leaf, and stumbled back toward the Manor House.

Tredienne met me and helped me into the house with my burden. She stayed at my side and lent me strength through the outpourings of grief from Gil and Jena and Hanna. Somehow I endured the long vigil beside Flora's withered body, the funeral ceremony the next morning, the early afternoon burial in what would become the Manor graveyard. I commissioned the carving of a tall pillar to mark her grave. Engraved on it would be a lily dying on a broken stem while from its drooping petals a bee emerged, ready for flight.

That evening I talked long with Tredienne about the lord line and how it must be preserved. The next morning I sought out Treden, Hanna's son.

Treden had grown into a tall, sturdy man, tanned and muscled from helping Gil in the fields. I called him into my study and shut the door. He shifted nervously from foot to foot and wiped sweaty palms on the hem of his tan tunic.

The awe with which his brown eyes regarded me was the general reaction of most of the younger valley dwellers. I'd performed no marvels among them in the years since my return to wed Flora, but the old stories circulated and grew with every telling. I studied his expression carefully, my silent scrutiny adding to his nervousness.

Beads of perspiration lined his upper lip, but his open face held nothing of the suspicion and resentment I'd come to see of late on many older faces, my supposed contemporaries, who wondered at and envied my lack of aging.

Some, I knew, accused me in covert whispers of having by sorcery taken my wife's years to add to mine. Thus they explained my youthfulness and her rapid aging. They could not know how gladly I would have transferred my agelessness to her if only I could.

But this was not the time for regrets. "You know, Treden," I said, "that you are to succeed to the lordship."

He blinked, tried to swallow, choked, and I had to pound him between the shoulders. When he recovered, he stammered, "I ... I'm a simple man, Lord. Dama Tredienne has tried to teach me, but ..." He dropped his gaze. His large peasant hands twisted his tunic.

I smiled. "You're more qualified than a slave I know to whom the deathright passed."

"Lord?" His brows knit in bewilderment.

"Never mind. Don't be afraid. You'll be a great lord. You'll build a fine Manor House to pass on to a long line of inheritors, you'll master swordsmanship, and you'll lead forces in victory against the Labonites."

"Lord, I don't know how to do any of those things."

"You will learn." I went to the door. Tredienne was waiting in the common room for my summons. She hurried in and stood silent, her back against the closed door.

"It is time," I said to her.

She nodded.

I drew out my fascinum, warmed it with my breath, placed it in front of Treden's mouth, and blew over it into his parted lips.

I reeled back, weak and dizzy. Tredienne leaped to my side. I clutched her arm.

Treden's eyes bulged. Gradually a look of comprehension settled over his face.

"I've given him most of my strength," I gasped. "Help me through the channel, Tredienne."

Again she nodded. Her arm around my back supported me. I raised a hand to Treden. "Hail, Treden Lord Terral."

A whisper over my fascinum opened the channel from the time of the first Lord Terral to that of the last. And though I had spent over twenty years in the time of the first, I hoped I'd arrive in the time of the last to find that little time had passed since I'd left.

Above all, I hoped that I could reach Divian in a time only shortly after he'd been sealed in the ice.

33

TURN OF THE CIRCLE

In my weakness, I needed a refuge in which to rest and regain strength for a confrontation with Koralie and, if I was to save my son, for an even more dangerous confrontation with Zera. Accordingly, I bade the channeler transport me not to the Manor House, but to the inn whose mirrored wall had first sent me back in time. I aimed for a time prior to all my previous visits.

From where I stood on the road that ran past the inn, I could see my goal a short distance ahead. Its sign was freshly painted, the building it hung from new and inviting. I headed for it.

A sudden memory stopped me. I recalled Derli's sniffs as we had neared it that first time. Vividly I remembered how I'd mocked her for claiming she could smell evil. I'd refused to listen to her then, to tragic results. How I wished she were with me now and could tell me whether the smell of evil already hung around this inn.

I remembered the trapper's cabin we'd passed on our way here and my stubborn insistence that it was the danger we'd been warned of. I'd been wrong then. Why repeat the mistake? I turned and headed away from the inn, toward that cabin, hoping to find it in this earlier time.

The walk was long and tiring, and I'd decided the cabin must not yet be built when I spotted it in a stand of trees that hadn't been there in the later time. Like the inn, the cabin was new, its rough log walls still smelling strongly of the sap that had recently run through the living trees from which they were cut.

I made my way to the door, and, after tucking my fascinum out of sight beneath my shirt, I knocked on the rough wood. Feeling a bit foolish for having given in to impulse, I almost hoped no one would answer. But the door swung open, and I faced a bearded young man who greeted me with a wide smile.

"I was advised to seek shelter here," I said.

"Oh? There's an inn just up the road a bit that offers more comfortable accommodations. But come in." He stepped back and with a sweeping motion of his hand indicated I was to enter.

I did so. The interior of the cabin was as rough as the outside. The furniture was crude: a handcrafted table and two chairs, a hammock swung from the roof beams, shelves built out from the side wall. A small stand held a pitcher and basin. A fireplace equipped with a metal spit and a hook from which a kettle hung provided his kitchen.

"So who told you to come here for shelter?" he asked, motioning me to one of the chairs.

"A nut gatherer," I said, withholding the fact that the advice would be given in a future time.

"Ah. Well."

"I can see you have no place for a guest," I said. "It would be an imposition—"

"No, not at all." He went to a pile of cloth in the corner and dug out a second hammock. Triumphantly he held it up for my inspection. "You see, I can string this up and easily make room for you. And as it happens, I've trapped a young boar. It will provide us with ample meat, and I've a small garden in back of the cabin that supplies me with more vegetables than I can eat by myself. So if you don't mind plain fare and the lack of the comforts the inn would offer, you're welcome to shelter here."

I accepted, assuring him what he offered was more than satisfactory. I didn't add that his accommodations were so reminiscent of my slave days as to make me a bit nostalgic.

I told him my name, Korth, and he gave me his, which was Meir. He asked to know no more about me, did not seem curious about where I came from or why I needed shelter. Grateful for this lack of curiosity, I settled in to enjoy my stay.

The hammock was comfortable, the food plain and delicious, the company pleasant and undemanding. Meir went off each morning to check his traps and spent each afternoon skinning his catch, cleaning and curing the meat, and preparing the pelt for tanning. If he'd brought back several small animals, as was often the case, I helped him with that work to the extent of my limited ability. I also helped in the garden, work at which I was competent, thanks to the knowledge beaten into me when I was a field slave.

Meir was not a conversationalist, so evenings were spent in companionable silence. Left to my own devices in the morning, I rested and exercised to build back my strength. The first morning I explored the cabin, which took little time. His belongings were few. His shelves held no books or papers, only utensils for cooking and eating, carpentry tools and the knives and scrapers used for his work, a few candles. Only one item stood out as incongruous in this rustic setting. On the end of the top shelf was a silver globe. A seam around its widest part indicated that it might open, but it did not respond to my twisting. Not wishing to damage what wasn't mine, I put it back where it had rested. And because my host had respected my privacy, I respected his and asked him no questions about himself or about the silver globe.

This pleasantly uneventful existence continued for many days. But the time came when I was strong, healthy, and growing bored. I knew it was time to move on to the tasks that awaited me: defeating Koralie and rescuing Divian. Tasks that could well destroy me, but I felt refreshed and ready to face them.

So I told Meir I'd rise in the morning when he did, and take my leave of him. I assured him I'd never forget his kind hospitality.

He went to the shelves and took from the top shelf the silver globe I'd wondered about. "Then I guess it's time to give you this," he said, placing the globe in my hands.

"What is it?" I asked, turning it about.

"I don't know. But I believe it is yours. Some time ago a man in strange clothing came to me and asked me to keep this until someone came here asking for shelter, even though the inn was close by. He said that if the man seemed content with what I had to offer and stayed here with no complaint, I was to give him this silver ball before he left. He never told me what it was for."

That was the longest speech I'd heard him make. I asked him to describe the man's "strange clothing," and by his response guessed his visitor to have been the juggler.

"Did he tell you how to open this?" I tried to twist apart the two halves.

"He said that you would know."

"But I don't. So maybe I'm not the one he intended it for, after all." I held the globe out to him.

He stepped back, shaking his head. "He said you would only be able to open it in a time of greatest need. He told me to insist that you take it."

I was mistrustful of anything that came from the juggler, but I was also curious. So I put the globe into my pack.

The next morning I left the cabin when Meir did, walked with him a short way, until our paths diverged, and he went off into the woods while I stayed on the road.

As I walked, I pondered the dilemma I faced. I'd promised Savnar that I'd return to him at the moment I left to go back to the time of the first Lord Terral. He'd implied that when I returned, I'd have to complete the transition to Makor. Was that true? I didn't want to break my promise, but neither was I ready to yield my life as Korth.

It had been some time since I'd felt Makor's presence, begging to be made whole and free. It had also been some time since I'd used my fascinum. Savnar had warned that it drew on Makor's power. Yet without Sunburst I had no other way of passing through time. I had two goals. I wanted to defeat Koralie and claim my rightful place as

Manor Lord. That goal I wanted to accomplish as Korth. The second goal was to free Divian from his icy tomb. I could do so only as Makor. To save my son I must lose myself and let Makor return fully to life.

Accordingly I decided to keep my promise, return to Vandesar in his guise as Ander the Innkeeper, and there convince him that I should cross the Rethe and as Korth assert my lordship over the Manor Lands.

I pulled the fascinum from beneath my shirt and let it warm in my hand. I pictured Ander as I had seen him last in the small office of the inn in Diakos.

He was gazing at me when I appeared before him in the exact spot I'd left from. He smiled. "You kept your promise, as I trusted you would."

"I did, but I'm not yet ready to cede myself to Makor." Ignoring his frown, I went on to explain my determination to wrest from Koralie the place that was mine by deathright.

I expected an argument, but he merely nodded thoughtfully. "Koralie's rule there has been overlong," he said. "Since Councilor Kast died, I've heard constant rumors about her cruelties. Here at the inn I've received refugees from the Manor Lands, who come lamenting the harsh conditions there."

"Can you gather these refugees?" I asked. "Any who are able and willing to fight for their rightful lord?"

"I can. I believe there will be many such."

"Do so quickly," I said, adding, "I trust you, Vandesar."

With a wide smile he rose from his chair and went down on one knee before me. "My Lord," he said. "I rejoice to do your bidding."

"I am not Makor," I cautioned. "I am Korth, and it is as Korth Lord Terral that I go to do this thing."

"You are not Makor," he echoed. "You are Korth. But Makor is strong within you. He lacks only one bit of his essence to become complete." With that he left to do my bidding while I pondered what he'd said.

As before, he'd offered me the hospitality of the inn, and I was headed for the dining hall when loud neighs drew me to the street outside. Sunburst cantered up to me, and I flung my arms around him. He whinnied a joyous greeting.

"So, Sunburst," I said. "You've come back to me. I thought I'd lost you as well as Derli." I buried my face in his mane to hide the tears that came with the memory of my lost love.

He turned his head and gently nibbled my ear. I drew comfort from his familiar horsey smell and from the rippling of his powerful muscles. "You must have sensed my need, my friend. Korth Lord Terral will arrive in the Manor Lands in a way befitting his station."

The fresh green-gold of spring velveted the fields through which I rode, enjoying these pleasant moments of solitude, Sunburst's matchless canter having outdistanced the escort Vandesar had recruited and armed. Vandesar had not joined us but had chosen to stay behind at the inn. I left my pack with him, but first removed the silver globe and fit it into my belt pouch, a tight fit possible only because the pouch was empty of coins.

The great red horse whickered and pranced, proud and frisky as a colt. I laughed and reached forward to pat the thick-maned neck. "You're right, my friend. It's been too long since we rode together. Go. Fly to the bridge. We'll wait there for the others to reach us."

The horse burst into motion. Air streamed past me with a solid force. Its chill reminded me of my obligation to Divian, an obligation I could fulfill only as Makor. Sunburst was Makor's horse. Was that why he'd come back? To let me know that it was time to let Makor emerge?

Sunburst slowed and halted, his front hooves thumping on the wood of the bridge across the Rethe. I caught my breath and dismounted. Shading my eyes, I scanned the fields through which we'd passed but could not spot the squad of men coming after us.

"We'll have a long wait, Sunburst." I frowned at the sight of two armed Manor Land guards at the bridge's far end.

They sighted me at about the same time. One guard put an arrow to his bow and took aim. Knowing I was out of range, I watched, unafraid. The other guard moved away, no doubt to alert a superior who would send word of my coming to Koralie.

He crossed the greensward and passed into the trees. Moments later he dashed out and ran toward his fellow as though a fiend pursued him. The archer loosed the arrow. It arced upward and curved gracefully down into the waters of the Rethe. He threw down his bow, and the two guards, as if driven, trotted toward me across the bridge. They drew near, their faces taut, their eyes great with terror. When they were no more than two body-lengths from me, a disembodied voice barked an order from behind them. "Halt and acknowledge your true lord, or I'll transform you into snails and throw you to the fish."

The two Manor guards paled and fell trembling to their knees in front of Sunburst and me. They moaned with fear.

Though it was disguised, I recognized the voice and fought to control the laughter bubbling up inside me. Derli! I had to keep my face stern. I did not trust myself to speak, but I could not control the radiance that burst from me for joy. Sunburst caught my excitement; his mane rippled into flame.

"Don't move!" The order to the prostrate guards vibrated with suppressed laughter.

I could bear it no longer. I tugged on Sunburst's reins. Sunburst gave a twisting leap over the two guards and landed sideways, blocking the bridge behind them. The guards started and scuttled directly toward my escort, now riding into view.

"Derli!" I loosed the laughter I'd held back, let it burst forth in torrents. Derli's joyous trills blended with it. Her pattern glowed around my face like a net of diamonds. I thrust my hand into it, and my fingers glowed with a witch-fire of dancing light. "My dear, dear love! How did you get back? The channels—"

"Were closed to me," she finished for me. "I forged a new one."

I glimpsed behind that casual boast a vision of suffering, loneliness, and grief. My shudder brought her dancing motes of light into a tight swarm around my face. "I'm with you again," she whispered. "That's all that matters."

My arms ached to hold her. I watched streaks of light dance across my fingers, and grew sad because I could not feel their touch.

My escort of two-score men cantered to the bridge, the two guards in their midst. The captain, a tall, solemn man, directed his horse forward and halted before me. "Sir, we've brought back the two who fled from you. What is your will for them?"

I gazed past him at the two frightened guards. "I am Korth Lord Terral," I told them. "I am the Lordslayer. The deathright passed to me when I performed the rite of Lord's-Kill on Lord Brid. Dama Koralie denied me my right of inheritance, but now I come to take up the lordship and end the dama's rule. Acknowledge me and join my men or cling to your allegiance to the dama and share her fate. Choose."

The two dropped to their knees and touched their foreheads to the ground. "Lord Terral," they cried.

"Rise," I said. "Reclaim your weapons as we cross the bridge."

I reined Sunburst to a halt before the massive iron gates in the newly constructed wall that blocked our way. Behind me clustered my expanded escort, its numbers quadrupled by the guards and freedmen who'd rallied to our cause as we rode unchallenged through forest, fields, and villages.

Koralie and those loyal to her had retreated behind this great wall she'd built around the Manor House. All around us we saw evidence of the haste of its construction. The ravaged gardens were littered with broken and discarded tools, chunks of stone, and twisted metal. The lovely lawns were trampled and rutted; the exposed earth was dusty and dry as the Desert of Labon.

Rage welled up inside me at the wanton destruction. My anger exploded into an aura of flame, causing my men to draw back in awe.

"Easy, Korth," Derli whispered in my ear. "Don't overdo it."

Her warning came too late. Makor emerged in a flare of light. In his strength I charged the gate. Sunburst hurtled against it, his mighty hooves crashing against the gate in a shower of sparks.

The iron gate shuddered and tore shrieking from its great hinges. Sunburst thundered over it and scattered the armed men massed behind it, allowing my followers to surge after us through the opening. The clash of metal against metal and the cries and shouts of combat told me the defenders had regrouped behind me to attack my men.

I didn't stop. At the great oak doors of the Manor House Sunburst reared. In front of the closed doors stood the aged dama, gowned in purple silk. One wrinkled hand held the staff with its resident fiend; the other held a large unlit torch. Her lips were set in a grim smile.

"I've come to claim the lordship, Koralie. Don't resist. I'll forgive you for sending Vicca to kill me. You may retain your position as dama."

She sniffed. "Vicca was a bumbling fool. I should have killed you myself."

"No doubt you should have. Now you can't. Will you acknowledge me?"

She stood firm. "You come too late for me, Korth, or whoever you are. I am withered and tinder dry. You come bursting with light and flame, as I guessed you would." Cackling, she held aloft the unlit torch.

A blast of light surged from me, drawn by witchery to the torch. It ignited in a wild explosion of flame. At the same instant, Koralie hurled the staff toward me. The fiend's batlike wings unfurled.

The spell I'd placed on it years before held firm. The released creature flapped around and cast itself at Koralie. Its talons sank into her frail form and lifted her up. She thrust at it the blazing torch she'd drawn from my own power. Too late I guessed her intent. The fiend clasped her, and the hungry flames engulfed them both. Behind them the oaken doors exploded into an inferno, sending sheets of flame streaking up the stone walls. Sunburst vaulted forward, drawn to the conflagration, flame to flame. I hurled myself from his back and rolled away from the fiery geysers.

I stood, and my men gathered around me. Intermingled with them were the men whom they'd been battling. All stared at the blazing Manor House.

"She bewitched it," said an awestruck voice behind me.

I nodded, neither knowing nor caring whether the speaker was one of my men or a Manor Guard. "This is her vengeance against me. She planned it all. I should have anticipated—" Dense smoke choked me, turning my words into a fit of coughing. I squinted into the inferno for a glimpse of Sunburst. The flames could not harm him, but not even as Makor could I have ridden him through Koralie's witch-fire.

Nothing could save the Manor House. It, its gardens, the wall Koralie had built—all were reduced to ash, caught up into the wind, and spread out above us, bringing early night. The intense heat and waves of smoke drove us to the safety of the Rethe.

Derli was uncharacteristically quiet, though the sense of her presence comforted me. She had warned me to take care. If only I had listened!

Boasting of my lordship, I'd been a slave to my rage, and Koralie had drawn that rage forth to kindle the fire. I viewed with sadness the devastation wrought by my folly. I had been using Makor's power, but at heart I was still Korth. I was not worthy to become Makor. Perhaps I never would be.

I bowed my head. The jingle of bells made me raise it again. The juggler sauntered toward me across the bridge. Derli gave a low whistle.

"Stay near me," I whispered to her.

I walked forward to greet the masked harlequin.

"A desolation worthy of you." He nodded toward the rising billows of smoke. In his hand he dangled by its hair the single remaining head.

"I should have known you'd come," I said by way of greeting. "You always appear in time to gloat over my failures."

"You have one chance left, one head to name—and save or cause to die." He tossed the head at me.

I caught it. "His name is Vandesar," I said. "He is not dead."

"He will be soon if Zera has her way. She believes he betrayed her."

"I left him safe at the inn in Diakos."

"So you did," the juggler agreed, not laughing now. "But Zera's reach is long. Zera whisked him to her palace."

"The temple on the mountain."

"Of course."

"Who are you, that you know these things? Unmask yourself."

"Who are you? You wear no mask. Can you name yourself?"

I straightened my shoulders and stood tall. "I am Korth Lord Terral."

An insouciant grin spread to the lower edge of his mask. "Are you really?"

His mocking words cut deep. I'd allowed Makor to emerge, but my failure to save the Manor house had suppressed him again. Did I dare call him forth once more?

Yes, but not here and not in a fit of pique.

"I am, and am not," I said. "It doesn't matter. I have urgent business elsewhere. If, as you say, Vandesar is in danger, I must do what I can to save him." I didn't add that I must also save my son. I merely grasped my fascinum, raised it to my mouth, and asked to go to the icy ledge where Divian had battled the Flux fiend and beneath which he remained entombed in an ice cave.

I arrived with a suddenness that sent me skidding over the ice, stopping perilously close to the edge. Derli gave a low whistle. I stepped back carefully and looked around. Her glittering sparks hovered above the pile of bones that were all that was left of the Flux fiend I'd slain.

"What's your plan?" she asked, and when I didn't answer, added, "You do have a plan, don't you?"

I couldn't tell her that my plan had simply been to get away from the juggler. Instead I reached out to place my hand within those sparks. I felt nothing. "I can see you now, but I can't touch you."

"I have no physical substance," she said softly. "You know that." Something like vibrations swept over my hand as she spoke.

"I came here to challenge to Zera," I said. "I must free Divian, and I hope to save Vandesar." I paused, finding it hard to speak that which we both knew. "If I can find a way to do those things as Korth, I will, but …"

"Do what you must," she said. "I understand."

I gazed at her a moment longer, then stepped closer to the edge, raised my head, cupped my hands around my mouth, and shouted, "Zera! Hear me, Zera!" I was prepared to stand here in the cold shouting for however long it took before she answered. But I hadn't long to wait.

"Who calls Zera?" came her voice from above.

"I, Korth," I called back, using the name she'd hope not to hear.

I looked up at her and caught my breath at her glowing loveliness. Splendid in a robe of gold and crimson, a diadem of pearls set in her ebony hair, she leaned forward, eyes sparkling. I'd judged Lisha beautiful, but Zera's mortal manifestation had no more been able to display the goddess's full glory than a small pond can manifest the full character of the ocean.

"And is your fala friend with you?"

Derli answered for me; I was too dazed. "I'm here. Your servant, goddess, as always."

"Always, fala? I think not."

"He's come to you, hasn't he?"

"He has not. He only wants his bastard son. You've betrayed me, Vandesar betrayed me, and Korth is as big a fool as ever."

"Spare Vandesar and I'll come to you," I shouted, suddenly eager. She'd understand what I left unsaid—I could only reach the temple as Makor.

"Korth, no," Derli's whisper roused me from my rapture. "That's too easy."

She was right. I'd almost made a terrible mistake. But I needed to know that Vandesar was still alive. I greatly feared I'd already failed to save him, as I had the others represented by the juggler's heads. Even if he still lived, how could I save him without sacrificing Divian?

"Ha! I'll slay him while you watch unless you leave your fala and come to me now."

"Is that any way to win back your consort's love?" The voice came from below. I looked down and was astonished to see the juggler balancing on a narrow ledge I hadn't seen before, just below the point where Divian was hidden. Possibly I could reach my son from there.

I drew my sword. "I'm coming down to you," I called to the juggler.

"And what have I done to provoke you to attack me with a sword?"

"You've provoked me in many ways, but the sword isn't meant for you. It's to chop through that ice to rescue my son."

"You'll never succeed at that," he said. "Only Makor can wield the sword in a way that would cut through the ice."

"Nevertheless, I mean to try." I leaned out over empty space, gauging the distance I'd have to jump. I reached for my fascinum. With its help …

"Korth, please be careful," Derli begged.

"How quickly you forget your vow, Korth," called Zera's voice. "Do you care so little for your liegeman?"

I looked up. Vandesar knelt before Zera, his hands bound behind his back. She held a jeweled dagger in her upraised hand.

"Try to break through that ice and Vandesar dies," she called down. "And you!" She leaned so far forward I thought she must surely fall. "How dare you come here?"

It took me a moment to realize she was speaking to the juggler. She knew him. But of course, she would.

It was time I did, too. I sheathed my sword, held the fascinum tightly in my fist, jumped ... And teetered on the edge of the narrow shelf. If the juggler hadn't grasped my arm, I would have fallen.

As he pulled me back, I reached up and snatched his mask from his face. A shiver of recognition shook my frame. A chill invaded my soul as I gazed on that darkly handsome and so familiar face.

Molor. Twin-Slayer.

He pushed me against the ice wall and grasped my throat. "I know this skill, too, brother," Molor said.

I wanted to tell him I was still Korth, not Makor. Not his twin. But I couldn't speak. Choking, I tried to push him off me.

Derli screamed, "Goddess! No!"

Had Zera stabbed Vandesar? Or had she turned her wrath against Derli?

With a loud crack the narrow ledge on which we struggled broke away. We tumbled through the air toward the ground far below.

I shut my eyes. Death was seconds away.

I felt myself lifted, heard the whoosh of great wings. I opened my eyes to see the ice mountain speed past as we rose higher and higher.

Molor had unfurled his powerful silver wings. We landed on the flat top of the mountain, next to Zera and Vandesar.

My liegeman still lived, but Zera held her dagger to his neck. "This is not the way you were to come here," she said to me. "And you are not Makor."

"And never will be," Molor said. "Not on the terms you've offered."

"Begone, Destroyer. You have no business here."

"The resurrection of my twin concerns me as much as it does you. More, I think."

"Not in the same way. You've done all you could to prevent it. I've come close to succeeding, but this vessel has resisted." At last she turned her gaze to me. "I could have given so much. You could have been so much. But you chose a fala over me. A fala!"

Taut with fury, she drew the dagger across Vandesar's throat. Blood spurted, disappearing into the crimson of her robe.

"No!" I fell to my knees beside him. I grasped my fascinum in one hand and pressed the other across the gash in his throat. "Live! You must live!"

"Too late!" Molor crowed. "You've failed again, fool!"

I refused to listen. Concentrating only on Vandesar, I willed the gaping wound to close, the blood flowing from it to return to its normal channels, breath to return to the laboring lungs.

Power flowed from me into the healing.

Not enough. The wound had closed. But his breathing did not resume. His heart did not pump.

"No!" I said again. And, "Makor!"

This time there was silence around me.

Silence except for a low hum. Something vibrated at my waist. I remembered the globe in my belt pouch. Still holding the fascinum, with my other hand I fumbled the pouch open and pried out the globe. I held it over Vandesar's mouth.

Nothing happened.

Molor leaned down and spoke into my ear. "Open it."

I released my hold on the fascinum and twisted apart the two halves of the globe. A violet haze rose from it, and I breathed it in.

With that indrawn breath came a power greater than any I had summoned as Korth. This time there would be no going back. I was Korth no longer. Again I placed my hands on Vandesar. No need for the fascinum now. I merely said, "Vandesar, rise."

He took a breath. And another. He opened his eyes, looked at me, and sat up. "My Lord!" he said.

"My Love," Zera said and dropped her dagger.

"My Twin," Molor said and stepped back, away from me.

I rose and lifted Vandesar to his feet. He bowed deeply.

I turned to Zera. Her face was radiant. "You are back!"

"Back from death, yes," I said, "and thanks to you both for that."

"But …?" Zera prompted.

"Korth believed he'd perish when I became whole. He opened that globe, Molor, knowing it would complete my release and believing it meant his death. Though you mocked him, twin, he was strong. Strong enough to survive. He is part of me now and forever."

I looked at Zera, my love, my wife. "Korth came here to save his son. He came knowing it was not within his power to save him. I would have to do it. And I mean to."

"I won't have him here," Zera said, her eyes blazing.

"And for Korth's sake I will protect Derli. And free the falas you've imprisoned in bird form."

Molor let out a whoop of glee.

Zera trembled with rage. "And will you protect humankind from the danger of their song?"

"Molor prepared the Manor Lands as a refuge for them. It has not been that for some time, but it can be again. Can it not, Brother?"

"It can if Zera will swear to respect the land as a sanctuary for the falas."

Her response was an angry sniff.

"We'll discuss this later," I said. "Divian has waited in the ice long enough." I didn't add that Derli, too, waited, on the ledge of ice where I'd left her. Perhaps Zera guessed. She whirled round and marched into the temple—not a temple, really, but the home I'd made for her. As I'd made the temple in the jungle, abandoned after she'd made it a hiding place for the transformed falas. To my shame, I'd let her do that, and because of it Molor slew me.

Now my twin leaped forward and embraced me. "I was wrong to trick and slay you. Zera was my foe, not you. If you'll renounce her—"

A vision of Zera in her full splendor filled my mind. I shook my head. "I won't. It was her love that would not let me die, her love that brought me back. She gave me Derli."

"She didn't intend for you to love the fala."

"Korth fell in love with Derli when she took on human flesh. It has always been Zera whom *I* loved. Yes, she can be cruel. She needs taming. But she can be gentle, and as a lover she has no peer. I will not renounce her. Yet I swear to you, the falas will be freed."

He hesitated, searching my eyes. Apparently he found truth there. He said, "You'll need my help."

"So we're a team again? Enemies no more?"

"A team," he affirmed and pounded my back. We both choked back tears.

"I must return and cleanse the Manor Lands. Will you join me, Brother?"

"Not yet. Though I am Makor, you created well in my absence. Do it again. Make the land fertile once more. And free the slaves."

"I will," he said.

"Will you reestablish the lord line? Korth received the deathright, but he cannot be lord. And with Koralie dead, who'll become dama?"

"As to dama, I have a replacement. Remember, I took Medara from you. As her patron, I took the responsibility of educating her." Molor chuckled. "I was not an easy taskmaster, but once I taught her to curb her tongue, the rest went quite well. She's slender again, as when you first met her, though with a more mature beauty."

"She's a good choice," I said. Medara had wit and courage. If adversity had given her wisdom as well ...

"But we need a lord," he said, giving me a questioning look.

Immediately the answer to the implied question came to me. Taking up the empty halves of the silver globe, I breathed into it, rejoined the halves, and held it out to my twin. "You gave this to a certain trapper for safekeeping. Meir is a good man. He'll make a fine Manor Lord."

"So he will." With a laugh he took the globe, threw it up into the air, caught it and pocketed it. "I'll be about my work as you must be about yours." He opened his great silver wings, and was gone.

I went to the mountain's edge and leaped easily down to the ledge where Derli waited.

"You'll free Divian now?" she asked, and raised no other question.

I answered by giving a single command that split the ice around Divian. Another command brought him, sputtering and fuming, to stand beside me on the ledge where we'd fought the Flux fiend.

He hurled accusations with every breath. "What a fatherly act! Sealing me in ice. I thought you came to save me. I thought you cared about me. I should have known better. How long did you leave me there? Days? Weeks?"

In truth I did not know how long it had been for him, though I knew it was far less than Korth spent after leaving here. "You needed a rest after your battle," I said and winked at Derli. "What matter whether for ten days or ten years? For you it was but a single sleep."

He looked around. "Where's Medara? What have you done with her?"

"Treated her more kindly than you did. She's safe, though you had little regard for her safety when you persuaded her to flee with you."

He scowled and his voice turned sullen. "I love her. You can't understand that, can you? You never loved me or my mother."

"I can understand love," I said, thinking of Zera.

Derli placed herself before my eyes. I saw her fully now, clothed in light beyond the range of human eyes, formed of sound, shimmering with glorious harmonies no human ear could hear. I understood why Korth had loved her, though he had never seen her full splendor as I could.

"It's you who know nothing of love, Divian," I said. "But how could you, growing up without father or mother? Let's not quarrel. Zera sealed you in the ice, not I. Until today I lacked the power to free you, though I did what I could to protect you from her wrath."

"Her wrath?" He stared in unbelief. "I was reared in her temple. Her priests were my foster fathers. I've looked on her as my mother. How did I earn her wrath?"

"Your presence in her temple was an affront to her, through no fault of yours." My eyes flickered to Derli, who'd channeled Medara and the infant Divian to the Diakan temple. Had she done so because the way to the temple was easiest to open, or had Derli used that means of wreaking a petty vengeance on her trapper? Some things not even a god may know.

My gaze swung back to Divian. "Your only crime was that of being born, and for that crime I fear Zera will not forgive you. She is not your mother, and she views you as the symbol of my unfaithfulness. But I'll plead your case before her."

"Must you go to her, Korth?" Derli's wistful voice cut like a dagger.

Gently I said, "Korth need not, but Makor must."

She sighed and her pattern dimmed. "Forgive me, Lord Makor. It was Korth who taught a fala the meaning of love. But I know too well to whom Makor belongs."

"Makor belongs to no one." My golden splendor blazed forth.

Divian, mouth agape, pressed back against the wall of ice. His legs folded slowly beneath him, carrying him to his knees among the bleached bones of the Flux fiend.

"Makor!" He breathed the awed whisper. He stared at me and pride replaced the awe. He scrambled to his feet. "Makor. My father. Even if Zera isn't my mother, I'm the son of a god!"

I shook my head. "You're the son of an ex-slave and a peasant woman," I said. "You must learn humility if you wish to be more than that."

Divian kicked savagely at the bones, sending them skittering over the ice with the tinkling sound of a beggar's bell.

Ignoring him while he conquered his hurt and anger, I turned to Derli. "You helped me find the scattered parts of my essence, knowing that when all were reassembled within me, I, Makor, would live again and would return to Zera."

"For a taste of freedom I swore to help Zera bring about Makor's rebirth. I hoped to win you over to the falas' cause. My people languish in their golden cages, but I—I found a trap of a different kind."

"To free your people, Derli, I must return to my consort. Stay here with Divian until I send for him."

"Stay here!" Divian exploded. "Why?"

"Because the way I go you cannot come." I stared upward at the mountain of ice.

"You're a god. Your power got you here, didn't it? Why can't it get us both up there?"

"Zera's power blocks it," I answered shortly without shifting my gaze from the wall.

"Blast your way through. You can, can't you?"

"I don't choose to. I go the way I must to appease Zera. And to free the falas."

Derli's pattern shimmered against the pale green ice. "You go the way you must to prove your love for Zera," she said.

I looked away and busied myself gathering the Flux fiend's scattered bones. The longer bones I hacked with my sword, breaking off their ends and fashioning rough points.

I sheathed my sword, gripped a bone, breathed on it to infuse it with the strength of finest steel, and drove its pointed end into the ice.

Using the bones as pitons, I slowly ascended the wall of ice. With a shout of triumph I pulled myself onto the leveled summit.

In the shadow of the temple I rubbed my arms and shoulders after the arduous climb. The golden doors swung open. Zera stood framed in the entranceway, gowned in red.

"Hail, Daughter of Time," I called, smiling. "I've returned to your temple."

Vandesar peered out from behind her, beaming with joy. I was relieved to know Zera hadn't done my liegeman harm while I delayed.

She stretched her lovely arms toward me. "*Our* temple, My Lord," she corrected with an answering smile that made me forget Vandesar. "And our home."

I crossed the space between us in a single stride.

Before I could embrace my fair consort, a sparkling presence flowed between us.

Zera's face clouded. She stepped back.

"Derli, I told you to stay with Divian," I said.

"I came to beg you, Lord, to bring him from that ledge." She spoke fast, her words taut with urgency. "In his present frame of mind, he's ready to cast himself off it to his death."

I looked at Zera, noted the tears of anger in her eyes. Her slender fingers caressed the jeweled hilt of the dagger in her belt. Vandesar retreated to the safety of the temple.

"Zera, as Korth's son he's my responsibility. I won't abandon him."

"I won't have him here."

"Let me bring him only long enough to speak to him once more. I make you this wedding pledge: I'll allow Mother Uta to spin him away to another world, to some place where he can find purpose and where he will disturb you no more."

Zera bristled with rage. Her black hair swirled. Her knuckles were white around the hilt of her drawn dagger. "You make a wedding pledge to me while this fala curls herself about you?"

Derli's shimmer stilled. Gathered into a tight, dim knot, she sank to Zera's golden sandals. "Goddess, I make no claim on your lord. I surrender my freedom. Cage me, but let Lord Makor save the boy."

Zera glanced down at the cluster of light and raised her eyes to me. "You've heard the fala's offer. What say you? Will you permit her to be caged to save your son?"

I swallowed hard and met her gaze. "I came here to renew my wedding vows, My Lady. But as your wedding gift to me I ask the freedom of the falas."

"You ask much."

I nodded. "I've learned much. Death is an excellent teacher, Zera. Your love refused to let me die. You created the slave Korth and set in motion the time twisting that gathered bits of my essence from many times and drew me from my aimless wandering on the timeless shore. Your plan was brilliantly devised, but your power alone was not enough to accomplish it. It required the intervention of Molor and the guidance of Derli."

Zera's shoulders slumped. She bowed her head. "True. I sensed and resented Molor's interference. Each time I trapped the fala and hid her away from you, he found a way to lead you to her. Only Vandesar's pleas prevented me from making war on Molor. It was Vandesar who made me see what Molor was doing when I didn't want to see and didn't want to acknowledge his help. Very well. I'll pay the debt I owe."

"Goddess," Derli's voice was low and soft, "I do not ask my own freedom. I'll keep my vow. It will be enough to see my sisters freed. But please, delay no longer to bring Divian here."

Zera looked at me. "You may bring the boy if in exchange you allow this single fala to be caged."

Helpless, not trusting myself to speak, I raised my fascinum to my lips, blew gently on it, and whispered my son's name. In an instant he stood beside me.

The temple garden is lovely by night, when the moonlight transmutes the golden benches to soft silver. The flowering trees sway in the cool breeze that mingles the scents of their blossoms.

Tomorrow Molor and my liegeman Vandesar will attend me as Zera and I reaffirm our vows. Tonight the goddess has retired to her chambers, leaving me to my sorrow after bidding farewell to Korth's son.

I sit under a tree hung with golden cages, all empty save one. In that one a bird with shining green-gold plumage regards me through knowing eyes.

"Divian's gone, Derli," I say. "Uta sent him spinning through the Flux to a distant world, where he'll have neither the handicap nor the advantage of being named Makor's son. He thinks me a harsh father, but if he learns to master himself, he may come to understand the love that lay behind the harshness. I suspect that, even though he's Korth's son, not mine, he has inherited enough of my spirit to find a place of power in the world to which he's gone."

I sigh and stare into the distance, where stars gleam down on the mountains' snowy peaks. "He wouldn't have thrown himself from the ledge. You knew that. Divian's anger has never been directed toward himself. You used that as an excuse to come here and persuade Zera— and me—to let you stay." I look back at the bird.

Head cocked, she listens, sitting on her perch, not a feather moving.

"I wanted you free with your sisters. I never wanted to see you trapped again. I would have missed you, but how can I bear to see you like this?"

The bird tips back her head. Her throat quivers, her beak opens, and a sad, sweet song pours forth.

I lean my head against the back of the bench and listen to the cascade of poignant harmonies. A wild, rich joy mingles with a rending sorrow. The notes twist my heart. Tears flow from my eyes. No mortal could listen to such song. His heart would burst or his mind would lose its reason.

But I am Makor. This song has helped me pass through death and return to life. My eyes close. I breathe deeply, taking in the melody, letting it carve into my soul.

I've been a slave, a freed man, and a lord. I've killed and I've healed. I've fought and I've made peace. I've loved deeply and suffered great loss.

Because I've done these things, because I've learned what it is to be human, I am a wiser, more compassionate god. Nor may I forget these experiences. I must relive them each time I hear Derli sing.

Her song is my deathright.

MANOR LORDS AND DAMAS

Terral founded the line of Manor Lords in what became known as the Year One. He served as Manor Lord 22 years. He named Tredienne as first dama, the dama being a woman with psychic abilities who had the responsibility to counsel and guide the lord and to select the lord's successor. As an infant Treden was named for Tredienne, establishing the tradition of the new lord selected by the dama bearing or being given a name related to hers. That custom reaffirmed the close relationship between lord and dama.

LORD	YEARS OF RULE, Dating from Year One	DAMAS
TERRAL	1 – 22	TREDIENNE
TREDEN	22 – 66	Damas Tredienne, Lonna
LONNESS	66 – 100	Damas Lonna, Gala
GALOR	100 – 171	Damas Gala, Ordell
ORDRED	171 – 205	Dama Ordell

METT	207 – 216	Damas Medara, Katrina
KADRY	216 – 247	Damas Katrina, Chevaise
[Interim]	247 – 266	Dama Chevaise, Regent
CHEVOR	266 – 278	Damas Chevaise, Ladala
LADIN	278 – 290	Damas Ladala, Massanne
MAXIN	290 – 374	Damas Massanne, Stamsine
STAMSEL	374 – 415	Damas Stamsine, Brinabeth
BRID	415 – 485	Damas Brinabeth, Koralie
KORTH	485 – 487	Dama Koralie

ABOUT THE AUTHOR

Like all children, E. Rose Sabin enjoyed fairy tales and stories of magical creatures, but her favorite book even in elementary school was *Bulfinch's Age of Fables and Beauties of Mythology*. As a child she found the book fascinating; as an adult she regards it and other reference works on world mythology as wonderful sources for story ideas. The Egyptian myth of Isis and Osiris provided her with the inspiration for *Deathright* and serves as the model for the myth she created as the novel's basis. Although *Deathright* is her only true mythic fantasy, myth infuses much of her work, and she hopes her readers will enjoy searching out the mythic elements in her other novels.

To learn more about Ms. Sabin, visit her web site at www.erosesabin.com or her Facebook author page, E. Rose Sabin's Books.